'TIL ENCRYPTION DO US PART

CATHLEEN COLE

FRANK JENSEN

C&J NOVELS LLC

Copyright © 2021 by Cathleen Cole

All rights reserved.

No part of this book may be reproduced in any form or by any electronic or mechanical means, including information storage and retrieval systems, without written permission from the author, except for the use of brief quotations in a book review.

Any references to historical events, real people, or real places are used fictitiously. Names, characters, and places are products of the author's imagination.

Publisher: C&J Novels LLC

ASIN: B0948LC347

Dedication

This book is for my family. Thank you for always believing in me and supporting me.

CHAPTER 1

Rat

A loud sound dragged me out of sleep—it wasn't restful, the dreams always ensured that—but it had been deep. I lay quietly in bed, trying to control my breathing, ears and eyes straining to take in my surroundings in the darkened room.

Rowdy laughter came from the hall and my eyes darted to the door, where the slim line of light glowed from beneath it. I recognized one of my club brother's voices as he tried to quiet another down.

The thud that knocked into my door had my heart galloping in my chest. I sucked in a breath and tried to find the doorknob in the dark, watching to see if it'd turn.

"You clumsy fucker. You're going to wake everyone up! If you can't hold your liquor, don't drink so much," Trip slurred, and I knew without needing to check that he was berating Drew. The two were practically joined at the hip.

The last fog of the dream faded away slowly as my heart calmed. I sat, still as a statue in my bed. I knew I was safe—for now. I hadn't always been, and I tended to wake up at any slight sound, listening for any sign that I needed to run or fight. It was a hard habit to break. Hard to accept that safety wasn't temporary.

Glancing over at the clock, I groaned and scrubbed my hand over my face. It was three a.m. and there'd be no going back to sleep. I could lay here, staring at the ceiling until it was time to get up, or I could do something productive with my time.

Mind made up, I flicked the light on next to my bed. The glow lit up my small room. I didn't have much use for a lot of space so the room I was given at the clubhouse was perfect for me. This had been my place for the last ten years when somehow Cade managed to convince Dagger—our former MC president—to accept a bedraggled street kid into the MC.

In fact, Dagger had given me my road name. He called me Street Rat so often, it stuck. Cade offered to give me a different name, but I wore this one with pride. Over the years it'd been shortened to Rat, but I'd never forget where I came from or how hard I worked to elevate myself.

Dagger hadn't let me officially join the club until I turned eighteen. Not that he was concerned with me being a legal adult, more like he was waiting for me to put on some weight and not look like a starved teenager. What he *had* done was put my tech skills to use from the day Cade and Riggs brought me home. They'd given me a place to live, safety, and a family. I'd never been close with Dagger or his officers, but there were many of the members I liked. Cade, Riggs, Steel, and Gunnar were the only four I trusted for a long time, though. Eventually, Axel came along, and he'd been added to our crew, and now Bass and I were like brothers.

I went over to my dresser and pulled on a t-shirt. I was already wearing sweats. I never slept naked. My formative years taught me that it was a bad idea. When you never knew who'd be sneaking up on you in the middle of the night you couldn't leave that kind of shit to chance, or you'd be running around the city with your balls hanging out. Ask me how I know…

Shaking the memories away, I tugged on my running shoes and

laced them. I crept down the hallway, careful not to wake anyone, even though Trip and Drew likely already had.

The gym in our basement was quiet and dark. I made it down without encountering anyone else and I was grateful for it. I hated letting the others see me after nights like these. The guys in my inner circle knew about my time on the streets, but that didn't mean I wanted to rehash it every time this happened, which was a few times a week.

Starting up the treadmill, I began running. Two things leveled me out, running and hacking. The physical exertion of pushing my body to the limits beckoned me more than fucking around online this morning.

Everything smoothed out inside my brain as my feet pounded against the track below me. The whir of the machine, the sound of my own breath in my head, chased the remaining memories back to the dark corner I tried to keep them locked in. I let my mind go gloriously blank.

I couldn't tell how long I'd been running—although I'd shucked my shirt already because it was drenched in sweat—when the door to the basement that housed our club gym was wrenched open.

My gait stuttered so hard at the movement that I almost ate shit. Cade paused just inside the door and shot me a hard look before he glanced down at the watch on his wrist.

"It's four a.m. Rat. Why are you awake already?" His eyes narrowed on my face.

I found my rhythm again and kept running as I spoke. "Couldn't sleep." I left it at that. It wasn't a surprise to see Cade down here this early, he seemed to sleep as often as me, and that wasn't saying much.

I'd been down here for an hour already and yet as soon as I'd focused, my mind was whipped right back into that tiny room where the twelve of us lived. We'd be out working the streets during the day, but at night we were forced to stay there, huddled together for safety and warmth.

Cade quietly crossed the room and set up the station he used to lift, but he kept shooting me speculative glances. The man somehow always knew what was going on in my head. It wasn't comfortable. Cade was like an older brother to me, though, and I trusted him with my life. He'd taken me on when no one else believed in me.

I'd been out, trying to meet my quota that fateful day. Joe Sullivan—or Sully as he made us call him—had a certain dollar amount he expected us to come back with. If we didn't, the punishment was brutal. At twelve, my amount was much higher than some of the younger kids and I often gave them whatever I managed to pickpocket in the morning so they wouldn't have to be out so long.

Earlier that morning, I'd tried to convince Sully that I could make him so much more money if he'd give me access to a computer.

"Fuck that technology bullshit! That's how they watch you," he'd screamed in my face. Even at that young age I knew something wasn't right in his brain. "Get out there and go to work and if I catch you at the library again, Seven, I'll make you pay."

He'd numbered us. I was the seventh kid he'd found—or taken, in the other kids' cases. He liked to crow that he'd found me, thrown out like the trash I was. Sully never failed to remind me that my family abandoned me to the streets when I was four. They'd left me huddled behind a dumpster in the pouring rain.

Thinking back on it, I guess I was lucky that Sully found me when he did. There's no telling what might have happened to me otherwise. At one point in time—before the MC—I used to wish that I'd been left to that nameless fate. What could have been worse than living for eight years with a paranoid schizophrenic who stole children and forced them to do his bidding?

My phone beeping drew me out of my dark thoughts. Cade had given up on pulling me into any kind of conversation and was grunting away as he rep'd a weight bar that probably weighed as much as I did. I'd been working out with my brothers, but I had a ways to go before I was as ripped as some of these guys. Pride swamped me. I'd always been a pretty lanky kid, but I'd managed to build an impressive amount of muscle in a short time.

I pushed the stop button on the treadmill and opened the text message. A smirk tilted my lips as I read.

Armando: 911, bro. Something crashed our bank of computers. None of us can figure it out. Can you make it over ASAP?

Making money was something that I'd been doing from a very young age. As soon as I was able, I started up a business fixing electronics. The club always encouraged entrepreneurship; it was an easy way to launder money. It was a pathological imperative that I be able to take care of myself. Those first years I did everything remotely. No one was going to pay to have a young kid fix their computer for them, so I couldn't show up in person.

Once I hit sixteen, I'd adjusted my paperwork to read eighteen and started taking on more jobs. I'd been working for this particular client for years and both Cade and I thought it was hilarious. They'd be horrified if they knew who they hired. Of course, they had no clue. Oh, they'd done their due diligence with background checks, but when you could make your history reflect anything you wanted it to, there wasn't much they could find. Since I didn't know jack shit about my history at the time, it was all made up.

"Gotta go do a job. Everyone will be on their own for breakfast," I told Cade. The majority of my jobs were still remote, so I spent a lot of time at the clubhouse. I'd naturally gravitated toward cooking for everyone. Shockingly, I had a knack for it and it was a way to force myself to spend more time around my brothers. I was a very solitary person, but when you were a part of an MC you were expected to be a part of the group.

"I'll spread the word," he grunted at me.

I paused before I scooped my shirt up. "I'll be over at 715 East 8th."

Cade racked his bar and sat up. A huge grin spread over his face. He knew all about this client. In fact, he was the one who insisted I take them on. It was beneficial to the club, and they paid well. I always gave the majority of my profit to the club. Cade had tried to decline at first, but it was one of the things I stubbornly refused to listen to him on. Once Cade took over, I'd given him all the back pay that I'd never handed over to Dagger. He didn't have my loyalty the way Cade did, so I'd never shared when he was in charge.

He chuckled and shook his head. "Let me know if you end up needing anything."

"Alright," I mumbled before I headed upstairs to shower and change.

* * *

I sat on my bike and eyed the Austin Police Department building. It didn't matter how much they paid, I hated coming here. There should be zero reasons for me to ever go into a police precinct without handcuffs. Cade was the boss, though, and the boss had put his foot down with this one. He had a point. Having the APD as a client allowed me access to their systems and I'd made sure to leave myself a backdoor I could access anytime I needed it.

I shrugged my cut off and locked it in my hard-shell saddlebag after I tugged my backpack out. I put on a shirt that said *Use the Force, Harry*, a little bit of nerd humor, and threw on a set of glasses. I looked one hundred and eighty degrees off from an MC member. Kind of the point when going into a police station. I shouldered my backpack, it had my laptop and all the gear I'd need to fix pretty much any problem.

Putting my bag on my back, I strolled in the front door of the police station. The cop sitting at the front welcoming desk glanced up and immediate relief washed over his features as I came walking up.

"Carl! Good to see you. Our computers completely shit out on us. We had to send our officers over to precinct three to do their reports. A complete pain in the dick."

I chuckled and leaned against the counter. "I'm sure I can get you guys set back up here pretty quickly."

"Who's this?"

We both glanced up as a detective walked over. I didn't recognize him. I never forgot a face, so I knew I'd never met the man before.

"Oh, Zane, this is Carl. He takes care of our tech issues."

"I thought our tech crew takes care of our tech issues?"

I watched the detective eyeball me. It was obvious he was one of those cops who did everything off gut instinct and his was currently telling him I was no good. I couldn't blame him. Typically, these guys and I fell on opposite sides of the law. Not today, though. Today I just wanted to find out which asshole had downloaded something that he wasn't supposed to and given their precinct a virus.

Zane's gaze dropped down to my shirt, then raked over my jeans until it stopped at my Chucks. There was a sneer firmly planted on his face when he met my eyes again.

"Oh, well, Carl is the one we call when our tech guys can't fix things," Larry said lamely.

I grinned over at him to try to defuse the situation. Larry was a pretty nice, mellow guy, unlike Zane. I'd chosen the name Carl to try to be as unassuming as possible. No one named Carl was a daredevil. You would be as likely to find a Carl in an MC as you would a Larry. The name helped me fit in a little better.

"This is how you show up for a job?" Zane continued on as though Larry hadn't even spoken.

"That's how all the techies dress," Larry piped up. Zane continued ignoring him.

I glanced down at my clothes. All the really strict ex-military types looked at me this way. It was all part of the act.

"What's your last name, Carl?" Zane asked. I could see irritation stamped all over his face that I hadn't said anything to him yet.

The easiest way to get under the skin of a guy like this was to match his loudness with silence. They hated that. Before I had a chance to respond to him, a harried-looking Armando rushed into the room.

"Ugh, there you are," he told me. He frowned at Zane, but motioned for me to follow him.

I shot Zane a smirk and walked with Armando toward the back.

"What do we know about that kid?" Zane didn't even try to keep his voice down, so it floated over to us before we left the room.

"Sorry about him," Armando told me as he waved his key card in front of another door that would take us back to the area I would need to access to fix their system.

"No problem. New?"

Armando made a face. "He just transferred in. Keeping a low profile doesn't seem to be his strong suit."

I snorted at that. Men like him could never keep their mouths shut or their heads down. They didn't go with the flow. Instead, they preferred to battle their way upstream. Sometimes, it worked for them and everyone loved them for it. Other times, you ended up with...well, Zane.

Ten minutes later, I had my laptop out and was wading through the eleventh precinct's internal system looking for the digital culprit. It probably wasn't too big of a deal. Some guy likely decided to look up some porn while he was bored at work and accidently uploaded a virus along with the video.

My phone dinged so I looked over. I wasn't quick enough to bite back the groan. Armando popped his head around a corner.

"Is it bad?" he asked anxiously.

"Sorry, man. It's not that, I just heard about another job I don't want to do." I shot him an apologetic smile. Armando was a nervous ball of energy at the best of times. He was a neurotic mess right now with the entire system down in the precinct he was in charge of. He mumbled something and disappeared around the corner again.

Eyeballing the spot to make sure he didn't pop out again, I picked up my phone and studied Cade's text.

Cade: You're meeting Sal and his daughters to get to know them. He's also set up a dinner for the end of the week. No excuses. We'll send a few others with you, but no more putting this off. Your time is almost up.

Last week our club entered into an agreement with Salvatore Giuliani, the biggest Italian Mafia Don in Austin. He wanted to align himself with us, and through us with our allies—the Zetas and the Bratva.

He invited us all over to his fucking mansion and dropped a couple of bombs I was still trying to absorb. I was the younger brother of Enzo Volkov, the Bratva's Pakhan. My name was Viktor—with a K. What the fuck kind of name was that? Stupid Russians and their ridiculous spelling. In order to form this alliance, I had two weeks to pick one of Sal's four daughters to marry. Well, I amended, now I only had a week left to choose.

I felt the blood drain from my face. The thought of marrying a stranger made panic claw its way up my throat. At the time, I'd agreed because I knew it was what had to be done to help our club. We'd just killed Miguel Guzman and his five brothers weren't going to be very happy about that when they found out.

Something told me they weren't going to care that Miguel started the beef with us by stealing Gunnar's girlfriend or that he'd ensured his own demise by trying to kill Diego Juárez—and by default since we were with him—myself and Ming. Axel, Diego's older brother, and our MC's Road Captain, hadn't been about to let any of that slide.

All of us were prepared to take on any of the remaining Guzmans who showed their face in Austin. The problem was the Guzman Cartel had vast amounts of soldiers. That was why we'd joined up with the Italians. It gave us greater numbers and a hope of standing against the Guzmans.

I hurried through and finally managed to isolate the virus plaguing the cops' system. I was right. It was porn. It didn't take me long to finish up and have everything back up and running again. Armando thanked me endlessly as he walked me back out front.

I straddled my bike and pulled my phone out of my pocket. It wouldn't be right to leave my president on read. I typed back a response before I pulled out of the lot.

Tonight, I'd be going on a date with my future wife. Fuck me.

CHAPTER 2

Rat

I parked my bike and sat looking out over the park. People milled everywhere and the smell of food from the grill made my mouth water. It was early evening and there were still a few hours of sunlight left.

The Giuliani family was attending a birthday party for a cousin—or something like that—and Celia had insisted this would be the perfect place for me to get to know the girls better. I was going along with her to keep the peace—for now. Something told me my future mother-in-law was going to be a pain in my ass.

My brothers in arms got off their bikes, and I sighed. Steel and Gunnar had volunteered to come with me—and since he could never pass up a free meal, so had Riggs. The big man eyed me as I sat there, debating on just backing my bike out and leaving.

"You could just flip a coin," Riggs commented.

I glared up at him.

Gunnar walked over, looking thoughtful. "That could work. They're all hot. It's not like you'd get stuck with an ugly-" He broke off on a grunt as Steel plowed his elbow into Gunnar's gut.

"Leave the kid alone. He's got enough to deal with today."

I shot Steel a grateful look. Riggs and Gunnar were just trying to lighten the mood, but I didn't fucking date. I had too many issues stemming from my childhood. They all knew I couldn't stand being around large groups of people either. There were at least seventy plus people in this park right now.

Quit being a fucking pussy. I was more sick of my quirks than my brothers were. Somehow these men got me. Knew what I needed, sometimes better than I did. Mind made up, I swung my leg off my bike.

"Let's go find-"

"Viktor!"

I winced at the squeal. It was Celia Giuliani. A grown woman shouldn't make sounds like that, if you asked me.

Celia hurried up, arms extended out. I neatly side-stepped her hug. It hadn't taken long to figure Sal's wife out. She was all about image. She'd hug you in front of a crowd, then pull the knife she stuck in your back out later in a more private setting. She frowned slightly then let a bright smile take over her face.

"Thanks for having us," I muttered, shoving my hands in my pockets.

"Come! I simply must introduce you to everyone."

Horror washed over me. I'd never get out of here if I had to meet everyone. I didn't give two fucks about most of these people. I was on a mission—one Cade had ordered. Get to know the four women who were my bridal prospects, then get the fuck home.

Gunnar stepped over and brushed his hand over Celia's arm. He stared down into her startled green eyes as a smirk formed on his lips. "I'd love to meet your guests. Maybe we could let Rat—uh, Viktor—spend some time with your daughters so that we can have some...alone time?"

Fuck me. Bridget was going to be pissed at both of us later when she found out about this, but I couldn't find it in myself to care right now.

I was going to owe Gun big time for this one. The fact that he was willing to not only deal with Celia for the next few hours to give me time to get to know her daughters in private—well as private as this could be—but risk the wrath of his fiancé? He was really doing me a solid.

"Go with him. Make sure the cougar doesn't drag him off somewhere," Riggs muttered to Steel.

We watched as Celia looped her arm around Gunnar's and dragged him off through the crowd. Steel followed after them shaking his head.

It didn't take us long to find the Giuliani women. They were standing around talking. I let my eyes sweep over them as we approached. Gunnar hadn't been wrong. They were all attractive women. Each was wearing a sundress and strappy heels. Summer was on its way out, that is to say, straight past fall and nearing winter. It was still warm enough for sundresses, though.

God bless Texas.

There was so much tanned skin and tits on display around me it was hard to focus. Riggs elbowed me with a grin, and I realized we'd stopped next to the girls, and they were staring at us.

It took me a moment to figure out that the oldest had said something to me. Having no clue what it was, I tried to cover. "Hey ladies." I'd watched the other guys hit on women often enough that I wasn't completely hopeless.

Alexandria giggled and scooted closer to me. She looped her arm through mine and started talking a mile a minute. I nodded at whatever she was going on about and took stock of her sisters. I'd been about to research them when Ming had found me and talked me out of it.

She'd told me to let it be organic and go into it not knowing everything about them right down to their social security numbers. The sarcasm had all but dripped from her voice, but she'd been right. At least this way I'd have questions to ask and it might not be so hard to talk to them.

I motioned to the girl who looked the youngest. "Want to get a drink?"

One of the others made a kind of strangled sound in her throat and stepped protectively toward her sister. I knew from the dinner that her name was Arianna and the sister I'd asked to go with me was Ada.

"Sure," she said quietly, giving two of her sisters an unreadable look. Alex was the only one who looked thrilled to be here, although less now that I was going off with Ada instead of her.

We walked over to tables laden with food and drink and I filled two plastic cups with whatever they had in a crystal punch bowl. Handing one to her, I walked with her off to a quieter area.

Had I thought—even for a minute—this would be easy?

"Ada, right?"

Her head shot up and she gave me a tight smile. "Yeah. Nice to meet you...officially." We shook hands then both looked away from each other.

This wasn't fucking awkward at all.

"How old are you?" It's something I'd been dying to ask. She looked young and that was the reason I'd asked her to go off with me first.

"Seventeen."

For fuck's sake! I choked on the punch I'd taken a swig of. "Your father is offering you up for marriage and you're not even eighteen?" The horror and disgust in my voice had her meeting my eyes for the first time today.

"Messed up, huh?"

"Hell, yes. No offense, but I don't date—or marry—minors."

Her face broke out into a smile. "None taken, and I hope you don't get offended, but I don't want to marry you."

We both laughed, relieved to have that out of the way.

"Well, you're safe from that," I told her, more relaxed now that the pressure was off. "Why don't you tell me about your sisters?" A thought occurred to me. "They're not under eighteen are they?"

"No. Although, Antonia is eighteen. Ari is twenty-one and Alex is twenty-two." She bit her lip and scrunched her nose as she thought about my request. "I probably shouldn't tell you anything about them since we don't know you, but you seem like a nice guy." She craned her head, looking around. "Toni and Ari are awesome. They're a lot of fun and always look out for me."

"And Alex?" I prompted, taking a drink of the sugary-sweet liquid in my cup. It was fucking disgusting, and I longed for a beer.

Ada rolled her lips between her teeth and bit down on them. That look told me a lot about her older sister. "Alex is…"

"Viktor!"

My name was squealed for the second time that day and I watched as the woman we'd been discussing hurried up. That wasn't any better coming from her than it'd been from her mother. It was like nails on a chalkboard.

"It's Rat," I told her and watched her brows pull low over her eyes.

"I prefer Viktor," she said with a toss of her head.

"Doesn't matter, it's still Rat."

"I'm going to go back to the others," Ada said and hurried off before Alexandria could say anything else.

Facing Alexandria, I tried not to cringe. She had a wild smile on her face and was eyeing me with obvious interest. She seemed to have had a change of heart from the dinner last week and I wondered why. Or maybe she was just embracing the inevitable. It was something I needed to do as well.

"Let's go over to the shade," she suggested and grabbed my arm. She tugged me over to some trees and I let her. The sun was still high in the sky and I was starting to sweat. Then again, maybe it was the way Alex's hand had suddenly left my arm and was sliding down over my abs that was causing the bead of moisture to slide along my spine.

I caught her wrist in my hand. "What're you doing?"

She gave me a provocative smile. "What do you think?" She licked her lips and her eyes dipped down to my dick.

Jesus. She was like a fucking wolverine. Dangerous. This woman was the kind of danger that you knew the minute you dipped your dick in her she'd find some way to trap you with her forever. I tightened my hold on her wrist, preventing her from grabbing my cock. I didn't need her wicked looking nails anywhere near my junk when I told her I wasn't interested in that right now. Most guys I knew would let her jack or suck them off whether they planned on marrying her or not. She was offering it and they'd happily use her. I wasn't interested in doing that. Without knowing which sister I'd choose, I didn't plan on touching any of them.

That wasn't the way I was going to start a marriage. I may not have grown up with parents showing me what a happy relationship looked like, but I'd seen a couple of the guys fall in love with their women and now they had eyes for no one else. I figured there was something to that. I wanted to do this right. Another thought nagged at me too, she was putting on a big show, willing to blow me at a party. But this was an arranged marriage, it had to be a show. Right? That's not how our marriage would be. What would she be like when she dropped the facade?

Alexandria pouted up at me. "No one has to know." She started to drop to her knees, but I used her wrist to drag her back up.

"Maybe some other time," I told her in a bored, slightly cold tone. She didn't seem offended at all. It was almost like my disinterest made her want me more. I sighed inwardly. Now that she was back on her feet I led her back to her sisters. I didn't want to give her any more of an opportunity.

Glancing around, I found Riggs at a nearby table chowing down on a plate of food. He grinned at me and took a long pull from a beer bottle.

Where the fuck had he found that?

Alexandria started babbling on about wanting to become a stylist for celebrities, pulling my attention back to her.

I frowned and interrupted her spiel. "You want to buy clothes for people?" Arianna snorted, trying not to laugh out loud.

"Famous people," Alexandria corrected.

I wasn't sure if we had any of those around here or not. I nodded and listened politely as she outlined her five-year plan.

"That's only if my husband wants me to work, of course," she said with a giggle.

Her mannerisms annoyed me. I couldn't figure out why she was suddenly so interested in me—in an arranged marriage. She wasn't trying to hide her interest in any way. That should've been a good thing.

It was almost too good of a thing.

The other women didn't look thrilled to be here and I was pretty sure they didn't want an arranged marriage. Which meant, I should seriously consider Alexandria, but she bothered the shit out of me. She was constantly giggling and fluttering her lashes. I hadn't missed the way she stuck her tits out and then leaned into me so they brushed my arm. My head started a dull throbbing.

Laughing green eyes met mine and the headache faded into the background. Ari bit back a grin, fully aware of the games her sister was playing and knowing that I knew, too. The corner of my lips kicked up in an answering grin.

"Arianna, want to go for a walk with me?" Any excuse to get away from Alex would've been enough, but now that I was focusing on Arianna, my interest was piqued.

Like her sisters, she had long dark hair. These women were so similar if you didn't look closely you'd think they were carbon copies of each other. Arianna's eyes were the biggest difference, though. Instead of an emerald green like her three sisters, hers were softer. The color of a glass bottle, broken and worn down by sand, sea, and time. A soft green glinting in the sun and they drew me in.

We walked quietly, ignoring the looks we were getting from her family. Vaguely I wondered about the family I'd just found out about. Did Enzo and I have this many relatives? I sure as fuck hoped not.

"Ada told us you said you weren't interested in her," Arianna said from beside me. "Thank you for that."

I looked over at her in surprise. "It's not a problem. Like I told her, I'm not into minors."

She laughed, and it was a warm, light sound, not the harsh grating giggle her sister kept giving. Technically, Antonia was of age so I could consider her, but she was still a bit younger than I was interested in. Which left me with Alexandria and Arianna.

I side-eyed the woman walking next to me. She was staring down at the ground. "Are you in school?" I asked.

Her eyes darted over to me before she looked down again. "Yeah, I'm going to the University of Texas."

She fell silent again, and I hated the fact that I wasn't good at small talk. "What for?"

"Computer Software Engineering," she said with a self-conscious smile.

My brows shot up and I stopped walking. "You're into computers?"

She'd stopped with me and she tucked a piece of hair behind her ear as she nodded. She was beautiful, but not overt about it like her sister. I bet she had all the guys in her college classes wrapped up in knots every time she walked in a room. Men who were into computers usually weren't used to seeing women who looked like her.

"What's your setup?" I asked her.

Her eyes narrowed on me as she started rattling off a setup that was very similar to mine. We fell into an easy rhythm talking about computers as we walked.

By the time we made it back to the group I was surprised to find I didn't want my time with her to end. "Arianna-" I started, grabbing her arm to pull her to a stop before we were within hearing distance of her sisters.

"Ari," she corrected, then smiled.

I opened my mouth to ask her if this was something she wanted. I hated the idea of forcing one of these girls into a marriage with me. It didn't matter that I was being forced into it, too. Before I could ask, Alexandria was back and chattering.

Irritation shot through me and I wanted to drag Ari off to the nearest secluded spot and stay there with her. Right off the bat, we had more in common than I did with any of her other sisters.

"Rat," Riggs said. He, Steel, and Gunnar all walked my way, faces grim. "We need to go."

I shot an apologetic look toward the sisters and left with them. Alexandria scowled while folding her arms over her chest and tapping her foot. I was grateful to be leaving her behind. As we jumped on our bikes I caught sight of Ari watching us leave. A grin split my face and I nodded to her. I was too far away to tell for sure, but I thought she might have blushed.

"There was some kind of mix up with one of our gun shipments," Steel explained. "Sorry to pull you away, but we need to go sort it out and Cade would fucking kill us if we left you there alone."

"Not that you can't handle yourself," Riggs said. "We wouldn't fucking leave anyone alone with Sal."

"Or his wife," Gunnar said with a mock shudder.

I barked out a laugh and shook my head. "It's fine. I was ready to go anyway."

Riggs paused in the act of backing up his bike. "The one in the yellow wanted to wrap her lips around your dick."

I choked on the laugh that burst out of my chest. Leave it to fucking Riggs to say that shit. "Fuck off," I told him and started up my bike, cutting off his response.

As we pulled out onto the highway, my thoughts drifted back to the women. I had a tough decision to make, but—as usual—Cade had been right. It'd been the right call to come here today.

CHAPTER 3

Rat

A knock on my door drew my attention away from the program I was working on. "Come in."

Cade strode in the door, and I felt my shoulders tense. "Hey Rat. I want you to take at least one guy with you tonight. I don't trust Sal yet, so I don't want you heading in there alone."

I nodded and stared down at my keyboard. At first I'd regretted asking to make my own choice between Sal's daughters. On one hand, it would've been a lot easier to just be given a bride, but then that would be two of us with no choice. Plus now, after meeting them, I was glad I was going to have the choice. The pressure was on me to choose someone, but somehow it felt less wrong for me to choose her myself. I was coming to terms with what I needed to do.

Bass and the others had been hounding me all week to tell them who I was going to pick. I hadn't decided yet, though. The easiest decision would be Alexandria. She'd made her interest in me and in marriage very clear. We just had jack shit in common.

"If you don't choose someone I'm sending Riggs with you," Cade warned, breaking me out of my thoughts.

Wincing, I shot him an annoyed look. Riggs was the last person I wanted coming with me tonight and Cade knew it. I loved the guy, but he would make it an even more miserable experience than it was already going to be. He wouldn't be able to keep his big mouth shut.

"I'll see if Bass can go with me," I told him.

"He can. Everyone's already volunteered to go. Including the women," he said with a chuckle.

Instantly, relief filled me. If we trusted Sal more I would choose to bring Ming with me. I'd love to get her opinion on the women I had to pick from. Our time down in Mexico had bonded us and I trusted her completely. She wasn't that much older than me, but I had never had a mother, or sisters either. I really appreciated how she took care of the group.

She'd know what to make of Alexandria and Arianna. I'd already dismissed the younger two women. My choice was between the older two. I wouldn't ask for Ming to go with me even though I could've used her opinion, though, because—like Cade—I trusted the Italian about as far as I could throw him. The last thing I wanted was to put any of the women in a possibly dangerous situation.

"You alright?"

I met Cade's concerned gaze. "Yeah, it's fine."

He sighed and folded his arms over his chest. "Look, this would be a lot for any of us to handle. You don't have to go through it alone."

"I know," I replied quickly. He knew I'd been hesitant on meeting Sal's daughters. He also knew I hadn't met with my brother yet. Cade somehow always knew what was going on around here.

I wasn't a big fan of changes, although I'd been getting better at dealing with them. I'd just needed some time to process everything before I could give Enzo a chance. "I'll deal with it. Can you tell Bass I want him to go with me and I'll be ready in an hour?"

"Sure, man. Let me know how it goes."

Cade left me alone with my thoughts. I was so grateful to him. He always seemed to know what I needed even when I didn't. He pushed me, but never farther than I could take.

I rested my head in my hands and let out a long breath. I would rather be back in Diego's basement facing Miguel Guzman and all his men than go to this dinner tonight.

* * *

BASS CLAPPED his hand on my back as we stood staring up at Sal's house. I clenched my jaw as the urge to turn right back around and ride away washed over me. I would never cut and run, though, because then someone else in the club would have to take over my responsibilities. I'd agreed to this deal and I would follow through.

"You ready, bro?"

I looked over at Bass. We'd gotten so close over the last year. He'd started prospecting for the club and we just clicked. "No," I said in a wry tone.

His laugh rumbled out like a diesel engine starting up on a cold morning. He'd gotten his road name because of his voice. "I can't say I envy you, bro. Marrying a chick you don't even know?" He made a face, and I gave a humorless chuckle. I felt the same way. "It's crazy that you're getting engaged." He shook his head.

I scrubbed my hand over my hair. "Let's go get this over with."

"Sure thing," he replied, following me up the stairs to the front door.

Ringing the doorbell, we glanced at each other as the sound pealed on the other side of the door. We were both nervous. This was why I'd asked him to come with me tonight. I trusted him and knew he'd have a lot of the same responses I did. Hopefully, his opinion would help me make this monumental decision.

The door opened and a butler stared down his nose at us. The man was in a suit and had slicked back hair. He looked offended at our jeans, t-shirts, and cuts. We weren't the dressing up kind. What you saw was what you got with us.

"Hey," I started after silence spread between the three of us, "we're here to see Sal."

The man moved back and allowed us inside the home. "Follow me."

Bass was craning his neck checking everything out as the butler led us to the dining room. I'd been here a couple weeks ago, so I'd already had a chance to scope it out. Bass met my gaze and his eyes widened comically. Sal was obviously very wealthy. His home was extravagant. I felt a weight settle low in my gut. Whichever daughter I chose was going to be used to being given everything she wanted. Judging by this house, I wasn't going to be able to keep up. I made a good living, but nowhere near this level. Not that I would ever choose to live this way even if I could afford it.

We walked in and froze when every eye in the room zeroed in on us. Bass coughed next to me and even though he was an outgoing, confident guy I know he felt the same tension I did.

Sal came forward to greet us and introduce his son. We shook hands with Abel, but my gaze kept straying to the three young women standing near their mother. I frowned, realizing Alexandria wasn't here.

"Come, sit, sit," Sal insisted, and everyone obeyed, sitting at the table. "Celia," he said and gave his wife a prodding look.

She excused herself and hurried from the room. We sat in uncomfortable silence while the staff placed food on the table in front of us.

"Alexandria," Sal said in a slightly annoyed tone as she swept into the room. I glanced at Bass out of the corner of my eye and saw his eyes almost bug out of his head. Alexandria was gorgeous. Her long dark hair was up in some kind of twist thing that left a few strands curling around her long, slim neck. The dress she was wearing was shimmering and flowed around her feet as she all but floated over to the table.

She shot us a winning smile as she sank down gracefully into her seat. While all eyes were on her, I watched her sister. Arianna—unknowing that I was studying her—rolled her eyes when her sister let out a breathy giggle.

"I'm so sorry I'm late." Alexandria fluttered her lashes at me.

"You're never on time," Arianna muttered, and her sister Antonia elbowed her.

Alexandria ignored them both. "Hi, Viktor," she breathed at me.

"It's Rat," I reminded her. The last thing I was going to allow was for her to steamroll me.

Her lips flattened out into a thin line. "Rat," she repeated although it sounded like she was forcing the word out.

Sal's other daughters looked bored. I got the feeling they all expected me to pick Alexandria. Ada at least had my reassurance that I wouldn't choose her. She shot me a small smile. Returning it, I glanced around and caught Alexandria watching me like a hawk.

Clearly, she expected to be picked, too. I wondered again what the appeal was for her? Why would she want to marry a stranger? Or was it just that she couldn't comprehend not being picked? It wasn't like I knew her well, but that seemed to jive with her personality—or what I'd seen of it so far.

"Thank you for joining us for dinner," Celia said.

"Yes." Sal put his elbows on the table and watched me with predatory eyes. "Why don't you tell us who you'll pick before we start?"

Celia shot him a horrified look, and I secretly shared the same reaction. Tell them and then have to sit through a whole dinner with potentially pouting women? My eyes shot over to Ari. I actually doubted she would pout, and I'd never gotten any time with Antonia. In fact, none of the other three sisters seemed anything like Alexandria.

"I'd rather use these last hours to continue getting to know your family," I told him as tactfully as I could. In reality, I wanted to blurt out who I was choosing and get out of there as quickly as I could.

Alexandria rolled her eyes. "Are you seriously considering any of them?" She froze then shot a worried look at her father.

My brows drew down as I frowned at her reaction. Sal just shrugged—though he looked pissed that I'd declined to tell him what he wanted to know. He was playing nice. Everyone at the table could tell, but I wondered how long he could hold on to that facade.

Bass bit the insides of his lips, and we exchanged a knowing look. Both Sal and Alexandria were having trouble hiding their true colors. There was no reason for Alexandria to assume I would automatically pick her. I'd rejected her at the park, but she'd conveniently ignored that.

She clearly valued her beauty. She'd spent a great deal of time on her appearance before dinner. What she didn't realize was her sisters were just as gorgeous as she was, if not as made up. That also wasn't going to be the deciding factor on who I would marry. Whoever it was needed to fit with me and my lifestyle.

Alexandria's emerald green eyes demanded an answer. "Yes, I am," I told her.

The pout grew heavier on her lips and I had to force myself not to cringe. This woman was used to getting her way. The thought of marrying her made dread crawl up my spine. There's no way she'd be happy with my way of life.

Celia spoke in a low voice to Alexandria and her daughter straightened up and wiped the pout off her face. Sal started up a conversation with us and his wife. Abel and Alexandria joined in, but I noticed the other three daughters sat quietly. Arianna was pushing food around on her plate, and occasionally glaring over at her father.

My lips quirked in a smile when she shot him another angry look. She fascinated me. She'd dropped a few hints while we talked that she didn't want to get married and wasn't happy with her dad's bargain. I wasn't thrilled with it myself, so we had that in common. That was the only reason Alexandria was still in the running. She was so wrong for me, but how could I make Ari go through with it when she wasn't willing?

Those soft green eyes met mine again, and the knot that was sitting in my gut loosened slightly. I couldn't explain the pull I felt for this woman.

Celia and Alexandria were chattering away. Celia kept talking up both Alexandria and Ada, and it was all I could do not to shake my head. What kind of woman was okay with sending her seventeen-year-old off in an arranged marriage?

"Ari is completing a Software Engine Degree," Celia said happily, finally

"Engineering, Mama," she whispered, then dropped her gaze down to her plate when my gaze shifted from her mother to her again.

"Well, isn't that a coincidence," Bass chuckled. "Rat is-" He grunted in pain when I kicked him underneath the table.

I was here to learn about the girls, but we didn't need to be giving Sal any useful information about me or the club. Not yet, anyway.

Bass cleared his throat and everyone around the table stared at each other. An awkward silence descended.

"I would looove to learn how to use a computer better," Alexandria said in a voice so chipper and high-pitched I was sure dogs would start howling at any moment.

That seemed to be the cue because everyone started talking at once. It was all nonsensical small talk, but the focus was off me.

I eyed Arianna speculatively. She was avoiding eye contact now. *This was such a weird family.*

Bass shoveled some food into his mouth, then gave me a sheepish look. Cade had warned us to watch what we said before we came over here tonight. I sighed. This was going to be a long night.

CHAPTER 4

Rat

"Excuse me," Arianna murmured and hurried out of the dining room after we'd finished with dinner.

I watched her leave. She was wearing jeans, a flowy blouse, and heels. I tried not to be a complete creeper, but the way her jeans stretched over her ass sent heat racing through my system.

"Would you like more dessert, Viktor?"

Jerking my gaze off her daughter guiltily, I smiled at Celia. "No, thank you. Everything was great."

Bass nodded happily as he plowed through another piece of chocolate cake. They'd used food to fill in the gaps of conversation and if I ate anything else, I was going to burst.

"Where's the bathroom?" I asked.

"Alexandria can show you," Celia chirped happily.

I fought back a groan, but gave Alexandria a smile. She came around the table and grabbed my arm, forcing me to bend it so she could loop hers through.

We left the dining room and took an immediate right, and went up the staircase. I clenched my jaw as Alexandria ran her free hand up and down my forearm. There wasn't anything wrong with her, but the longer I spent around her the more convinced I became that I couldn't marry her.

She'd barely held herself together during dinner. Her true self kept peeking through during the meal, despite the fact that her family was sitting all around us. I'd now gotten to see her on her 'best' behavior and what she was like alone. Neither inspired much confidence that she and I would get along. She was constantly sniping and chiding her sisters, and she'd made it very clear that she was Sal's favorite—except maybe for Abel—and that he gave her everything she wanted.

We stopped outside a door and she smiled at me. I opened it and frowned when I saw a bed with a canopy over it. There were a ridiculous amount of pillows resting at the head of the bed.

Small hands shoved me inside the room and I watched her warily as she closed the door behind us.

"Alexandria," I said with an irritated sigh.

"I just wanted us to be able to get to know each other a little better without my parents around," she said softly, walking toward me. "We hardly got any time together at the park."

I stood my ground even though I wanted to back away from her. Her hand ran down my chest, and I grabbed her wrist to keep her in line.

"What's wrong?" she asked breathlessly.

Jesus. What wasn't wrong? I didn't know her. I was pretty sure I didn't like her, and I wasn't about to let her feel me up in her bedroom with her parents waiting for us downstairs. I'd never been big on people touching me to begin with and her hands on me didn't change my mind.

"Nothing. I need to use the bathroom," I told her in a clipped tone. Stepping around her, I beat a quick retreat out the door. Once in the hallway, I didn't stop because I knew she'd be coming after me. I stepped inside the nearest door to wait for her to go past.

"Why are you in my room?"

I froze as Arianna's voice wrapped around me like silk. Turning my head, I spotted her sitting at a desk. She was sitting in front of a computer set up that actually made my dick twitch. I'd been right, her computer set up and mine was damn near identical. I wasn't sure whether the hardware or the woman was responsible for my chubby, but either way I was drawn toward them like a moth to a flame. I wasn't sure what it was about Ari that was different. The thought of her touching me had me hardening even more. I knew which sister my body was voting for, I just needed to wrap my head around taking her choice away from her.

The knock on the door had me freezing in my tracks again. Arianna's brows went up and a small smile played over her lips. She jerked a thumb toward a door and I gratefully stepped into her bathroom.

"Is he in here?" Alexandria demanded. Her voice floated through the door and I shuddered at the waspish sound. Now that she wasn't on her best behavior it came across clearly.

I leaned against the wall, next to the door, and blatantly listened in.

"Keep your grubby little hands to yourself, Ari. He's mine."

"I never said I wanted him. If you want to be sold off, then be my guest," Ari responded.

"Don't be such a child. Papa explained all of this already, and it's not like we didn't know this would happen one day."

"Just because he raised us with the expectation that we'd be shipped off in arranged marriages doesn't mean we have to be happy about it," Ari grumbled at her sister.

I felt bad for them. Well, for Arianna at least. Not that I was in any position to feel sorry for her since I was in the same dead-end situation.

"If it's not him, it'll just be someone else, Ari. At least he's hot." I heard a door open. "And by the way… It won't be him for you. I'm the oldest, I will be getting married first." The door slammed shut.

I silently counted to ten before I came out of the bathroom. I hadn't really needed to use it, I'd just wanted to get away from the oppressive atmosphere downstairs.

Ari watched me grimly. "She's gone," she told me when I hesitated in the doorway.

"Thanks."

We stood, staring at each other. Her gaze was calculating. "Why are you doing this?"

I raised a brow at her in question.

"Getting married. It's being forced on us—well maybe not Alex—but why are *you* doing it?"

She'd been at the meeting, but I doubted Sal shared his secrets with his daughters. It hadn't occurred to me that she may not know much about what was going on. I was surprised she hadn't asked at the park when we talked. My only guess is with the deadline looming this was becoming as real for her as it was for me.

"Our club needs to align with your father," I told her, watching for her reaction. "This is his price for peace."

She sighed. "I figured it was something like that."

"Oh yeah? Why's that?"

"You're too gorgeous to need an arranged marriage." She shut her mouth so quickly her teeth clacked together. Red crawled up her neck.

I had to bite back the laugh even as I flushed a color that matched her own. She obviously hadn't meant to be *that* honest with me. I let my gaze roam down her body. It was nice to know that she was as attracted to me as I was to her.

The club girls who hung around at all the parties the MC threw had come onto me more than once. Usually, after they'd been turned down by one of my brothers. Between that and not wanting my first time to be with someone who'd slept their way through the MC, I'd refused them every time.

I was twenty-two and a fucking virgin. I suspected my brothers in arms knew, considering I didn't socialize, but it wasn't something I talked about. Being a red-blooded male I had the urges, I just hadn't been able to drop my walls around any females long enough to lose my V card. Instead, I spent entirely too much time watching porn. It did the trick and made it so I didn't have to open up to someone else. Being vulnerable wasn't a position I was fond of. I'd had too much of that as a kid.

My gaze landed on Arianna's again. Here was a woman who didn't care about the club—or my status in it, for that matter. That was appealing to me.

Despite being gorgeous, her older sister only induced mind-numbing panic and a need to fucking run when she looked at me. Arianna on the other hand had me going from half to full mast with one embarrassed glance.

What I'd heard after ducking into the bathroom made me hesitate, though. Arianna didn't want to get married. She didn't want to be forced to take a husband. I'd suspected it, but having it confirmed made me feel damn guilty.

The silence had stretched on too long between us, but Arianna was studying me as intently as I was her. She had the same confused look that I was sure was on my own face.

A door slamming out in the hallway made Arianna jump. For once, the sound didn't evoke a flight or fight response in me. I sucked in a breath and watched the woman in front of me. She held her breath, listening hard at the door.

Footsteps pounded past, then another door slammed. "She's going to search this entire house for you."

My eyes were drawn back to hers. She was like a magnet, pulling me in. I stepped in closer to her. My heart was slamming inside my chest. Arianna's eyes widened and she tipped her head back to keep eye contact with me. My gaze dropped down to her lips as they parted.

The door wrenched open at her back, and I stifled a groan as I saw Alexandria standing there glaring at us.

"I knew it!" She shoved her sister out of the way, grabbed my arm, and pulled.

I let her drag me out into the hall, but my eyes stayed on Arianna. She looked down at the ground and worried her lower lip between her teeth. That was the closest I'd ever come to kissing someone, and it looked like she'd been just as affected by it as I was.

"Come on. Papa is looking for us," she said, while towing me along. Her strength surprised me. Not that I couldn't have easily stopped her if I wanted to. I let her take me out of Arianna's room because I didn't trust myself to be alone with her. Something told me Sal wouldn't like me messing around with his little girl under his own roof.

Then again, maybe he wouldn't give a shit. The man was hard to read, and I prided myself on that ability. He had two faces, the one he showed the world, and one only his family—and maybe enemies—saw. I could tell by the way Celia and her children reacted to his movements and were constantly watchful of his moods that he wasn't the more jovial version he showed everyone else. It was like they were terrified of him. Abel was the only one who seemed calm although distant in his father's presence.

Sal watched Alexandria and I closely as we came back into the dining room and I felt that knowing tingle as it raced down my spine. I'd spent my life around men like him. I didn't know him yet, but my gut told me he wasn't trustworthy. Not that our club trusted him. He had a lot to prove before we'd extend him that courtesy. That didn't mean we wouldn't use him for our own gains.

Arianna hurried in as I was slipping into my seat. Bass gave me a nudge with his elbow and a questioning look. We'd been gone longer than was normal for a bathroom break.

"So… Viktor…"

I focused on Sal, who was studying me. I returned his hard stare with one of my own.

"Yes?"

"Who will you choose?"

I darted a quick look over at Arianna. She refused to look up from the table. Movement caught my attention as Alexandria shifted on her chair.

"Come, tell us now," Sal insisted.

I considered telling him to fuck off, but he was right. I had made up my mind. It wasn't going to change and if I made my choice now, I could get out of this house. "Arianna," I said firmly.

What happened next would've been hilarious if it wasn't for the fact that this was real life—my life. Alexandria jumped up so fast her chair flew out behind her. She let out a screech that would've made a pterodactyl proud and tackled her sister from her chair to the ground.

My jaw dropped. A deep rumbling sound came from my side and I glared over at Bass who didn't have the same issues with laughing at the women rolling around on the rug.

"Girls!" Celia hissed, trying to restore some order. It didn't work.

Alexandria was on top of Arianna and was ripping at her hair while screaming, "He's mine!" at the top of her lungs.

It was a bit of a stroke to my ego, I wouldn't lie, but I also didn't want these women fighting over me. I wasn't sure Arianna was fighting for me so much as trying to keep her sister from yanking her hair out of her head.

I stood up and shot Sal a glare since he was just passively sitting there, letting his girls duke it out. Nothing phased the man, it was an incredible lesson in self-control. I caught a hint of malice and glee in his gaze and realized that the man may not be completely sane.

Going around the table, I was just about to pull Alexandria off my fiancée when the sickening sound of crunching bone made everyone freeze. Abel grabbed his sister when I hesitated and pulled her off Arianna.

Alexandria was holding her nose and sobbing as blood poured from between her fingers. "You stupid bitch," she wailed, then jerked out of Abel's arms and ran out of the room. Her mother hurried after her.

I held my hand out to Arianna. She eyed me warily, but took it and I pulled her up to her feet. "Nice shot," I commented.

Her lips twitched as she tried to repress a smile, and Abel chuckled.

"Welcome to the family," Abel said and stuck a hand out for me to shake. When I took it, he pulled me in a little closer and whispered, "I'll deny it if she asks, but you chose the better sister." He winked at Arianna, then turned and strode out of the room.

My mind was blown. Just like that—apparently—everything was done. I glanced over at Arianna. I couldn't tell from her expression if she was pissed or not. She'd completely shut down after the smile she'd given me. I didn't know her well enough to gauge her mood, and wasn't that fucked up? I was marrying a stranger. Worse, I was forcing her to marry one as well.

"Congratulations," Sal said, approaching now that his daughters had settled their skirmish.

I hadn't grown up with a normal family and my MC brothers fought shit out all the time, so who knew? Maybe this was normal amongst siblings.

"Thanks," I muttered and tried not to flinch when Arianna tensed next to me.

"Papa-"

Sal cut Arianna off with a steely look. Guilt overtook me. I hated taking her freedom of choice away from her.

"I'd like to set a long engagement," I told them. "It'll give us time to get to know-"

"No."

My brows shot up at his clipped response.

"I'll work it out with your president, but the quicker you get married, the better for everyone," he relented and gave me the explanation I'd silently asked for.

"No," I parroted. His eyes narrowed dangerously. My heart started beating so fast I could barely hear anything over it. "You'll work it out with me. Here and now." Sal had already gotten his way in multiple situations. Besides, from what I'd seen of him tonight, if I didn't start this marriage by standing my ground I'd be a slave to him forever. I may not be the most assertive of my brothers, but I was still a Viking and a man, and Sal would respect that, or I'd make him.

Sometime in the middle of our talk, the two younger girls had left the room. I felt Bass come and stand at my back. Arianna moved to stand next to me. It was the three of us squaring off against Sal.

"You'll work it out with *us*," Arianna said. I could finally tell how she felt about this. She was pissed. I didn't miss the slight tremble in her hand, though. Standing up to her father wasn't easy for her. A protective instinct filled me and I shifted slightly so that our shoulders brushed, a sign of solidarity. If Sal wanted to take us on, he'd be fighting against us both.

CHAPTER 5

Ari

I shot both my fiancé and my father a dark look, daring them to argue with me. It made my stomach churn. Papa had taught us early on that arguing with him was a bad idea. We even knew better than to argue with Mama in front of company. Neither would let the action go unpunished. Papa thought it made him look weak to have his children anything other than under his complete control, and Mama would be embarrassed by misbehavior.

Neither man said anything. Papa motioned for us to sit back down. I noticed Mama had run off after Alex. No surprise there. My sister was a spoiled, bratty woman, and I didn't like her much. My two youngest sisters, though, I'd give my life to protect.

Instant gratitude had pummeled me when Ada had told us Rat wouldn't be choosing her. Papa would've let him, if that's what it took, so I was thankful it hadn't come to that.

I sat down across from the two men, while Papa took his seat at the head of the table. It was only the four of us in here now. I'd never negotiated an arranged marriage before, so I wasn't sure what to expect.

Were they going to exchange chickens for me? How many barnyard animals was I worth?

The thought made my lips thin out into a flat line. I had a maelstrom of emotion causing chaos inside me. I didn't want to get married. Or rather, I didn't want to be forced into it. I'd always had this childhood fantasy that I'd marry for love. For most women these days that would be the expectation. For my sisters and I, we'd been told from a young age that we'd be paired off to men of my father's choosing. The lack of choice in the matter grated at me and I wanted to deny the match just out of spite.

I peeked through my lashes at the man who would become my husband. He wasn't exactly jumping for joy either. Everything he'd told me upstairs and what I'd heard at their meeting indicated he was only doing this for the good of their club. That had a strange feeling of disappointment mixing in with the other emotions churning in my chest.

When he'd said my name, excitement and more than a little smugness had sparked within me. Being smug, I understood. Alex had been positive that she'd be chosen. In fact, we all thought she would. She was the oldest daughter and beautiful. Men had been falling all over themselves chasing after her for years. Not that Papa would allow us to have boyfriends.

Papa would lose his mind if he knew his precious Alexandria wouldn't have been a blushing virginal bride. I'd caught her with one of Papa's Capos. Leave it to Alex to choose a man twice her age to lose her virginity to. At least when I'd lost mine it was with a boy from school. Our first time had been fumbling, but sweet. We'd had a summer fling and I'd thought myself in love at the time. The feelings faded— as they tended to do with young love— but I'd forever be grateful to him. He'd given me the opportunity to take control of my life— not something that Papa often allowed.

If we'd been caught-

I shoved the thought away as ice filled my veins. I'd played a dangerous game with that boy's life and possibly my own. I doubted my father would've actually done anything to me, but we were only willing to push him so far.

"Celia and I would like the wedding to take place in October."

My father speaking pulled me back into the conversation happening in front of me. I couldn't help gasping. October was only a couple weeks away. I stared at Papa in shock, then peeked over at Viktor.

His face was cold, hard, and I had to suppress a shudder. He'd seemed really nice and sweet when we spoke at the park, but right now he was showing a new side. He looked as dangerous as I supposed guys who belonged to a motorcycle club probably were. It just reminded me that I had a lot to learn about this man.

"That doesn't work for me," Rat replied coldly.

Both men remained silent for a few beats while they studied each other.

"November," Rat said.

His voice had a ring of finality to it and I felt a vise clamp around my lungs. It was getting harder to breathe.

Papa's face broke out into a grin. "Agreed."

"You can pick the date."

I looked over and found Rat's intense blue eyes watching me. *Gee, lucky me.* I didn't get to choose to become engaged or decide the month or year in which I'd be married, but I had full control over which day it would be. Folding my arms over my chest, I inwardly sighed because that wasn't true either. My mother would hound me unmercifully until I picked whatever day she wanted.

Mama was going to be livid that she had to plan a wedding in six weeks. I held on to the small amount of joy that thought gave me. It wasn't that I didn't love my parents—on some level I did, but I also resented them. It was probably pathetic that I was desperate for their love and approval. I just couldn't seem to help it. After years of basically being ignored—unless they were telling me what *not* to do—I still needed that validation from them. It was fucked up and I didn't understand why, but there wasn't much I could do about it. I'd tried to write them off and it hadn't worked. It didn't matter that I was terrified of Papa most of the time and that Mama was the cloth Alex was cut from—and that they both pissed me off.

Abel was the heir, Alex was the princess and Ada was the baby. Both Antonia and I had pretty much been left to our own devices unless Mama or Papa needed something from us. Abel had been more of a father to me than my own had over the years. My love for him was pure and I knew he returned it—in his own way.

It had mostly been for the best. It meant I got to pursue my own passions without Mama constantly harping at me that 'a lady shouldn't behave that way.' I saw what Alex went through, and though she seemed to love it, I would've hated growing up like that. Instead, I got to take things apart just to learn how they went together and learned everything I could about computers. I was able to duck the responsibilities—and negative attention—both my parents gave Abel and Alex.

"...can take her home tonight."

What? Had my father just offered for this man—who I don't know—to take me home like I was a stray puppy? I stared at him in shock. Viktor seemed as lost for words as I was. His friend's head was bouncing around like he was watching a ping pong match as he looked between the three of us.

"I will not be going home with him," I said stiffly.

Papa's eyes met mine and something dangerous sparked there. I was furious, though, so I didn't care. I was convinced I got my temper from him— although maybe mine wasn't as precarious. Once I was angry, I was willing to bring his wrath down on me and screw who it burned.

"You'll do as I-"

"I won't," I insisted as I cut him off. "I will move in with him once we are married."

Papa's fist slammed down on the table, rattling the leftover dishes that the staff had left here—presumably they'd all made themselves scarce during the fight. He and I had our gazes locked, a silent battle of wills.

"You will, or so help me…"

He didn't finish the sentence, but I felt fear trickle down my spine. I knew exactly what my father was capable of. He'd never hurt one of us before, but that's because we all fell into line whenever he commanded it. He had it in him, though. It wasn't hard to read the violence in his eyes.

Viktor cleared his throat and our eyes snapped over to him. "She will stay here until the engagement is announced. Then, she'll come to live with me."

There was that commanding voice again. I bit the inside of my cheeks to keep from telling him he could screw all the way off. I sat stewing in my chair as my mother hurried into the room.

"I'm so sorry. What did I miss?" She was breathless and excitement flickered in her eyes. This was a dream come true—for her. Sure, she was probably disappointed that it wasn't Alex getting married, but she'd gotten over it quickly enough. I ground my teeth as she sat daintily next to Papa.

"The engagement party will be next Saturday," Papa told the room.

Mama gasped. "Salvatore, you expect me to get a party together in that amount of-"

Papa's hard look had her snapping her jaw shut and sucking in a deep breath. She smoothed out her features before she smiled at me then at Viktor. "I'll see that it happens and it will be beautiful."

My stomach lurched so hard I felt like I was going to throw up. Once we announced it, it was going to be very difficult to break the engagement off. I needed to do something before Saturday to press pause—or stop it completely.

My mind was racing too fast to pay much attention to the rest of the conversation. Before I knew it, everyone was standing.

"Walk your fiancé out," Papa ordered.

I followed Viktor and his friend out onto the front porch. The second guy went to wait by their motorcycles. I thought his name was Bass—it would make sense with that deep, dark voice he had—but the whole night had been a blur, so I wasn't sure.

"Viktor-"

"Rat," he reminded me, gently. He sighed as he stared down at me.

As a girl I'd sprouted up quickly and topped out at five-nine, but Rat had a good four inches on me. I had to tip my chin a bit to look into his troubled eyes.

"Look. I'm sorry for putting you in this position, Ari."

He paused, then gave me a nod. "If there was any other way I would've chosen it."

Frowning, I searched his face while I tried to deal with the conflicting emotions welling up inside of me. I hated the mafia life. I wanted to be free of it, and not through marriage. The idea of marrying a stranger, just because Papa told me I had to, made me feel like destroying something in a bout of rage. But hearing what Rat was saying made me feel insecure and unhappy. I couldn't possibly be upset that this guy wasn't thrilled about marrying me either—could I?

"Maybe we could talk some sense into my father?" I asked hopefully.

Rat shook his head. "It's done. As sorry as I am about it, I won't go back on my word and I've promised to marry you."

I've had a lot of practice hiding my emotions. You learned to do so very quickly when your father has no qualms about killing people who pissed him off. That didn't mean I was a doormat, though. Rat's words had a wash of red hazing my vision.

"Well, I'm sorry, too," I hissed at him. I wasn't sure who I was more pissed at—him for basically admitting he didn't want me or myself for caring.

Rat's eyes widened, then his brows drew together in a frown. "Wait...what-"

I didn't hear the rest of what he was saying because I'd already spun around and slammed my front door in his face. Hurrying across the foyer, I glared at my parents who came out from the dining room.

"Arianna," Papa growled, but I ignored him and raced to my room. I locked the door just in case.

My parents didn't bother to come check on me, and that was fine —typical. I sat down at my computer and started looking into the man I was going to be marrying and his club.

* * *

I wasn't sure how much time I'd lost while I'd been digging around on the dark web. All I knew was I was in deep fucking shit. My heart was racing, hands clammy, and it felt like I was going to throw up what little dinner I'd eaten.

When Papa had first brought home these bikers, I hadn't paid much attention to who they were. Once we found out he was arranging a marriage with one of them, everyone assumed Alex would be the one chosen, so I still hadn't bothered to look into them.

If Rat and his club found out who I was—what I'd done—they'd kill me. If I refused to marry him, Papa might kill me. I was caught in the middle. I'd just found out quite a bit about how Rat's club operates —despite the impressive security blocks someone had thrown up to hide their activities. Everything I'd found told me they'd have no qualms about killing someone actively working against them. Desperation was bubbling up inside of me.

I logged into my bank account—or rather Audrey Heyburn's—and sighed in relief when I found my little nest egg untouched. It'd been necessary to hide the money I'd been saving for the past four years. If my father found it, who knew what he'd do.

Once I'd started college, I began picking up little side jobs I could do for other students—homework, helping fix their computers, stuff like that. I'd squirreled it all away with every intention of fleeing this life with Antonia and Ada. That meant I had to wait until Ada was eighteen. I couldn't risk taking her before then.

I'd never asked my father for permission to take a real job because then he'd know I have money. Plus, there was no way he'd have allowed it. He already had his men following us around campus as it was—for our own protection, he always said. I never really knew if it was that, or to keep us in line.

My plan was to go to my Uncle Nico in New York. He would take us in. I was closer to him than I'd ever been to my own father. I had to be careful, though. Uncle Nico was a mafia boss, too. As much as I loved him, those kinds of men—men like my father—ruled over their little worlds like dictators. The kind of power they had made them feel like they could do anything they wanted with anyone's lives and get away with it. Sadly, they did get away with it.

Uncle Nico knew what the relationship was like between my father and I. I used to dream that he would come rescue me from this life. As I got older I began to understand that if he did, it would cause a war between our families. That'd been the last thing I wanted, so I never blamed Uncle Nico for not doing anything. We weren't his kids —his responsibility.

Things were different now. I was an adult and my sisters would be as well. If I couldn't convince Uncle Nico to help, he would send us back home immediately. The consequences didn't bear thinking about. It would be worth it, though. If it worked, we'd be free. Free to live how we chose, marry who we wanted, and never have an overbearing family member or husband tell us what to do again.

My door opened and I glanced over my shoulder into the worried face of my sister. She and Ada were the only two who had keys to my room. Even Abel didn't have one. Antonia shut the door behind her—locking it again—and came over to me. I rose and we hugged.

"What are you going to do?" she asked, her voice muffled from having her head buried in my shoulder.

I stroked her dark hair. "I don't know," I admitted.

"You should go." She pulled back and our eyes locked. There were tears in hers, but there was a grim set to her mouth.

"I can't leave you and Ada." The thought made me want to sit down and cry. As much as I loved Ada if she chose not to come with us I wouldn't worry about her. Ada was Mama's baby and she'd make sure nothing bad happened to my sister. Antonia and I had always been extremely close, though. "I won't leave you," I repeated.

She frowned and went to sit on my bed. "We could go then. Just you and I—tonight."

I sighed and sat next to her burying my head in my hands. Tugging on my hair, I tried to come up with a plan. "The wedding changes everything."

"How?"

"Uncle Nico might have kept us in New York if we asked even against Papa's wishes. Papa most likely would've kept it quiet to prevent any kind of gossip." I raised my head and looked at her. "I don't think he'll let us stay if some motorcycle club is going to come pounding on his door looking for a runaway bride." Not to mention Papa would demand that Uncle Nico return me and it could start that war. I wasn't willing to drag Uncle Nico into this mess.

"We can make him understand that you had no say in the matter-"

I couldn't help but laugh. Antonia's face screwed up as she thought about what she'd said. "There's no way. He'd hand me right back over to the Vikings and you to Papa. I wouldn't be around to protect you from the consequences I caused."

"This is our choice, too," Antonia said firmly. "You gave both me and Ada a chance to make up our own minds about going with you or staying. We decided to go."

Abel and Alex were the only two who seemed to want to live this way. The rest of us wanted out.

"Maybe it won't be so bad being married to a biker?" Antonia said. Her tone was hesitant, but hopeful. Neither of us knew much about motorcycle clubs. We'd been overly sheltered growing up. Papa had kept his family safe from outside threats. I was pretty sure it had more to do with reputation than because he cared for us. He'd always been so hard and strict we were terrified of him. Instinctively, we knew if we pushed too hard he'd end us. Such was the mafia way. I'd never known any different.

"It's trading one type of imprisonment for another," I told her. I wanted to be free to make my own choices, live my life, and what I was getting was another man who was embroiled in the criminal lifestyle. There could be good men in this way of life. Uncle Nico and Abel had proven that, but I had no idea on which side of the line my future husband fell.

I swallowed. I hadn't shared much about the work I'd been doing for Papa with Antonia. The less she knew the safer she was, but I needed advice. "I'm in a lot of trouble, Sis."

CHAPTER 6

Rat

Bass and I pulled into the clubhouse as the sun was rising. I'd told him to go home, but he'd insisted on keeping me company as I rode around the city. The cool breeze had helped me clear my head. Bass had taken care of letting Cade know what happened. I hadn't been ready to talk about it.

As we walked into the kitchen and I saw Ming sitting there, staring sleepily into a bowl of cereal I suddenly felt an overwhelming urge to spill my guts to her. It was crazy. It'd taken me years to fully open up to my brothers, but after only a few months I trusted this woman just as much. More really. I considered speaking with one of my happily paired off brothers about my troubles, but something told me a female's perspective would be more beneficial.

Bass grunted a goodnight to us as he loped up the stairs toward his room. I sat down across from Ming.

She smiled at me. Curiosity filled her eyes, but she didn't ask me any questions. This, this was why I wanted to talk to her. She somehow understood my moods and quirks. She was almost as good at figuring me out as Cade was. She knew when to stay quiet and listen and when to lay into me and tell me what I needed to hear.

"I chose Arianna."

Ming listened quietly while I detailed what'd happened last night. She chuckled when I told her about the fight and Ari punching her sister in the face. "She sounds like she'll fit in perfectly around here."

I closed my eyes and sighed. "Hopefully. I want her to get along with everyone."

Ming covered my hand with her own. "We're all going to love her and welcome her here."

"Will that be enough? She didn't choose this, and she didn't choose me. And that's not the worst of it." It meant so much to me that I could count not only on my brothers to accept my new wife, but their women too. That would make this transition a little easier. I frowned and opened my mouth to ask Ming something before thinking better of it.

"What is it?"

I looked up at her and grimaced. "I pissed her off."

"Arianna?"

"Yeah, only I don't know what I did wrong." I told her what'd happened on the porch before Ari had stormed off.

Ming groaned and I felt heat flush up my neck. She already knew what wrong step I'd made and she hadn't even been there. "Those were the exact words you used?" she asked, sounding like she hoped I would deny it.

I nodded.

Ming shook her head, but gave me a soft smile. "You have a lot to learn about women, Rat."

I knew that.

"The way you phrased that, to her makes it sound like you're sorry you have to marry her."

Frowning, I stared down at my hands on the countertop. "I *am* sorry-"

"I know you, so I know you're sorry that you're forcing her to marry you. The way you said it made it sound like you didn't want her —specifically."

My jaw dropped and my eyes darted up to hers. "That's not at all what I meant."

"I know that, sweetie, but if I didn't know you, that's how I would've taken it too."

Well, fuck me.

"Okay...how do I fix this?"

"Go talk to her. Use a few more words to explain why you're sorry to be marrying her." Ming chuckled, and I felt another flush spread over my skin.

I was so fucking underprepared for dating a woman, let alone marrying one. I had too much baggage I was still dealing with. "Thanks, Doc."

"Anytime." We both looked over as Axel walked into the clubhouse kitchen.

He frowned then looked at his watch. "I thought you left for work already?"

"I'm going now," Ming said, sending me a wink. She kissed Axe then walked out the door.

Axel narrowed his eyes on my face. "Everything good, Kid?"

I nodded, told him goodnight, then beat tracks up the stairs. His voice floated up after me. "Goodnight? It's fucking six a.m."

* * *

I STROLLED across the University's campus. It hadn't taken me more than an hour to dig up some information on Ari's life once I'd woken up. Glancing at my phone, I noted the time then leaned against a tree to wait. She should be passing by soon, heading from one class to another.

It'd occurred to me that I'd never gotten her number. My digging this afternoon fixed that. She'd done some basic level shit to hide her identity, but nothing I couldn't work around in a few minutes.

Straightening up when I spotted her, I watched as she crossed the courtyard. Her head was down, dark hair covering her face as she typed away on her phone.

I fell into step beside her and she glanced up then started when she realized who I was. She stopped and blinked up at me.

"How-"

"Hey," I said softly. I was trying to keep an eye on our surroundings, but those soft green eyes kept pulling my focus back onto them.

Her mouth twisted into a frown and I hardened as my eyes fell to those lush lips. I had a flash of her on her knees in front of me, wrapping them around my cock. Clearing my throat, I shoved the visual away. I'd never reacted to a woman this strongly before.

"What are you doing here, Rat?" she asked suspiciously.

"I wanted to see if we could talk. Want to get some lunch?"

"I have class," she glanced over her shoulder toward the building she'd been hurrying toward.

"Come on. Have lunch with me. Your GPA can handle skipping one class." I gave her a playful grin.

Her eyes narrowed. "How do you know what my GPA is?"

I put my arm around her shoulders, ignoring the way she tensed, and started leading her toward the lot I'd parked my bike in. "If you want to find that out, you'll have to come to lunch."

She huffed out a laugh and stopped fighting me. "Alright, you win." Her step stuttered when she saw a man in a suit walking toward us.

"Where are you going, Arianna?" The man spoke in a low voice as he approached us.

"We're going to get food," I told him, turning her a little so I was between her and this guy. He was too old to be a student, so I was guessing he was some kind of bodyguard. "Alone."

His eyes narrowed. "Who the fuck are you?"

"Bene, this is my fiancé," Ari said from behind me. "Check with Papa, he'll be fine with it."

We waited as he stepped away and spoke quietly on his phone. After listening he walked over and handed the phone to me.

"Yeah."

"You didn't clear coming to see my daughter with me." Sal sounded pissed.

"Didn't know I needed to," I said, adopting a bored tone. I motioned to Ari to wait and stepped away from her.

"There are rules-"

"Why do you care? You already tried to have me take her home," I asked, cutting him off.

I could hear the smile in his tone. "And you declined. From now on, clear it through me. Since I have you on the phone, I need a favor."

This guy was a complete dick.

"What kind of favor?"

"I have a friend—he's more like family—who's having trouble tracking someone down in New York City. I told him my future son-in-law could help with that."

Pausing, I considered the request. Having Sal owe me—owe the club—was a good thing. Not that I wanted to help him in any way. "Send me the information. I'll give my card to your man here. If I decide to help you, I'll let you know."

"You'd also be helping Nico Romano. Look him up." His chuckle was dark and knowing, as though the minute I looked up whoever the fuck that was I'd trip over myself to help.

Dick.

"I'll let you know."

"Have fun with Arianna." It sounded more like a warning than anything.

Handing back the phone, I pulled a card out of my wallet. The guy was almost as big as Riggs. He glared at me, but finally turned away.

I smirked as I watched him leave. "What the hell kind of name is Bene?"

"An Italian one," she said grinning. "Besides, what kind of name is Rat?"

"A road name," I told her. The corner of my lips tipped up at her teasing tone.

"What happened?" Her green eyes lit with curiosity.

"He wanted me to help a friend find someone," I told her casually.

She frowned and looked like she was going to say something. After a moment of indecision, she finally asked, "Where are we eating?"

"You tell me. What's good around here?" I didn't pry to try and get her to tell me what she'd been about to say. I'd deal with it later.

Arianna grinned and gave me an address. We stopped by my bike and I typed it into my GPS. After a few minutes of studying the map I put my phone away. I knew the streets well, even after all these years. It wouldn't be a problem to find the place. I watched Ari as she ran a fingertip along my bike. Swallowing hard, I had to keep my mind from conjuring images of her running it over my body. Something about her spoke to me in a way no one else had. She made me feel comfortable—well, except behind my zipper. It usually took me a long time to warm up to people, but with her it felt like I'd known her forever. It didn't matter that I hardly knew a damn thing about her.

"Your motorcycle is beautiful."

"Thanks. Have you ever ridden one?"

She shook her head, but I caught the gleam of excitement in her eyes. At least she wasn't afraid. I opened up the saddle bag and took out my extra helmet.

Ari frowned. "Where's yours?"

"I don't like wearing it." I took the helmet out of her hands and set it on top of her head, securing the strap.

"Then why do I have to wear one?"

"Because I like how smart you are. I want to keep it that way."

She snorted at me, but let me finish adjusting the helmet. I straddled my bike, started it, and backed it out of the parking spot before I motioned for her to climb on. I couldn't help the chuckle that escaped as she exuberantly clambered on behind me. It was nice that she wasn't scared. In fact, she seemed downright giddy to be going on a ride with me. It was a good first step to making this easier.

As soon as she wrapped her arms around me and pressed against my back my dick kicked painfully. Jesus. I needed to remember to jerk off before spending time with her again. It'd make things a lot less painful.

CHAPTER 7

Ari

It felt like we were flying. The wind whipped my hair behind me as we rode along city streets, weaving in and out of traffic. Papa hadn't even allowed us to get our driver's licenses. Instead, he had his men drive us everywhere.

I started to wonder if marrying Rat would give me some of the freedom I craved. Antonia and I had sat up late last night, going over possible plans. All but one had us living a life on the run from both the mafia and an MC. Even if The Vikings would eventually stop looking for me, there's no way Papa would. He'd find me, just to make me face slighting him, if nothing else. So, we'd made the decision to stay. I'd marry a man who didn't really want me and my sisters would stay in our father's home until he found men that he wanted them to marry. It was downright depressing, but we couldn't see any other way out.

Rat pulled up in front of the little pizzeria I'd given him the address for. I loved this place. I hopped off the bike, trying to ignore the way my body protested being removed from the hard line of muscles in Rat's back. He wasn't buff like the jocks that walked around on campus, but the man was ripped. He didn't have an ounce of fat on his body and I'd felt the definition of each of his ab muscles under my hands as I held onto him. My body warmed and my nipples stiffened as I watched him dismount his bike.

Turning away, I tried to gather my wayward thoughts. What the hell was wrong with me? Sure, I enjoyed a pretty face and a ripped body as much as the next girl, but I'd never had this kind of reaction before. Rat wrapped his arm around my shoulders again and led me into the restaurant. I lost against the urge to shiver as his body brushed against mine.

"Are you cold?" As he shrugged off his cut, then tugged off his sweatshirt his t-shirt caught on it flashing me a view of tanned skin and just as many abs as I suspected he had.

It was the end of September, but still in the seventies during the day. I wasn't cold. I wasn't about to tell him why I'd shivered, though, so I took his sweatshirt and put it on. He put his cut back on over his t-shirt and I tried to ignore how good the leather looked on him.

"Thanks," I murmured as we found a table and sat. I realized immediately that putting his clothes on had been a mistake. His scent surrounded me and I had to press my thighs together under the table to control the bolt of lust that shot straight down to my core. What was wrong with me? I wasn't supposed to want this guy. I was being forced to marry him and vice versa. He didn't want me. It'd be humiliating to throw myself at him and be rejected.

"Ari!"

The voice calling my name broke through my thoughts and I smiled at Mary as she walked up. I'd been coming to this place since I started college. I was usually here at least once a week. Mary was the owner and she was the sweetest lady I'd ever met. "Hi, Mary!" I stood and we hugged.

"I didn't see you last week. I thought maybe you'd finally gotten sick of my cooking."

I snorted at her and shot her an unamused look. "As if that could ever happen. Sorry, things have been a bit hectic. I won't miss another week, promise." Even as I said it, I hoped it would be true. I didn't know what kind of restrictions Rat might put on me once we were married. The only good thing about living with my parents was I knew all the rules and how to circumvent them when I needed to.

Mary's curious gaze swept over to Rat. "Who's your friend?"

"Oh, this is Rat. Rat, Mary."

He stood up and shook the woman's hand while she eyeballed him like she expected him to snatch me away and do wicked things to me.

If only. I cringed at that thought. I needed to get the horny voice inside of my head to shut up. It wasn't helping.

"Your usual?" Mary finally said, after she finished studying Rat.

"A large," I said with a smile. We sat back down as she bustled away. "Oh...I guess I should've asked before I ordered-"

"Whatever it is, is fine. I'm like a black hole."

A grin stretched across my face at his description. It seemed accurate. He was pulling me in, despite my best efforts to remain aloof around him.

"Look, I wanted to explain about last night."

I tensed. I knew I'd overreacted about what he'd been saying. Drama wasn't typically my thing, that was Alex's area of expertise, but it'd been a long, stressful night. Being chosen and rejected in the same hour was a little taxing. Out of habit, I almost apologized about how I'd reacted, but something stopped me. I wanted to see where he would go with this. How he'd act and whether he'd manipulate the situation to guilt trip me. That was my family's MO. This would be a good chance to see what this man was about. When I didn't say anything he continued.

"I wasn't trying to upset you. I didn't mean to imply that I didn't want to marry *you*." His blue eyes were intense on mine. I had to fight not to drop my gaze. "I meant that I was sorry to be taking away your choice in the matter."

Blinking, I searched his gaze. He seemed genuine. The coiled tension in my shoulders eased a little. "Thank you. For what it's worth I'm sorry too. Both for how I reacted and because it doesn't seem like you have much say in this either." Although, he did have a bit more than I did. "Why *did* you pick me?" I'd been wondering all night.

He sighed and looked at the table for a moment before looking up.

"A few reasons. One, as I said already, Ada is too young. Two, Alex is...awful."

I chuckled at this and smiled at him. He relaxed a bit and smiled back. I could have melted in my chair.

"Three, I... well, this is selfish, but I realized that if I didn't choose *you*, someone else would. Someone that wasn't me. Who isn't like me."

What the hell does that mean? I nodded, not really sure what to say.

He nodded back. "It's going to take some time for us to figure each other out. I'm looking forward to it, though."

He leaned back in his chair and we both sat quietly as Mary dropped a large pizza in between us. It was slathered in extra cheese and topped with just about every type of meat known to man. My mouth watered.

"My kinda girl," he muttered, before he picked up a piece and shoved the piping hot slice into his mouth.

I watched, transfixed as he licked his lips. When those eyes met mine again and heated I took the coward's way out and looked down.

It should be illegal to eat pizza the way he did. My mouth went completely dry as he licked sauce off his thumb.

This time, when his scorching gaze landed on mine, I held it for a few seconds. I watched as his eyes narrowed then dropped to my lips. I lifted a piece onto my plate and started cutting into it with a fork. Silence stretched out around us and my head snapped up only to find Rat watching me with confused fascination.

"What?"

"You eat pizza with a fork?"

I blinked at him, then down at my food. "Yes?"

"I don't think this is going to work," he muttered.

"Huh?"

"I can't marry someone who eats pizza with a fork." The teasing smile on his face completely transformed it. He looked so mischievous, I couldn't help the laugh that slipped out.

"Well, maybe I can't marry someone who eats most of the pizza." I watched as he snagged a second piece.

Rat chucked, but continued eating. "So, tell me more about yourself." When I just stared, he rolled his eyes and elaborated. "Favorite color? Food? Movie?"

I smiled. The idea of having this conversation—one that would usually happen on an awkward first date—now, after we're already engaged was funny to me. Although, I guess this was technically our second date—if you counted the time we spent together at the park.

"Blue, pizza, Titanic," I responded, tucking my hair behind my ear.

He fought against the grin that was forming on his lips. "Titanic?"

"Yes," I said firmly. "It's got a great love story, but I also enjoy the history itself." I fought the blush that threatened to build. "What about you?"

"Green," he said softly, holding my gaze. I swallowed and wondered why his gaze was so searching. "Mushroom Risotto, and Taken."

My brows rose. "Mushroom Risotto?"

"I like to cook."

I had to fight the urge for my jaw to drop. A biker who cooks Mushroom Risotto? I had a feeling there was a lot to learn about Rat. The rest of the meal was light-hearted and we exchanged small talk, getting to know each other on a surface level.

Neither of us was ready to take it deeper yet. It didn't matter that our engagement party was less than a week away and our wedding was barreling down on us.

* * *

WE PULLED up in front of my home. I sat for a moment, staring up at the house I grew up in, arms wrapped around the man who was going to take me away from that life. I just had no idea what kind of life I'd be moving into. It couldn't be worse than the one I was leaving, could it?

I realized I was still clinging to Rat, and I scrambled off his bike. "Thanks," I told him. "I had fun."

He reached up and brushed his knuckles over my cheek. My eyes widened slightly because it looked like he was going to kiss me. I wanted that—so badly—but another part of me wasn't ready to take that step.

Rat must have been able to read the indecision in my eyes because he only nodded to me and started up his bike. "Bye, Ari."

I waved as he rode off. Antonia came out the door. "He is really hot," she said, slinging an arm around my shoulder. She sighed dramatically. I laughed and looped my arm around her waist as we walked inside.

CHAPTER 8

Rat

For the second time today, I sat outside a mansion on my bike. I'd rather go back to Sal's. At least there, I'd be able to keep getting to know Ari. She was so beautiful, it'd been hard to keep my hands off her.

I'd wanted to kiss her, out in front of her house, but I wasn't going to push either of us too quickly.

"Viktor."

Looking over, I sighed as Enzo walked over.

"Enzo."

"Thank you for meeting me."

I nodded and swung my leg off my bike. It'd been time to man up and come speak to my brother. I'd ignored his every attempt to reach out for the last couple weeks.

So much of my childhood had been chaotic. I never knew where the next meal was coming from and knew exactly where the next beating was. Even living with The Vikings for the last ten years I hadn't outgrown my dislike for change. I was a creature of habit. Routine was how I kept the dark memories at bay. Finding out I had a brother and that I was getting married had catapulted me back into the shadowed, miserable areas within my mind. Everything kept playing back while I slept.

"Come inside, please."

I followed Enzo inside his home. He brought me to a library and motioned to a seat across the desk from where he sat down. We sat, studying each other, for a quiet moment.

"You must have so many questions."

I did. There were so many times, I imagined sitting here with my family. Demanding answers. Why had they left me? Why was I behind that dumpster? Had no one looked for me? Sitting in front of Enzo now, I wasn't sure I wanted to know the answers anymore. They wouldn't really change the past. I shrugged my shoulders in response to his statement.

Enzo's lips twitched as though he were holding back a smile. He steepled his fingers together on the desk in front of him as he continued studying me. "Then let me start by asking some."

I folded my arms over my chest and waited.

"How long have you been with The Vikings?"

"Since I was twelve."

Enzo's brows pulled together in a frown. "That young," he murmured, more to himself than to me.

"I found Cade and Riggs one day and convinced them they needed me." They hadn't. The club could've gotten by without me just fine. I'd been the one who'd needed them. Somehow, Cade had been able to see that.

Enzo nodded, looking thoughtful. He didn't seem to be in a hurry to ask another question, so I decided to ask the one that'd burned itself onto my soul.

"Did you look for me?" I'd been working on my quirks a lot lately, so I held his gaze while I asked the question. The old me would have looked down, if I'd bothered to ask it at all.

Anguish flashed in Enzo's eyes. *They were the exact shade as my own,* I realized.

"Every day. I never gave up looking for you, Viktor." His deep voice had gone hard. "Father looked too, until he died."

I could see the determination in his face. He hadn't had any luck finding me, but he'd tried—they'd tried. That made something deep inside me warm. Someone had wanted me. The taunting words Sully had thrown at me for years were nothing but lies.

"You have to understand...you and I were close, before you went missing. The gap in our ages didn't matter to me. You were my brother, my friend. You were my shadow, following me everywhere. I loved it, loved you. I would have died for you." Enzo's eyes were tortured. "Not knowing where you were—if you were safe, for I never doubted that you were still alive—was hell for me."

I couldn't imagine how hard that must have been for him. I'd had a fucked up childhood, sure, but I hadn't had to live with the knowledge that someone I loved was missing and probably living in messed up conditions. I truly didn't know which would be worse. I didn't know how to respond to him, so we sat in silence for a few moments.

"Where-"

I shook my head, and he cut off the question. I wasn't ready to explain to him where I'd been, how I'd grown up. To be honest, I wasn't sure if he was really ready to hear it either. Not after what he'd just told me. Enzo must have noticed how much it hurt. He didn't press me further on it.

"Alright, then tell me, which girl did you choose?"

My brows rose. It was going to take some getting used to, having yet another person interested in what was happening in my life.

"I'm hoping you picked well," he said with bitter amusement.

"I chose Arianna."

He looked relieved. "Thank fuck you have a decent head on your shoulders and don't think with your dick. If you'd chosen Alexandria I might have had to disown you."

His grin was fast and sharp, but I had a feeling he wasn't joking. Little did he know I was sort of thinking with my dick. It just turns out my cock isn't into spoiled princesses, but computer geeks. The realization wasn't a shock, really.

"She seems like a good girl," he told me.

As if I needed his approval. I shoved the errant thought down. "There's an engagement party on Saturday...if you want to come, you can."

A genuine smile spread over Enzo's face. "Yes. I would."

I had no idea if I was supposed to be inviting people to the party. Though, if Sal and his wife thought my MC brothers weren't going to be there, they'd be mistaken. It felt wrong to leave Enzo out of it, too.

We spent the next few hours doing pretty much what Ari and I had done earlier that afternoon. We got to know each other a little. I'd basically had two awkward first dates today.

* * *

I GROANED as I pulled into the club parking lot and five sets of eyes swung my direction. The whole crew—minus Bass—was standing around on the front porch, shooting the shit and smoking.

The last thing I wanted was more interaction with people today. I'd used up my quota of patience. The look on Riggs's face told me there was no way I was getting out of talking to them, though. Cade looked understanding, but determined as well. Steel and Gunnar kept exchanging knowing looks as I walked up. Axel was the only one who looked like he didn't want to be here anymore than I did. I felt an odd kinship with the man. It'd taken us years to become close because neither of us wanted to be around other people or speak to anyone.

"Hey, Kid," Riggs greeted me as I walked up.

I frowned suspiciously at all of them. Steel handed me his pack of cigarettes and I pulled one out, waiting for them to start hounding me with questions. We all stood around quietly, and I felt myself starting to relax. It hadn't been a bad day. Just one that was very out of habit for me. Somehow, my brothers recognized that and were letting me decompress.

Steel whistled as though he were impressed by something. We all looked at him in confusion. "I don't know if I've ever seen my brother stay quiet for this long when there was something he was dying to find out."

I chuckled and took the bottle of beer Axel passed over to me. "Go ahead. Ask," I said to Riggs. He did look like he was getting ready to implode.

"How'd it go?"

My brows shot up at his question. I'd been expecting something more like 'well which chick are you marrying?' "Good." I told them which sister I chose.

"I would've taken the oldest," Gunnar said, taking a drink of his beer.

Steel rolled his eyes. "No shit, dumbass. We all knew that's who you would've chosen."

Gunnar frowned and looked around at all of us while we grinned at him. "What? How the fuck would you know that?"

Axel snorted. "Because she's Bridget with dark hair?"

"Bridget's not quite *that* bad," I muttered.

"Bass mentioned that you negotiated with Sal?" Cade said to me while watching Steel and Gunnar wrestle with each other. They'd started going at it after Axel mentioned Alexandria and Bridget's similarities.

"Yeah…" I hesitated.

"Good for you," Cade said, low enough that only the two of us heard it. Axel and Riggs were too busy trying to pull the other men off each other. Their good-natured wrestling had turned into an all-out brawl.

I ducked my head under the weight of Cade's stare and chugged my beer. It felt good to have his respect. Standing up for myself was something I was going to need to do more often. It wasn't going to be just me anymore. I was going to have a wife to look after. Ari made this possessive, protective, nature awaken inside of me. I'd be fucking damned if anything was going to harm her while I was around.

"So, when do we get to meet her?"

The guys were done fighting and now they were all either sitting or leaning against the railing, trying to catch their breath. I met

Riggs's dark eyes and realized I hadn't told any of them the details about the marriage yet.

"Shit. The engagement party is Saturday," I told Cade.

"We'll be there," he assured me.

"I'm not fucking dressing up, though," Riggs said, continuing on and muttering something about a monkey suit.

I wondered if they even made suits in his size. "The wedding is going to be sometime in November. Ari's picking the date."

They all fell silent and stared at me. I felt all my past insecurities skitter down my spine as I held their gazes.

"Fuck me. That's soon," Steel said.

"Congrats, though, bro. You're going to be the first one of us to get married," Gunnar said, coming over to slap a large hand on my shoulder.

That didn't make me feel any better. I should be the last one to get married—if I ever did—certainly not the first. I needed someone else to make all the mistakes so I could learn from them. *Fuck my life.*

"Looks like we all know who to come to when we need advice about our wives," Axel said with a smirk. It was like the fucker was reading my mind.

I set my beer down on the railing and swallowed hard. My gut twisted sharply and I wondered if I was going to puke.

"Alright, leave him alone for fuck's sake," Cade muttered. "Give us a few minutes," he told the others and they wandered off.

Cade and I stood watching them leave. Steel and Gunnar started their match back up once Riggs and Axel disappeared around the back of the building.

"Rat, I know this isn't easy…" he started.

I sighed and rubbed a hand over the back of my neck. "It's fine. I'll figure it out. But Cade…"

"Yeah?"

"Her dad wanted her to come home with me last night. I compromised and said she'd come live with me after the engagement party." I searched for a way to phrase my question. As usual, he beat me to it.

"The construction crew has about a week left and they'll be

completely finished. After that, you two can move into one of the officer's apartments."

I glanced over at him. "Really?"

He nodded. "Yeah, there're plenty of them now. You do the job of our treasurer. It's time we made it official and you got some of the perks for it." He looked thoughtful for a minute. "Besides, you and your old lady will need a bit more space than your current room has."

The tiny room had done well for me, but he was right. There was no way the two of us could live there permanently. "Thanks, Cade."

He thumped a hand on my shoulder. "Let us know what time the party is." His smile was wolfish. I had a feeling Celia wasn't going to appreciate the way my family partied. In fact, this was going to go over as well as bringing a bunch of backwoods rednecks to a fancy tea party.

CHAPTER 9

Ari

"Stop fiddling with it," Mama said, slapping my hand away from the hem of my dress.

The cocktail dress was much shorter than something I would have chosen for myself. Unfortunately, I'd lost my temper early in the week and had told Mama and Alex I didn't care about the party tonight and that they should just plan it. Alex had bought my dress for me.

"You look gorgeous." She wasn't being nice. Her voice was smug, as if to say anything she'd chosen would have made me look good, not the other way around.

Saturday had come way too quickly. One minute I'd been told I was being chosen to marry Rat and the next I was standing here as guests started pouring into our backyard. Mama had outdone herself. She'd transformed the garden area into a sea of glittering lights. There was nothing surprising about it, though. She lived to entertain and rub people's noses in Papa's wealth.

The sun was sinking, casting the sky in beautiful shades of reds and oranges. I smiled as someone called out a hello, but I had to wipe my palms on my dress to dry them. I wasn't used to being the center of attention at these events. Everyone already knew why we were here tonight, though, and Mama had me standing over here on the terrace like I was the freaking Queen of England.

"Once a few more people get here, we'll make our entrance," Mama said. Her voice was breathy and excited.

Rolling my eyes, I met Antonia's gaze and she stifled a giggle. I wanted to turn around, go back to my room, and ignore everyone here tonight. Well, almost everyone. Of course, my elusive fiancé wasn't actually here yet. My stomach did a little flip at the thought of seeing him again. I scolded it and told it to behave. I hadn't heard a peep from him since our date. The man was very hot and cold and I wasn't sure what to make of him.

"Smile, dear," Mama muttered.

I dutifully pasted a fake smile on my face. We waited a couple minutes then she announced it was time to go meet everyone. My feet twinged in the high heels I'd been forced into. I was used to wearing sneakers, not heels, and I was paying for it already.

Just as we were coming down the few stairs—I was desperately clinging to the railing so I didn't roll my ankle in the stupid sky scraper heels—a commotion started up around the side of the house. I couldn't help the laugh that escaped as I watched Rat and about thirty some odd bikers and their women come into the backyard.

While everyone from my side of the family were in fancy dresses and suits, his men were in jeans, t-shirts, and cuts. The women were dressed in sundresses and I gazed longingly at one girl—who looked to be about my age—who'd paired sneakers with her dress.

Mama made a little sound of distress in the back of her throat, but Papa was already moving across the lawn to greet his newest allies.

I came forward and stood next to him in time to hear the man standing near Rat tell one of the waiters, "Hey, keep these coming." The man was a giant and the poor waiter's mouth dropped open as he snatched up two champagne glasses. He raised his brows at the waiter and finally the servant scurried off to get more champagne as ordered. The man turned and his gaze latched onto another waiter. He strode forward and snagged the silver tray full of finger foods out of that man's hands. "Thanks," he muttered. He handed the glasses off to a beautiful dark-haired woman standing near him and tossed one of Mama's hors d'oeuvres into the air before catching it in his mouth.

The woman next to him shook her head. "You're such a savage, Riggs."

His eyes flashed and turned molten as he stared down at her. "You know you love it, babe."

She scoffed and walked away from him to go stand near a group of women and bikers. Rat, his president—I was pretty sure his name was Cade—and Papa had been talking while my sisters and I were watching Riggs's performance.

"Jeez, that guy is huge," Antonia whispered to me.

I tore my gaze off Rat and looked over to where Riggs was polishing off the tray. I snickered as I watched Mama hurry over to try and distract him as he started for the table laden with food that no one was supposed to touch yet.

"He's the tallest guy I've ever seen," Ada said.

"I bet he has a huge-"

"Alex!" Antonia glared at her.

"What?" she asked with a shrug. "Look at him." She waved a hand to indicate him. "He's got huge everything. You know his...package is probably proportionate." She'd adjusted whatever she was going to say for Ada's sake. My youngest sister's face was beet red.

"Hey."

We all jumped when we realized Rat had come and stood next to us. "Hi," I said, shyly. I wondered if he'd heard any of our conversation.

My sisters hurried away, but before she left Antonia whispered into my ear, "He's looking at you like he wants to devour you."

A blush crept over my face and I shoved her to get her moving. I looked back at the man standing next to me. My sister wasn't wrong. Rat's gaze was roaming over my body. It shouldn't be surprising, enough of it was showing in the skintight, short dress. I tugged on the hem as if that would make it sprout a few more inches.

"How're you?" Rat asked.

'TIL ENCRYPTION DO US PART

"Good, thanks." Ugh, this was so awkward. Why was it so weird? We'd left things on a good note after our lunch date. Of course, then it'd just been the two of us.

I opened my mouth to make more small talk when someone approached us.

"Ari! Let me be the first to congratulate you."

"Thank you." His arms went around me and I hugged him. "Uncle Riccardo, I'd like you to meet my fiancé, Viktor." I shot Rat an apologetic look for not using his road name.

If it bothered him, it didn't show on his face. "It's nice to meet you," he said, politely shaking Riccardo's hand.

"And you as well." Riccardo reached over and patted my cheek. "We all love Ari and expect you to take good care of her, my boy."

Rat nodded solemnly. He frowned when Riccardo handed him a thick, white envelope before he headed off to the banquet. That started a parade of people who made their way toward us.

"What...the...fuck."

Rat's shocked mutter forced my attention off the crowd heading toward us and onto the envelope of cash he was holding in his hands.

"What is this?"

"Money," I told him dryly.

"Why-"

"Ari!" The call cut him off and he shoved the envelope into his back pocket. I chuckled to myself, knowing he was going to need a lot more pockets before the night was through.

A couple hours later everyone had happily gorged themselves on the banquet with Mama and Papa lording it over their guests, looking thrilled. Even Rat's crew looked pleased. Rat on the other hand looked shell-shocked. He was holding about fifty envelopes in his hands.

"How many fucking uncles do you have?" he whispered to me.

The laugh burst out of me before I could stop it. Mama frowned over at me, but then went back to speaking with another prim and proper looking lady. I couldn't remember her name for the life of me.

"We're Italians. We call everyone uncle," I told him.

"Seriously, though..." he held up the envelopes in confusion.

I smiled. "It's tradition. Those were all of Papa's officers. I've known them all since I was a little girl. Whenever their kids get married they give the couple a gift. It's almost always cash."

"I can't accept all of this."

Patting his forearm, I continued smiling at him. "You have to, Rat. It'd be a huge insult to them if you tried to return it. They give it happily. To them, it's their way of helping the new couple get on their feet."

"I don't need help taking care of you," he growled.

Frowning, I searched his gaze. He was agitated and had a restless look on his face. Turning my head, I spotted my parents across the yard busy speaking with my actual uncle. I grabbed Rat by the arm and pulled him along behind me.

He followed me quietly as I led him upstairs to my room. Taking the envelopes from him, I set them down on my dresser. I inhaled slowly before I turned to look at him. "What's wrong?"

"What do you mean?" he snapped. When I cocked a brow at him he sighed and rubbed a hand over the back of his neck. "Sorry. I don't do well around large crowds."

That surprised me. He'd handled the swarm with self-assurance and projected confidence as person after person approached us. I'd had no idea he'd been struggling. "I'm sorry, I didn't realize."

"There's a lot you don't know about me, Ari. I..."

He snapped his jaw shut, cutting off whatever he'd been about to say. "You, what?" I prompted.

Rat shook his head. "No. Not tonight. We'll talk about it later."

My fiancé was a mystery and with every minute I spent near him, I wanted to figure him out more and more.

"You look beautiful."

Our eyes clashed and he gave me a long look before letting them drop to take in my dress again. I felt my face heat up.

"Alex picked it." I plucked at the hem nervously.

His hand covered mine, stopping me from tugging at the fabric, and I froze. I could feel the heat from his fingers on my leg through the thin material. Then he brushed his fingers lower, over my bare thigh and it felt like pin pricks of fire licked along my skin where he touched. I sucked in a breath and his eyes shot back to mine.

Rat smiled and stepped even closer to me. I backed away quickly until my back hit the door and I was forced to stop. He stepped in front of me, crowding into my space. He didn't touch me other than to tuck a strand of my hair behind my ear. My eyes fluttered closed as his fingertips trailed lightly down my neck. Little sparks were dancing over my sensitive skin wherever he touched me. I could feel my pulse trying to beat its way out of my neck as his finger brushed over it.

My lips parted involuntarily and my body felt heavy—achy. There was no denying my attraction to Rat. It'd been there since the first day he and his MC had walked through the front door of my papa's house. Thinking of Papa had my eyes snapping open. It reminded me of the dark secret I was withholding.

I'd been debating on coming clean to Rat for the past few days, but it ultimately boiled down to the fact that I didn't know him. Therefore, I couldn't trust him. Just because my body yearned to be close to his, didn't change that fact.

Rat lowered his head, giving me plenty of time to move if I wanted to. I should, but I didn't. I needed to know what a kiss between us would feel like. Marrying this man ensured I would get that opportunity at some point. That didn't mean I wanted our first kiss to be in front of the hundreds of people Mama would be inviting to the wedding.

His lips brushed lightly over mine and though they were gentle I couldn't stop the gasp from slipping out of my mouth. Those sparks I'd felt earlier tingled on my lips then drifted lower until I wanted to grind myself against him.

Warm, large hands cupped my cheeks as Rat deepened the kiss. His tongue thrust into my mouth and brushed against my own. The moan was dragged from my chest and it surprised me as much as it seemed to excite him. He shifted closer and I felt his hard dick against my belly. It took everything inside of me to let my hands settle on his biceps instead of reaching down to grab his rigid length.

What the hell was wrong with me? This man went to my head like a shot of tequila. I could throw all caution to the wind and see where this took us—here and now—but if living in this home had taught me anything it was how to be cautious.

Breaking the kiss, I leaned my head back against the wall. A smile tipped my lips when Rat tried to follow to continue the mind-blowing meeting of lips. My hand on his chest stopped him and those intense blue eyes focused on mine.

"We should get back before anyone notices we're gone."

He nodded and held out a hand for me. I hesitated slightly before I took it. This marriage was happening. I needed to get to know my husband, to learn if I could truly trust him, and the only way to do that was by spending time with him. We walked quietly back to the party and I wondered if his heart was racing the way mine was.

CHAPTER 10

Rat

Cade's gaze found mine from across the party as Ari and I rejoined the crowd of people. He grinned at me, and I didn't miss the way my MC brothers were all shooting smirks our way.

"Viktor. Introduce me to your bride-to-be."

Enzo materialized out of the shadows like he was a fucking ghost. Hiding my surprise, I tugged Ari forward. "Ari, this is my brother." They'd seen each other before, I wasn't sure why he wanted a formal introduction.

"It's nice to meet you, officially, Enzo." She smiled and shook his hand, then her eyes widened when he flipped her hand over and brought it to his lips.

"The pleasure is mine."

I frowned at them as jealousy clawed its way from my gut to my chest. I'd never figured I'd be a possessive kind of guy, so why was I feeling this way watching my brother touch my fiancée? My eyes narrowed as Enzo smiled charmingly down at Ari. Apparently, I was a jealous man, I'd just never had the opportunity, or reason to be. Until now. This woman was mine and fuck anyone who thought they were going to make googly eyes at her in front of me—even if it was my brother.

Reaching over I grabbed Ari's hand, jerking it out of Enzo's grasp. Ari looked at me, startled, then her gaze bounced between me and my brother.

Enzo—the fucker—just had an amused, if slightly knowing, grin on his face.

"Arianna, may I have a moment alone with my brother?"

Ari nodded and pulled her hand from mine. We both watched as she walked over to stand next to her sisters.

"She's beautiful, Viktor. Congratulations."

I eyed him suspiciously. "Thanks?" I didn't know what game he was playing, but I had a feeling the scene that'd just played out was some kind of test for him. I didn't know much about Enzo yet, but I'd been digging into his life, learning what I could. He was cultured, devious, and brutal, according to everything I'd found. "Thanks for coming."

"I wouldn't miss it." We stood there quietly for a moment before Enzo pulled something out of his pocket.

I took the ring box from him when he held it out and opened it. My brows shot up as I stared down at a wedding set that probably would've set me back a few years' pay. "What-"

"It was our mother's. She'd have wanted you to have them." Enzo shoved his hands into his pockets and stared down at the rings.

"I can't accept these."

"Mother would've wanted you to have them," he repeated. I started to speak, but he cut me off. "Also, I'll need you to come back by the house so we can discuss your bank account."

"My... What?" Enzo was staring off across the yard completely oblivious to my confusion.

"Your account. I need to get you access," he murmured. I followed his line of sight, but couldn't see who'd caught his attention.

I stepped in front of him, forcing him to return his gaze to me. "I have no fucking clue what you mean," I growled.

He blinked at me as though he'd forgotten I was here, despite the fact that we'd just been speaking together. It made me wonder again who he'd been watching.

"The night you disappeared I started up a fund for you."

"A fund?"

"It's all the money you'd have received growing up if you'd been home with me—where you belonged."

It felt like someone hit me in the solar plexus. I wasn't sure what to say.

"It's a decent amount. So, we'll both need to be present in order to get everything transferred properly."

"I don't want your money, Enzo." I wasn't a fucking charity case. I already felt guilty as shit taking money from the majority of the men here tonight. Ari insisted I had to accept, and that was chafing at me. Now my own brother—who I barely knew—was essentially doing the same thing.

"It's not my money. It's yours." There was a note of finality in his voice.

One thing he was going to learn about me was I could be just as stubborn as he appeared to be. "Why didn't you bring this—and the rings—up while I was over the other day?"

One side of his lips kicked up in a smirk. "You wouldn't have stuck around." There was a hint of a question in his tone.

"Fuck no, I wouldn't have," I confirmed.

"Then there you go." Without another word he turned and walked away, melting into the shadows at the edge of the yard.

I stood there, mouth slightly open in stunned silence, and watched him go.

"Everything alright?"

Glancing over, I watched Cade stroll up. I shook my head and searched the yard again, but Enzo was gone. "Just a disagreement."

Cade's brows went up and he followed the direction I was looking. "Over what?"

I handed the ring box to him and smiled in aggravation when he whistled under his breath. "Enzo wants me to give those to Arianna and apparently has a boatload of money to give me."

Cade's eyes narrowed as he handed the rings back. "You know, there aren't many men out there that get this annoyed at free money and jewelry."

I stared down at the rings in the box. I'd gotten Ari a ring. In fact, I'd meant to give it to her already. Despite that, there was something tempting about the thought of giving her my mother's ring. I didn't remember anything about her. There'd been years of anger and feelings of betrayal because she'd never come to find me. I'd had the opportunity to ask Enzo about her the other day and I'd frozen. Then it hit me, if this was her ring, she wasn't wearing it.

After all this time, I knew for sure that she was dead. My mouth went dry. I could chase down Enzo and ask him what'd happened, but I wasn't sure I was ready to find out. "I don't need his money, and it feels like he's paying off his guilt."

Cade's look was quick and sharp. "Hasn't Enzo told you what happened the night you disappeared?"

I shook my head. "He started to... I-" I fell silent, unwilling to admit out loud I was too much of a coward to face the emotions that would come along with knowing.

Cade put a hand on my shoulder and waited until I met his eyes. "You need to know, Rat. This will eat you alive, if you let it. At least, if nothing else, you'll finally know the truth about how you were separated from your family."

I couldn't hold his gaze anymore, so I looked down at the grass at our feet.

"I won't be the one to tell you everything, it's not my place. I can say...it's not what you think it is."

With that, Cade went back over to our crew and gave me some space. I stood there, emotion swelling inside of me as I tried to decide what to do.

"Is everything okay?"

My head snapped up. I'd been so deep in my own thoughts I hadn't heard Arianna walk up. I nodded and made a split-second decision. Plucking the engagement ring from the box, I held it out to her.

Ari's eyes widened and her mouth fell open in shock. "Wha-"

"It was my mother's. I'd like for you to wear it." I frowned. "Unless it's not your style?" I didn't know shit about style, or rings, or any of that girly crap.

"I love it," she assured me. "Are you positive you want me to have it?"

"Yeah." I slid the ring on her finger and it just felt right seeing it sit there on her hand. I didn't know my mother, but somehow it felt like she'd approve.

Celia rushed over and dragged Ari off by the arm telling her she had to show everyone the ring. It hadn't dawned on me that people were watching us that closely.

I tried not to let my irritation with my brother spoil the rest of the event. Even though it was way fancier than anything we would've ever put together, we still had fun. Arianna was being pulled in so many different directions by her mother I didn't get much time with her.

I grabbed a chair at a table with the rest of my crew. "Don't worry, sweetie," Ming said as she sat down next to me. "We'll throw her our own welcome party when she comes to the clubhouse."

"A barbeque," Riggs said, polishing off another silver platter of finger sandwiches. "None of this tiny shit that it takes fifty of to fill you up."

"Agreed," Bass muttered and continued chowing down on the plate of food in front of him.

I chuckled and shook my head. Guilt was plaguing me because I knew I should be over with my fiancée facing her family with her, but people weren't really my thing. I'd make it up to her later.

"When is she coming to stay?" Remi asked.

"I was planning on picking her up tomorrow afternoon."

Bridget clapped her hands together. "I'll plan the party," she volunteered.

I bit the insides of my lips to hold in my smile. If Bridget planned it, it'd end up looking more like the party we were currently at. "Maybe we should give her a few days to settle in before we throw everyone at her all at once?"

"It's not like she's not going to meet us over the next couple of days. All the men live at the clubhouse and most of the women are there the majority of the time," Bridget pointed out with a pout.

"No, he's right," Cade said. "This way she can meet everyone slowly instead of in a huge crowd. We'll have a barbeque next weekend to welcome her."

Bridget sat back with a huff, but everyone was nodding in agreement. I shot Cade a grateful look. I didn't want to hurt Bridget's feelings, but a second huge party for an event that we'd had no control over seemed like a lot in two days.

"Oh my God," Bridget gasped, and I cringed hoping she wasn't going to try and insist on a party. "What is Uncle Bobby doing here?" Her wide eyes shot around our group and I turned in my chair in time to see the Austin Police Chief strolling through my engagement party. His eyes flashed over to our group and his lips lifted in a challenging smile. He nodded to Bridget, but kept walking.

Sal and Abel—with multiple of their men at their backs—strode over to confront him. Their conversation was quiet, but you could feel the tension across the yard.

"Should we go help?" Remi asked.

"No," Cade said, watching thoughtfully as Sal escorted the man out of the party.

"Do you think they're working together?" Axel voiced the question we were all wondering.

"I'm not sure, but I'll be finding out," Cade responded. "Let's get out of here."

I'd bet every dollar I had that Agent Flynn would be stopping by again at some point.

I went and got Ari to tell her we were leaving. The appearance of the Police Chief had put an abrupt halt to the party and we weren't the only group heading out. I knew without a doubt, he was who Enzo had spotted when we'd been talking and the reason my brother had made such a quick exit.

She peeked up at me through her lashes and I couldn't help the smile that formed on my face. We still had a lot to learn about each other, but with every passing minute I spent near her I knew I'd made the right choice.

"I'll pick you up tomorrow?"

She nodded in agreement. We'd spoken earlier about her coming to live with me. I could tell she was nervous, but I didn't know how to lay her fears to rest. Hell, I was nervous about it too.

Stepping closer to her, I cupped her cheek and laid a soft kiss on her lips. They parted slightly as she sighed and I fought the urge to deepen it. As much as I wanted to keep kissing her, I didn't want to do it out in front of her family.

I hopped on my bike and pulled out onto the street. I'd told Cade not to wait for me. It was going to be another long night of clearing my head. A lone bike waited in the darkness, just up the road. I tensed and tried to identify it. The Lycans had run off with their tails between their legs when Sal had killed Blaze, but that didn't mean they wouldn't show back up.

My shoulders relaxed slightly when I recognized Bass. Looked like he was waiting for me and was going to be my shadow again tonight. He pulled up beside me and we gunned the engines, taking off with a squeal of tires. I didn't need to tell him that I appreciated him being here. He knew it.

CHAPTER 11

Rat

Sighing, I knocked on Enzo's door Monday morning. I'd spent all weekend riding around the city with Bass. It wasn't possible to outrun my demons, so it was time to face a couple of them.

I stuffed my hands in my pockets as Enzo answered the door. He was in tailored slacks and a crisp white shirt. I was glad I'd taken the time to shower and change into a new pair of jeans and t-shirt before I'd shrugged on my cut and come over. There'd been no point in trying to sleep. With all the stress happening I'd only been getting a few hours anyway, and after the party last night I was still feeling wired.

"Viktor, please, come in."

He was always so formal. "Is there any way I could get you to call me Rat?"

"No." There was a hint of a smile on his face when he said it, but his tone told me it'd never happen.

He brought me to the same office that we'd talked in before. I sat down and barely waited for his ass to hit the chair before I started in on the speech I'd worked on most of the night. "Look, Enzo. I appreciate you giving me Mom's ring. I gave it to Arianna, and she loved it." He started to speak, but I cut him off. I needed to get this out. "I don't, however, want or need your money."

His eyes darkened, and his jaw clenched. "I told you. It's not my money, it's yours. It's what you would have had growing up had I been able to find you earlier."

"It seems to me it's a way to relieve you of your guilt." I raised a brow at him.

Fury snapped in his gaze. He didn't say anything for a long moment and I wondered if I'd pushed too far. I didn't know this man and really, he didn't owe me anything. I knew—as the head of the Bratva—he could easily make me disappear.

"Perhaps it is, in a way. I failed you. Be that as it may, it's yours and I will be transferring it into your name. Give it away if you don't want it, but it's yours." With that he picked up the phone on the desk and dialed.

I frowned when a woman rattled off the name of a local bank here in Austin. It wasn't worth fighting him on this. I had more important things to settle.

"How may I help you?" she chirped.

It took about twenty minutes and only a few yeses from me and Enzo had transferred a staggering amount of money into my name. There were so many zeroes on the end my eyes nearly popped out of their sockets when the woman gave me the balance of the account. I nearly told her to cancel everything, but the look on Enzo's face promised retribution if I did.

"Fucking hell, Enzo," I told him as soon as he hung up the phone. I wasn't sure what I'd been expecting—a couple hundred thousand dollars, maybe. Not a number in the millions—multiple.

His lips quirked up. "Our family is very wealthy."

That was being fucking modest. I already wanted to go back home and bury my head in the sand about all of this and I wasn't even close to finished.

"You'll be receiving a monthly stipend as is fitting for my brother." His tone was formal and warned me not to argue.

It hadn't taken long to realize arguing with this man was pointless. He did what he wanted, so I acknowledged his statement. Sucking in a deep breath, I took a moment to calm myself. Cade had forced me—a few weeks ago when all this started—to start going to therapy. I wasn't sure if a biker in therapy was a rarity or just a regular necessity, but it was clear that I needed more help than Julie was able to provide. She was going to make an excellent therapist one day, but she hadn't finished school yet. She'd talked to me a few times and had been pushing me to seek out additional help as well.

There were a few calming techniques my therapist had given me that seemed to help, but the idea that I had to go and talk to someone about my problems, someone not in the club, embarrassed the fuck out of me. Cade had promised he wouldn't say anything to anyone else, but had insisted that I should've been going long before this. He probably wasn't wrong about that—he wasn't wrong about much.

Enzo leaned forward and steepled his fingers together on the desk.

"Would you tell me what happened that night?" I forced myself to look him in the eyes.

I saw him stiffen at my request, but he gave a curt nod in response. He quickly ran me through the feud that'd existed between our family and another Russian family and how they'd attacked that night.

"Father sent you and Mother away with some of his most loyal men."

I waited quietly when he didn't continue. The look on his face told me he was far away, reliving that night. I was pretty sure I had the better end of that deal, not being able to remember it.

"We found the car. It'd been forced off the road," he finally continued.

"It was only later, when Father and I had tracked down Pyotr Sidorov and I had him under my blade, that he told me what'd transpired that night. After they ran all of you off the road, they killed the Bratoks—our soldiers—who were there to protect both of you.

Mother used the distraction to run with you. Our men gave their lives to give her the time she needed to hide you." Enzo was staring down at his hands. His knuckles were white with how hard he was clenching them together. "When Anatoly Sidorov—the head of their family—found her, she'd deposited you somewhere. She refused to give him the location."

"What happened to her then?" I knew. I knew before coming here. I knew as soon as he gave me her rings.

His eyes met mine. He must have seen the unwavering determination in my eyes because he told me the rest, as requested. "He raped her in some back alley and slit her throat." Our gazes were locked, neither willing to flinch away from the horrific end a woman we'd loved endured.

"We searched for you. That night, the next day, for weeks we looked in every place she might have had time to hide you." His voice cracked slightly. What'd happened to his family—our family—that night, clearly haunted him. It was what happened after that night that ate at me.

"It wasn't your fault. I'd probably already been taken by the time you figured out where the car was." For all I knew Sully had watched them rape and kill my mother before he'd taken me out from behind the dumpster I was stashed behind. All these years thinking that my mother hadn't wanted me, only to find out she'd endured horrific things in order to protect me. A new wave of guilt washed over me. I'd been angry at her for so long, and she hadn't deserved it.

I swallowed, not wanting to think about that right now. "Do you have a picture of her?"

Enzo stood and walked over to the fireplace. He handed me a framed photo when he came back to the desk and sat beside me. I stared down at the picture. I was just a baby in it, my mother, father, and brother were all grinning widely at the camera. We had her eyes, but were both the spitting image of our father.

"What happened to him?"

"Heart attack," Enzo responded. "The toll of losing you both ate at his health. I think the hope of finding you was the only reason he outlived her death."

I sat silently, staring down at the photo. We looked so happy. I couldn't help wondering what would've been different if I'd grown up here with them.

"Where were you?" Enzo asked in a low voice.

I shook my head. I wasn't ready to talk to him about where I'd grown up. "I'll tell you someday, but not today."

His eyes hardened and his jaw clenched as he ground his teeth. I didn't need to ask to know he wasn't angry that I wouldn't tell him. He was pissed that it was obviously bad enough I couldn't talk to him about it. I put my hand on his shoulder and gave a light squeeze. My way of telling him it wasn't his fault. That I didn't blame him.

Maybe once I knew him better, although I wasn't sure if I'd be ready even then. Cade was the only one who knew some of my story, and even he didn't know the half of it.

"I'd better get going," I said, standing up.

Enzo walked me out. "I'm hoping we can get to know each other, Viktor. Be a family again."

I nodded. "Yeah, I'd like that." We both stood there awkwardly until I said goodbye and got onto my bike. I wasn't sure why it was so hard for me to be around people, but I was looking forward to going to pick up someone it didn't seem difficult to be myself around.

* * *

THE DOOR OPENED, and I smiled when I saw Arianna standing there. She gave me a shy smile, and I wanted to scoop her up, toss her over my shoulder, and take her somewhere where we could be alone.

"Hey."

"Hi, come on in." She held the door open wider so I could enter. "Give me just a minute and I'll be ready, okay?"

I nodded and watched as she turned and she and her younger sisters fell into each other's embrace. There were tears and babbling, promises of calls and visits. Shifting on my feet, I wondered why the obvious affection between them made me uncomfortable. I thought back to this morning and the way Enzo and I were around each other. Of course, there were some massive differences. We were men, for one. We hadn't grown up together, and we both kept our emotions tightly controlled. It seemed I came by that trait genetically, if my brother was any indication. It'd shocked me when he'd said—flat out—that he wanted us to become a family again. Something told me that hadn't been easy for him to say.

When the women approached, I picked up the bags sitting next to the front door. Antonia sniffled and knuckled away the tears on her cheeks. "You'd better take care of her...or else." Her glower was menacing.

My brows shot up. I planned on taking care of her in every way she needed, but I was curious. "Or what?"

All three women looked shocked. Antonia's lips thinned out into a flat line. "I grew up in the mafia. If you think I don't know how to dispose of a body, you'd be mistaken."

I barked out a laugh. "Alright. You win. I promise to take care of her. I was going to sell her to the carnies at the county fair, but I guess not." They glared at me, trying to repress a smile. I looked back at Ari, "I bet they'd give me one of those oversized stuffed puppies for you."

"Or a Rat..." Ari retorted, scrunching her nose at me.

Antonia grinned, gave her sister one last hug, then went up the stairs. Ada followed us out onto the porch, looking forlorn. I felt my gut twist. I wished I could take all three with me. My gaze swept the outside of the house. It was obvious they grew up with a lot more than I had, but I still sensed sadness and longing in these three women. It made me ache to rescue them from it.

I tossed Ari's bags into the back seat of the cage ride I'd swapped my bike out for before I'd come over. Opening the door, I held my hand out for her to take as she got into the truck.

Ari's brows rose and a small smile formed on her lips. My eyes dropped down to them. Soon enough, she'd be mine and we could do whatever we wanted. The idea made my dick harden. At the same time apprehension filled me. She probably didn't think she was getting stuck with a twenty-two-year-old virgin who had major trust issues and a whole slew of other problems. I shoved the thoughts away as I climbed behind the wheel. There was no point in worrying over it. We'd have to talk about it soon enough.

CHAPTER 12

Ari

As soon as we pulled out onto the highway my heart sank in my chest. It hadn't occurred to me to ask where Rat lived. It should have, but I'd never imagined anyone would choose to live outside the city. I was a city girl through and through.

"Where do you live?" I asked when we'd been traveling for about ten minutes.

"Down by San Marcos," he responded. He must have heard something in my voice because he kept glancing over at me with an unreadable expression on his face.

My heart settled in my stomach like a rock at the bottom of the ocean. I had never learned to drive. I didn't have a car and we were going to be living about thirty minutes south of Austin. Not only did that present a problem for me getting to and from class every day, but it severely limited the freedom I wanted. Not that I'd ever had it. I guess I just felt that by leaving Papa's house I wouldn't be a prisoner anymore.

Rat cleared his throat. "I live at the clubhouse with my MC."

I was speechless. They all lived together? The only thing I could picture was a dorm, like the ones at the colleges. I'd been desperate to live there when I'd first started at the University. There was no way Papa would've allowed that, so I let the idea go. I wasn't sure how I felt about living in a crowded space with my soon to be husband. I tried to imagine a bunch of bikers living in a college dorm, with togas and beer pong tables. My brain kept rejecting the idea. I would just have to wait until I saw it to understand.

When I didn't say anything, Rat continued. "The room we have right now is small, but by next weekend we'll be moving into a bigger space. They're just finishing up building it out."

I didn't want to be ungrateful, or a brat, but that made me feel a little better. "Will there be space for the rest of my stuff?" I didn't have a bunch of things, but Rat had said we'd go back in a few days and pack everything else up. That must have been why he told me to hold off on packing everything. He was waiting for the space to open up.

"Plenty of room. Promise." He shot me a reassuring smile.

He was lucky in that regard—if he had chosen Alex, nothing short of a mansion would hold all her clothes.

I nodded and stared out the window. My palms were sweaty and I didn't want to have to ask my question. "I...don't have a car. How will I get to classes?"

Confusion spread over Rat's face. "Your dad never bought you a car?"

I shook my head, but didn't elaborate why. I could see the considering look on his face. He was trying to figure out how I lived in such a nice house and was given so many nice things, but never a car.

"I'll buy you one."

His answer floored me. I had enough in my savings to buy a junker car. "That's really sweet, Rat. I don't want you to have to spend your money on me."

"You're my wife. If you need a car, I'm buying you a car," he said firmly.

I didn't bother to point out that we weren't married yet. It was basically a done deal anyway. "I..." I sucked in a breath, miserable I had to admit this. Teenagers knew how to drive for God's sake. "I don't have my license."

Now he was staring over at me incredulously. I licked my lips nervously, my gaze bouncing between his face and the road in front of us. He wasn't paying attention to it anymore. All of that intense focus was on me. I liked it, but maybe not while we were going eighty miles an hour.

"Okay… I can take you to the DMV."

Mentally, I smacked myself in the forehead. He was being so sweet, and I was only giving him bits and pieces of information. I couldn't tell if he was judging me or not, but it was time to rip the Band-Aid off. "Rat. I never learned how to drive. Papa wouldn't allow us to go anywhere on our own. Safety reasons," I said in a deep voice, mimicking my father. "It's so nice of you to offer all these things, but maybe I'll just Uber."

He was staring at me again, blinking slowly. "You can't Uber out here every day, Ari. That'd be expensive as fuck. Besides, don't you want to drive yourself? Not rely on strangers?" He blew out a breath. "For now, I can take you to class. You shouldn't be driving around the city alone right now anyway. And I'll teach you how to drive, then we'll get you your license and a car."

A determined look flitted over his face. He'd solved the entirety of the problem, but I was stuck on something he'd said. "Why shouldn't I be driving alone?"

A muscle ticked in his jaw. Had I made him angry? That was the last thing I wanted. There were so many things we needed to talk about.

"I'll tell you that later. Not while we're driving."

I nodded quietly and watched the scenery fly by outside the window. The rest of the drive passed quickly and soon we were pulling into a gravel parking lot. There was a huge building off to one side, and two homes behind it. A forest filled the property on one side.

"It's beautiful," I murmured. Maybe I could see the appeal of living outside the city, now that I saw what was out here. The sun was still shining brightly, but I couldn't wait to watch it sink below the horizon.

Rat grabbed my bags out of the back.

"I can help with those."

He just gave me a look that said there was no way in hell he was letting me carry them. Something warm fluttered in my belly. I'd always been a sucker for an overprotective gentleman. I wasn't sure if that was what I had here, but he was sure acting that way.

I followed behind him as he led the way into the clubhouse. I peeked around corners as we made our way through and up the stairs. It was a lot less...busy than I thought it'd be.

Rat must have noticed me looking around, because as he opened a door in a long narrow hallway he said, "I asked everyone to clear out and give us some space while you settle in. They're all dying to officially meet you and get to know you more. I just thought maybe you'd like a tour without being introduced to thirty plus people."

He was right. This was all so overwhelming. The last thing I needed, the last thing I could handle, would be that many new people rushing me.

I stepped into his room. It was small and sparse, with just a bed and two desks that held all his computer equipment. "That was very nice of you," I responded. "I don't mind meeting new people, though, so I can't wait." I *could* wait, but there was no need to tell him that.

He set my bags down in the closet. "I know it's not much, but I'll show you the room we'll be moving into at the end of the week."

"It's just fine," I told him. It had its own bathroom, which was a huge plus in my book. "I appreciate this." I sat down on the bed and caught his amused look.

"What? That I'm having my wife move in with me?"

"We're not married yet. You could've told Papa he had to wait to kick me out."

He cocked his head and leaned against the wall. My gaze dropped to where he folded his muscular arms over his chest. Just sitting on his bed made my skin tingle and my breathing quicken.

"It doesn't seem like you and your dad have a great relationship."

He didn't ask a question. He was leaving it up to me whether I wanted to expand on his statement.

"We don't. I-" I paused, not sure if I should tell him everything. Internally, I reminded myself that I needed to get to know this man and hopefully start trusting him. "We've always been afraid of him—of what he might do," I said, a little ashamed of being a coward. "I wasn't one of his favorites, and even they—Abel and Alex—don't test him often. I was lucky that he mostly ignored me." I shrugged my shoulders. It was something I'd come to terms with when I was young.

Rat frowned. "Is that a thing? Picking a favorite and then ignoring the others?"

He'd tensed when I said that I was afraid of Papa. I was thankful he didn't bring it up, though. I didn't want to get into it right now.

It was my turn for my brows to knit together. I studied him, the strong brow, straight nose, full lips. My sisters had told me more than once—not that I hadn't noticed for myself—that he was gorgeous, and they weren't wrong. The man standing in front of me was almost beautiful. His muscles, tattoos, and attitude kept him from being feminine in any way. There was something about him, though, that seemed almost...broken. Sad. I could see it there in his eyes.

"Sure. Probably not in every family, but I suppose it could happen. You just click with some people more...you know?" It was more than that, I'd always felt it, but had been so desperate to feel loved I lied to myself. Now that I was older, I was more honest about my family dynamic—at least to myself.

He nodded thoughtfully as he came to sit next to me on the bed. He didn't look over at me. Instead, he kept his eyes firmly planted on the Converse sneakers he was wearing. "You were my favorite."

My insides melted as my head snapped over and I studied the side of his face. "Thank you," I whispered. Warmth flooded my system. It wasn't until this moment that I realized it was what I had been craving—who knows how long, probably my entire life. I wanted to be picked, simply for being me. His admission also made me realize he *had* chosen me for that reason. My breath shuddered out.

He must have heard it because he finally met my eyes. He trailed his thumb over my skin as he cupped my cheek. When I didn't pull away he brushed it over my lips. They parted involuntarily as the pad of his thumb soothed back and forth over my lower lip.

I didn't know what came over me, but I used the tip of my tongue to lick him. His deep groan echoed in the room around us and I had to squeeze my thighs together when the sound sent a zip of pleasure straight down to my core.

Rat smirked when he noticed the movement. He cupped the back of my neck and brought his lips to mine. Gently, he nibbled, seeking entry. This time we both groaned when my mouth parted and our tongues met.

He pulled back and I saw him shift, trying to ease the hard-on in his jeans. I bit the insides of my lips to keep from laughing at his discomfort. I was glad I wasn't the only one who was undeniably attracted. Despite the fucked up situation, we both seemed to be fairly happy with his choice to marry me.

A small voice in my head asked me if we'd still be happy once he found out the secret I was hiding. I locked the voice away. I didn't intend for Rat to ever find out about that.

"...for a tour?"

I looked back into his eyes and caught the rest of what he was saying. "Yes, please."

We got up, and he held the door open for me. Stepping out into the hallway, he pointed. "This is where half the rooms are. Once we go over to the other side you'll see the others. Over there is where we're building more of the bigger apartments. Steel's is at the end of the hall there. If you need anything and I'm not around you can go to him." He paused as though he were thinking about what he said. "In fact, you could go to him, Cade, Riggs, Gunnar, Axel, or Bass."

I blinked at the flood of names he tossed at me. Cade was the only normal one, and I latched onto it. I'd felt bad that I hadn't really had a chance to get to know his guests from last night. He'd introduced me, but Mama kept dragging me away to show me off to all her guests. Rat had insisted it was fine, that his crew was happy to sit and eat and drink.

"I'll introduce you to everyone and you'll pick up on the names pretty quickly. All our brothers are good men, and their women will welcome you," he told me. "The only time I need you to be careful is when we have parties and outsiders come into the club, or Nomads are here."

"What's a Nomad?" I was going to need to study up on MC life.

Rat led me down the stairs. "What do you know about MCs?"

It was like he knew what I was thinking. I blushed. "Next to nothing."

"No problem. I'll teach you everything you need to know." He stopped in a large living room. It was so big it was almost like two had been shoved together. "This is the common area. We hang out here a lot, have parties, get-togethers and shit like that."

Next, we stepped into the kitchen. "Self-explanatory. I do the majority of the cooking."

I looked at him in surprise and he grinned at me. "I told you I like to cook. Plus, I'm here most days. It's practical."

I glanced around as he hurried me back into the common area and we stepped through another door. I hesitated at the top of the stairs, but he nudged me gently and we descended down. He'd hit a set of lights at the top, so at least it wasn't pitch black. As soon as I stepped off the last stair my eyes widened.

"Our gym. You're welcome to use it anytime." He smiled down at me. "None of the guys will bother you. If they do, just let me or one of the officers know and we'll take care of it."

My head was spinning, so I just nodded. He was throwing out terms that were natural to him, but I didn't understand. I wasn't going to stop the tour to ask, though. I'd research it later. It was just so much to take in.

CHAPTER 13

Ari

"This is the other side of the building I was telling you about." Rat held open another door and I stepped into an empty apartment. The smell of wet paint slapped me in the face.

"This one will be ours."

I stood in the middle of the room and looked around. The living room was plenty big, there was a kitchen and I assumed the bedroom was through the door off to my right. "It's nice."

Rat was studying me, gauging my reaction so I smiled at him. It really was a nice place. There was enough space for the two of us here. "Does everyone in the club live here?"

"Mostly. There are a couple of guys and their families who live in the city. The majority of us prefer to be here."

I was going to ask another question when someone knocked on the door.

I studied Cade as he walked in. He was older than us—although not by much, maybe only five to ten years—and he was drop dead gorgeous. He moved with a stealthy grace. I'd seen him at the party last night, but there hadn't been time to get to know anyone.

He flashed a smile at me, his green eyes meeting mine. "Sorry to interrupt. I'm Cade."

"Arianna, but you can call me Ari," I told him, shaking his hand.

"It's nice to meet you, again."

"I'm sorry we didn't get a chance to speak more last night-"

"That's no problem at all. You were busy and I certainly wouldn't have wanted to be dragged around with you," he told me, cutting off my apology.

We shared a smile. So, they'd noticed how miserable I'd been, being paraded around in front of my parents' friends.

Cade turned his attention to Rat. "I need to have you look over something for me." They both glanced my way and I took the hint.

"I'm going to go wait outside."

Rat frowned. "Don't wander off, it's a big property."

I rolled my eyes, but smiled at him. "I won't." I wondered if he was always this overprotective or if it was because I was new here. Getting to explore the grounds on my own was more than Papa would've allowed, though, so I counted it as a win.

Stepping outside, I sucked in a deep breath of the fresh air. The smell of grass and outdoors greeted me. I walked behind the clubhouse, and past the houses back there. Someone had a lone chair sitting out on top of a small slope that overlooked the back of the property.

I trailed my hand over the wooden arm as I walked past. It was a nice spot to sit. I wondered whose it was and if they'd be willing to share the spot when they weren't out here.

Folding my arms over my chest, I fought against a shiver. It was late afternoon and the nights were beginning to cool rapidly. Winter would be here soon. I didn't mind. It was my favorite season.

A scream caught in my throat when something heavy landed on my shoulders. My heart was galloping in my chest when a man stepped up next to me, staring out over the land. He'd dropped his heavy leather jacket over my shoulders. I clutched the edges to keep it from falling off while I stared at him in shock. I hadn't even heard him come up behind me.

"Tha-thank you," I said. My voice wavered a bit.

He inclined his head at me, but didn't say anything else, just went back to looking in front of us. I examined the side of his face. He was older—maybe fifties—but still handsome and in shape. Some gray peppered his hair. It didn't detract from his looks at all. In fact, I could see why younger women fell for older men, if they looked like this one.

It's too bad I hadn't known about bikers earlier. They were so sexy. I wasn't sure if it was the leather vests, I mean *cuts*, or the attitude, but I was a fan. A devilish thought entered my mind. I needed to let Alex know about these groups of gorgeous outlaws. She'd drive Papa mad with all the trouble she'd cause. He'd deserve it, too.

The man next to me gave me a nod and turned to leave.

"Wait, your coat-"

"Keep it for now. You can't stand out here and freeze." With that he left.

I was only out there a few more minutes when Rat came out to where I was standing. I had no problem hearing him approach me. The grass and leaves rustled under his sneakers. Why hadn't I heard the other man?

"Where'd you get the jacket?" He asked, eyeing it.

"Some guy gave it to me. He didn't tell me his name."

"That's Hush's jacket," he told me. There was a note of shock in his tone.

"He scared the crap out of me. Didn't say anything, just appeared behind me and put it on me."

Now Rat's mouth was hanging open. He closed it with a click and cleared his throat. "It is getting colder out here. Want to go inside?" He didn't say anything more about the man or the coat.

The sun was starting to sink. As much as I wanted to stay and watch the sunset, I didn't want to disrupt his routine. "Sure."

"Have a seat," Rat told me as we walked into the kitchen. "I'll make us some dinner."

"Are the others joining us?"

"No, the other guys took some of the girls out. It's been a little hectic around here lately, so they were happy to get a night out."

Disappointment filled me. I wasn't sure why. It was so sweet that Rat had gone out of his way to make me comfortable, but now I'd almost rather just meet everyone up front—get it over with.

It might have been nice to have a distraction, too. I watched as Rat shrugged out of his cut and hung it on the back of the chair. The white t-shirt he wore stretched over his back as he started working at the stove.

I'd never really dated, Papa would've lost his mind. I'd only had my one affair with Neil that summer. So, I was a bit awkward around men. Add to that I was marrying this stranger, and it put a whole different level of stress on me. All I could do was take the time to get to know him, but I sort of wished we could fast forward past this stage and get to a place where this wasn't so uncomfortable.

"What do you do, Rat?"

"I own a tech business."

I had to stop myself from jumping forward with excitement. Instead, I sat forward, leaning my arms against the island. "Really?" I asked nonchalantly. Now I was interested. *Very* interested. He'd have to have some kind of skill to own a company, and the thought was incredibly sexy to me. We'd talked about computers that day in the park, but knowing he had a business revolving around them and didn't just game online was completely different. I'd noticed his set up when we'd been upstairs in his room, but hadn't wanted to snoop. It'd killed me not to.

"Yeah," he said in amusement. "I'm a bit of a computer geek."

"Me too." I smiled at him when he glanced over his shoulder. His gaze raked over me, and my breath caught in my throat.

"Hottest geek I've ever seen," he said it so low I wasn't sure if he'd meant for me to hear him. He turned back around, missing the blush that crawled up my neck.

We chatted all through dinner and the cleanup. I'd insisted on helping wash the dishes.

"What time is your first class in the morning?" he asked as we headed back up to his room after we were finished.

"Seven a.m.," I told him sheepishly. "I'm a bit of an early riser."

"No problem, so am I."

I stopped on the stairs and he bumped into me. His hands reached out and locked onto my hips to steady me. There was a question in those intense blue eyes.

"Sorry…" Standing a stair above him put us level. It'd be so easy to lean forward and kiss him. I'd liked having his lips on me, but I didn't kiss him. I wasn't sure what the expectation was going to be for tonight and I wasn't ready to sleep with this man. My core clenched at the thought. *Alright, some of me was ready.*

"Why'd you stop?"

Oh, right. "It just always seems like early risers end up together with night owls. I was just surprised that we have so much in common," I finished, feeling lame. He was so cool and aloof, and I felt like a bumbling idiot around him.

Rat chuckled and inclined his head, indicating for me to keep moving. That was when I realized we were still standing close together with his hands on my hips. They slid off as I turned and started up the stairs once more.

My heart started thudding as we entered his room. The bed was only a queen size, but the implications of sleeping in it with him made it feel like it was swallowing the room.

"I can sleep on the floor-"

He gave me a sharp look. "No. We're both sleeping in that bed." He pulled off his shirt and walked into the bathroom. My mouth went bone dry at the sight of him shirtless. I clasped my fingers behind my back to keep from reaching out to touch all that tanned and tattooed skin.

"We're going to be married and I refuse for either of us to be uncomfortable in the upcoming weeks until we make it official," he said, coming back out. He'd splashed his face with water and his blond hair was standing up in short spikes.

I nodded and bit my lower lip as a stray drop of water slid down his neck and over his chest.

"Ari." His voice was softer, but insistent.

I looked up and met his gaze. "This doesn't mean we have to have sex tonight. We'll wait until you're ready for that. I won't force you to do anything you're not ready to. But tonight, we sleep here, in comfort..."

Relief almost overwhelmed me. Some combination of his generous sensitivity and the fact that he was in total control was incredibly sexy. I was insanely attracted to Rat, but being forced into this entire situation was strange and I didn't want to move too fast and have us end up regretting anything. We were already being rushed into the marriage itself.

"Thank you." I smiled at him.

His return smile was gorgeous. His face relaxed, as though he'd been worried about having that talk with me. Things were finally settling between us and the air wasn't charged with that awkward tension. The sexual tension was still there, but that was manageable. *For now.*

"You want to shower?"

"Yes, please." I went over to my bag and dug around inside for a pair of sleep shorts and a t-shirt. The sooner I could get clean and get to sleep, the better.

CHAPTER 14

Rat

I messed around on my computer while I waited for Arianna to finish in the bathroom. It was like a lead weight had lifted off my shoulders. I'd been trying to figure out all day how to set her mind at ease and discuss what the expectations for sex would be. The smile she'd given me had damn near knocked me on my ass.

If she waltzed out of that bathroom right now and wanted to go a round, I'd be down. I'd be ready whenever she was, but I didn't want her to feel pressured at all. This was something that was going to be totally within her control. We'd already taken away so many of her choices, I wouldn't pressure her.

I'd waited this long, a few more days or weeks wouldn't kill me. The shock of being able to touch her without feeling uncomfortable was still there. Things were so different with Ari. That told me I'd made the right choice. There was just something about her that was sweet and made me want to trust her. I wasn't about to complain about the fact that I felt more comfortable with her faster than I had with any other human being I could remember.

It didn't take long before we were both showered and stood staring down at my bed.

"Want to watch a movie?"

She brightened at my question. "Sure!"

I brought my laptop over to the bed. "Climb on in."

She crawled over toward the wall and laid down. Flicking off the lights, I settled in next to her. With my laptop sitting on my chest, we scrolled through Netflix until we found a comedy we both wanted to see.

I started the movie and set the laptop up on the dresser. Grabbing the remote, I hit a button and a projector screen came down on the wall at the foot of the bed.

She looked up at the projector wide eyed. "Okay. That's a nice set up," she laughed.

I grinned at her, hit another button and the surround sound boomed to life. We laid there, shoulders propped against the headboard, laughing along with the show.

The next thing I knew my eyes were snapping open as Ari shook me awake.

"I'm so sorry...you were yelling..." her eyes were wide and she looked worried.

The screen was flashing through movie previews, lighting up the room with a haunting glow. The fact that I'd fallen asleep at all was a testament to how little I'd been sleeping lately.

My heart hammered against my chest and my mouth was bone dry. I cleared my throat and rolled off the bed, escaping to the bathroom. I knew throwing off my routine would bring the nightmares to the forefront of my brain. It was only a matter of time before Ari saw this side of me. I'd just been hoping to get through the first night without it. But like the world's biggest Band-Aid, I would be ripping it off much sooner than I wanted to.

Splashing cold water on my face, I looked up into the mirror. My breathing was slowing as the memories faded. I'm sure Ari was freaked the fuck out, and leaving her without saying anything didn't help, but I couldn't talk about it directly after an episode. I needed a few minutes to remind myself that I wasn't in that dirty, abandoned building anymore. That wasn't my life. I'd escaped it.

I hung my head over the sink and scooped water over the back of my neck, letting it trickle over my skin. Tearing my shirt off, I used it to mop up the dampness then tossed it into the hamper. I walked back into the bedroom in just my sweats.

Ari was kneeling in the middle of the bed, with the blanket clutched to her chest. Her eyes followed me from across the room as I opened my dresser and pulled another t-shirt out.

"I'm sorry-" she started.

"Don't be. I'm sorry I woke you." I cringed inwardly as my tone came out gruffer than I meant for it to. She had no idea what was going on. I wasn't intending to take it out on her, but it sort of sounded like I was. Flicking the light on, I went and sat next to her on the bed.

Her eyes were a softer green and sympathetic. Usually, I hated anyone feeling sorry for me, but it didn't seem like that was what she was doing. She looked...concerned. Genuine. It helped to put me at ease.

"Sorry," I sighed. "I can't tell you everything yet, but I had a fucked up childhood. I should've warned you before we fell asleep. I wake up this way a couple times a week when I'm under a lot of pressure or stressed."

It killed me to have to admit this to her. I felt weak and useless. How could she trust me to protect her, to take care of her when I couldn't manage something as simple as sleep?

Her warm hand covered mine. I glanced up and found her examining me. "There's nothing to be sorry for. Is there anything I can do to help?"

The vise around my heart loosened considerably. I wasn't sure how she was going to react, but she was perfect. She didn't pry, or go on about how awful it was. She just wanted to help.

"You can say no..."

She cocked her head at me in question when I hesitated.

"Can I hold you?"

'TIL ENCRYPTION DO US PART

The smile started small, but quickly spread over her face. "I'd like that."

Nodding, I stood and flicked the lights off again. I shut down the laptop, leaving us in the dark. As I laid down, she scooted over and settled against me. Her front was pressed to my side and her hand and cheek were resting on my chest. I wrapped my arm around her and felt the last of the dream fade away. Strange how holding her in a protective way made my heart feel protected from the demons that plagued me.

My therapist had been harping at me to 'take comfort in others' during these times when the past collided with my present. If I'd known this was what she meant and that it'd feel so good to do it, I might have listened to her sooner than this.

The image of Riggs and I cuddling floated through my head and I had to choke back a laugh. Maybe I'd needed to wait until now to find someone who could offer me that kind of comfort. I rested my cheek on the top of her head and let peace steal over me.

Ari's breathing evened out as she fell asleep in my arms. It took hours for me to finally fall back to sleep, but when I did there were no more dreams.

* * *

I GLANCED up from the stove as Ari hesitantly padded into the kitchen.

"Morning," I called out to her. "Have a seat and I'll have something for you to eat in a few minutes."

"Thanks," she said softly and sat at the table we hardly ever used.

Typically, we used either the kitchen island or just balanced our plates on our laps in the common area. We weren't the most sophisticated bunch.

"Coffee?"

"Please," she responded next to my shoulder. I hadn't heard her come over. She was already searching through a cabinet for cups. I pointed the spatula at the one she needed, and she grinned at me. She was just settling down at the table again when the tornados that were my crew blew in.

"Oh good! It's too fucking early. I was worried you wouldn't have coffee on yet," Riggs said as he stumbled toward the coffeepot. Everyone filed in behind him, all chatting, laughing, and passing around the liquid that was more important to them than gold.

I glanced over and saw Ari sitting off to the side, eyes wide. We'd gone from just her and I to twelve extra people in the span of seconds. There was probably some girl-related fear of meeting people while in pajamas…and probably some concern of make-up, too. It was too late to address any of that.

"Why are you up so early, bitching in my clubhouse?" Cade asked Riggs.

"This fucker made a seven a.m. appointment at the shop. Then he has the fucking balls to ask me if I can do the repair because he had something else pop up," Riggs grumbled, grabbing his brother Steel in a headlock. Steel fought the hold, sloshing his coffee everywhere, until Remi snagged the cup from him and set it down on the island.

"Guys," Ming called out. Everyone ignored her and kept up the banter and fighting.

"GUYS!" Now Ming had everyone's attention. She glared at all of them, then tossed her head in Arianna's direction. She walked over to my fiancée with a smile. "Hi, I'm Ming."

Ari stood and self-consciously tugged her sleep shorts down as she reintroduced herself to everyone. I couldn't help but let my eyes wander down smooth, tanned legs as she was passed around from person to person. They'd ignored her outstretched hands and pulled her in for hugs.

"What's Hush's jacket doing in here?" Steel asked, munching on a pancake.

I glanced over at the plate where I'd been stacking them, noting that at least two were missing. I'd only taken my eye off them for a minute. I glared at Steel, but the asshole just gave me a grin. Feeding everyone here was like wrangling sheep. They were always underfoot, sticking their noses where they didn't belong, and crying about being hungry.

"Oh, I'm returning it to him."

Everyone fell silent. Ari glanced at me in confusion as they stood staring at her incredulously. Steel had his mouth hanging open, half eaten pancake forgotten in his hand.

"Returning it?" Julie asked her.

"Um, yeah. He let me borrow it last night when he told me-"

"I'm sorry, wait," Remi interrupted her. "He let you *borrow* his jacket?" Ari blinked around at everyone as they continued staring at her.

"And...spoke to you? Like actual words...that others could hear?" Bridget asked.

I chuckled under my breath. That'd pretty much been my reaction, too. Hush didn't let anyone touch his shit. He was fiercely protective of it. It was well known in the club that if you found something random laying around, you'd better ask who it belonged to before picking it up. Hush had damn near castrated a prospect with his knife a while ago because the poor kid had been cleaning up after a party and found that knife and sheath in the common area. The clip had come off Hush's belt and he'd found the kid waving it around. The prospect never made that mistake again, but it'd taken Cade interfering to calm Hush down.

Before Ari had a chance to say anything the back door opened and the man in question stepped into the kitchen. All eyes shot to him and he paused.

"Morning, Hush," Cade said with a grin.

Hush's eyes narrowed, but he gave his president a friendly nod—or friendly for him.

Arianna, being out of the limelight, hurried over to the chair she'd hung his jacket on. "Hi," she said quietly, approaching him.

Riggs came over and leaned against the counter next to me as we all watched the scene play out in front of us.

"Mornin'."

All the girls'—except Ari's because she wasn't in on this game—jaws dropped.

"Thank you so much for lending me your jacket last night." She handed it to him, and he took it and shrugged it on. "I took good care of it." She smiled at him and to everyone's amazement he grinned back at her.

"You're welcome." With the exchange over, Hush grabbed a cup of coffee and strode out of the clubhouse, leaving everyone behind in stunned silence. The girls all looked like a bunch of goldfish, eyes wide with their mouths opening and closing, but no words coming out.

"When's the last time anyone saw him smile?" Gunnar asked, looking around.

"When was the first time anyone saw him smile?" Riggs chimed in.

The men collectively shrugged and began searching around for more food.

"Shit," I muttered. I'd scorched the eggs watching the ex-marine interact with my fiancée. There was a story there. For some reason he responded to Ari. I sort of understood it. I responded to her in a way I hadn't expected. She had this soft, accepting demeanor. Somehow you knew she wouldn't judge you. Not that she was a doormat. She'd knocked her sister for a loop with that right hook of hers. I paused and considered how Alexandria would've handled everything last night and this morning. I snorted and shook my head. I doubted it would've gone well.

Handing Axel the plate of pancakes, I started scooping eggs onto a platter. Everyone was settling in over at the table, since that's where Ari had chosen to sit.

"He's never spoken to me before," Bridget commented.

"That's because you're a loudmouth," Ming said with a laugh. Remi and Anna cracked up at that, and Julie just shook her head.

"Seriously, though. You've been here for one night and I think he's said more to you than any of us," Julie told her. "That means he likes you."

"He talks to me," Axel said with a shrug of one huge shoulder.

"Sitting outside not talking isn't a conversation. You have to actually speak for it to count as *talking*!" Ming yelled at him.

Huh. I wondered if that was the reason Hush and I got along so well? It'd never occurred to me before that it was because we hardly spoke.

Breakfast was a loud, boisterous affair, and I watched in amusement as Ari's head swiveled back and forth like she was watching a tennis match as she tried to keep up with all the conversations. She'd soon realize there was always plenty of activity happening here. My family was already treating her like one of us, and surprisingly were on their best behavior. Which is to say, being loud, pushy, and all around not behaved at all. It was nice to see everyone so relaxed and already accepting her.

CHAPTER 15

Ari

Everyone cleared out as quickly and noisily as they'd entered and I sat there a bit shell-shocked. Our family dinners were always quiet and refined—and let's face it, dull. Mama would be horrified if any of us acted like these men and women had while eating. *Everyone* was talking with their mouths full, spitting food everywhere.

More than one piece of breakfast had gone flying across the table when someone had flung it at another person. And. I. *Loved* it! I couldn't wait for the day where I wasn't the new girl and could join in on the multiple conversations—well, shouting matches—that were happening all at once. This was what I suspected a real family was like. It was how Antonia, Ada, and I behaved around each other, constantly laughing and having a good time.

By the time the kitchen fell back into silence it was only me, Cade, and Rat sitting at the table. It looked like a hurricane had ransacked the kitchen. "I can help clean up," I told them.

"Thanks, but the prospects get clean up duty," Rat said, shooting Cade a look.

I couldn't read their expressions, except I knew they were serious.

'TIL ENCRYPTION DO US PART

Unease unfurled in my stomach as I waited. This was how Papa always looked when he had something to speak to me about and it usually wasn't something I wanted to be involved in, but had to in order to appease him.

"Ari, we're very glad to have you here with us," Cade started.

I gave him a small smile, but didn't interrupt. My fingernails dug into my thighs, below where my shorts ended. The idea that maybe they'd found out what I was hiding made me feel sick.

Rat gave me an encouraging look and brushed his hand over mine. He frowned and his gaze dropped down where I knew he'd felt my nails biting into my skin. He grabbed my hand and gently removed it from my leg, holding onto it in his big one.

Relaxing slightly, I shot him a grateful smile.

"There's been a lot happening around here for the last... Fuck has it been six months?" Cade shook his head in disbelief when Rat nodded.

"We know you've grown up in a similar lifestyle, but I thought I should go over some ground rules. Just so you know what to expect."

His green eyes met mine and I found myself unable to look away. He was a lot like Papa. Cade wore his authority like it was a natural part of him. Time would tell how he handled miscommunications and mistakes. That would truly tell me how much like my father he was. He seemed like a nice man, but they always did until you made them angry. And he was going to be angry if he ever found out what I'd done.

"We have a lot of enemies, especially right now." The men gave each other another look that would've spoken volumes to someone who was in on their secrets. "It's not safe for you to be traveling around the city alone."

I nodded and glanced down at my lap. I'd been let out of my gilded cage, only to be stuck in another one.

"It's our job to protect you. Rat mentioned your father had a bodyguard watching you, so I'm sure this isn't anything new."

I shook my head and chewed on my lower lip.

"It's not forever." I raised my head at Cade's words. "Just until things calm down a little. We're doing the same for the other women."

"And they all hate it," Rat said, chuckling. "They weren't used to having someone watch over them at first, but we're all settling into a routine."

"Rat will be taking you to and from school for now. If he's unable to, we'll assign someone else to go with you."

I frowned. "Do you have enough people to watch over everybody all day?"

Cade laughed. "No, most of us have businesses and jobs we have to get to, but until you settle in, we'll have someone stick with you. Typically, our guys just drop the other women off and pick them up for the ride home."

My heart sank. They were keeping an eye on me until they could trust me. I knew how to read around the political talk. *They have zero reason to trust you yet,* I reminded myself. In fact, if they'd known what I'd done, they never would.

"Okay."

Rat looked over at me uncertainly and squeezed my hand in reassurance. "These are just precautions. It won't be long before we can relax our guard and life gets back to normal."

I'd never had a normal life. I wanted to believe him. To believe them. I smiled at him and nodded.

"Great, in the meantime, if you need anything you can come to any of the people who were here for breakfast. We want you to be comfortable here," Cade said, standing.

I stood as well and saw Rat trying to hold back his grin.

"Thank you, Sir."

Cade grimaced. "It's just Cade. You two have a good day." With that he strode out the door.

"You alright?"

I looked down into Rat's face. "Yes. Like you said, it's not anything I'm not used to."

"There's still a lot we need to go over, but if I don't get you to class you're going to be late. We'll talk later."

* * *

THE DAY PASSED IN A BLUR. It should've been just another day, but for me so much had changed. Rat's promise of a talk had my stomach tied in knots. He'd met me during each break and walked me to my next class. When I'd asked him how he was supposed to get his own work done he'd just laughed and said he almost always could work from anywhere.

We were back at the clubhouse, and he was busy making dinner. There were so many people hanging around, and I'd already forgotten most of their names. It was becoming overwhelming again.

I stepped out the back door and sucked in a deep breath of the cooling night air. I'd thrown on a sweatshirt this time and I wandered toward the back of the property. Yesterday, I'd spotted a chair facing the woods. I headed that way, thinking it would be more relaxing, but someone was sitting in it so I changed directions. I ended up near a huge grill and some picnic tables. Sitting down on one of the benches, I faced the back of the property and watched the wind ruffle the tree branches. My phone startled me when it went off.

"Hey! You didn't call me this morning," Antonia pouted when I answered.

"Sorry," I told her with a laugh. "It was a busy morning."

"Soooo? How did last night go?"

"It was fine," I replied. It had been a good night until Rat's nightmare. I'd woken up to him yelling and thrashing around and it'd scared the shit out of me. I'd thought something was wrong. Then when he disappeared into the bathroom I'd worried that I'd embarrassed him. There was so much I needed to learn about him and this life that it felt daunting.

"It was fine, or it was *fiiiine?*"

I chuckled at the inflection in Antonia's tone. "Nothing happened. Don't be a perv."

"Bummer." She sounded so disappointed. "I have to live vicariously through you. You know how Papa is."

"Rat was very sweet, but I'm not ready to take that step yet."

"I get it. You guys need to get to know each other, learn to trust one another. Then it's going to be bow-chica-bow-wow," she sang.

"Oh my God, Toni! You are so bad." It felt good to laugh, though. Doubts and fears had been plaguing me all day. I glanced around to make sure I was still alone. "They've got Rat following me around."

Antonia sucking in a breath was audible over the phone. "Do you think they know?"

"No. They said it was for my protection because they have enemies."

"That's Papa's tired excuse, too." I could all but hear her rolling her eyes. "Strange how over the years we've never once seen these enemies."

I agreed wholeheartedly and was just as sick of it all as she was. "I know, but I'm playing along for now. This is their place, their rules."

"Wait. Their place?"

"We're living at the clubhouse."

"That's so cool. Can I come visit?" she asked breathlessly.

"You'd better...but Toni?"

"What?"

"No hitting on the bikers."

"Well, that's no fun," she pouted.

"Most of them are taken anyway...I think. At least no hitting on them until I figure out what's what. We don't need some biker chick kicking your ass for cozying up to her man."

"Fine. I guess I'll only come to visit you." She paused for a minute before continuing, "Is everyone being nice?"

"Oh yeah, they're great. In fact, we're about to have dinner. I'd better go. I'll call you later?"

"Sounds good. Love you, Ari."

"Love you, too," I murmured, turning to watch over my shoulder as Rat walked up to me.

"There you are. Everything okay?" His worried blue eyes raked over me.

"Yeah, I was just talking to my sister."

"Gotcha. Dinner's just about done if you're ready to come back inside."

I stood and brushed off the back of my jeans. When I looked at him again Rat had his hand out and I hesitated before taking it. His long, warm fingers wrapped around mine and I felt something heat low in my belly. He was doing a really good job at making me feel like he wanted me here—like I belonged. It had my heart threatening to melt into a puddle at his feet. I couldn't allow that, though.

Just because I'd given up on my plan to run away and was getting married to him didn't mean I could let my guard down. For all I knew he was lulling me into a false sense of security before he dropped the hammer and completely took over my life. I was still trying to find out everything I could about his club and their dealings. Maybe once I knew what to expect I could relax and start trusting, but for now I steeled my resolve to keep some distance. That meant I had to smack my fluttering heart into compliance.

CHAPTER 16

Rat

"Fuck!" I grabbed the 'oh shit' handle in the truck and mashed my boot down on the invisible brake. I was stuck over on the passenger side of the cage ride, though, while Arianna did her best to give me a fucking heart attack. "Watch out for that-" I groaned as she accidentally hit the gas instead of the brake and popped up onto the sidewalk in the parking lot we were in.

She gasped and took both feet off the pedals.

"No, don't-"

The truck lurched to a stop, engine dying. I took a deep, calming breath, and wondered why I'd let Riggs talk me into teaching her to drive on a manual. There was so much more for her to learn and remember driving a stick shift. Joke was on him though, since he would be the one to replace the burned-up clutch when we were done.

"I'm sorry," she mumbled as red crawled up her neck.

"Hey," I said softly and waited until she looked over at me. "It's not a big deal. If you burn the clutch out in this thing, Riggs gets to fix it." I grinned at her. Her answering smile wavered a little.

"I don't think driving is for me."

I barked out a laugh. "You've only been doing it for ten minutes, Ari. It takes time to learn—especially a manual. You'll get the hang of it."

She huffed out a breath, mashed the clutch back into the floorboard, and started the truck up again.

"Good girl."

She darted a quick, surprised look over at me then looked back out the windshield.

I'd brought her to an abandoned parking lot to practice. I was glad I had now. I didn't need her crashing into any parked cars.

It took about an hour, but soon she was driving around the lot. Her shifting was smoothing out and she was gaining confidence. The grin on her face made the first terrifying ten minutes worth it.

We sat parked, engine idling. Ari'd been living with me for a week. She was settling in at the clubhouse and was starting to get to know everyone, but I could tell she was holding back—from me, from the others—I just didn't know why.

"Tell me something about you," I requested.

"What?"

"Anything you want."

She chewed on her lower lip, and I had to bite back a groan. I wanted to suck on that lip so bad it was hard to keep my hands to myself and stay on my side of the vehicle.

"I don't know what to tell you," she said with a laugh.

My lips tipped up in a grin. "Favorite childhood memory?"

"That's an easy one. My seventh birthday party. Alex convinced Mama and Papa to rent a petting zoo for me." Her smile slipped a bit. "It wasn't long after that when Alex stopped hanging around with me. It wasn't cool to have your little sister tagging along." She rolled her eyes at me. "But that birthday was perfect. Mama wasn't thrilled because—even then—she liked things to be fancy. They had to drag me away at the end of the night, and I was plotting on how I could sneak one of the bunnies back home."

I chuckled and tried to picture a young Arianna smuggling a stolen rabbit into her house. I barely knew her folks, but it didn't take a rocket scientist to know her mother would've flipped her shit.

"How about you?" She asked.

The question was innocent. And I should have expected it, since I asked her first. There was an eagerness in her eyes I didn't want to stomp out by telling her I didn't have any fond memories. Well...there was one.

"The day I walked up to two bikers and convinced them to include my scrawny ass in their MC. Of course, while I was convincing them, I had lifted their wallets and the keys to their bikes. It helped make my point."

She frowned. "How old were you?"

"Twelve," I said, meeting her eyes.

Those gorgeous, soft green eyes widened. "I knew-" She licked her lips. "I heard at dinner that night, they said you were separated from your family?"

I gave her a curt nod.

Her eyes searched mine. "Where were you before the MC took you in?"

I'd known it was coming and still the question hit me like a boot in the gut. "That's a story for another day," I told her after a lengthy pause. "We need to get over to your parents' house to get the rest of your stuff. Do you want to drive over?"

"Hell no!" she snapped. "I'm not ready for the freeway."

Laughing, I opened the door and we switched places. "Fine, but I'm not taking it easy on you. You'll be driving in no time."

Ari smiled at me and clicked her seatbelt. "Thanks, Rat."

I shot a couple of our prospects a text to meet us at the address then pulled out onto the road.

* * *

I APPRECIATED a woman who packed light. Other than her clothes, shoes, and a few other odds and ends, the only thing Ari brought was her desk and computer equipment.

The officers had stayed behind and moved all of my stuff from my smaller room to the apartment we'd be staying in from now on.

"Thanks guys," I told them as Scout helped me lug Ari's desk up from the parking lot.

"Anytime," Cade said cheerfully.

"Gave us a chance to dig through your shit," Riggs said, holding up a pair of my boxers.

Rolling my eyes, I continued maneuvering Ari's desk into the living room. I put it right next to mine. Our place wasn't going to be full of furniture and all the other things normal couples had. It was a nerd's wet dream in here.

"How did you manage to find the one girl who has as much of a hard-on for computers as you do?" Steel grunted as he carried a portion of Ari's equipment through the front door.

"Fucking lucky, I guess," I said with a grin. "Put it over here."

With everyone pitching in, it didn't take long to have everything set up in our new space.

"Thank you all so much," Ari told them. She shot Hush a bright smile, and I swore the man's face flushed a dull red.

Before anyone could respond, Remi and Bridget came through the door. "Okay! Now it's our turn."

Ari looked confused and I bit back a smile. I hadn't told her what the women had planned. I was hoping it would be a good surprise and help her relax a little more.

Remi grabbed one of Ari's arms while Bridget grabbed the other and they started marching her toward the door.

"What's going on?" she asked, her eyes finding mine across the room.

"We're throwing you a bachelorette slash welcome to the club party!" Remi said excitedly.

"Women only, no boys allowed." Bridget shot us a wild-eyed look and arched a brow. No one said a word, but everyone was grinning.

"Steel, we'll need you to open the gates up for the strippers we ordered," Remi said, batting her eyelashes.

"What the fuck?!" Steel started forward and Remi took off into the hall. Her laughter floated back to us.

"Um...I don't want any strippers," Ari mumbled.

"There are no strippers," Ming said, walking through the door. "Why the hell would we pay for guys to take their shirts off when we could get these guys wasted and have that for free?"

She had a point. We'd had a barbeque a while back and Trip had ended up stripping down to his boxer briefs. The women loved it. They'd started shoving singles down his shorts.

Bridget dragged Ari out the door without another word.

"Don't worry, we'll take good care of her," Ming told me.

I had no doubt about that.

We watched as Ming left, closing the door.

"Who wants a beer?" I asked the room. Every hand went up. The least I could do was feed them and give them alcohol when they'd just helped me move.

CHAPTER 17

Ari

"I can't believe you went to so much trouble for me," I said, looking around at the women seated at the outside picnic tables. "Thank you so much."

"Oh sweetie," Ming said, softly. "It's no trouble at all."

"We're just sorry more of the wives and girlfriends couldn't make it. It was sort of a last-minute idea," Remi said, grabbing another slice of pizza from the middle of the table.

"We wanted to be the first to give you a bachelorette party," Bridget smirked.

There was no way Mama would have given me a bachelorette party, but I groaned knowing I'd be stuck with a bridal shower. "You're all invited to my shower. I'll have to get the date, but I know Mama is already planning it."

They all grinned. "We'll be there," Anna said, and happiness washed over me. These five women had gone out of their way to make me feel comfortable here.

"Gift time," Julie sang out and plopped a bag in my lap.

My mouth dropped open. "You didn't have to buy me anything!"

"I think I got your size right," Bridget muttered, eyeing me like I was a piece of roadkill and she was a buzzard.

To give myself something else to do, I pulled a teddy out of the bag. My face went up in flames of embarrassment. It was black and completely sheer. I turned it around as the women around me laughed and elbowed each other.

"That's from me," Bridget said proudly.

"I...um...thank you, Bridget." I had to force myself not to ask where the rest of it was. What was the point of wearing something that hid nothing? Bridget's wicked smile answered that question for me.

I made my way through the presents, overwhelmed that they'd thought to buy me gifts. I didn't tell Rat earlier, but one of the reasons the petting zoo birthday had been my favorite was because my parents had forgotten my next two birthdays. It'd happened to Antonia once, too. I wasn't sure how a parent could forget their child's birthday, but they'd managed it. The fact these women, practically strangers, went through so much effort and put so much thought into this made me feel more loved than I did with my family.

"Thank you, seriously." I blinked back the tears as I looked around at all their smiling faces.

"Now it's time for margaritas," Julie rushed into the nearest house and came back out with a frosty blender full of the liquid and a bunch of red plastic cups.

The next thing I knew we were one—maybe three—drinks deep, and I was so drunk I couldn't stand. Thankfully, I wasn't the only one.

"I'm mad at you," Remi told me with a serious look on her face.

My alcohol-soaked brain was horrified. "Why?" I clutched my hands to my heart, ready to burst into tears. *Must be the margaritas.*

Anna filled my cup to the top again and I blearily wondered if I should stop drinking. *Ah what the hell, when in Rome.*

"You're getting married before me," Remi pouted, then shot me a wink.

I softened with relief and laughed. "I would say sorry about that, except it wasn't my idea," I slurred.

The others chuckled.

"Have you set a date yet?" Ming asked. She went to set her drink on the table and then watched, seemingly annoyed with the cup, as it missed and fell to the ground, spilling its contents everywhere. "Aw, I wanted that."

"We have plenty more," Bridget shoved another cup into Ming's hand.

I wasn't sure how she'd had the time to fill it since only a few seconds had passed.

"That's okay Remi. You'll be Mrs. Steele soon enough," Julie told her.

"Sure, if Steel will stop dragging his feet and let me pick a date," she grumbled into her cup.

"Hang on," I said, and every eye locked onto me. "I'm sorry..." My addled brain was performing a task it really shouldn't be —thinking.

"Is Steele his last name?" They all nodded, and I started laughing so hard I snorted. Now they looked at each other in confusion.

"Remi, is your name short for Remington?"

She grimaced but nodded. "My dad was a Marine," she explained.

"So, your name after you get married is going to be Remington Steele?" I asked in between peals of laughter. It probably wasn't that funny, but I was no longer in control. The giggles had me now, and there was no stopping them.

The others were quiet for a beat of time and then they started howling along with me. Even Remi couldn't hold the disapproving frown she'd been giving us.

After we'd calmed down about that and talked about obligatory wedding plans, we sat there in silence for a bit.

"We're really glad to have you here, Ari," Ming told me, interrupting the comfortable silence we'd fallen into. "Rat, well, he deserves to be happy. And you're such a good fit for him. I know you two will be madly in love before long."

"Yeah," Anna said, raising her head from where she'd been resting it on the table. She was swaying slightly, despite the fact that she was sitting. "Glad. Madly."

I snickered. They were going to feel like shit come morning. *And so are you.*

"And lucky you, you got to come when things settled down and weren't so crazy," Bridget told me.

"Crazy?"

"Oh man, don't get us started on the bullshit that's been happening lately," Remi muttered. They proceeded to tell me the whole thing.

By the time they were halfway through, my eyes were as big as the plates in front of us. "That's insane. I mean, I grew up in a mafia family and I don't even have a story like that."

"Psft, that's not even the end," Anna said. "When they were down in Mexico this last time, there was some kind of mix-up and all the guys went after Miguel Guzman, except for Rat and a couple of the Zetas-"

"And Ming," Julie interrupted her.

"Right, and me," Ming said, holding up her cuo in a drunken salute.

"Anyway, by the time they got to where Guzman was supposed to be, it turned out he'd somehow tricked us and was already on his way to the Zetas' compound."

"Some asshole looped the security feeds and set it up to look like Guzman and his goons were there when they weren't," Remi spat.

Every ounce of blood drained out of my face.

Ming must have noticed because she patted my hand. "Don't worry. We were all fine, and the guys took care of Miguel Guzman."

"Yeah, and it wasn't the guys' fault, it was our families'," Julie said mournfully.

I wished the idea of Rat and Ming being in danger was why I suddenly felt like I was going to throw up. It upset me a little, but the real reason I was feeling this way was because...I was the asshole who'd messed with Guzman's security feeds.

"Okay, that's enough!" We all jumped as Steel's voice boomed out from behind us.

My heart thudded in my chest as the rest of the men came up, all grinning.

"Shit, they're completely wasted," Riggs laughed. He caught Anna as she fell backward off the bench.

Rat's laughing eyes met mine as the men started scooping up their respective women and hauling them off. Rat's brows pulled low over his eyes when he noticed the look on my face.

"What's wrong?" he asked, stepping over to me.

"N...nothing. I'm suddenly not feeling well."

"Okay, let's get you up and into bed then," he replied. He helped me stand and let me lean on him. My legs were like wet noodles and I had to concentrate on where I was stepping. That was hard though, with all the super-charged thoughts running through my head.

Rat gave up and swept me into his arms. My world spun and I tucked my face into his neck to make it stop. Guilt and worry plagued me as he carried me up to our room. This was the secret I'd been hanging on to. I knew it was going to come back to bite me in the ass.

I'd had no idea when I did it that I was helping some asshole cartel leader, or that I'd be putting anyone in danger. Hell, I hadn't even known the Vikings then. I'd just done what my father demanded. It made me wonder how many deaths I was responsible for due to all the times I'd helped him in the past. And there was another thought clamoring to reach the surface, damn the alcohol. Why? Why help the cartel if he was going to marry me to their rival?

I couldn't hold back the tears, the guilt was too much. Rat glanced down at me as they wet his neck and t-shirt.

"Hey," he said, alarm coating the word. "Hey, hey, hey." He set me down on our bed and crouched in front of me. "What's wrong? Why are you crying?" When I just sat there sobbing he said my name sharply, "ARI, are you hurt?"

"Noooo," I sobbed. I'd probably be embarrassed about my behavior later. "I have to tell you something," I whispered, then hiccupped. I was miserable, because I knew he'd push me away after this. That used to be what I wanted. Now, I didn't know what I wanted anymore. What if Ming was right? What if I could love him?

"Okay, what is it?" He wiped the tears off my cheeks and our eyes met.

"You're so pretty," I told him.

He barked out a laugh. "That's what you wanted to tell me?"

It hadn't been, but my brain was having a hard time hanging on to what I had desperately wanted to say.

"Go to sleep," he murmured, laying down beside me and pulling me back against his chest as he wrapped his arms around me.

I couldn't fight it. I dropped off into sleep.

CHAPTER 18

Ari

Oh God, someone kill me now.

My eyes parted and I groaned. My mouth was filled with cotton and my head pounded behind eyelids that snapped closed. What the hell happened last night?

No sooner had the thought run through my mind than the answer followed. It all came back in a flash and so did the guilt. I rolled and looked at Rat. His face was peaceful. The clock over his shoulder said it was five a.m. Apparently, even hung over I couldn't sleep in.

I found blue eyes watching me with a hint of worry when I looked back at him. "How are you feeling?"

"Like crap."

He chuckled and rolled out of bed. Rat went into the bathroom and then came back out with a glass of water and some Tylenol.

"Thanks," I muttered as he handed them to me.

"You girls sure know how to party." He sat down on the bed next to me.

"Tell me about it," I groaned, causing my head to throb.

"How did it go?"

I froze. The entirety of the night came to me all at once. "Great. They're so sweet." The guilt was eating me alive.

"Yeah, they're awesome," he replied.

"I'm going to shower," I told him and escaped to the bathroom. I let the hot spray pound over my aching head while I considered my options. I could try to keep this secret forever, and maybe I'd be able to move past it someday, or I could be an adult and explain what happened to the club. The thought made my stomach roil. I had no idea how they would respond.

Only a week ago I thought they'd kill me if they found out what I'd finally determined to reveal to them. Now I wasn't so sure, but I didn't know if I could take Rat's response. In a very short time, he'd started wriggling his way past my defenses.

When I came out of the bathroom I found Rat laying on the bed, scrolling through his phone. He looked up at me and a smile lit his eyes. "Feel any better?"

I swallowed. "A little. Hey, um… Can I speak with you?"

His brows shot up.

"Well...with you and Cade?"

Those intense blue eyes narrowed on me. "Sure." He tapped on his phone then stood and walked over to the dresser.

I waited patiently while he pulled on jeans and a t-shirt.

"It can wait since it's so early-"

"Nope. Now is good." He didn't bother to ask me what was going on. His face was a blank mask. I couldn't determine how he was feeling. He'd obviously picked up on the fact that whatever I wanted to talk about wasn't good news and he'd locked everything up in preparation of dealing with it.

Anxiety filled me as we walked downstairs. He led me to one of the two houses on the property.

Cade answered the door when he knocked. "How many times do I have to tell you not to knock? Just come in." He shook his head at Rat, then his speculative gaze landed on me.

I silently followed them into Cade's kitchen then sat when prompted. This probably should've waited until I was feeling a little better because between the hangover and my nerves it felt like I was going to either throw up or pass out. Or both, and not in that order.

Both men focused on me and my mouth went dry. I struggled to swallow, and twisted my fingers together in my lap.

Despite his casual pose as he leaned back in the chair, I could tell Rat was tense. His eyes were narrowed and watchful.

"The girls told me what's been happening with Miguel Guzman," I started.

Rat frowned. "They weren't supposed to say anything to you." His hard gaze softened when my eyes widened.

Shit. Now I'd gotten them into trouble.

"I was going to tell you," he explained. "I don't want you worrying about not being safe living here with me."

I opened my mouth, then promptly closed it. This was a mistake. They were going to be furious with me—rightfully so.

"Whatever it is, just tell us." Cade's voice was even and calm.

I took a deep breath. "I was the one who adjusted Miguel Guzman's video feed at his compound," I blurted out. Immediately I wished I could reach out and grab the words, shove them back into my mouth.

Rat's mouth dropped open, but Cade didn't flinch. He sat still as stone. I held Cade's gaze because I wasn't sure I'd be able to get the rest out if I saw the hurt that was likely there in Rat's eyes.

"I swear I didn't know who he was. Or that he was your enemy." I frowned. "Or who your club was at the time," I stated, feeling like an idiot.

"Why?" The fury in Rat's tone made me flinch. Up until this point he'd been nothing but sweet and patient with me.

I finally met his eyes and the cold, barely suppressed anger I found there had my heart dropping into my stomach like a lead weight. "My father," I wet my lips, "he asked me to." More like ordered, but I left that out.

"And you just do anything he asks?" Rat snarled.

"Rat," Cade said so calmly we both ended our staring match and looked over at him. "She didn't know."

"That's no fucking excuse! She nearly got us killed-"

"I didn't mean to!" I interrupted. "If I could take it back I would."

A dark cloud settled over his features and I knew there was no taking it back. There was a possibility of no forgiveness judging by the look on his face. "You know your father's a fucking criminal. Any job you do for him affects someone."

Anger ignited within me. I wasn't feeling overly protective of my father, but I didn't like his hypocrisy. "I'm sorry...aren't *you* a criminal?" I asked with icy politeness. His head reared back as though I'd slapped him. "Whatever your club is involved with can't be any worse than what my family is, or you wouldn't have crossed paths in the first place. Furthermore, my father always kept me in the dark about what he was doing, but I tried to figure it out before I helped. I didn't see any harm in looping a security camera feed, so I did it."

"You did it to help yourself," he growled at me. "So, you could stay in your daddy's good graces."

Tipping my chin up, I held his gaze unwaveringly. "You're right. That's exactly why I did it. Now, if you'll excuse me, I'll let you two talk." I stood and swept out of the room with the grace of a queen. It seemed I'd picked something up from Alexandria and Mama after all.

I went up to our apartment and grabbed a backpack and started stuffing some clothes into it. It was weird to be packing again after only having officially moved in the night before. There was no way Rat was going to marry me. Not after the way he reacted. Cade had barely gotten a word in edgewise with the two of us arguing, but he hadn't seemed quite as angry. If anything, I sensed a general feeling of disappointment coming from him.

Walking downstairs with my things, I glanced around the parking lot. I wasn't sure how I was going to get home. Home...I didn't know where that was anymore. I shuddered to think what Papa would do once he found out. Maybe it was time to put my original plan into action. If Rat wasn't going to be pounding on Uncle Nico's door, demanding I be returned, I could go to New York.

With that part of the plan settled, I watched as someone pulled in on their motorcycle. Relief coursed through me when I saw it was Hush. I walked up to him.

Hush watched me with a suspicious gaze as I approached. His eyes dipped down as he noticed the bag I carried.

"Hi," I tried to keep my voice bright to hide the turmoil within me.

"Mornin'."

"Would you be able to bring me into the city?"

His eyes narrowed. "Where's Rat?"

My bottom lip trembled, so I bit it to keep it from giving me away.

Before I could answer, Hush got off his bike and took my bag from me. He set it on the seat of his bike and motioned for me to follow him.

"Where are we going?" I asked, puzzled.

He didn't bother to say anything, so I followed him out back to where the picnic tables were. His brow rose when he saw the mess we'd left from the night before. Hush sat on a bench that was empty.

I started cleaning the mess—stacking cups and plates until I could grab a garbage bag. I needed something to do with my hands. Hush didn't stop me.

He sat in silence, watching me for a minute before he spoke. "What happened?"

I glanced over sharply. "What do you mean?"

"Why're you runnin' away?"

That pulled a derisive laugh from me. "I'm not running away, Hush. I'm not twelve-years-old."

He cocked his head. "Looks like runnin' away to me." He folded those huge arms over an equally bulky chest.

Sighing, I paused what I was doing and stared down at the wooden table. "I...made a mistake a while ago. Before I knew Rat—or anyone here—but I had to tell them what I'd done. It hadn't been my intention to hurt anyone." A tear slipped down my cheek. I rubbed at it with my knuckles, horrified that I was crying in front of someone who was basically a stranger.

"I just didn't know if I could live with the lie. Now I wonder if I should have. Did I only tell them to absolve myself of the guilt?"

I shook my head and continued on before Hush had a chance to say anything. "You can't start a relationship with a foundation of secrets and lies. Then again, I'm pretty sure my relationship is over, so what does it matter?" I sat down with a sigh. It felt strangely good to get all that out. Peeking over, I tried to gauge Hush's reaction. Nothing had changed. He hadn't moved.

"You think the kid is going to send you back to your family?"

I nodded, misery building inside me at hearing him voice my fear. How could I have changed so much over only a week? I'd been planning on leaving at the beginning. How could I want to stay so badly now?

Rat had been nice to me. He seemed like he cared about me. I groaned inwardly, disgusted with myself that I craved connection with someone so badly, that I'd given him this kind of control over me.

I hardly knew the guy, so it wasn't love. Somehow though, he'd touched a piece of me that I'd locked away, thinking no one would ever reach it.

"Nothin' good ever came from runnin' away, Girl."

I looked over at Hush. He looked stern, like I imagined a father scolding his child would. It's never how my father looked. My father scared the living hell out of me most of the time. Hush looked...disappointed, but kind and patient.

Ugh. I was sick of disappointing people this morning.

"It beats waiting around to be told to leave," I whispered.

Hush laughed. It was a husky, deep rumble and pleasant to the ears. "If you think that kid is lettin' you go anywhere, you're an idiot."

I bristled at that and glared at him. I wasn't an idiot.

He arched a brow at me clearly reading my thoughts on my face. "What do you call someone who runs away because she pisses someone off and doesn't want to stick around to see what the consequences are?"

A coward.

I liked that even less than being called an idiot, but I saw his point. I sighed and plucked at a paper plate sitting in front of me. "I guess I kind of have to face up to it, huh?" My tone was just hopeful enough that he smirked at me.

"Yup."

Groaning, I stood up. "Fine. I'll go get my bag and wait for Rat," I muttered.

Hush walked me back out to the front. He grabbed my bag and held it out for me.

My hand had just touched the strap when the sound of a door slamming echoed across the lot. I glanced over my shoulder and my eyes widened as I saw Rat stalking across the yard. The look on his face was murderous.

His eyes flashed between me, Hush, and my bag. "Where are you going, Ari?" He grabbed my arm and jerked me toward him.

"Ow, you're hurting me," I told him quietly, ignoring his question. I tried to keep a lid on my temper. Rat was justified in his anger toward me. That didn't mean he had to tear my arm out of its socket. I also needed to control my own emotions because—growing up in my home—we'd gotten into fist fights more often than not. Well, us girls had. Mama hated it. She thought it wasn't lady-like, Papa had just laughed and let us fight it out.

Rat squeezed my bicep a little harder before my words penetrated his anger and he loosened his grip. "Answer me."

"I was about to go up to the apartment to wait for you."

Hush cleared his throat and set the bag down by my feet.

"Is there a problem here...brother?" Rat snarled at Hush.

The other man just chuckled and walked away. My mouth was hanging open. It didn't matter that I hardly knew this man, I didn't know he was capable of this kind of anger. It made me worry about the type of man I was marrying. The last thing I wanted was another version of my father.

Rat picked up my bag with one hand and tugged on me until I followed him toward the clubhouse. I allowed him to pull me inside.

"Morning," Anna grumbled as she poured a cup of coffee. She looked like she woke up feeling as terrible as I had. Her brows drew together when she saw Rat yanking me along. "Hey, what are-"

"Leave them alone, Anna," Riggs said quietly from across the room. He'd just entered the kitchen from behind us.

I glanced over my shoulder and the man's usually jovial expression was cold and hard. I grimaced and focused on the back of Rat's shirt.

"He can't just drag her around like that, Riggs." We were already through the door to the other side, so I couldn't hear his reply. Anna's shout made it through the door just fine, though. "You guys are such cavemen!"

That made my lips twitch. I appreciated her defending me, but I wasn't sure she'd want to after she found out what I'd done. Obviously, while Hush and I had been talking, they'd brought Riggs into the meeting and told him my secret.

Rat finally let go of me once we were in the privacy of our bedroom. I sat down on the bed and watched as he stalked from one end of the room and back.

My emotions were all over the place. At first, I'd feared Rat sending me away. It wasn't what I wanted. After seeing the way Riggs responded to me and imagining everyone reacting the way he and Rat were...maybe it was for the best.

CHAPTER 19

Rat

I couldn't seem to get a grip on my anger. The intensity of it was unsettling, but in the moment I didn't fucking care. She'd betrayed me. Betrayed my club. Worked for our enemy. Worst of all? She'd lied to me about it. A lie of omission was still a lie.

Somewhere in the back of my mind a voice tried to reason with me. Shit, both Cade and Riggs had tried to explain to me that it wasn't necessarily her fault. I'd calmed down a little by the time I left Cade's to go find Ari. Then I spotted her handing over her bag to Hush. If she thought she was going to fucking leave me, she had another thing coming.

I glared down at her. She was sitting calmly on the bed. The only indication she was nervous was the wringing of her hands where they sat on her lap. I looked away and took another lap around the room. I needed a minute to calm the fuck down. I was overreacting, but I couldn't seem to stop myself.

Ari waited me out. She didn't try to appeal to me or explain. That actually helped my heartbeat slow from the frantic pace it'd set. Finally, I stopped and faced her.

Her head rose and she met my gaze steadily. There was a spark of anger and stubbornness in her eyes. I loved that she wasn't weakly backing down from me. *Not the reaction I was expecting from myself.* Her chin jutted forward slightly, waiting on me.

"What were you doing with Hush?" I demanded.

She blinked in surprise. Whatever she'd been expecting me to say, that wasn't it. Her mouth opened, then closed. Then she took a breath and blurted out, "I was running away...according to him."

It was my turn to feel surprised. "Why?"

Her laugh was mocking and she motioned to me. "Look at you, Rat. You hate me. It's easy enough to see that." Her lips turned down into a frown. "I thought you were going to return me to Papa. I figured I'd save you the trouble."

Return her? What, like she was a fucking puppy I was taking back to the pound? I narrowed my eyes on her unhappy face and ground my teeth together.

"Was he going to take you?" We had barely started talking and already things had taken a turn towards the unexpected. I needed to determine if I had to talk to Hush about this. I wasn't sure how I felt about it. I liked that he seemed to like Arianna and felt protective of her. That didn't mean I wanted him trying to protect her from me. I'd never hurt her, no matter how angry I was. That wasn't the kind of man I was. I didn't hit women. *Well, not unless they were trying to claw your eyes out over half a hamburger you pulled from a dumpster, but that's a story for another time.*

"No. He talked me out of it. He was giving me my stuff back so I could come inside when you saw us."

The knot in my gut loosened slightly. I should've known better than to question the loyalty of a brother, but this woman had me so twisted around I didn't know how to feel.

It didn't matter that we'd only been together for a week. I'd begun to trust her. My mistake. I should've realized with her computer skill —not that I'd known the extent of it—and her father being who he was, he'd probably dragged her into some of his business.

"Is there anything else?"

She looked at me in confusion. "Huh?"

"Is there anything else you haven't told me? About the work you've done for your father?" I couldn't seem to soften my tone. Even when she flinched at my sharp words, I couldn't do anything about it. Later, once I'd calmed down, I'd probably feel bad. For now, I was riding that wave and couldn't get off. It would be better if I waited to have this conversation with her. I knew it, but I wasn't going to take the chance that she'd bolt. She'd already tried once.

"No. Or...not that I know of," she said softly, dropping her gaze down to her hands. "I only remember that one because Papa let Miguel Guzman's name slip. He usually kept me in the dark about what I was doing."

That made me feel a little better. "Did they tell you everything that happened? With Guzman?"

Her face paled a little, but she lifted her chin and recited what the women had told her. It was a story to her, but we'd lived it. My own life hadn't mattered to me at the time and the risk of losing it wasn't what made me angry now. It was that Ming had been put into danger. If Ari hadn't tampered with that feed, I would've known Guzman wasn't at his compound and the full force of our men would've been there to meet Miguel head on when he snuck into town.

"It's likely we'll find more things in the future that you didn't realize were connected to us. When you do, I need you to tell me about them."

Ari nodded in agreement. "When I do, you need to handle it better," she told me in a steely tone of voice.

She wasn't wrong. What was her motivation to tell me if this was how I behaved each time?

"Agreed." I turned and walked out of the bedroom. I'd already opened the door to the apartment before she caught up to me.

"Where are you going?"

I turned my head and looked at her. She looked miserable. I wasn't sure if that was from the hangover or everything that had happened this morning. Maybe both.

"I have something I need to take care of."

Her hand landed on my arm and I paused.

"Shouldn't we talk about this more?" Her voice was uncertain.

"Oh, we will Ari," I told her, spinning around and stalking her so that she took a step back with every move I made toward her. "We're absolutely talking about it. I have to go to church first, though."

She let out a little squeak of surprise when I backed her into the kitchen island. Before she could move, I pressed my body against hers. I cupped her chin and tilted her head up, so she had nowhere to look, but into my eyes. "This isn't over."

She swallowed and her eyes widened, but she held my gaze. "Are you going to send me back to Papa?"

"Fuck no," I snarled at her. "You're mine. You fucked up, but we'll get past that. Make no mistake about it, Arianna. You belong to *me*. There'll be no running away or racing back to your father every time we have a fight."

Her eyelids fluttered closed as I leaned in and kissed her hard. Her breaths were choppy and uneven by the time I pulled back.

All the blood rushed from my head and my dick hardened. It wasn't easy to step back and leave. I wanted to lift her onto the counter and give in to my body's demands. There wasn't time for all the things I wanted to do to her, though.

"I'll be back in about an hour. Stay here," I warned her before I shut the door behind me.

I'd just stepped off the back porch when Hush materialized from around the corner. I sighed. This was going to continue to be a shitty morning.

"I don't know what you've got goin' through your head, Kid. Just know there's nothin' between your girl and me," Hush told me in a low voice.

Cocking my head, I stared at him. "I know, but why have you taken such an interest in her?"

"She reminds me of someone." He stuffed his hands in the pockets of his jacket to ward off the morning chill. "Just thought she needed a friend."

I nodded. "I appreciate that, Hush."

He gave me a curt nod in response and left. That was all it took. Everything was settled between us. I groaned when I was stopped again only a few steps later.

"Follow me," Cade told me as he passed.

Huffing out a breath, I went with him. We stopped out behind his house.

"Look. I know you're pissed. Shit, I would be too-"

"I know I'm overreacting," I muttered, interrupting him.

Cade smirked a little and folded his arms over his chest. "You are, but I get it. You still planning on going through with the wedding?"

"Shit, you too? I made a commitment and I'm sticking to it. What she did doesn't change that."

"It should help knowing she didn't do any of it knowing what would happen," he commented.

"It does." I sighed. "I'll get over it."

"Good. Let's get to church."

I hardly paid attention during the meeting while Cade explained what Arianna had told us this morning. The girls were unusually quiet. I wasn't sure whether to blame that on their obvious hangovers or if it had to do with Ari.

Ming's eyes found mine from across the table and understanding shone in them.

Remi groaned, and everyone looked at her. "Well now I don't know if I'm mad at her, or if I feel bad that I said some asshole messed with the video since she was that asshole." She dropped her head into her hands. "My brain hurts too badly to think about it."

Almost everyone chuckled at that. Remi was always good about breaking the tension.

"Why would she do that?" Julie asked.

"She did it for her father," I told her. "Because he told her to."

"I know what she did put some of our people in danger, but to be fair Arianna didn't know that's what would happen. Her father is… let's just say he has a reputation," Cade told everyone. "It's well known that he keeps his family firmly planted under his thumb. I doubt she had much of a choice in the matter."

That would make sense. She'd flat out told me she was terrified of her father. Suddenly, I felt even worse about my behavior. She'd said she hadn't seen the harm in looping a video feed. To her, it was probably easier to just do as he asked rather than take a stand over something so insignificant. My anger cooled rapidly, thinking about that.

They moved on and discussed other things while I was lost in my thoughts. Before I knew it Cade had released us. Everyone gave me my space as I headed back up to our room. I wasn't sure if that was because they could tell how angry I was when I'd first come in or if Anna had told them what happened.

Ari was sitting at her computer, headphones on, tapping away when I walked in. She froze, eyes still on her screen. She took a deep breath and turned around to face me. She studied me, quietly waiting.

"Why did you do it, Ari?"

She pulled the headphones off her head. "I told you-"

"I mean, why would you go along with what your father wanted?" I didn't care if she was doing anything illegal. She'd been right to call me on my hypocrisy there. I just wanted to confirm my suspicions.

Ari bowed her head, debating on whether to trust me enough to answer me. I didn't blame her. I hadn't exactly handled the previous news she'd given me very well.

"The first time he asked me to help him... I told him no." She still refused to look up. She was staring at the carpet. "He threatened to hurt my sisters."

I swore and shoved my hands in my pockets. I wanted to wrap them around Sal's neck. Never would I have thought that the man would hurt his own kids. And worse than hurting Ari directly, threaten to hurt her sisters instead. Something about what Cade had said during church told me he knew, though.

"I swear, Rat," her eyes shifted up to mine. "I only took on the jobs that I thought were harmless. I didn't want to do anything for him. I told him if he tried to hurt my sisters I would kill him in his sleep," she whispered. There was fear in her eyes. She thought I'd judge her for saying that to her father. All I felt was pride.

"The fact that you stood up to him at all is fucking impressive, Ari."

She blinked back tears. I could see them shining there in her gorgeous eyes. The idea that I'd helped put them there made me feel like shit.

I sighed. "Look. I get it. You did what you had to do to protect yourself and your sisters. There was no way for you to know that you were putting anyone in danger." Relief washed over her face, but she let me finish. "I'm sorry about the way I reacted. It's still a touchy subject for me. Can we put this behind us and move forward?"

She nodded. "And like you said earlier. If I come across anything else, I'll tell you. I would've told you about this sooner, but-"

"You didn't trust me," I finished for her. When she looked guilty, I shook my head. "I don't blame you. We don't know each other. There are still things I'll need to tell you and all I can say is you'll have to give me time."

I took her hand and pulled her up out of the chair. Wrapping my arms around her I pulled her in close, inhaling her scent. She smelled like something fresh and sweet, but I couldn't place what it was. I liked it. I hoped this hadn't set us back too far. We didn't have much time before we'd be bound together in marriage.

CHAPTER 20

Ari

The wedding was only three weeks away and every time I thought about my wedding day my stomach felt like a mob of butterflies were trying to escape it. Looking into the mirror, I stared at my reflection. The huge, poofy wedding gown was hideous.

"Oh, you look stunning," Mama sighed softly when I came out of the back to show them.

Antonia's eyebrows shot up and we exchanged an amused glance. I looked like a yeti. There was no way in hell I was wearing this thing down the aisle. Ada had an expression on her face that made it seem like she was sucking on lemons. At least my sisters had similar taste as me. Alex hadn't bothered to come. That was fine by me. We weren't friends. She had the unique talent of being able to agree with Mama while simultaneously being condescending and making me feel awful.

"I think I'll try something else," I said as tactfully as I could.

Mama frowned, but the sales lady bustled me off quickly to try on another choice.

It'd been about a week since I told the club my secret. Things had been strained with Rat and I, but we were slowly working past it. We hadn't had a solid foundation to begin with, so something like that coming out had rocked us a bit.

Everyone else had been quiet around me as well. I wasn't sure if they didn't know how to feel about what I'd done or if they were taking a page from my book. I'd been avoiding everyone as much as possible— including my fiancé. At least no one had gotten in my face and started screaming at me. No one had so much as said a mean thing to me. It was like we were all just tip-toeing around each other.

I slid the next dress on and my eyes widened when I looked in the mirror. My lips parted as I ran my hands over the satin covering my hips. It was perfect. Simple, elegant, gorgeous.

"Absolutely not," Mama said as soon as I stepped out.

I turned and looked at the simple A line in the mirror again. It fit me like a glove. The thin spaghetti straps connected to a modest bodice that had pink embroidery on it, giving it just a small pop of color.

"I love it," I said.

Mama sighed. "You're only saying that because I don't like it," she pouted.

"No, really, Mama." I met her eyes in the mirror. "I want this dress."

"I like it, too," Antonia said firmly. It was nice to have backup.

Ada raised her hand as a third vote then went back to playing on her phone.

"Arianna. Don't you want something fancier?" She stood and circled me like a shark. "A princess dress?"

I fought against making a face. Hell no, I didn't want a big poofy ball gown with yards of sequins. This dress was understated and a little sexy.

"It's her wedding, Mama," Ada said, looking up from her phone. Her eyes trailed over me. "Besides, her new husband is going to swallow his tongue when he sees her in that dress."

"That's because it looks like a nightgown," Mama insisted.

It didn't. The material was thin, but it gave the dress a delicate look, not a trashy one.

Before Mama could say anything else her phone went off. We all watched as she stepped outside and started shouting at the caterer.

"Thanks, Ada," I told her, sitting next to her on the ottoman. Having Mama's favorite in my corner was sure to help.

"You look beautiful," she said, giving me a side hug.

I picked up the glass of champagne the sales lady dropped off. Ada took one as well and I smiled over the rim of my glass when she quickly downed it as Mama came storming back in.

"I really wish you'd picked the end of November," Mama grumbled at me. "It would've given me a few more weeks to prepare."

I didn't care about the wedding. At the beginning I hadn't wanted it. Now, I just wanted it to be finished. Mama was stressing me out. She'd called and woke me up at two a.m. last night to ask whether I wanted blush pink or rose pink as an accent color. I didn't even know what the difference was between the two. She wouldn't listen when I told her I didn't want pink. I fully intended to use that to my advantage to get my way.

"It even has your color of pink on it, Mama," I said, indicating the dress.

She frowned down at it. Her phone rang again and she rolled her eyes. "You want this one?"

I nodded, holding my breath.

"Fine. What?" she snapped as she picked up the phone.

All our eyes widened and we laughed together as we listened to her barter with some other vendor.

"Let's go girls." She held a hand over her cell phone while she spoke to the sales lady. "She'll take that dress. We'll need to pick it up within two weeks. Arianna will come back in to have it fitted." Mama sailed out the door, and I had to scramble to the back and rush out of the dress and into my clothes.

I gave the sales lady an apologetic smile on my way out. "I'll call to make an appointment for a fitting."

She smiled at me and said goodbye.

* * *

"*This is where you're living?*" Mama's face twisted into a sneer as we pulled into the club's parking lot.

"I had zero choice about it, Mama," I reminded her.

She pretended not to hear what I said. Acknowledging that I was sold off might stop her from making more complaints about the club. I wasn't going to bother getting into an argument by telling her that despite the mishap of me helping Papa, and inadvertently helping the MC's enemy, they'd treated me better here than I ever had been at home.

Things were slowly starting to get more comfortable. From what I could tell most of the members and their girlfriends didn't blame me for what happened. Rat was the only one who'd freaked out over it. I couldn't really blame him, since it was his soon to be wife who'd betrayed him.

Hugging my sisters goodbye, I looked over as Mama rolled the window down before I could go inside. "Don't forget. The bridal shower is this weekend." They drove off before I could respond. I groaned and headed inside.

Rat glanced up as I walked into our apartment. He jerked his chin at me in greeting as he spoke to someone on the phone. "Yeah… it's fine. I can do that for you. Uh huh…" He typed something out on the computer in front of him. "Yeah, see you then."

He stood as he hung up and walked over, pulling me into his arms. Even though things had been off between us, he went out of his way to hug me, touch me, and ask how my day was. It was his way of keeping a connection while we weren't in sync. We hadn't really had a chance to find that groove yet before my confession had thrown it off kilter, but we were both making an effort. That was all we could do for now.

I didn't mind it. It felt good to have his strong arms wrap around me. I sighed and buried my face in his shoulder, soaking in the heat from his body.

"How'd it go?"

My groan was muffled against his shirt and he laughed.

"That good huh?"

"She's a nightmare."

He knew I meant my mother. I'd been bitching about going wedding dress shopping for the last few days. The entire checklist my mother sent to me was stressing me out. She was making this wedding a huge affair when I'd asked her to keep it smaller. To be fair, the one-hundred-and-fifty person guest list was little to her. The first time she'd shown it to me there'd been over four hundred people on it. People I didn't even know.

"I have to go do a job on site," he said. "You going to be alright here for a few hours?"

I laughed. "I'll be fine." Most everyone was still at work or school, so I was looking forward to a little alone time.

"Hush will be here if you need anything." He pulled a sweatshirt on over his head before shrugging into his cut.

"Okay." I grabbed my laptop and followed him downstairs. He brushed my lips in a kiss before he headed out the door.

Making myself comfortable on the couch in the common area, I soon lost myself in research. I'd been using my spare time to look up everything I could on the MC lifestyle.

When something brushed my foot I couldn't contain the yelp that spilled from my lips. Big brown eyes looked up at me. The puppy sat her butt on the floor— something that was clearly hard for her because she kept trying to wiggle her little nub as she sat there.

"Oh, you're sooo cute," I told her, reaching forward to scratch her velvety soft ears. She took that as an invitation and jumped up onto the couch next to me, curling up, and instantly falling asleep.

I glanced around the room, but it was still empty. Shrugging, I went back to my computer, smiling when the dog started snoring softly.

CHAPTER 21

Rat

I wanted to run. The urge to haul ass out of Sal's home and never look back was almost instinctual. Panic gripped me with steel claws. I damn near jumped out of my skin when Riggs slammed a huge hand on my shoulder. He'd come to stand next to me and we both stared at my reflection in the mirror.

My gaze slid over to his reflection. "I don't know how they managed to find a suit in your size."

His grin was wide and he tugged on the lapels. "Custom made," he said proudly.

"You look like a monkey," Steel retorted from where he was reclining on an ottoman.

"Fuck you. I make this look damn good."

It was my wedding day and none of us were thrilled to be dressed in suits. I'd put my foot down on tuxes. There was no fucking way I was wearing one of those. Ari'd had six bridesmaids, so I'd asked my six closest brothers to stand up there with me. Bass and Gunnar were in a corner, deep in discussion, and Axel was leaning against the door looking like a guard dog watching every move anyone made. His uptight attitude wasn't helping me relax.

Celia had pitched a huge shit fit when she found out I wasn't Catholic and therefore couldn't be married in a church. Not that anyone wanted my brothers packed into one. The place would burst into flames. So instead, we were having the ceremony and reception outside in their sprawling backyard. We weren't thrilled to be stuck in Sal's house for the day, but the spectacle my mother-in-law was about to put on wouldn't have worked at the club's property.

Swallowing hard, I returned my attention to the mirror. The need to escape washed over me again.

"Nervous?"

My eyes met Cade's in the mirror. I gave him a sharp nod. My mouth was too fucking dry to say anything.

"Don't be. It'll be great." Cade grinned at me, but it didn't reach his eyes.

"What's up?" I asked. He'd been more restless than usual the last few weeks. I doubted anyone else had noticed, but keeping a close eye on those around me and their moods was a leftover childhood habit. It was the difference between dinner and getting beaten.

Cade sighed. "It's nothing."

"Talk to me."

"I'm just waiting for those consequences to roll into town," he muttered.

That made sense. We never got a break. Not once since Dagger—the previous club president—was run off.

The guys were laughing and drinking the whiskey someone had left in the library for us. I frowned at the liquor cabinet, which was standing open. Perhaps someone liberated it. Either way, Sal was going to have considerably less alcohol by tomorrow. Steel shoved a glass into Axe's hand and told him to lighten the fuck up.

"I've been keeping an eye on Marco's activities like you asked. He's still in New York."

"I know." Cade ran a hand through his hair, making it stand up in spikes. "I just want to get it over with...you know?"

I nodded. I knew exactly what that felt like. If I could fast forward through the rest of the day, I would. Hell, I wanted the inevitable fight that was coming our way to be over, too. Waiting sucked balls. But knowing Cade, something bigger was bothering him. An upcoming fight was bad, but not enough for him to be noticeably anxious.

We'd discussed it extensively and it was the consensus of the group that the Guzman brothers weren't attacking yet because of our new connections. The alliances we'd formed with the Zetas, the Bratva, and the Italian Mafia made us a lot more of a threat than we were before.

"Enough of all that. Today is your wedding day," Cade said with an evil smirk.

The fucker.

He watched as my eyes darted to the door and crossed his arms over his chest. "Would you want to leave and let her get married to someone else?"

The anger that seared through my chest was surprising in its intensity. "No."

His grin grew wider. "You two are going to be solid once you're past the getting to know you stage and what happened. I have zero doubts about it."

I hoped he was right. I'd been a dick. Sure, Ari had fucked up, but in all fairness she had more than enough reason to protect herself and her sisters. I'd been trying to set our relationship right. It was slowly getting there.

"Ah fuck," I muttered, voice strangled when someone knocked on the door. That was our cue to head downstairs and go wait at the altar. A drop of sweat rolled down my back.

"Let's get this over with," Axel said darkly.

"You're such a mush," Bass said, rolling his eyes.

Axe narrowed his eyes on Bass, but before he could say anything Riggs grabbed him by the shoulder and bodily shoved him out the door. "No fighting on the kid's big day."

"I'll remind you of that later," Steel chuckled, following his brother.

They cleared out, leaving me alone with Cade.

"You know I'm fucking proud of you, right?"

Shit. I wasn't used to people telling me things like that. I shifted my weight from foot to foot. "Right."

Cade chuckled. "I won't go on and embarrass you. Just wanted you to know that." His silence afterwards said everything he was staying quiet about so it didn't make me uncomfortable. There was a reason he was my best man. No one else had ever given a fuck about me until the day he had. He'd pulled me out of a situation so shitty no child should ever have to endure it. I still didn't know if he knew how grateful I was. It wasn't like I could adequately tell him. Maybe someday.

Cade shoved me out into the hallway. We made our way downstairs. As soon as I stepped out into the backyard, every eye swung my way and I had to fight the urge to flinch and go back inside. Balling my hands into fists, I walked down the aisle and stood up near the altar.

"At least it's not July," Riggs muttered as Cade and I stepped over to where the others were standing. "We'd be sweating our fucking balls off."

The priest gave us a sharp frown as he overheard Riggs's comment. Gunnar laughed and arched a brow at the man. He quickly turned his attention back to his bible. We may be dressed in suits, but there was no doubt about the type of men we were. Our tattoos and hard demeanors were a dead giveaway.

A slight breeze picked up, cooling off the afternoon even more. It was November and despite the sun shining down on us, it was comfortable.

Celia had outdone herself. This was a bigger, fancier wedding than I would've ever chosen for myself. Neither Ari nor I had wanted to fight that battle. There were other hills we would choose to die on, and my mother-in-law could have the fancy wedding and reception.

I stared out into the huge crowd of people on Ari's side and wondered if she knew all of them. My side was much sparser. Enzo arched a brow at me when our eyes met. I was pretty sure he knew what was running through my head. He was as perceptive as Cade. It seemed to be a trademark for the type of men they were—leaders.

His daughter, who I hadn't met yet, was sitting next to him playing on her cell phone. Cade had started pushing me last week about making more of an effort with Enzo. He was right, I needed to. There was just too much going the fuck on for me to focus on my brother right now. Once this damn wedding was out of the way I'd hopefully be able to establish a new normal. Build a routine that could include two new people in it. Until then, all I could do was put my head down and force myself to do what needed to be done.

Everyone was getting restless—myself included—I glanced at the watch on my wrist. We were five minutes from the official start time. They were all still staring at us and I could feel the judgement rolling off the crowd in waves.

Riggs wiggled his fingers at someone in a wave and I glanced over. He was giving this intense look to some woman in the crowd. I rolled my eyes because she was sitting next to her glowering husband.

"Seriously, if you start a fight at this thing I'm going to make you deal with all of Celia's hysterics," I growled at him.

He smirked at me, but avoided looking back at the blonde, who was practically jumping to her feet trying to catch his attention again.

The violinists started playing soft music. I was praying to a God I didn't believe in that it'd mark the appearance of my soon to be wife.

Ari and Sal stepped up to the beginning of the aisle and everyone rose. Women gasped at the sight of her. The music switched over to the wedding march.

My mouth went bone dry, but not because that overwhelming urge to run was back. My eyes were glued on Arianna. She was in a simple white and pink wedding dress that hugged her curves perfectly. My eyes dropped down to her tits and lingered until Cade elbowed me—hard.

Guiltily my gaze shot back up to her eyes. There was laughter in those green depths. Her hair was dark and loose, cascading waves that reached almost down to her waist. My swallow was audible. How the fuck was I getting so lucky? I certainly didn't deserve this kind of luck. Any of it.

Pretty much from that first date, I'd been hooked on her. I wished there could've been a different way to meet her. One that would've made this her choice. I wasn't an idiot, though. We'd have never met. Our worlds never crossed except for through her father. It wasn't like I went out looking for women or dates. Because of that, I couldn't find it within myself to feel bad about this anymore. This had turned from something I'd been forced into, to something I wanted.

Ari'd been prepared to go back home—to a house she hated and a neglectful family—once I'd found out what she'd been keeping from me. At that point, both of us had made the choice to be together. That was when we'd taken control and made the decision to marry each other.

She was standing next to me now, staring up at me. I'd missed the part about Sal giving her away. The preacher's voice was a muted drone off to my right. I was thoroughly caught up in her.

I gave in to my instinct and reached up, rubbing my thumb over her cheek. Her eyes widened slightly and her cheek pinkened under my thumb. The smile that she gave me melted some piece of me that I kept buried away.

Ari's brows shot up and she gave me a questioning look. My focus snapped back to the wedding. The preacher cleared his throat and repeated. "Viktor, repeat after me."

Somehow, I made it through the vows, the kiss, pictures, and the millions of other things that were expected to happen at an event like this. It all passed like a blurry haze. The only thing I wanted was to get my wife—Jesus, I had a wife—home.

There were speeches, food, and cake. The only part that came into sharp focus for me was the first dance. I pulled Ari into my arms and we swayed together on the dance floor that her mother had somehow gotten set up out on the lawn.

"Are you okay?" Ari asked me, eyes searching my face. "You've been really quiet."

I smirked down at her.

"More than usual," she amended with a laugh.

"Yeah, I'm just ready to be done with all of this." I frowned when I realized that sounded dickish. "I mean-"

"No. I agree." She smiled up at me. "I wanted something smaller...less..." she trailed off and bit her lip, looking around.

"Exactly. I'm ready to just be us."

Her smile returned to her face. I pulled her in a little closer and saw the flare of heat in her eyes.

We hadn't moved forward on making our relationship physical. There was too much that'd happened and it had been too soon. With everything evening out and all of us—my brothers and their women included—relaxing around her I wondered if tonight could hold that possibility.

Strangely, as much as I was looking forward to it, I was dreading it too. Would she be disappointed that I wasn't more experienced? I wasn't sure how women felt about that kind of thing.

After the dance we settled down at our table, which looked out over all of our guests. It was like we were royalty and the peasants had to come to us to congratulate us. It was pompous and annoying.

Drumming my fingers on the table, I stared out over the crowd. I was debating on how long we'd have to stay.

"Let's get out of here," Ari leaned over and whispered near my ear. The way she said it...it was a suggestion, and a demand. My suit pants tightened uncomfortably as her breath washed over my neck.

"Seriously?" I asked her. Hope was practically crushing me beneath its weight, but this was her wedding. I didn't want to ruin it for her. "Is the reception even halfway over?"

"I don't care. I don't even know most of these people." She grabbed my hand and pulled me up.

Quickly, I adjusted my dick as subtly as I could. I didn't want to walk across this room full of people with it tenting my pants.

"Darling," Celia called, sailing over. She'd mostly been ignoring my bride all night, instead fussing over Alexandria and Ada and speaking with her guests. "Where are you going?" Her smile was bright and completely fake. She shot Ari a sharp glance.

"Thanks for the great wedding and reception, but I'm taking my bride home now," I told her firmly.

Celia's smile faded. "Oh, but it's so early-"

"We have our own celebrating to do." I gave her a wolfish smile. Let her read into that if she dared. Both she and her daughter's faces went red.

I walked over and shook Sal's hand, then steered Ari away from the crowd with my hand on her lower back.

"Good food," Riggs grunted at Celia as my brothers all passed by. Little did she know that was high praise coming from him. My family formed a small group and we left together.

"Leaving so soon?" Enzo asked, appearing out of the shadows.

How the fuck did he do that?

"Yeah, this isn't our type of partying."

Enzo chuckled. "Congratulations," he told Ari and lifted her hand, kissing her knuckles.

She smiled, but looked super uncomfortable. "Enough, Enzo." I muttered, and he finally let her hand go.

"You're a lucky bastard," he said, slapping me on the back.

Didn't I fucking know it?

"You're welcome to come out to the clubhouse. We're throwing our own celebration," I told him.

He looked thoughtful for a moment. "Thank you, but I'd better get Alya home. She's bored," he said with an exasperated sigh. "I'd love to have you both over for dinner. You can meet your niece." His eyes narrowed on my face as he searched my expression. I hadn't given him much in the way of reconciliation. This was something I could do.

"Sure. Just let me know when."

With that we said goodbye, and I helped Ari slip into the limo her mother had rented for us.

CHAPTER 22

Ari

A sigh of relief escaped me as soon as the car pulled out onto the road. I leaned back in the seat and closed my eyes.

"Hey, what's wrong?"

I opened my eyes again and stared into Rat's frowning face. I beamed at him. "Nothing. Everything is perfect... I'm free."

His frown deepened.

Laughing, I shook my head. "It'll probably sound stupid, but that house—my parents—have been like this shackle. They kept me locked up—chained to a wall. I hated it." I peeked up at him through my lashes. "I just feel...free."

The smile Rat shot me made my heart stutter in my chest. We'd eased into a routine at the clubhouse. He drove me everywhere and all the time together had forced us to get over our fight. Despite that, and despite the loud chaos that was the clubhouse, it was a more relaxed way of living than I'd ever had before.

Rat had managed to ease all my fears about marrying him. Even him being angry with me hadn't lasted long and I'd never once feared that he'd kill me and dump my body in the river. The idea that he'd return me had been my biggest fear and he'd given me no doubts that despite any fights in the future he'd never do that.

The clubhouse was starting to feel like home. The house I'd just left was like a bad dream and I was happy to leave it behind to fade into distant memories.

My brows drew together and I sat up in my seat as we pulled up to the clubhouse. Lights were on everywhere and throngs of people were milling about.

"What-"

"I wasn't lying when I told your mom we had our own celebration to get to," Rat said with a smirk.

I'd thought he'd meant something else. The idea of being alone with my handsome biker, married, with the expectation between us that we'd consummate our marriage made me feel breathless.

"We can skip it, though, if you don't want to deal with more people tonight."

"No! This is great." They'd gone to the trouble of planning a party for us. A real party, with people having real fun. Something warmed in my chest.

The door next to me jerked open and I flinched. Rat's hand covered mine, comforting and warm.

"Come with me!" Bridget grinned, excitement written on her face.

"Um, where are we-"

She was already tugging me out of the car. I glanced over my shoulder at Rat, who just shrugged.

"We're going to get ready at my place," she huffed as she dragged me behind her. "You don't want to be wearing a wedding dress all night." She stopped so abruptly I slammed into the back of her with a grunt of surprise. "Unless you do...want to wear your dress?" Her blue eyes found mine.

"Uh, no, thanks." It had been everything I wanted in a wedding dress, but it was time for it to go.

She graced me with the full power of her smile, and I blinked. If I was into girls, Bridget might be my type. Apparently, I had a thing for blondes. Lucky for my new husband I preferred men. My eyes strayed to her ass as she led me into her and Gunnar's apartment. That didn't mean I couldn't appreciate a beautiful woman's assets, though.

"Oh good! You're here," Remi said, coming in the door only steps behind us. "I can't help with the clothes or make-up, but I brought wine." She held up the bottle and grinned at me.

"Yes, please," I groaned.

"Did you enjoy your wedding?" Ming asked, shoving me down onto the couch.

I paused and considered her question. "It was kind of like someone else was getting married and I was along for the ride." My father's daughter got married.

The women's eyes widened so I rushed to explain. "Not that I'm not happy to be married, or to be with Rat. It just wasn't how I would've done it."

Anna cocked her head and took a drink from the glass Remi handed her. "Why didn't you get what you wanted?"

Before I could answer there was a knock at the door. Julie answered it and glared at Bass. "Nope, no men allowed. We'll be down in a few minutes."

Bass grimaced. "Like I'd want to hang out up here with you… lovely ladies," he amended his statement halfway through when Julie's eyes narrowed dangerously. "I have a surprise delivery. A present from the groom to his bride."

The smile Bass shot me was panty melting. Why were all these people so beautiful? It sure fucked with a girl's head…and confidence. I stood and went over to the door just in time for Bass to shove someone through. He left even as I gasped in pleasure and hugged Antonia.

"Okay, does he belong to someone?" My sister asked, her arms wrapped around me, but her eyes following Bass down the hall.

"That asshole is mine," Julie informed her, somehow annoyed both at the question and at the answer.

"Damn, but I figured he'd be taken," Antonia laughed. Julie chuckled right along with her.

"He's pretty, right?"

Antonia nodded and fanned herself.

"The only ones really left are a bit too old for you, honey," Bridget said.

"What about Scout?" Anna asked. They all paused and considered that.

"Yeah, I guess the prospects are available and most are young," Bridget amended. She held up a shirt and squinted at me.

The thing was covered in sequins and despite its expensive quality was too garish for me. I shook my head at her. Bridget's mouth formed a pout, but she scampered off to her bedroom to choose something else.

"What are you doing here?" I asked Antonia.

"Your husband-" Her eyes widened and met mine. "That's *so* weird."

It really was.

"He convinced Papa to let me come celebrate. I get to stay the whole weekend...without any of his men following me." Excitement shone on her face.

"We'll keep you safe, sweetie," Ming said, taking away the wine glass Remi had shoved into Antonia's hand.

"Hey!"

"You can't possibly be old enough to drink."

"She's not, but we always snuck into Papa's liquor cabinet," I told Ming. Handing Antonia my glass, I gave her a wicked smile. "This isn't our first time."

Ming shrugged. "What the hell? It's a party."

"You know, we just got in a few new prospects," Anna told Antonia, wrapping an arm around her shoulders. "We can go check them out together."

"You don't have your own biker?"

"She does," Bridget said with a devilish grin.

Anna flipped her off.

Even I'd seen the sparks that flew whenever she and Riggs were in the same room together. I wasn't sure why the woman was denying how she felt for the huge biker, but who was I to judge?

***

Forty-five minutes—and ten outfits—later, we stepped down onto the main floor of the clubhouse.

"There are so many people," I murmured.

"Oh yeah, the guys' parties always draw a huge crowd," Remi said. "You've got the members, their wives—unless they had to stay home with the kids—members of the community-"

She cut off as a woman pranced by in a skirt that showed a peek of ass cheek with every step. Remi rolled her eyes. "The patch bunnies."

I couldn't help the laugh that slipped out. "The what?"

"Chrome crickets," Ming said with a smile.

"Chopper hopper," Bridget piped in.

"Patch pouncer," Anna told me.

"Fender fluff," Julie laughed.

My mouth was hanging open. "I have no clue what you guys are talking about."

"Those are the women who come to these parties and sleep with bikers in the hopes that one of them will make them their old lady," Julie explained.

Antonia and I exchanged a glance. "That's a thing?" she asked. "'Cause I was only sort of kidding around about finding a biker."

"Oh, trust me," Anna said, putting her arm over Antonia's shoulders. "We wouldn't let you become a sweet butt."

"These terms," I groaned.

"Right?" Remi said, rolling her eyes. "You're old lady material and not the type to bounce from biker to biker so you have nothing to worry about."

"If that even crosses your mind," I told Antonia, "I'd kick your ass."

"Nope, not interested, thanks," she said, shaking her head. "Good for them for knowing what they want, but I'm not down with it."

After that everyone split up to go enjoy the party.

"You go find your husband and have fun. I'll watch out for her," Ming told me, steering Antonia toward where Axel was standing glaring around the room.

It didn't take me long to find Rat. He was leaning back against the wall. He and Bass were deep in conversation and I paused long enough to admire the way he filled out the t-shirt and jeans he'd changed into. It'd been weird to see him in a suit. He looked great in it, but I preferred him like this.

My eyes narrowed and anger had me clamping my jaw tight as the girl from earlier swished her way over toward the men. She stepped between them and leaned into Rat, putting her hand on his chest.

I imagined her laugh was husky and low as she gave him a suggestive look. To Rat's credit he looked furious. He gripped her wrist and removed her hand from his body, since it'd started slinking lower over his abs.

This morning, when I'd been getting ready for my ceremony, I'd made myself a promise. I was done going with the flow and letting others dictate my life. My parents had held control over me for far too long. I was the daughter of a Mafia Don and I had a weird mix of talents. Papa had taught us all about The Life—even his daughters—in the event we married into it. Abel had worked with me on my shooting and fighting skills long after Papa had stopped. I not only could make you disappear digitally; I knew exactly how to dispose of a body for optimum efficiency.

Storming across the room, my eyes met Rat's. Shock and unease flashed in the bright blue depths. Before he realized what I was doing, I'd grabbed the woman by the hair and yanked her back a few steps. She stumbled in her high heels.

"Why are you touching my husband?" I snarled at her.

Her scream was piercing enough that every eye in the room turned to us. Someone shut off the loud, thumping music.

"Who the hell are you, bitch?" She cried out when I twisted enough to yank her hair tighter in my grip.

"Me? I'm your fucking worst nightmare if you touch him again." I nodded over at Rat then put my face in hers. "Got it?"

She eyed me speculatively. I saw the exact moment she decided to call me on my bluff. Reminding myself of who I was, and that shock and awe usually made more of an impression than giving second chances, I swung her around by the hair until she hunched in front of me. She was a lot taller than me in her six-inch heels.

"Who the fuck do you think you are?" she shouted again.

I didn't bother to answer—verbally anyway. My fist connected with her face, sending a fountain of blood spewing onto both Rat and Bass. The men look shocked, but amused. Little half smiles were on their faces as they watched the woman screech and grab her nose. I finally let go of her hair.

"You broke my nose," she sobbed.

Rat grabbed me and pulled me back against his chest, wrapping his arms around me. I wasn't sure if he was holding me back or comforting me. "Yeah, my girl's good at that." I could hear the smirk in his voice.

"What are you *not* going to do?" I asked her, ignoring the man behind me and the way our bodies were pressed together. My tone was filled with disgust.

Her brown eyes flicked from my face to Rat's over the hands cupping her nose. "Touch him."

"Good. I'd suggest you don't forget that. Now, go away." I put my hands over Rat's forearms where they crossed my stomach.

"That was awesome," Bass chuckled as she ran out of the room, dripping blood onto the floor.

"Sorry about your shirt," I told him with a smile.

He glanced down at the blood droplets on his white t-shirt. Shrugging, he took a drink of his beer. "Worth it for the show. I think I'm going to try to find another patch bunny to hit on Rat..."

I glared at him, but he just winked and strolled off.

Rat tugged me into a more private corner. "Ari, I wasn't-"

"I know, I saw you push her away. I wasn't about to let her—or anyone else—think that they could get away with hitting on you in front of me," I paused, then added, "or when I'm not around."

The corner of his mouth kicked up. "Jealous?" he asked, sweeping a lock of my hair off my face. He brushed his thumb over my cheek, the same way he had during the wedding. All the women in the audience had sighed in longing when he'd done that and my heart had melted into a puddle at his feet.

If you'd told me two months ago that I'd be forced into an arranged marriage and would start to fall for my husband this quickly I'd have told you to jump off the nearest bridge. It was happening, though. Something about Rat just spoke to me.

"Just claiming my territory," I responded loftily. His laugh was loud and surprised. "Do you have a problem with that?" I asked him with a dangerous look.

"Even if I did, I wouldn't test you by telling you that. I'd hate to end up with a broken nose." He tugged on my hair, tipping my head back so he could plant his mouth over mine.

The moan that escaped—unbidden—from my lips was swallowed by his, and he pulled me closer. It was like the sound kick-started the heat that'd been shimmering between us for weeks now.

"Get a room!" someone shouted.

"Fucking Riggs," Rat growled, pulling away.

I had to fight the urge to pull his head back down to mine. He'd just started brushing his tongue over mine, and my body was already aching for him.

"They're married," Steel commented, loudly. "Doesn't that mean the sex is supposed to stop?"

"Shut the fuck up," Riggs gasped in mock horror. "Don't give them any ideas."

We watched in amusement as Remi stepped over and drilled a finger into Steel's stomach. The man grunted hard and laughed as she did. "Is that why you're dragging your feet on picking a date, Steel?"

We winced at her tone. Steel got a look on his face that said he knew he was stepping onto dangerous ground. "Uh-"

"Because if that's what you're worried about," Remi fluttered her lashes at him, "there's no need. I won't wait until we're married to deny you sex. That starts now." She grabbed Bridget's arms and pulled her friend away into the crowd.

Steel's jaw dropped as he watched his fiancée disappear. "What?" Horror was etched on his face.

I smothered a laugh behind my hand, still wrapped up in Rat's arms.

"Let's go upstairs," he murmured into my ear.

Shivers raced up my spine and my nipples tightened at hearing his low, gravelly voice. Our eyes met, and I saw the lust there. I felt it too. He must have sensed hesitation.

"Don't worry. I'm still not going to force you to do anything, Ari. We'll go at your pace. I'm just tired of sharing you with all these assholes."

I snickered and nodded my head. I wanted to be alone with him. I wanted to have sex with him. There was no logical reason for me to feel a moment's hesitation, so I let the feeling drift off.

Rat grabbed my hand, linking our fingers, and walked me upstairs. There were whistles and cheers, but the last thing I heard made me smile and—oddly—made me feel special.

"Shut the fuck up, all of you," Cade bellowed at them. The jeers stopped abruptly as everyone quickly got back to drinking and dancing. The music was turned on again at eardrum splitting levels.

I wasn't sure if Cade's protective streak was just for Rat or if it included me, but I was going to pretend it did.

CHAPTER 23

Rat

Closing the door to the apartment behind us, I watched as Ari walked to our bedroom. The look she tossed me over her shoulder had my already aching cock leaking pre-cum into my boxers. I groaned under my breath as I followed her.

"Hey, we should-"

One minute she was standing near the bed, the next her body was plastered against mine. Her mouth was voracious, all tongue and teeth, and my heart kicked into high gear. My hands went—of their own volition—to her ass to grind her against my hard-on. Our tongues danced, and heat raced through me. Moving her, I pinned her against the wall, so I could keep moving against her while my hands slid up her front.

Her tits weren't huge, but they were a perfect handful. My brain was shutting down. The little breathy moans she was making had my blood boiling. There was something we needed to talk about, though.

The last thing I wanted to do was pull away, but while I still had some blood left in my brain, I forced my body to comply. Stepping back, I raked a hand through my hair.

"What's wrong," she asked, still leaning against the wall, panting.

My breath was as choppy and uneven as hers. My dick was painfully hard, and fuck if I didn't want to bury myself balls deep in my wife. I needed to be fair to her, though.

"I have to tell you something. Then if you still want to do this...we can."

She crossed her arms over her stomach as uncertainty flooded her face. "Okay."

Motioning for her to sit on the bed, I blew out a breath. I'd never looked forward to having this conversation. There was every possibility I'd make excuses not to have it, so I blurted out, "Ari, I'm a virgin."

There was a heartbeat where she didn't move a muscle. I wasn't sure if she was processing what I'd just said or stunned. Then she blinked. "Okay..." The tone of her voice was asking why we'd stopped to talk about this.

I rubbed a hand over the back of my neck. "I just thought you should know before we-" I gestured lamely at the bed.

Her smile was quick and bright. "I don't know how you managed to get to twenty-two without women throwing themselves at you."

Some had.

"It doesn't bother me." A frown formed as a thought occurred to her. "I'm not a virgin...does that-"

"No," I interrupted her before she could finish. "I don't care that you've had sex. Fuck, it's probably better that one of us has." I grinned, trying to relieve the tension.

She stood up and cocked her head at me. She moved slowly toward me, and my eyes narrowed on her face. "I kind of like it."

"Like what?"

She shrugged. "That you're all mine."

I chuckled as she grabbed me by the shoulders. Letting her shove me down onto the bed, I watched as she crawled her way up my body.

"I don't like sharing," she murmured as she pulled my shirt off. Her hands traced the tattoos on my arm while she kissed those on my chest. I let my head fall back onto the bed and closed my eyes. She paused as her fingers brushed over the long, gnarly scar the tattoo on my forearm hid. Her questioning eyes met mine.

"I'll tell you about it later."

She ducked her head and brushed her tongue over my nipple, and I groaned. "I don't either," I told her. She peeked up at me through her lashes, a question written on her face. "Share. So, from now on, you're all mine."

I felt her lips form a smile on my skin. "Deal."

Her lips brushed down over my abs and the blood that'd been rushing in my ears flooded south. I grabbed her by her long, dark hair. Raising my head, I looked down at her. "I'm not going to last if you do that," I warned her. Our first time together didn't need to end—prematurely. It was already going to be tough not to come as soon as I sank into her.

She gripped my wrist and lightly pulled until I released her hair. "That's the idea. You don't need to last."

I glared down at her, and she laughed at the expression on my face. "We have the rest of our lives for sex. Let me...have my fun."

My head dropped back again, and I took a deep breath. Her dirty words had my dick kicking hard.

It was all the encouragement she needed. Her hands quickly undid my belt and jeans. Raising my hips so she could drag my clothes off, I stared up at the ceiling. If I watched her pink lips wrap around me, I was going to embarrass myself.

I hissed out a breath when her hand gripped me. Swallowing, I scrubbed my hands over my face.

Fuck, fuck, fuck.

"Tell me if I do anything you don't like." Her voice had dropped and it was husky—turned on. If she liked doing this as much as I knew I would enjoy receiving it, I was going to be one lucky fucker.

Her hot, wet mouth encircled the tip of my dick, and a long groan tore out of my throat. "Fuck, baby that's-"

I lost all ability to speak for a minute as she slid her mouth down, taking me deeper. My hand went back to her hair, gripping it tight, but letting her dictate her movement. I just needed to hold onto her.

She worked her hand, mouth, and tongue in a rhythm that nearly had my fucking eyes crossing.

"Arianna," I growled. She slowed, but didn't stop working her mouth on my cock, and I could feel the muscles in my stomach tightening.

She moved her mouth off me with a wet pop and I lifted my head. Our eyes met as her tongue darted out to lap up the pre-cum that was leaking from me. My breath shuddered out at the sight. She was going to fucking kill me.

Ari went back to sucking my dick after that as though it was her fucking intent to suck my soul out.

"Ah, fuck. Baby, I'm gonna-"

She let out this loud, muffled moan, and mumbled around my dick. "Come in my mouth."

Fuck my wife was dirty and so fucking hot. "You want me to pump your throat full of cum?" I asked, voice gravelly.

"Mmmhhmmm," she moaned.

Both of my hands entangled themselves in her hair and I helped move her head up and down on me in a motion that had me blowing my load in her mouth. I'd jacked off plenty of times. This blew every previous experience out of the water. There was no comparison.

Ari crawled up my body again and lay down beside me, her cheek resting over my thundering heart. All I could do was lay there, sucking in breaths.

She lifted her head, kissed my chest, then laid it back down before running her fingers over my ab muscles. "You have such a sexy body."

I was pretty sure that was supposed to be my line. I grabbed her hips, but before I could roll us so I could feast on her body she stopped me.

"Let's just lay here and cuddle."

"You're...sure?" I frowned down at her.

"Mmmhhmm," she stretched lazily against me.

I ran my hand repeatedly down her back, over her shirt. I hadn't even gotten her undressed and I was laying here butt-ass naked. She'd just rocked my world and now she was falling asleep in my arms. I'd set the expectation early on that we'd only do what she was comfortable with. I'd extend that until we officially had sex. After that, I had plans for my gorgeous mafia princess.

Laying there, listening to her breathing even out in sleep, I wondered how a nobody like me had gotten so lucky. She hadn't cared about my virgin status. It made me wonder how she'd feel about the rest of what I needed to tell her.

The session with my therapist two days ago had been tense. She'd told me I needed to come clean with Ari about my childhood. She'd recommended I do the same with Enzo.

If it was just embarrassment holding me back, I'd man up and tell them. Mostly it was that it brought me back to that place in my mind, and I never wanted to go there again.

Talking about it takes power away from the memories, I remember my therapist saying. There was only one way to figure out if that was true.

CHAPTER 24

Ari

Something crashing downstairs woke me. Glancing up at Rat, I held my breath until I saw his chest continuing to rise and fall in rhythm. I laid there, wide awake now, brain spinning. It'd been a crazy day—good, but crazy.

Sliding from bed as carefully as possible, I crept into the closet and took off the party clothes I'd fallen asleep in. I put on a pair of Rat's sweats, tied the cord in the waistband so they wouldn't fall off, and tugged on one of his sweatshirts. His scent surrounded and comforted me.

I eased out the door, tip toeing until I was out of the apartment. Rat was a light and troubled sleeper. I didn't want to wake him up, and there was no way for me to shut my mind off enough to fall back asleep right now.

Going downstairs, I peeked my head through the door to the other side of the clubhouse. There were still a few die-hards that were partying. I went outside and found myself standing at the picnic tables.

"I guess this is my spot," I mumbled.

"It's a good one," a deep voice said from behind me.

Gasping, I whirled around. It'd never occurred to me to worry about my safety here at the clubhouse until now. Standing outside at two in the morning, with no kind of weapon wasn't my brightest idea. Abel had taught me better than that. He'd gotten me a beautiful switchblade and it was sitting up in my room, useless to me now.

"Just me," Hush said, stepping into the light that shone above the barbeque area. It was the only lamp post out here and shone all night.

I relaxed and let out a relieved breath. "That's okay. It just occurred to me that it might not be a good idea to wander around at night."

"Probably not, but the prospects patrol the grounds most nights. Especially when we have a party."

"What happens if you don't have enough prospects to do that?" I asked.

"Then our members do it."

That made me feel a lot better. I sat down on top of the picnic table and peeked over at Hush. He stood with his hands shoved in the pockets of his jacket.

"Want to join me?"

He grunted at my offer and sat on the table next to me. We stared out into the darkness for a few quiet minutes.

"Congrats." His voice was gruff, almost sad.

"Thank you."

I felt him look over and study my face before leaning forward, resting his elbows on his knees. "What're you doing alone out here?"

"I just needed to clear my head and didn't want to wake Rat." I smiled over at him.

"Everything good there?"

"Oh, absolutely. Rat is...perfect." I cringed at the fact that the last word came out as a sigh. *What was I, twelve?*

Hush chuckled. "He's a good kid. Got lucky with you. Heard about your show earlier."

I blushed remembering fighting with the woman in the clubhouse. I shrugged my shoulders because I couldn't think of anything else to say.

"Like I said, lucky kid." He hesitated before continuing. "Wasn't always so lucky."

Glancing over at him, I felt my heart skip a beat. "He told you about...everything?" I wasn't sure what he was hiding in his closet, just that he said he planned on telling me. That'd been my first night here, but he hadn't said anything yet. I hadn't pushed because he'd tell me when he was ready. That didn't mean I wasn't dying of curiosity.

Hush shook his head. "Nope...but like recognizes like."

I sucked in a breath, examining his handsome face. He'd let his facial hair go beyond stubble and was sporting a short beard. His blue eyes crinkled when he smiled, but they normally looked sad. Like now. They were haunted. His hair was slightly longer on the top and dark brown with threads of gray. It was tousled, like he'd been running his hands through it.

"What brought you out here tonight, Hush?"

He was quiet for so long, I almost thought he wasn't going to answer. It would've been fine if he hadn't.

"Couldn't sleep," he finally said.

"Any particular reason why?" A muscle in his jaw twitched. "Anything you tell me is told in the strictest confidence. Think of me like a priest," I joked.

He snorted and shot me a glower. "No way I'd talk to those fuckers."

I laughed. "Alright, no priests. Still, as friends, you can share and know I won't judge you. We can also just sit here." I patted his back a little awkwardly. When your father kept you cooped up your entire life and taught you to regard anything new with distrust and suspicion, you tended to not be the best at making friends. *And when your chauffeur is also a two-hundred-and-fifty-pound gorilla in a suit it tends to make kids not want to play with you.*

I was thankful for the quiet man beside me, though. He never made me feel like less, even after finding out about my betrayal. He'd extended his hand in friendship, though I had no clue why. According to everyone here, they'd never seen him act this friendly toward anyone. He even steered clear of Cade and the other officers unless they needed something.

I had a feeling Cade knew why. That man had a thumb on the pulse of everything happening in this club and with his people. It was impressive. It probably shouldn't be since Papa had been the same with his men. That was just part of the role of being the leader.

"Anyone tell you I only joined this chapter about six months ago?"

I shook my head and leaned back on my hands, staring up at the stars. Something told me this would be easier on him if I wasn't looking directly at him.

"I was a Nomad. Came into town with a few others." I peeked over and noticed his face was screwed into a snarl of disgust. "Three of 'em ended up causin' a lot of trouble for the club. Steel took care of it. Good riddance," he muttered the last more to himself than to me. "Anyway, this seemed like a good crew of men, so I stayed. Reminded me of some...old work buddies."

"A Nomad is someone who travels." I'd been studying biker terms and was proud of myself for knowing that one.

"From chapter to chapter within the same club," he agreed. "I'd been travelin' across the U.S. for about a year before I landed here."

"That must have been lonely." Another peek showed that he wasn't angry anymore. He just looked tired and sad. I wished I could wipe away the hurt.

"It was the only thing I could do."

We fell silent again. I waited. It was like comforting a wounded animal. You had to wait patiently for them to come to you—to trust you enough to help.

"They tell you why my road name is Hush?"

"The only thing anyone told me about you is that you never talk," I said, looking over with a smile.

He chuckled. "My ole' lady was responsible for my name."

Surprise bolted through me. I knew from the other women that old ladies were wives. It'd never crossed my mind to ask if Hush had family.

"I used to be a real chatterbox. She was always tellin' me to 'hush up.' The other guys in my original club picked up on it and started calling me Hush."

"Where is your wife now?"

"In Tucson."

Something in his voice told me there was more to it.

"In the Sunny Oaks Cemetery."

The gasp tried to claw its way out, but I shoved it down deep. It sat there, aching in my stomach as my heart plummeted down to meet it. "Oh, Hush. I'm so sorry." I knew it didn't mean much, but I wasn't sure how else to vocalize my heartbreak for him. I sat forward and wrapped my arms around myself, watching his face. Gone was the need to give him space to tell his story.

"What happened?" My voice was husky with unshed tears.

His eyes closed briefly then opened again and focused on some point out in the darkness. I wasn't totally sure that he wasn't there with her in his mind as he recounted the story.

"D had been buggin' me to get her a bike. Daphne was her name," he said quietly. "She'd grown up around the club, but she'd never gotten on a bike. She wanted to learn to ride. So, I surprised her for her birthday. Got her a gorgeous Indian Challenger, signed her up for classes, and watched her like a hawk until she rode like a pro. We had some great rides together, cruisin' across the desert." He scraped a hand through his hair. "I got stuck at the shop one night. The note she left said she'd gotten restless and went for a ride. It wasn't unusual."

Every fiber of my being welled with sadness for what I knew was coming.

"The August heat in Arizona brings monsoons. They're beautiful to watch. The desert doesn't do a great job of suckin' up the amount of moisture those bad boys can dump on an area, though. A storm blew in fast, floodin' a good part of the city. D had been crossin' a wash when a flash flood hit her. There'd been no warnin'. A couple cars got caught in it too." He blew out a breath. "Other motorists tried to help. There wasn't anythin' they could do. She and another car got swept away. Three dead." He trailed off.

I put my hand on his back, and when he didn't flinch or pull away,

I rubbed circles there. I'd always liked to be comforted with touch. The last thing I wanted was to cross a line, but my hand seemed to pull him back.

Hush smiled over at me although it didn't reach his eyes. "It wasn't long after that I went Nomad. I couldn't stay. Couldn't be around my brothers—the memories. Her brother was the president of our club. It wasn't any easier on him. He never blamed me, though. In fact, he called in a favor to every chapter I stopped at and asked that they accept me if I chose to stay. Didn't know that until Cade told me."

It didn't surprise me. Cade seemed like a really nice guy. I hadn't spent much time around him yet, but it didn't take long to see that he really cared about his people. "Why would her brother blame you?"

Hush shook his head, grief etched in every line on his face. "If I hadn't bought her that bike…if I hadn't been runnin' late."

I turned so I was facing him. "The bike probably made her really happy…right?"

His frown deepened, but he wouldn't meet my eyes.

"If that's what she chose to do when she was feeling restless she must have loved it, and you for gifting it to her. You can't blame yourself for an act of nature, Hush." My voice hardened a little and he glanced over.

"So I hear."

"Would she want you to blame yourself?" I didn't want to be a bitch, but he'd given it to me straight when I'd been trying to run away and needed the truth more than coddling.

His laugh boomed out and started me. "Hell no. She'd be pissed that I was sittin' here feelin' sorry for myself."

"You're grieving. You loved her very much." He didn't need to tell me that. It emanated from his very being. "She'd have been fine with that, any woman would, but eventually she'd want you to move on. You're still young."

He smirked at that. "I'm fifty. Too old and ornery to move on."

"I'm not saying you have to find love again, although I think you deserve to. I just mean, move past the guilt and the destruction so you can heal."

That muscle was ticking in his jaw again as he clenched his teeth. "I suppose you're right." He glanced down at his watch. "I've kept you long enough for tonight. The kid wakes up and finds you gone he's gonna shit a brick."

He was done talking and that was okay. I leaned over and gave him a peck on his whiskered cheek. "Thanks for keeping me company, Hush."

The low light prevented me from being able to tell for sure, but I thought he might have blushed. He walked me back to the clubhouse.

Quietly, I slipped back into our bedroom and shucked the clothes I had on. I climbed onto the bed and straddled Rat, who was laying on his back, his arms tucked behind his head. Running my hands over his chest, I admired his tattoos.

"Jesus fucking Christ!" He jolted awake and grabbed my wrists.

"I'm so sorry," I gasped and tried to jerk out of his hold.

He sat there, half upright and holding my wrists for a few seconds getting his bearings. "No, it's fine." His heart was racing under my palm, and he was panting as though he'd just run a mile.

"I didn't mean to-"

"Why are your hands so cold?" His handsome face frowned up at me in the darkness. The moon shining in through the window provided the only light, and it was meager.

"I took a walk-"

Rat swore. "You shouldn't be out walking alone at night, Ari," he growled. When he'd first startled awake his eyes had darted around the room. Now, they pinned me where I sat on top of him, and I realized he was angry and worried.

"Hush found me and escorted me," I told him with an apologetic smile.

Rat's muscles relaxed under my palms. He'd trapped them on his skin when he'd grabbed me. I couldn't complain too much. His chest was so warm it almost burned me. I shifted a little and his eyes narrowed when my heat grazed his suddenly growing erection. He only now seemed to be aware of the fact that I was naked on top of him.

Leaning over him, I brushed my lips over his. The hardened tips of my nipples scraped over his skin and we both groaned when I wiggled on him again.

"Ari-" he said as I released his mouth.

Placing my finger at his lips, I lightly sucked on the side of his neck. His breath huffed out, moving my hair with its force.

His strong arms went around me, and I couldn't help the squeal that escaped when he abruptly rolled me.

"Not this time," he said with a devilish look in his eyes. "I've been waiting a long time to try this." His smirk was easily discernible in the moonlight.

There wasn't time to ask what he meant because he'd already slid down my body. He threw my legs over his shoulders and attacked my clit like a starving man who'd found a buffet.

"Oh!" My eyes rolled to the back of my head, and my hips arched off the bed involuntarily when he sucked it into his mouth and flicked his tongue over it. One heavy arm moved over my hips and anchored them to the bed so he could keep driving me mad.

"How-" I broke off with a moan when he slid a long finger inside of me. "How do you know how to do that?"

His head raised, pale light glinting off his golden hair. "Seriously? You want to ask me a bunch of questions right now?" His gaze held mine as he added a second finger and thrust them inside me.

I gasped, but nodded.

Rat shook his head. "Porn." With that, he went back to eating my pussy.

There were no more questions. All I could do was scratch at the forearm that held me down as he played my body, building me up toward the stars.

With a cry, I broke apart, shattering into a million pieces. As I drifted back into self-awareness I heard a crinkling sound and watched as he rolled a condom onto his dick.

He notched it at my opening and I slapped a hand on his chest to stop him.

Rat's eyes were questioning, but he paused at the movement.

"If porn is your teacher, you should know, I don't want you to just slam it in. That'll hurt." My voice was low, and I was panting again. I could feel how wet I was for him.

He leaned his head down and rumbled into my ear, sending shivers skating down my body. "You don't want a little pain with your pleasure?"

I wrinkled my nose at him when he lifted his head to stare down into my face. "No. I haven't tried it, but it doesn't sound like fun to me."

"Hmmmm, I like that we're going to get to explore our limits together."

I wasn't sure what he meant by that, but he'd had enough talking. He slowly entered me, filling me until I wondered if I could stretch far enough. The man I'd had a summer fling with hadn't been well endowed. Not that I'd known that. I hadn't had anything else to compare to at the time.

Rat's forehead dropped down to my shoulder as he bottomed out. "Fuck, baby. You feel so...you feel better than I imagined." His voice was a little strangled and happiness shot through me. I wanted him to feel even half of the delicious sensations he was creating within my body.

He slowly withdrew and in a steady motion filled me again. The friction was incredible—intense—and I wrapped my legs around his hips, trying to get closer. We moved together, reaching for that end goal.

Rat shifted and sucked my nipple into his mouth while he kept up the rhythm that was torturing me. It wasn't until his hand slid between us and began rubbing my clit that I broke apart again. He grunted hard in surprise when I clenched around him and dragged him into the void with me.

CHAPTER 25

Rat

We laid there afterwards, Ari in my arms, letting our heart rates return to normal. She snuggled closer into my side, and I wondered how I'd gotten so fucking lucky. When this whole arranged marriage shit had been presented to us, I'd thought it was crazy. Then Sal said my name. I'd never expected it to be me.

Now that we were here—husband and wife—I wouldn't have it any other way. I trailed my fingers up and down Ari's spine.

"Thank you," she said softly.

I glanced down at her. "For what?"

She hesitated before responding. "For not sending me back. For forgiving me. I'm really glad to be yours." She laid a soft kiss on my chest.

My eyes closed, and I stroked my hand over her silky hair. The therapist had told me that I'd know when the time was right to open up to Ari about my past. I couldn't believe this was that moment. I didn't want to ruin what we'd just shared with my fucked up memories, but something prompted me.

I cleared my throat. "I- There's something I want to tell you."

She smoothed her hand over my abs and rubbed circles there. It was easier to get it out if I paid attention to that motion.

"I'm sure you remember from the dinner that I was separated from my brother when I was a kid."

She nodded, but didn't say anything.

"I don't remember the night I was taken, but the man who found me always liked to taunt me. He told me he'd found me stashed behind a dumpster. Thrown out like trash."

Her shoulders tensed, but her hand remained relaxed, continuing the soothing pattern.

"I didn't know why my family had abandoned me—not then—and eventually it stopped mattering why." I sucked in a breath and stared up at the darkened ceiling. "I didn't have a good childhood, Ari, not from that point on."

"How old were you?" Her voice was calm. If she'd gotten upset or freaked out, I wouldn't have been able to tell her more. It was like she knew exactly what I needed.

"Four."

She sucked in a breath. "You were so young."

"I didn't find out until a few weeks ago what'd happened that night." I went back to trailing my fingertip over her supple skin. "Enzo told me that some war broke out between our family and a rival. They snuck into our home to kill us all in our beds. While my father and his soldiers fought, he had others take my mother and I away. We were going somewhere safe. We never made it. The family found us and killed our guards. The fight gave my mother enough time to hide me before they took her life, too. That's when Sully found me." I frowned. "I've wondered, over the last few weeks...how many minutes was the timing off? How long passed between him taking me and when Enzo and my father found the car. Imagine if it were only a few. A few minutes could've been the difference between growing up with them —happy, and...well, what I had."

"What happened?"

I didn't want to tell her. There wasn't any reason for that kind of darkness to touch her. She was sweet and light, I didn't want to corrupt her, but she'd already seen some of the weird quirks I had because of my experiences.

"Sully was a paranoid schizo. He was delusional, but not stupid. And just paranoid enough to stay off of Law Enforcement's radar. He never did so much that they caught him. Part of the way he laid low was he collected children."

Her eyes flashed up to mine, and I read the horror there. She pressed her lips together in a grim line and laid her head back down, resuming the circles. It was her way of asking me to continue.

"He used us to steal, beat us when it wasn't enough, and terrorized us in between. We were forced to live in an abandoned building where a bunch of other homeless people were. Some were nice, others oblivious, but some…" I broke off, sweat popping out on my brow. My heart was thudding hard against my chest. Retelling the story always meant I relived it.

"How many of you were there?"

"Seven when I first got there, but twelve in all before it was over. I wasn't the first kid he took and I wasn't the last, but he got more ballsy the longer he had us. There were a few he snatched right out of their strollers when their moms were busy with something." I wiped the sweat away and focused on my breathing. It was one of those quack techniques the therapist insisted on me doing. Strangely, it seemed to work.

"They were so young when he brought them home. He still brought them even knowing that a few of the men living in the building had a thing for young kids."

Ari's hand slowed, then stilled. "Did-" she looked up at me and hesitated before asking, "Did they?"

"Not me." I gave her a wry grin. "I was too fast for them to catch. Had to learn to sleep really light, though." I brushed my thumb over her bottom lip. "Before he started taking kids from loving homes, he only collected street kids. The ones who'd been abandoned, or whose parents were too strung out to care if they never came home. One of them was the only one to get…" I couldn't say it. "He'd been ten at the time and I'd already lived with Sully for a few years. None of us could fight the guy off, though we tried."

I took her hand and pressed her fingers over the scar she'd found earlier on my forearm. She traced it silently. Most people didn't notice it because of the tattoo and I preferred that. "Beer bottle. Fucker nearly gutted me with it after he flung me off his back." I shook my head, trying to clear the memory. I could feel the bite of the glass, the gush of blood.

"Where the hell was that awful man?"

"Sully?" I shrugged. "Who knows. He rarely slept and liked to wander the city, always sticking to the shadows."

"So, you were forced to watch as…?"

I nodded. "Yeah, although I passed out halfway through due to blood loss. I kind of think I was lucky for that. None of us spoke much again until the younger kids started coming in. We banded together to protect them, and ourselves."

"How did you stop the bleeding?"

"One of the women who lived there. Her sister was a nurse. She brought me and the other boy to her to get us cleaned up."

"And she didn't do anything to help you?"

I sighed. This part was always so hard to explain to people. They'd never been in situations like that, so they couldn't understand the fear and suspicion. Why would we choose to run back to what we knew rather than take the helping hand that'd been extended to us?

"She tried. We'd been fed lies for years, Ari. If we told anyone they'd take us and experiment on us. Shit like that. The guy wasn't right in the head and he filled us so full of bullshit we didn't know what to believe. We couldn't trust that anyone would truly help us. So, we left with the drug addicted sister and went back to our shitty lives. Sully was reliable, in a horrible way. He always came back for us, which made us believe him."

I sucked in a breath, determined to finish it. "I'd been with Sully for eight years before I took a chance. I was older—twelve at the time —and had finally seen enough to understand that there were good people in this world, despite what he'd told me. I found Cade and

Riggs scoping out some guys. I walked right up to them, bold as you please. Told them they needed me, that I could help them." I chuckled. "The look on Riggs's face was priceless." Their reaction—there'd been no anger or threats, even though Riggs had been shocked—when I'd returned their wallets had been all I needed to see to know I could trust them.

Her laugh drifted over my skin. "I can only imagine." She paused. "No, I really can't. I'm so sorry you had to go through all of that, Rat." She refused to look up, but her voice had gone husky.

I tipped her chin up to force her gaze to mine. "Don't waste your tears on me, Ari." I wiped one that dripped off her lashes.

She turned her face into my palm and kissed it. "Thank you for telling me that. It couldn't have been easy."

I grunted and released her chin.

"Rat?"

"Hmm?"

"How did you get your road name?"

He huffed out a laugh. "Well, Sully numbered us. So, Seven had been my name. I didn't remember that it was Viktor. The MC refused to call me by my number. They didn't know what to name me. Dagger —the former president—took to calling me Street Rat."

Ari sucked in an angry breath.

"It just sort of stuck. Cade insisted on changing it, but I refused. I wanted—needed—to remember what I was. Every year, around my birthday—I chose the day I joined the MC to celebrate it—he asks me if I want to change my name. I don't, I'm fine with it."

Ari moved and sat cross legged near me. "Now I feel like a bitch for complaining about my family…"

"Don't do that," I told her firmly. "We all have our experiences and just because mine was what it was doesn't negate yours."

"How are you so damn smart?" She broke off and slapped a hand over her mouth. "Oh my God! I'm so sorry, I didn't mean it like that-"

I barked out a laugh because she looked truly devastated. "Don't worry, baby. I've got damn thick skin. One of the ladies living in our building taught a few of us to read—those who were interested. I just had a natural affinity toward electronics.

Once I was old enough, I started spending a few hours a day in a local library. The librarian there always let me in and let me stay on the computer as long as I wanted. She'd chase anyone off who tried to get me to move." I cocked my head. "Thinking back, I owe her a lot. I was an unwashed homeless kid and certainly didn't pay for a library card and she still let me in every day. She started bringing me lunch." I shook my head, something warm filling me as I thought back. The librarian and the nurse had been momentarily bright spots in a pretty dim time in my life.

"Oh...I should tell you. I'm in therapy." Shame and doubt tugged at me. Despite seeing the therapist for a while now, I still couldn't shake the feeling like I was wrong for sharing all this with someone.

"There's nothing wrong with that." Her hand covered mine. "Is it helping?"

I sat up in bed and shrugged my shoulders. "I don't know. It's a lot of fucking talking and 'sharing my feelings'," I said in disgust. "Maybe," I conceded when I realized that even six months ago finding my brother and gaining a wife would've sent me into a downward spiral.

"Good. Then I hope you keep going." She lunged forward and wrapped her arms around me. I chuckled and tucked her in close.

We chatted for a while longer, settling back down onto the bed. It wasn't until she'd fallen asleep in my arms that I let my guard completely down. It hadn't been easy to reveal all that to her, but she hadn't judged me for it once. She'd just seemed sad for me, but not pitying. I'd seen more pity in my life and I never wanted anyone to feel that for me again. I'd worked hard to have the life I wanted and it seemed like things were finally going my way. Closing my eyes, I drifted off with Ari's comforting weight on my chest. And for the first time, since...ever, I didn't wake up screaming.

CHAPTER 26

Ari

The weather seemed to be mirroring my mood. Dark, gloomy rain clouds had moved in, putting a damp chill in the air. My heart had been aching. It'd been a month since I'd heard not one, but two devastating stories from men that somehow had latched themselves onto my heart and still I hurt for them.

My professors had sounded like Charlie Brown's teacher all day today—wah, wah, wah—for all the attention I was able to pay to my classes. Rat had tried to get me to take the day off since he couldn't bring me to the campus. Instead, I had some fresh-faced looking blond following me around. His name was Scout and it fit. He looked like a boy scout. I couldn't believe he was in an MC.

He had his hands shoved in the pockets of a jacket, head downturned as fat drops of water began to fall from the sky. I stopped and lifted my face, letting the cold rain splatter on my cheeks.

In typical Texas fashion, it went from beginning to rain to a torrential downpour in moments and we bolted into the library for cover.

"I have a free period," I told him. "I'm going to spend it here in the library if you want to go get lunch or something?" I felt so bad for him. He probably didn't want to be stuck following me around all day.

Scout flashed a smile at me, but his eyes strayed over to where a group of freshmen walked past, throwing him suggestive looks and giggling to each other.

I bit the insides of my lips to keep from laughing. "I'll stay right over at that table until you get back," I told him when indecision warred on his face.

"Alright. One hour and I'll be back." He strolled over to the group of girls and I shook my head. These guys oozed confidence and charisma. It wasn't any wonder women tossed themselves at them.

Settling in at the table, I pulled my laptop out of my backpack. Instead of getting to work, though, I stared out the window at the rain coming down in sheets. It'd been clear the night Rat had told me about his childhood, he'd said all he wanted to on the matter and I hadn't wanted to bring it up. So, I'd decided to get some answers on my own.

It hadn't taken me long—fingers flying over the keys—looking for anything that would clue me in to what'd happened to Sully. I'd been hoping to find a death certificate—if anyone deserved to rot in hell it was him, along with the other men who'd lived in that building and thought it was okay to touch children. My heart had raced as I'd accessed the Austin Police Department's database. I typically tried to stay out of their systems as much as I could.

It had been a risk, but one I'd taken in order to find out what I wanted to know. After about twenty minutes of digging, I'd found what I was looking for. Joe Sullivan was arrested—not long after Rat'd been taken in by the MC—within that same year. He was currently serving time in the Texas State Penitentiary.

I'd searched through the case notes, desperate for any crumb of information I could find. The things he'd done to those poor children. It still made me sick to think about. They'd found eleven children living in that abandoned building, the youngest at the time was four years old and had been abducted at the age of one from his own birthday party.

I shuddered, remembering back to what I read. I could only imagine the guilt and terror those poor parents had felt. Sadness filled me, so I thought back to the articles detailing the return of most of the kids to their families. In each article, the parents mentioned a young man who'd helped give them back their children. Some called him a guardian angel, others were less poetic, but not one of them would give his name or any details about him other than how grateful they were that he was there to help their children during and after the ordeal.

My heart twisted in my chest. I wondered if Rat was still in contact with the families even though it'd been ten years. I'd searched multiple times in the month that I'd been looking into Rat's background, but found nothing in the police records about any of the homeless that were living there. That was disappointing. At some point, I'd bring it up and ask Rat what'd happened to them. It'd been so hard for him to open up to me, I didn't want to push and cause him more pain.

As I drifted back to the present, I noticed it was a lot quieter in the library. A glance at the clock on my laptop told me I still had about fifteen minutes to kill before Scout would be back for me.

Glancing out the window beside me, I realized the rain had stopped and almost everyone had cleared out. I had one class left for the day and then I would get to go home. Home. I'd have never believed that the clubhouse could become that so quickly. That Rat could be that for me.

Someone sat down next to me and I smiled over at him, expecting to see Scout. My smile died when Bene gave me a dark look.

"I need you to come with me."

My mouth fell open. "What? I'm not going with you, Bene."

He jiggled something in his hand, under the table and I sucked in a breath as he waved the gun that he had pointed at me. "You are and if you cause a scene this school is going to have an active shooter situation on its hands."

"You're insane," I whispered, shocked to my very core. "Papa is going to be furious when he finds out."

His dark brow arched and his lips twitched in humor. "Who do you think sent me, Ari?"

I shook my head in disbelief. Why was Papa sending Bene—the man who'd spent years watching over me—to threaten me?

"If he wanted me to come visit all he had to do was ask," I told him icily, rising from my seat to shove my laptop into the backpack.

Bene shrugged one muscular shoulder. "Not my place to question the Boss."

"Of course it's not," I said, disgust lacing every syllable. I couldn't blame him though. I'd gone along with Papa for far too long myself. It'd make me a hypocrite to hold it against Bene. Head lifted regally, I followed him out to the car that he had waiting in the parking lot.

As I slid in the back I saw Angelo was driving. Before closing the door, Bene held his hand out. I glared at him, but dropped my cell phone into his waiting hand. Papa had sent two of his men after me which told me he knew I was being protected by the MC.

The drive to my parents' house was silent. I didn't bother to try to use my laptop to ask for help. They'd hear me on it and I didn't want Bene to get pissed and toss it out the window. I wouldn't put it past the man. He had a wicked temper.

We rolled to a stop and I shoved out the door as soon as Angelo unlocked them. I didn't bother to wait for the guards as I stormed into the house.

"Papa!"

Mama's gasp sounded from the doorway of the main floor library. I swerved left and stalked past her.

"What are you doing here, Arianna?"

"Don't ask me," I told her bitterly. "Ask him." I stopped in front of where my father was standing. Folding my arms, I lifted a brow. I was done pandering to him.

"Salvatore?" Mama asked.

Before Papa could answer, my siblings entered the room. "Ari!" Antonia and Ada rushed over and hugged me. Alex sailed past me and went to sit on a chaise lounge in the corner. Abel gave me a side hug before taking a seat as well.

"I need a moment alone with your sister," Papa said, his voice tight, but controlled.

Alex rolled her eyes and continued texting. No one left the room.

"Why am I here, Papa? Your idiot guards took me without letting me tell my friend that I was going. If you don't think he's going to tell Rat, you're mistaken."

Papa's eyes narrowed on me. "Out!" he bellowed. Every breath caught and all of us watched him warily. My sisters all started to head toward the door.

"The MC is going to think you kidnapped me," I continued. His face was turning red, a very bad sign, but I was past the point of caring. "Either tell me why you wanted me here or I'm walking out that-"

I broke off when he lunged toward me and backhanded me so hard I saw stars.

"Sal!" Mama gasped, but she grabbed Ada, who tried to rush past her to get to me.

Antonia ran over to check on me. I held my arm out to her, keeping her a safe distance from me as I faced my father. Alex was silently watching from the corner and Abel had disappeared. Disappointment in my brother mixed with anger as my face throbbed.

"You force me to come back to this hell hole, then hit me for simply asking why?" I spat at him.

Papa's eyes narrowed.

"Arianna, respect your father," Mama hissed. There was fear in her eyes.

My laugh trilled out, high pitched and slightly manic. "Why Mama? Cause you're all afraid of him?" I turned my head and locked eyes with her. There was sadness and pity swimming in her gaze.

"No," I said, interrupting her before she could answer, "I get it, trust me. I tip-toed around him for my entire life, too." My eyes found Papa once more. "That ends today. Either tell me why you brought me here, or I'm leaving." I clenched my hands by my sides to still the shaking in them.

"You're going to do a job for me," Papa finally said after a heartbeat of silence following my speech.

I took a deep breath. "No, Papa, I'm not."

His hand darted out and grabbed me by the jacket lapels, pulling me in close until we were nose to nose.

I'd seen him like this many times before. He was close to losing his cool. Despite having struck me he hadn't quite given in to his temper yet. This was the first time he'd laid hands on one of us, but it made sense that it was me and it was now. I was no longer his responsibility. He'd still claim me as his daughter, but only so he could keep using me. In his mind, I belonged to the MC so he could treat me the way he treated his men, not the way he treated his family.

His hand started to raise again. I tipped my chin up, waiting for the blow I knew was coming. I refused to cower before him or give in. Another arm shot in front of my face and I stared over at Abel, slack jawed as he gripped Papa's wrist in his hand.

Abel was about two inches taller than Papa, and had packed on a lot of muscle over the years. He'd always been respectful of the man standing in front of us because he was our father and the Don. I was happy to have my brother standing up for me, though. I hadn't heard him come back into the room.

"Don't you fucking touch her again," Abel told Papa. The two men were tense, staring each other down.

Papa had been grooming Abel to take over as the next Don pretty much his whole life. I didn't want to speculate on what this was going to mean for Abel.

CHAPTER 27

Rat

I finished executing a command on my keyboard before I picked up my ringing cell phone.

"Fucking finally, bro," Riggs barked into my ear.

"Sorry, I was-"

"No time. Get your ass over to Sal's place. He took Ari from the campus."

I froze as I realized Riggs was bellowing because he was calling while riding his bike.

"Scout was with her." Worry clogged my throat. If that slimy ass mobster had done anything to them, I'd never forgive myself.

"He's fine. Everyone is heading over now. No clue what's going on, but Cade got a call from Abel," Riggs barked, then hung up the phone.

"Fuck," I muttered. I was at a long-time client's house, so he took it pretty well when I tore out of there like the hounds of hell were on my heels.

I was grateful not to have been at the clubhouse. Being at this client's place meant I was only ten minutes away from Ari's childhood home. Likewise, most of my brothers in arms were coming from their various businesses around the city, so we all showed up about the same time.

When I pulled in, Steel and Riggs were fighting with two of Sal's men. The match was fierce, but short, ending before I had a chance to get down the long driveway and park my bike. Bass, Trip, and Cade had pulled in directly behind me. Bass grabbed some rope from his saddlebags and tied the men up.

"Don't want them crashing the party," Bass said with a grin.

"You're disturbingly good at that," Trip muttered, watching as Bass expertly made his knots.

Bass smirked, then puckered his lips in a kiss aimed Trip's way.

I was already moving up the porch. Not bothering to knock or check if anyone was behind me, I entered the house. It didn't matter to me if anyone else was showing up. I'd take on Sal's whole operation alone if I had to.

I paused in the foyer. Muffled voices came from behind a door to my left. I barged in and made my way across the room. Ari was standing facing away from me. Stepping up behind her, I wrapped an arm around her waist and pulled her back against me. She laid a hand soothingly on my forearm. My body was practically vibrating with my fury.

She and her brother were facing her father, and I lent my support. I could tell I'd walked into a tense situation, but my anger was drowning out all the other emotions in the room.

"Sal," I growled, trying to let go of the rage I felt. "Want to tell me why you took my wife from the campus without saying anything to me?"

Ari shot me a perturbed look over her shoulder that I caught out of the corner of my eye. I kept a steady gaze on Sal. He was the one I needed to keep an eye on. Yeah, I sounded like a possessive, controlling dick, but that was the only language that her father understood.

Sal's eyes narrowed, then shifted behind me. I didn't need to look to know my brothers were standing at my back.

"Celia, take the girls and leave."

Ari's mother did as she was instructed and bustled their three other daughters out of the room, closing the door behind them. Ari stayed firmly planted in front of me. I maneuvered her body so that she was tucked up under my arm. If Sal pulled any shit I'd be able to shield her better this way, but she got to be a part of the crowd staring down her father. I saw him motion toward the doorway and knew more of his men were making their way into the room. They shuffled inside, but stayed out of our way—for now.

"You too," Sal snarled at Ari.

"No. She stays. You wanted her badly enough to take her. Now we want to know why," Cade said, stepping to the other side of Arianna.

Relief washed over me that he was backing my decisions and including my wife in them as well. She was still new to this club and her father clearly wasn't trustworthy—although we'd known that from the minute he'd back stabbed his other partners and killed them in front of us.

Sal swallowed hard, his gaze shifting between our faces. This was the first time I'd seen him nervous.

"There's more going on in this city than you realize."

Cryptic. Cool. Still didn't answer our questions. I tugged Ari a little closer and waited. No one else moved a muscle.

Sal sighed. He glanced around the room as though he expected someone to be skulking around in the shadows, listening. "You saw the chief of police at the engagement party?"

We all nodded. The others shifted around, forming a line with us. A united front against this man.

Sal's mouth gaped open as he started to speak, then he shook his head. "I can't tell you everything," he hurried on when Cade's eyes narrowed. "I don't know everything, yet," he corrected himself. "Just that something's going on."

"With the cops?" Riggs asked.

Sal gave a sharp nod. "Bobby Miller—Precinct Five's Chief of Police—has been keeping a close eye on me. Closer than normal. I needed Arianna to look into it for me." He shot her an angry look. He said it so casually, like kidnapping her was a normal response to needing help.

My gaze slid over to Cade's and we shared a silent look. I didn't need him to tell me it was up to me how I wanted to proceed.

"She won't be helping you anymore." I continued on before Sal had a chance to say anything. "If you need something you come to me. I'll help where I can, but leave her out of your business."

"She's my daughter." His unspoken words were 'she's my property'.

"She's *my* wife," I told him in a low voice that brooked no argument. "Every time you include her in these fucking situations you put a target on her back. I won't allow that."

Silence filled the room as Sal eyed me. His calculating gaze was hard as stone, but finally he nodded in agreement.

"I have business to take care of today, but we'll stop by tomorrow and go over the rest of this. I'll see what I can do," I told him, taking Ari's elbow and prompting her to move as we turned our backs on him and walked to the door. Everyone was tense. I'd dismissed Sal as though he worked for me, completely disrespecting him in front of everyone. He didn't object. That in and of itself told me how desperate he was. As we passed, Ari held out her hand, giving Bene a dark look. After shooting Sal a glance, Bene dropped her phone into her hand and we continued.

We did everything as a cohesive group, and not one of the men surrounding us contradicted my directive. It was fucking weird, but they were letting me take the lead since it was my wife and her father. The only comforting thought was knowing I wouldn't be staying in charge. Leadership was the last thing I wanted. I hated having to do it here, but it was a necessity.

As we all piled outside, I blew out a breath, trying to release the pent-up frustration and agitation inside of me.

"Good job, Kid," Riggs said with a grin.

"What do you think he meant 'the cops are watching him'?" Steel asked Cade.

Cade shrugged, but his green eyes were speculative. He glanced down at his phone curiously before putting it back in his pocket. "Do you know?" he asked Ari.

She shook her head. "He never tells us anything. The only one who may know is Abel."

"I'll speak with him," Cade said. His tone was distracted. "I'll see whatever other lines I can tug on, too."

I knew he'd be contacting Flynn. None of us knew what her endgame was yet. One minute she's trying to put us in jail, the next she takes a bullet for Ming. Either way, Cade wasn't above asking for help when necessary. We'd use any advantage we had and if that meant dealing with fallout later, so be it.

The cops sniffing around Sal was technically the mobster's problem. Except we'd hitched our wagon to his—for now. We didn't need the police looking into any of us when we knew for a fact Marco Guzman was about to make his move.

I'd notified Cade this morning that it looked like Marco was gearing up to confront us. He'd been sitting back, gathering intel, and now we were about to go into another war. I'd intercepted an encrypted email from him to Miguel's second in command—now the leader of the cartel down in Reynosa.

Whoever Marco had working for him in cyber security wasn't the best, by far. One week. He'd be coming to Texas in a week and we had that amount of time to make ourselves and our allies ready. With Sal causing trouble and this new information about the police digging into him—and ultimately us, it put more pressure and stress on the club.

"We need to talk," Cade muttered, passing by to head to his bike. "Catch your girl up on everything and bring her to the meeting room in an hour."

I nodded and motioned for Ari to climb on behind me after she got her backpack from the car she'd come in. Her arms wrapping around me alleviated some of the anger burning inside of me. The ride back to the clubhouse should've taken care of the rest of it, but for some reason the closer we got to home the more jacked up my nerves got.

By the time we parked, I was shaking. I was so pissed off. The fucker had balls of steel to think that he could get away with taking my wife. The only reason we hadn't rained hell down on his head was because we still needed him. If he wasn't careful his treachery would outweigh his usefulness and we'd end him.

Threading my fingers through Ari's, I brought her up to our home. It wasn't until we entered our apartment that I turned to look at her. As soon as I did, the words withered in my throat. A low growl tore out as I cupped her chin and tipped her face so I could see it better.

She had a light bruise forming on her cheekbone. Her jaw clenched, but she met my furious eyes. "I refused to help him. He didn't like it much."

"I should've pounded his fucking face into the ground," I growled. Anger punched me in the gut. At him, for hitting his daughter, at myself for not paying closer attention when I got there, and at Abel for allowing it to happen. "How the fuck can he justify hitting his daughter?"

"He doesn't consider me his daughter anymore—unless he needs to use me for something. To him, I'm the wife of a biker, his ally—for now. You can't trust him, Rat. I've seen it too many times. He only cares about himself and his empire. He'll step over me, you, the club, to get what he wants."

"I know that," I told her, brushing my thumb lightly over the bruise marring her smooth skin. "We know working with him is dangerous and temporary."

Ari's eyes widened as she searched my face. "You knew you wouldn't be working with my father long-term and you still accepted his conditions?"

She meant marrying her. "Yes. Because in the short-term it provided us with what we needed. Plus, I got you out of the deal." I grinned at her. "I won, hands down."

The corner of her mouth tipped up. "What if you'd picked Alex?"

"That would've been a fucking nightmare, but I would've dealt with it."

She shook her head and snorted in disbelief. "Alex is so far in Papa's pocket you would've had a spy in your camp. Her loyalty will always be to him."

I tilted my head and watched her expression as I asked, "And what about you?"

The shock and hurt that filled her gaze would've been enough of an answer, but I hadn't really needed it. "That's what I thought," I murmured before she could answer. "Your loyalty is to me. You proved that today." Leaning in, I brushed my lips over hers.

Before I could take it deeper, she pulled away with a frown. "How do you know what I did today? Besides what I've told you?"

"Abel."

She blinked, confusion growing on her face.

"You think Cade went into a deal with your father without having his own spy in that camp?" I asked in amusement, repeating her phrasing.

Her jaw dropped. She looked so fucking cute, standing there, stunned.

"Abel wouldn't betray Papa…"

"Wouldn't he?" I asked when she trailed off, considering the possibility. "You said it yourself. Your father only looks out for himself. Fuck, I bet he'd sell your mother and sisters out to save his own ass. Abel realizes that too. He was all too happy to come to an arrangement with us."

She looked unconvinced but didn't argue with me.

"Come here," I led her over to the couch and we sat. "I need to fill you in on the rest of the shit show we have going right now. The only way to keep you safe is to keep you informed. I would've told you earlier-" I broke off, wondering if my wife was the kind of woman who'd get upset if I told her we'd had to work out whether we could trust her or not. If her flashing eyes were any indication, she'd already figured out what I hadn't said.

"I promise you, Rat. My loyalty is one hundred percent to you and this club."

I nodded. We knew that—now. She gave me a smile in return and I tried to school my features to not let the surprise ripple over them. The other women—with maybe the exception of Julie—would've been tearing into me for insinuating that we didn't trust them. Not my woman. She understood it. She may not know much about MC life, but she knew about *this* life. The one that involved criminal activity and what it took to keep all the balls up in the air and off the ground. Her father may not have intentionally included her in it, but she'd paid attention. My girl wasn't anything if not intuitive and intelligent.

It didn't matter how close I was to the other women. I was grateful for Ari's calmer, more reasonable nature. We seemed to be meshing well, and I knew day by day I was happier than I could ever explain that things had worked out the way they had. That she was mine. Who knew that an arranged marriage could give me the best thing that'd ever happened to me?

I pulled out my phone and glanced at the time. "I have a lot to tell you and not much time to go over it. Then we have to meet with Cade."

Her brows shot up. "You're taking me to your meeting?"

"Cade's orders," I told her with a grin. "Welcome to the club."

"But how-"

"I told you. We know you're loyal to us."

"It just seems like after what I did...that it would've taken longer to accept me."

I shrugged. "No one—other than me," I admitted guiltily, "blamed you for that. They knew that was your father. Turns out Cade knew more than the rest of us all along. He usually does."

With that, I went over the last six months of troubles that had been plaguing our club. Parts of the story required me to delve further back into our history, so by the time I was finished we only had a few minutes to head into the room that was finally finished and designated for Church and all the rest of our meetings.

Scout shoved off the wall, where he'd been leaning and waiting for us.

"I'm so fucking sorry," he said, blue eyes shifting to Ari to include her in the apology before he focused solely on me. "If I would've known-"

"Where were you?" I growled at him. He'd shown up as we'd all been leaving Sal's house. I'd seen the regret on his face, but hadn't stopped to hash it out then. Looked like we were taking care of it now.

Ari placed a hand on my forearm and I looked over at her. "I told him he didn't have to stick around. I had some work to do in the library-" She broke off at my furious look.

"Give us a minute," I told her.

She grimaced, then shot Scout an apologetic look before going into the meeting room.

I arched a brow at Scout. "None of the women want us tailing them. That doesn't fucking mean you can leave her alone!"

"I know," he muttered. "Seriously, Rat, I fucked up. I didn't think her dad would do something like that and… FUCK!" He scraped his hand through his shaggy blond hair, making it stand up in spikes.

Sighing, I tried to rein in my anger. Scout was younger than me by a few years—his age was the main reason he was still a prospect. We trusted him and he'd be a good brother, but he was impulsive and reckless. Of course, that could describe most of my brothers. This kid could practically be Gunnar's baby brother with all the common traits they shared.

"It's fine. She's fine, but next time-"

"There won't be a next time. This will never happen again," he said eagerly.

I knew there wouldn't be. You only made this kind of mistake once. I gave him a curt nod, and he strode down the hall. Shaking my head, I walked into the meeting room.

CHAPTER 28

Ari

I froze after I turned from closing the door behind me. Rat and Scout's voices floated through the door, mostly muffled, but I could tell Rat was pissed. All thoughts of him fled my mind, though, when Abel rose from the table and walked over to me, pulling me into a hug.

My eyes met Cade's perceptive gaze and held until I averted them. Riggs was sitting next to Cade, tipped back onto the back legs of his chair and watching us, looking deceptively relaxed. I wasn't sure whether his suspicion was for Abel or me.

"Are you okay?" Abel asked, searching my face. Anger flared in his eyes when they landed on my cheek.

"I'm fine. You've seen better days, though." I lightly touched near the split in his bottom lip. It looked like he was going to end up with a black eye, and when I'd hugged him, he hadn't been able to hold back the wince of pain from his ribs. "Was that from Papa?"

"Easy for an old man to kick your ass when his men hold you down," he said with a sarcastic tilt of his lips.

"Oh, Abel. I'm so sorry. Why is Papa acting like this?"

Abel shrugged. "It's not the first time. Something has him spooked. He...doesn't handle fear very well."

I examined his eyes. They were identical to mine. There was a resignation in them, as though he hadn't meant to say that to me.

"What do you mean? What's not the first time?"

Abel's lips flattened out into a thin line before he shook his head. "It doesn't matter."

I was sick to death of everyone leaving me in the dark. "Give us a minute?" I said firmly, glancing at Cade and Riggs. Rat chose that moment to walk through the door. The tone of my voice—and maybe the fact that I was bossing his president around in his own clubhouse —had Rat's eyes widening slightly. "Alone!" I barked when no one moved or said anything. They just sat there, staring at me like I was insane. I hated when people did that. React, speak, do something, don't just stand there staring.

"Sure," Cade said, with a hint of amusement coloring his voice. He elbowed Riggs hard enough that he almost sent the man crashing backward in his precarious seat.

Riggs caught himself just in time to prevent landing on his ass and glared at Cade. Neither man said anything else as they left the room. Rat eyeballed me for a moment before he too left us alone.

"Ari-"

"What did you mean, Abel?" I folded my arms over my chest and gave him the same look Mama had always given us as kids. The one we knew meant we were in deep trouble.

Abel sighed. "He's been using me as his punching bag since I was eight years old."

My jaw dropped. Had I been so oblivious that I'd never noticed?

He must have read the question on my face. "They were mostly body blows. Easier to hide that way." His eyes hardened. "It was better me than..."

Us. He'd been protecting us. Thinking back on it—now that I knew—I could see Abel gingerly walking to the table for dinner after Alex had riled Papa up over something. After I'd ignored his orders and done what I wanted. Guilt threatened to capsize me like a ship on the sea. If we'd known the price for disobeying—and that we didn't have to pay it—we would have rethought a lot of our little rebellions over the years.

"Why?" I asked him, tears filling my eyes.

"What? You think I'm the kind of man who would let him beat on my sisters?"

"Surely he wouldn't have hurt Alex."

"Probably not," he conceded, "but that wouldn't have saved you or Antonia."

I sucked in a sharp breath. He continued before I could say anything.

"I was already used to it. In his mind, I wouldn't be ready for leadership unless I could take a beating." Abel shrugged. "I waited years for my chance to return the favor." He gave me a malicious grin. "I kicked the fuck out of him on my fifteenth birthday. Ever since, he's used his men to make sure it's not a fair fight."

"Why would you put up with that?" I cried. "Why not leave?"

"I'd never leave you and Antonia. You two are...unbroken. I couldn't risk letting him hurt you. Besides, it's my fucking birthright." Something dark passed over his face. He moved around me and jerked the door open. "We're ready," he told the three men who were lounging in the hallway outside their own meeting room.

I swallowed and sat next to Rat at the table. Abel refused to look at me, so I focused on Cade.

"We'll go over this in church too, but I wanted to let you two in on it before then," Cade started. "I approached Abel after making that deal with Sal and he agreed to work with us." Cade crossed his large arms over his chest.

It'd never really occurred to me—until now—how big the man was. He wasn't quite as large as the guy sitting next to him. Riggs was a giant even among these men, but Cade wasn't small by any means. His muscles rippled as he shifted. He reminded me of a tiger. Calm, cool, waiting for his time to strike. There was a keen intelligence in his eyes that told you it didn't matter where you ran, he'd find you and eliminate you.

I shivered and caught the last bit of the story Abel was telling. "Can't be trusted, we all agree on that."

"Today proves your father's desperation," Cade said, his eyes finally leaving my face and focusing on my brother. He'd been fully aware of me taking stock of him.

"He's paranoid. I haven't been able to dig any information out of him. You guys found out more today than I've been able to since the engagement party," Abel explained.

"Where will helping your sister out today leave you with him?" Cade asked.

Abel shrugged. "Sal is used to me sticking up for Ari and Toni."

"Not like today," Cade insisted. "You called me. He wasn't able to use your sister's...talents, because you brought us in. The beating you took tells us he knew it was you."

Able looked thoughtful at that. "True."

"What's going to happen now that you've shown loyalty to us?"

I narrowed my eyes on Cade. His tone of voice was slightly bored, as though he knew the answer, but he needed Abel to come to the conclusion on his own.

Abel shifted in his chair. "He'll kill me."

Unable to help it, I gasped. Abel's confession showed me that I'd been right to fear my father all these years. I only wished I'd known what my brother was doing for me so I hadn't wasted that time desperately wishing for Papa's affection. My childhood had been a lie. Abel had ensured that a pretty glass bubble surrounded us at all times, never letting the ugly truth come to light.

It felt like someone had knocked the wind out of me. I had my brother to thank for having a decent childhood. Sure, I'd always felt left out, but I'd never been beaten. I guess being left out wasn't so bad. He couldn't say the same. If that was what it took to be in Papa's good graces, I didn't want any part of it. I wondered if Alex had ever had to sacrifice.

"There's no leaving the mafia," Abel said flatly. "Especially not when you know as much as I do. If he suspects there's an agreement between us, he'll kill me." He was explaining it for me, but I already knew it. How many times over the years had I heard the speech from Papa? Loyalty, Honor, Servitude. That's what he expected from his Underboss all the way down to his Soldiers. He didn't mind ruling with an iron fist and fear.

We were sitting around a table calmly talking about my father murdering his son—my brother. My stomach roiled at the thought. Riggs and Rat both nodded in agreement with Abel's words.

Cade countered with another question. "What's your plan?"

Abel frowned. His brows were pulled low over his eyes. Eventually, he shrugged.

"You're going to let him kill you?" Cade's voice wasn't sharp or judgmental, just inquiring.

"No," Abel said firmly. His eyes met mine. "I guess if my baby sister can stand up to that asshole, so can I." His lips twitched in a small smile. "I'm going to fucking de-throne him." Abel's voice rang out with certainty. "It's been my plan all along. I just wasn't expecting the time to be now."

My eyes slid over to Cade, who wore a self-satisfied smile. The man was a chess master. I wondered how many people had gone along with his plan without ever realizing it.

"You want Abel to kill Papa and take over in his place." It wasn't a question.

Cade shrugged. "Killing him would ensure that he couldn't come back and cause trouble in the future."

"Fucking cold to ask a son to kill his father," Abel said conversationally.

I was shocked at the lack of emotion I felt at the statement. Papa had ensured that I never felt close to him. The nail in his coffin was finding out that the one man living under our roof—the only one I remember showing me affection—had protected me from him for so many years. No, any loyalty I had to my father withered and died in that moment. The MC and my brother were my future, and I fully embraced that knowledge.

"I don't think I can swing that even though I want to. As it is, I'm going to have to convince the majority of his Capos and Soldiers to forsake him and follow me. If I kill him, they'll never switch to my side."

I listened to them talk about how to overthrow my father and I felt nothing. Abel would do a far better job than Salvatore Giuliani ever did. The MC could count on him to be loyal and a true ally.

"What about Mama? And the others?" I asked, interrupting their planning. Rat's warm palm covered my thigh and squeezed reassuringly. My voice had been shaking. It didn't register that it had until my husband offered me comfort.

"They'll have to make their own choices," Abel said coldly. "I'm going to try to get Ada and Antonia out." A grim look settled on his face.

"I can help with that," I told him. "You have enough to deal with."

Abel's eyes narrowed, but slowly he nodded. "Keep them safe."

"Of course."

I'd never seen him in this light before. Growing up, he'd been reserved, but had always had a grin for me. Knowing now what he'd been through in order to protect me, it was a wonder he ever smiled as a man. My heart cracked a little. I wished he'd have told me. There wouldn't have been much I could've done, but somehow knowing might have made it easier on us. Then again, maybe it wouldn't have.

My brother was an incredible man. I would've expected there to be resentment shining there in his eyes. Who knew how many beatings he took that were earmarked for Antonia or me? Odds are Papa wouldn't have stopped with us. It would have eventually bled over onto Alex, Ada, and likely Mama if it hadn't been for him. Understanding was what I found in those green eyes. My entire world view had been upended and shaken out like a drawer that you were certain contained the item you'd lost.

"Did Mama know?"

Abel's eyes clouded and darkened. It was all the answer I needed. How could she have let Papa do this to him? I pursed my lips together to keep from asking more questions. He wasn't ready to answer, and he certainly wasn't going to air our dirty laundry in front of the others. What'd happened growing up in our house didn't pertain to this meeting.

"Sorry I'm late." Enzo's deep voice echoed through the now silent room and I turned to watch him walk in, bold as you please. The resemblance between him and Rat was there, if you knew where to look. Enzo's hair was a few shades darker, but those eyes were a dead ringer.

Riggs grumbled under his breath as the head of the Russian Bratva sat down next to Rat, across from my brother.

Enzo steepled his fingers together and eyed Abel. "I hear we're taking out your lying, murderous father."

I huffed out a breath. These men were all so intense. They spoke of death so casually, like it was inconsequential. It wasn't like I'd never seen death. The first time had been when I'd snuck down to the basement. I'd hidden in a vent shaft and seen far more than any kid probably should. I'd been so eager to be a part of the family I'd had grand notions of joining. Abel had found me afterwards and made it abundantly clear that Papa would never accept a woman into his organization, least of all his daughter.

Papa had made his bed and as far as I was concerned he deserved what he got. Was it a little bloodthirsty? Probably, but I was his daughter after all. As they caught Enzo up and began discussing how Abel could convince Papa's men to flip on him, I wondered how anyone could live in a life like this permanently. It seemed violent and short. My eyes slid over to Rat, who sat watching intently, adding suggestions here and there. He seemed to thrive here, with this group of men, and I'd never take that from him. But how could we begin a life, a family, with all this danger?

That thought pulled me up short. A family. Kids. Panic clutched at my throat, and I had to force those thoughts from my mind. The idea of children didn't scare me. Raising them in this life did. Even more scary was the thought of being a mother. How could I do something so important when my own parents had made such a mess of things? I had no decent role models and Rat hadn't even had the luxury of shitty parents like I'd had.

He was watching me. Somehow, he was so in tune with me already, he could tell the turmoil that was blazing through my veins. I cleared my head and focused on the conversation once again. After a moment, Rat's gaze shifted off my face.

"It's a long shot," Enzo offered. "Sal isn't going to let his empire go easily. You won't convince Stefano to double-cross him. There are others that are one hundred percent loyal as well. Like Bene, Tony, Carson, and Valentino."

Enzo must have seen the shock on my face. He spoke the names of my father's Underboss and some of his most trusted Capos as though he knew everything about them. Maybe he did. They'd been enemies for so long who knew how many times they'd come up against each other over the years. Enzo's lips tilted up into a knowing smile.

"I know they're a lost cause," Abel agreed. "But the others are tired of Sal betraying every ally he takes and putting them and their families in danger."

"Whatever you're going to do, you'd better do it quickly," Riggs muttered.

"Trust me, Sal's already put a hit out on me, guaranteed. I won't be taking my sweet time to make a move," Abel said good-naturedly, as though they were talking about the weather.

I wondered how long he'd been calling Papa by his given name. I'd never heard him do it before today, but something told me it was more natural for him to use it than father anymore. The meeting adjourned then.

"Stick around," Cade told Rat and Riggs, "we're having church right after this so we can catch the others up on this and the Guzman situation."

Abel gave me another hug. He squeezed me tight and whispered in my ear. "We'll talk more about all of this once the dust has settled."

"I'm with you," I whispered back. "Anything you need just let me know."

Abel pulled back with a frown and stared down into my face. "I don't want you involved in this Ari."

"You're my family. I'm already involved."

"No-"

"Abel," I interrupted him. "I *have* to be a part of this. I *need* to help you. To make up for...everything."

His frown deepened. "We'll talk about it later." Cade was waiting to escort him and Enzo off the property.

Rat came over and wrapped his arms around me from behind while we watched them walk down the hallway.

"You okay?"

"Yeah," I sighed. "I know you have church, but can we go somewhere afterwards?"

"Sure, and *we* have church."

I looked up at him, and he grinned. "Welcome to the club." He repeated, then kissed the top of my head and pulled me back to the chair.

CHAPTER 29

Ari

Silence filled the room despite the amount of people in here. Everyone was staring at me, and I had to fight the urge to hunch my shoulders. Cade had just finished explaining what'd happened that afternoon.

"Welcome to the club," Bridget said with a sardonic smile.

How many times was I going to hear that? I was happy to be included, but maybe not in this way.

"Yeah," Remi piped in. "The MC and *our* club." Her tone was a mix of disgust and sarcasm.

I frowned at her in confusion.

"The 'our families are pieces of shit and betrayed us in the worst way possible' club," she explained.

The memory of her and Bridget explaining how her uncle and Bridget's father had gotten them into some pretty hot water, and how Ming and Julie's father was blackmailed by his own sister-in-law, filtered through my confused and chaotic mind. My situation wasn't exactly the same, but close enough.

"I guess—technically—Abel and I are the betrayers in this

scenario," I said with a self-deprecating laugh. "We're the ones who will be stabbing Papa in the back and taking his empire after all."

Rat glanced over at me sharply. "*You* aren't doing anything," he declared.

I narrowed my eyes at him and he returned my dangerous look with one filled with pure stubbornness. "If you think I'm going to let Abel do this all on his own-"

"Besides," Cade's voice boomed from the head of the table, making me jerk in surprise and fall silent. "Sal brought this all on himself. If he hadn't dug himself in so deep there'd be zero chance that Abel could pull the support of his Capos away from him."

Cade had effectively stopped the argument between us, but I shot Rat a look that promised we'd be discussing this later. His blue eyes darkened to a deeper blue. They shifted with his moods. His eyes were his own personal mood ring and super convenient for me. Not that I needed them right now to tell me my husband was seriously pissed off at me for wanting to insert myself into a mafia war.

A small warm hand picked up mine—where it'd been clenched in a fist on top of my thigh—and then both Julie's hands were covering it. I glanced over into her soft brown eyes. My hand relaxed in her comforting hold, and the tension ran out of my shoulder as we locked gazes.

"We'll help you in any way possible," she told me softly. I followed the quick look she shot at the other women and saw them all nodding enthusiastically. "We're kind of pros with this sort of thing now." Her soft voice flowed over me, further easing my consciousness and urging me to open up to her.

Riggs's voice jerked me out of the spell Julie was weaving around me. "You'd be too late to help anyway," he said, tossing some peanuts into the air and catching them in his mouth. Riggs grunted heavily when someone—presumably Anna since she was giving him a death glare—kicked him in the shin under the table. His knee hit the underside of it and lifted the heavy oak table a couple of inches before it crashed down again, making it well known what'd happened. "Jesus fucking-" he glanced over at me then frowned at

Anna while he bent to rub his shin. He opted to keep his mouth shut after that.

"What does that mean?" I asked, watching both Rat and Cade. Riggs wasn't about to open his mouth again and earn another kick.

"You heard Abel. He's not going to sit on this," Rat said, as if that meant anything to me.

I gave him a look that properly translated the mix of emotions swirling inside me. Confusion. What the hell did that *mean*? Disgust. Speak English please, for the love of God. Anger. Why was I sitting here when my brother needed me? And frustration. How had everything spiraled out of control so quickly?

Bass chuckled as I sat there quietly pinning Rat with that look and everyone's glare shot over to him. He choked on the sound and averted his eyes in guilt.

"He's meeting with your father's Capos now," Cade explained.

"How?" I sputtered. "There hasn't been enough time to even…" That's when it hit me. Today was just the straw that broke the camel's back. Abel had been planning this for a while. How else would he know that Papa's Capos and Soldiers were unhappy with how he'd been running things? He'd been campaigning before this. My heart squeezed painfully. All these years I'd been selfish and stupid, thinking I was alone and not a part of my family. In reality, I'd had Antonia and Ada.

Abel was the one who'd truly been alone. I'd always assumed he'd had Papa's favor so his life was perfect. In reality, he'd been completely isolated. His hatred for Papa was palpable. How he'd managed to hide it from everyone for so long was a mystery. Who could blame him? The man had been beating him for years. I was shocked he didn't hate us—his clueless, ungrateful sisters whom he'd been protecting from the shadows for so long.

There wasn't anything I could do about the past, but I could help Abel now. I quickly shot off a few texts as the meeting was wrapping up. I could feel Rat's heavy gaze on me, but I focused on the others. We'd have it out soon enough. First I had something more important I needed to do.

* * *

"Give me a minute, okay?" I murmured to Rat and Bass and was grateful when they stopped short, giving us space. Rat shoved his hands into the pockets of his jeans, his intelligent eyes sweeping around the park.

I did my own quick scan of the park for the hundredth time before hurrying over and embracing Antonia and Ada.

"What's with all the cloak and dagger?" Antonia asked, since I'd sent the text to a burner phone. Since the plan had been for us to run, I'd made sure we were prepared.

"Something's up. I need you both to come with me," I told them. Rat and Bass were surely keeping an eye out from where they were standing, but I couldn't help checking out our surroundings again.

"What's going on?" Ada asked. Both of their eyes were wide as they watched me nervously look around again.

I shook my head. "I can't tell you here. Trust me, it's not safe. Did you bring your clothes?"

"One bag of clothes is not nearly enough," Ada said with an uncomfortable laugh. She was trying to lighten the mood. I wasn't about to relax until we were gone from this place. It was too open; we were too vulnerable.

One bag was what I'd allowed them to bring. Anything more and Mama and Papa would notice. I'd made them walk to this park to avoid any of Papa's made men following them. That was why I was so on edge. Any minute we could be discovered.

"Come on, get in the car and I'll explain," I told them, leading them back to where we'd parked.

We all froze as we saw Bene and another one of Papa's soldiers standing near our car.

"They must have followed us," Ada whispered.

"I'm so sorry, Ari, I tried to make sure we weren't spotted leaving the house," Antonia told me.

There was no point in blaming her for anything. We'd been trying to duck the guards Papa had put on us over the years and the men had gotten keen to our tricks.

Rat's hand went to my bicep, pulling me to a stop as I stepped toward Bene.

"Let me try to talk to him," I pleaded with Rat. The last thing I wanted was a fight.

He let go of my arm, but stepped up with me as I went to face my former bodyguard. "Hi, Bene." Bass stepped up to my other side and they sandwiched me between them while keeping my sisters behind us.

The man glared at me. I was positive he'd never liked me. Probably because he got stuck babysitting me and my sisters instead of doing whatever it was he really wanted to be doing.

"Look. Ada and Antonia are going to come spend the week with me."

"Did Sal okay it?"

"Yes," I said without hesitation. Then I prayed that he wasn't going to take the time to check. His eyes bored holes into mine as he tried to ascertain the truth. I refused to do anything other than maintain eye contact with him. He'd see anything else as a lie or weakness.

"Why didn't you pick them up from the house?"

I shrugged. "Things have been a bit tense with my parents. I wanted to avoid any conflict."

Bene glared at me. "Bullshit. They wouldn't have snuck away from the house if they had permission."

"I don't give a fuck what you think," Rat growled at him. "You heard my wife. Her sisters are staying with the MC this week. Get the fuck out of the way."

There was no circumventing this. Bene wasn't going to let us go with the girls and I wasn't leaving without them.

Bene's eyes narrowed. He was weighing the pros and cons of fighting us. The soldier next to him wasn't smart enough to realize there were consequences to consider. It didn't occur to him, as he lifted the gun he'd pulled from behind his back, that if he shot the

Boss's daughters, it might piss off Sal. *Clearly Papa wasn't hiring based on critical thinking skills.*

I wasn't so sure if Papa would be angry or not. At this point he was so far off the rails I wasn't convinced that he gave two fucks about us anymore. He was a drowning man and he was willing to pull anyone and everyone down with him.

Rat shoved me back behind him and he and Bass closed ranks, drawing their guns.

Chaos exploded with the first crack of the gun. I grabbed my sisters and we ducked behind a nearby parked car. Rat and Bass were calmly moving toward cover now that we were out of harm's way, and Bene was screaming at his own guy.

I wasn't sure who's bullet killed the mafia soldier, but silence fell and I peeked my head over the hood of the car. The man was dead on the ground and the other three had their weapons trained on each other.

"Like I said," Rat repeated, "get the fuck out of our way."

"Unless you want to join him?" Bass motioned to the dead man.

Bene made an executive decision and put his gun away. We waited while he dragged the man to his vehicle and shoved him in the trunk. Still we waited until he pulled out of the parking lot.

"Hurry up," Rat shouted, and we dashed for the car. We piled in and took off out of the lot with a squeal of tires. We didn't need the gunshots to be reported and get caught by the cops. We also didn't need Bene bringing my father back here.

For the last few weeks Rat had been working with me on my driving skills, but I let him take the wheel. I was far too shaken to drive. Rat eyed my sisters in the rearview, or maybe he was checking behind us for my father's men.

"Everyone alright?" he asked.

"That. Was. Crazy!" Ada said breathlessly, but excitement lit up her eyes.

As Rat pulled out onto the highway, I turned in my seat and found Antonia's grim stare. I could see Bass following closely behind us through the rear windshield. Antonia and I glanced over at Ada who was far too exuberant considering we'd nearly gotten killed. She'd always been an adrenaline junkie. She was the first to head toward trouble—even as a small child—it was usually her fault when we got involved in something we shouldn't.

By the time we'd gotten to the clubhouse, I'd told them everything. Antonia was crying silently, but had her jaw set in determination. Ada looked like she was ready to burn down the world. She and Abel had always been close. In fact, it had always amazed me how he'd managed to have a tight knit relationship with each of us, but never made it seem like he preferred one of us over the others. We all loved our brother unconditionally. He'd stepped in as that father figure for us more often than not.

"How can we help?" Antonia asked.

"We choose Abel," Ada said at the same time, venom all but dripping from her tone. "Fuck Mama and Papa both!"

Her outburst didn't surprise me or Antonia, but Rat shot a wide eyed glance at me. Bass was looking at her in shock, too. Ada was so much like Papa. Her emotions ran hot and cold. When you first met her she was calm and quiet, but piss her off? All bets were off. Thankfully, there was enough difference that she wasn't as cold hearted as Papa. She just loved Abel so much she was willing to do what was necessary for him. On top of that, the man had been protecting us for so many years, we couldn't help feeling an intense loyalty to him. Ada may have had Papa's wild mood swings, but she wasn't a sociopath.

Ada's steely emerald eyes met mine, leaving zero doubt of how she felt. She was reminding me why I felt such a close connection to them and always had. They loved as hard as I did. Of course, they were enough like me that I knew they were going to hate this next part.

"There is something I need from you two. Something that will help," I told them carefully.

Excitement shone in Ada's eyes, but Antonia looked suspicious. The look I gave her pleaded with her. Behave.

"I need you to go stay with a friend of the club's-"

"You can't send us away!" Antonia shouted and I sighed.

I didn't blame her. I'd had pretty much the same reaction when both Abel and Rat told me I couldn't help.

"If you want to help," I told her, "you'll do this for me."

"How is that helping?" Ada's chin jutted out as tears of frustration filled her eyes.

"Abel needs you somewhere safe until this is over. So do I," I added.

"Why can't we stay with you and the MC?" Antonia asked.

"There's an enemy of theirs that's about to strike. It wouldn't be safe for you and there's not enough men to watch you. That's why we're sending you to friends who can protect you." Both of them folded their arms over their chests. "It's only for a few weeks. Swear." I told them. Everything in me relaxed when I saw Antonia sigh.

"Fine, but we're not happy about this," she muttered.

Rat chuckled from the driver's seat. "Noted."

I was grateful he'd stayed silent and let me handle my sisters. We could all be a bit stubborn and I knew the best way to get them to concede.

We pulled into the parking lot of the clubhouse and I hopped out of the car and stepped over to where Hush was waiting by another running vehicle.

"I can't tell you how much this means to me, Hush." I cast a glance over my shoulder as Rat and the girls dragged their bags out of the trunk. "If anything happened to them-" I broke off as a sob threatened to escape.

"It won't. No one'll be lookin' for us. Just a father and his daughters, takin' a road trip to Arizona."

I eyed him. With his dark hair and features it was believable enough that my sisters could be his kids. I gave him a quick hug, then turned to my sisters. Their bags had been loaded into the new car.

Reaching into my pocket I pulled out a new burner phone and handed it to Antonia. "My number is in there. Call me every night." We hugged and chattered amongst tears. It didn't matter that they were only going to be gone for a short time. I wasn't going with them and it killed me.

Rat would love nothing more than to ship me off, too, but I'd refused. I wouldn't leave him and the others here to deal with everything on their own.

Handing Antonia a manila envelope, I swiped at the tears on my cheeks. "For anything you may need. There are new identities in there and a credit card. I'll pay it off, so buy what you need." I also handed her a fat stack of cash and her eyes widened. "Try to use this before the card if you can."

Hush reached over and wrestled the money away from Antonia. "I'll hold onto that for the drive," he rumbled.

Antonia shot him a pout, but then focused back on me. "What about you?"

"I'll take good care of her," Rat promised, wrapping an arm around my shoulders.

After another round of hugs and tears Hush finally growled, "Enough, let's get on the road."

"Oh!" I grabbed a bag out of the car we'd arrived in and pulled something out of it. Plopping the baseball cap onto Hush's head before he could say anything, I tilted my head and surveyed my work. "That'll do." I put hats on both girls as well. "You can take them off later," I told them, ignoring Hush's open mouthed incredulous look.

He muttered something under his breath before turning and opening the door. "Get in the car!" he barked, and the girls jumped to comply with my surly friend.

A month ago, my only worry had been marrying a stranger. Oh, to go back to those simpler times. *Simpler times like when Papa beat Abel and threatened my sisters so that I would do work for him.* I internally rolled my eyes. Out loud I told Rat, "I want to go to Abel's meeting with Papa."

He wrapped his arms around me and pulled me back against his chest as we watched the taillights disappear down the road. He chuckled, the sound vibrating through my body. "I wouldn't call it a 'meeting'.

It took a minute to understand. Of course, this wasn't like one company buying out another. There wouldn't be anything civilized about this take over. "I still want to help."

"Sorry, it's over."

"What?" I pulled out of his arms and stared at him. "What happened?" The speed at which Abel had reacted and gone after Papa was dumbfounding.

Rat gave a wicked smile. "We got what we wanted—a war."

CHAPTER 30

Rat

It'd been a long-ass Saturday already. My head was pounding from the tantrum Ari had thrown when I told her I wouldn't take her to go meet with her brother. He'd called yet another meeting between all our allies to make sure everyone was on the same page. This life was a constant chess match, one where the pieces might suddenly change sides. Making sure all the players were where you needed them to be often decided whether you'd win or lose. Only losing here meant people got killed.

Ari had already been through enough, finding out what she had about her brother and father, then having to send her sisters away. I didn't want to add to it. Also, there was the fact that Abel specifically said not to bring her.

My wife sure could pitch a fit, though. I wondered why I'd ever thought she was more mild-mannered than the other women. Sure, it took more to bring it out of her, but it was there.

I glanced over to where Bass was riding next to me, feeling his eyes on me. He arched his brow and I nodded, letting him know I was fine. There were zero doubts that everyone had heard our fight. It hadn't been a quiet one, but I'd finally won and Ari promised to stay behind at the clubhouse while we went to go talk to our newest allies.

We'd known as soon as we got back to the clubhouse that it would end up being the day Abel took over as Don. That's why it'd been so important to catch Ari up to speed and then to get her sisters the fuck out of town. The only leverage Sal held over Abel was those three women.

Ari hadn't bothered to give Celia or Alexandria any warning. We knew which side they'd be on and alerting them would've given Sal an early warning. Abel would've made sure to get his mother and sister out of the house before he and his crew had gone in.

Antonia and Ada were on their way to Tucson. Hush would drop them off with his prior chapter then head right back. He assured us the girls would be safe there with Lockout. He was Hush's brother-in-law, and apparently Cade knew him pretty well, too.

Sal wouldn't know where to look for his girls if he tried. Especially not since Ari had taken care of getting them new identities to hide with. When I'd asked her how she'd gotten them so quickly a guilty look had passed over her face. She explained that they'd been planning to run for a while, before we got married. I couldn't blame them. They hadn't had a lot of say in how their lives were going before now.

We pulled into the parking lot for the building where we'd agreed to meet with Abel and his new crew. As we walked in, all eyes swung our way. Glancing around the room showed that every one of Sal's former Capos—minus those Enzo had named—had decided to follow his son. It was fucking impressive and spoke to the trust these men had for Abel. That must be a huge blow to Sal's ego.

Unfortunately, the man was still alive. Abel hadn't gone in with the intention of killing him, but if it'd happened in the heat of battle it would've been better for everyone. Cut the head off the snake and the body wouldn't know where to strike. Those loyal to Sal would've eventually drifted out of our lives.

Ming rushed over and started administering to Abel's men. Most of them had flesh wounds, but a few were more serious. She focused on them first. Axel hadn't been thrilled to bring her along, but no one could refute how useful she was after a fight. It often meant she got to tag along with us when the other women stayed home.

Walking over, I crouched down next to her. "Anything I can do to help, Doc?"

"Put pressure on this," she snapped.

I complied, and pressed down on the man's thigh. He was leaned back against the wall and he groaned at the motion.

Abel came over. "Tell us what you need and we'll help," he told Ming.

The grin came unbidden as I listened to Ming start ordering around a bunch of mafia guys. The woman had balls of steel and I loved her for it. When there was an emergency it didn't matter to her who you were. You fell in line and helped or you got the fuck out of her way.

It took about forty-five minutes to get everyone patched up and for Ming to finally wave us away. "I'll finish taking care of them. You guys go have your meeting." She jabbed a guy with a needle and attached an IV to the port.

Cade had set up a connection that allowed us to get unlimited hospital supplies. They came in handy when paired with our resident doctor. Every man in our organization was happy to let Ming take care of them and avoid the hospitals.

Enzo arrived and came to sit next to me, his men lining up against the wall behind us. He held his tongue, but I could see the satisfaction there in his eyes. He'd never had an issue with the Italians, his beef had always been with Sal. The fact that he'd set that grudge aside to find out my identity was even more surprising now that I knew how much he hated the man. Enzo was getting exactly what he wanted now, though. Hell, we all were—all except Sal. Like Cade had said earlier in the day, Sal had brought this on himself.

Diego and the Zetas were the last to arrive. Axel and his brother hugged. Cade took over introducing the Italians and Russians to the Zetas.

"Thanks for coming," Abel said, and all eyes swung to him at the head of the table. "This isn't the best time for a coup, but there's not much we can do about that."

"Since when does anything ever happen on our timeline?" One man, sitting to Abel's right chuckled. That must be his new Underboss.

Abel and everyone else laughed along with Gio. He'd been one of Sal's younger Capos, so it made sense that Abel would've promoted him. The man was close in age with his new Don and clearly Abel trusted him.

"Did you lose any men?" Cade asked.

Abel's eyes darkened. "Five," he replied. We could all see the weight of that burden, it was written all over his face.

"They lost more, though," Gio said, and that got a few chuckles. Death was a constant in this business of ours. Whether it was a one percenter MC, Mafia, Bratva, or Cartel, it didn't matter. We all dealt with the same situations. There was always another enemy, or a rival looking to take what you had. You mourned your lost brothers, but all you could do was keep moving forward.

"My father escaped into the city. We won't rest until we find him. That doesn't mean we won't be helping with the Guzman threat," he told Cade. "We're behind you on that. Just let us know when and where to show up. Hopefully, we can take out the threat my father poses before Marco goes on the attack. He refused to leave quietly when I told him to," Abel explained.

We'd offered to help Abel with the original takeover yesterday, but he'd said he needed to do it on his own—him and his men. He wasn't wrong. They needed to trust that their new Don could lead them, without the help of anyone else, allies or not. The wolfish smiles from around the table were enough to know more bullets had been exchanged than words. Danger was an aphrodisiac to men like us.

"Is he holed up in his home?" Riggs asked.

"No. That belongs to me now," Abel told him. "From this point on our meetings will be conducted there. I just wanted a more neutral space for this first one."

More likely he wanted somewhere his father couldn't rally and get the jump on him before he and his men were ready.

"You think he's going to slink away like a kicked dog?" Enzo asked.

"No, he'll retaliate, and at the worst possible time for us. Expect him to attack whenever Marco gets to town." Abel gave Cade a knowing look.

"I expect they'll be working together, to be perfectly honest," Cade replied.

I'd bet my new found fortune that Cade more than suspected it.

Abel nodded. "I suspect as much as well." His eyes shifted to me. There was a question there that he didn't need to voice.

"They're on their way." I kept it cryptic, but knew he needed to know his sisters were safe. Theoretically, everyone in the room was on our side, but until the dust settled you couldn't be sure.

His shoulders visibly relaxed. "Thank you for that."

The meeting was quick. With the wild card—Sal—out of the picture it was easy to get all the men updated and eager for what was to come.

"Any news on the Guzmans?" Diego asked, his eyes flashing.

"Lorenzo just got to New York yesterday. That puts Marco, Raul, and him there. The twins are still in Chicago," I told him. Eyebrows shot up all around the table.

"I wonder why Lorenzo would leave California," Diego mumbled, shooting Axel a questioning look. The Juárez brothers knew the Guzmans far better than any of the rest of us. Diego had been pissed when he'd woken up and found out that we'd already killed Miguel. He'd wanted his own revenge on the man.

"Either they're grouping before they come here, or they ran into some kind of trouble over there," Axe said with a shrug. "Either way, we'll be ready when those fuckers come to town."

"It'll be any day," Cade said. His confident statement had men shifting in their seats. Our MC and the Italians were already spoiling for a fight. It didn't take much to get the other two groups of men ready. They'd already been living a constant battle day in and day out.

We split up after that and Diego came over and clapped a hand on my shoulder. "I have much to thank you for, it seems."

I grinned at him and shook my head. "I just did what any of us would have. How's Aarón?"

"Good, good. He finally gave in and took a position with me as our doctor."

It didn't surprise me. The older man was cool under fire and a damn good doctor—for a veterinarian.

"Come. I'll buy you a drink," Diego offered.

"It's not buying him a drink when you're staying with us and using our alcohol," Axel muttered.

Everyone chuckled as we headed out to our bikes. We'd sent the prospects down with a few cage rides to pick up the Zetas for this meeting. With the chance that the Guzmans would be coming to town soon they'd be staying with us. That was another reason Ari's sisters couldn't stay. We were full up. Last thing we wanted were gangsters of some sort chasing them around and flirting when we needed to be focused on a fight.

"Enzo, you're welcome to join us," I told my brother, and to my surprise he accepted.

The Italians were going back out to patrol the streets, so we didn't expect to see them. They'd only stopped hunting Sal and his men long enough to meet with everyone. It was going to be a busy few weeks, but we were all ready for it. It was past time to get this over with.

We'd gotten in a few new shipments of guns and passed those around as men left the building. I hadn't been kidding when I'd told Ari this was war.

* * *

Once we got back to the clubhouse everyone went directly to the living area. Trip started pouring drinks and we all sat around bullshitting. There wasn't much that would bond men together better than fighting on the same side. When you didn't have an enemy to fight yet, booze would work as a close second.

I wanted to go up and check on Ari, but we both needed some space to cool down. She'd been furious with me when I'd left. Despite her anger, she'd given me a kiss that bordered on vicious and told me to be careful.

Grinning, I lifted my beer bottle to my lips. She could be feisty as fuck. It turned me on. There'd been a time when I would have walked away from someone like that. Now—thanks to the other women—I knew how to handle it.

"Looks like marriage suits you." Enzo dropped onto a chair next to me.

I grunted in agreement and took another swallow from my beer.

"Where is your beautiful bride?" He brought his scotch up to his lips, not bothering to hide his shit-eating grin.

It hadn't taken long for Enzo to figure out I didn't like him fawning over my woman. Now he was doing it just to piss me off every chance he got. We may not have grown up together, but he acted just like my brothers in the MC. Affection filled me even as I told him to fuck off.

We were quiet for a moment, watching the men milling around talking and drinking.

"She's upstairs—pissed."

Enzo said something in Russian. It was guttural and I had no clue what it meant. If I had to guess, I'd say he'd muttered, "Women."

"Sorry to interrupt. Can I have a minute with you two?"

We looked up at Cade. I frowned. He looked...resigned, as though he didn't want to actually speak to us. My gaze dropped down to a manila envelope he was holding.

"Yes," Enzo said, standing.

I followed them out back. My curiosity was eating at me. Why was Cade pulling us out here to talk?

"Abel wanted to give this to you himself, but with everything happening..." Cade handed the envelope to Enzo. "He found it this morning once he had a chance to go through Sal's office."

Enzo flipped through the papers and his head slowly lifted. "You're sure this is true?"

Cade shrugged. "Abel found it hidden in Sal's office."

I looked over at the sound of paper crinkling and watched Enzo's fist ball up the documents. At my movement he realized what he'd done and handed the wad of paper to me.

Smoothing them out, I quickly scanned the pages. My heart felt like someone had curb stomped it. It was documentation of what had happened the night our family had been attacked.

"How did Sal get this?" I murmured. A name stuck out on the page and I slid a glance over to Enzo. His face was turning a mottled red. Ivan—our father's, and now Enzo's, advisor—had sold out our family. According to this, he'd been the one to tell the Sidorov's that we were home that night and gave them additional information that allowed them to bypass our father's security.

"Sal must have found this when he was looking for you," Cade said carefully.

My eyes narrowed on my president. He'd made some kind of connection that I'd yet to see. As soon as it clicked I felt my face pale. "She would have told me once she recognized our last name."

"Rat," Cade's voice held a note of caution. "She may not have been the one-"

I was gone before he could finish. My boots slammed against the wooden stairs as I took them two at a time up to our apartment. The door smacked into the stopper so hard it rebounded when I flung it open. I had to slap a palm on it to keep it from nailing me in the face.

Ari's response would've impressed me, if I hadn't been so pissed. She'd been sitting at her computer, typing away on a paper I knew she had due in a few days.

She didn't scream or panic. She ripped the headphones off her head, slid out of her chair and faced me in a fighter's stance. Confusion replaced the hard-edged look that had been on her face before she'd realized it was me busting in on her.

Her hands dropped down to her sides as she watched me warily. "Rat?" Her voice was soft, but uncertain.

CHAPTER 31

Ari

My husband had nearly given me a heart attack bursting through the door like he had. Now he was just standing there, breathing hard, staring at me with a wild look in his eyes.

I hadn't noticed the papers in his hand until he tossed them my way. They fluttered to the ground between us. Still, he said nothing, just watched me.

Biting back my irritation, I scooped up the papers and quickly read them. My eyes widened with every sentence.

"Abel found them in your father's office," he snarled.

My eyes shot up to him. Was he mad at me because Papa had these? They were devastating. It was some kind of correspondence between one of Enzo's men and the head of the rival family Rat had told me about. The family that had broken into their home and ultimately raped and murdered his mother and set him on a path to be raised by a psychopath.

"Oh, Rat. I'm so sorry. Do you know who this man is?" I looked down at the name again.

When he didn't answer my question my blood chilled in my veins. My eyes slowly lifted as the reason for his anger clicked inside my brain.

"Did you fucking find this for him? Did you find me for him?" Rat's voice was cold, detached. The fury that'd been burning hot a few minutes ago had morphed into a chilly hatred.

I think I preferred the blazing anger to this new emotion he was showing. It scared me. Not that I thought he would hurt me physically, but emotionally he could destroy me.

"I didn't." I shook my head with the admission. "I promise. I would have told you. I don't know how he got this." I lifted the papers.

Rat was still breathing hard, like he'd run a marathon. He moved toward me with the grace of a jungle cat and something tightened in my belly. I couldn't tell if I was terrified or turned on—maybe both. The way he was watching me was unsettling.

I turned my head as he started circling me like a shark in the water. I tipped my chin up and focused on those eyes, refusing to bow down to his mood. They were blue-gray right now. Usually, they were a deeper blue when he was angry. I couldn't read the emotion on his face and I didn't like it.

"Would you stop that?" I finally asked, exasperated. "You can be mad at me if you want, but I didn't do-" I broke off with a gasp when he bulldozed me into the wall.

His hand cupped the back of my head so it didn't smack into the plaster and his mouth latched onto mine before I had a chance to comprehend what was happening.

A moan bubbled up from my chest as his tongue fought with mine. This wasn't sweet, or tender. He was still pissed, although I didn't think it was at me anymore, and this was the way he was releasing some of that building frustration.

Wrapping my arms around his neck, I gave as good as he did. If this was what he needed I was fine with it. We'd all been stressed and in a constant state of turmoil for weeks now and a little 'I'm sorry that I accused you of betraying me, but I'm still really pissed' sex might be just the thing to help us unwind. I shoved him away a little and he let me. Then I shoved away from the wall and jumped into his arms, wrapping my legs around his waist and attacking his mouth with mine again.

Rat groaned and pressed me back into the wall so he could grind his length against my pussy. The pressure had need—molten and all consuming—pooling low in my belly. I could feel how wet I was.

He shoved my legs, and I slid down his body. Before I could ask what was wrong he unbuttoned my jeans and shoved them down to my feet before doing the same with his. He didn't bother kicking his boots off or fully taking off his pants.

I stepped out of mine just in time because he picked me back up, forcing me to wrap my legs tightly around him for balance. I let out a squeak of surprise and he growled into the skin of my neck. This was primal, there would be no sweet nothings murmured. If there were any words at all from him I'd be surprised.

We both still had our shirts on when he plunged into me.

"Ahhh!" I cried, screaming in delighted shock as he sank in, filling me. It didn't matter, I was ready for rough. I could feel the wetness dripping down my body.

He paused, pulling his head back and pressed his forehead against mine so he could look down into my face. His was a hard mask, but I caught the flicker of worry in his eyes.

Kissing him, I leveraged off the wall and bucked against him. It made us both groan and was all the assurance he needed that I wasn't hurt.

Rat's hips pulled back and slammed into me, pushing me further against the wall, trapping me between it and his hard chest. From there it was a race—and one with no rules. There was licking, sucking, biting, scratching—most of this from me—as we both strained and fought to come.

I wanted him to lose control. Even with the wild way this had started I could tell he was still holding tightly to a level of control that I wanted him to release. He was a dangerous man and I wanted him to fuck me as hard as he could. I wanted him to set this beast free. The slap of our flesh was loud in the silent room. Our breaths were coming like a freight train. I raked my nails over his shoulder blades and bit down on his shoulder simultaneously. His rough growl had my core clenching around him. If he wanted angry sex, I was more than capable of giving that to him.

Over the last month he'd more than made up for his original lack of experience in sex. I hadn't gotten a full night of sleep since our wedding night. It was like he felt he had to make up for lost time. The physical connection was helping us grow the emotional side of things that much quicker, which was a bonus. Plus, my husband knew how to get me off. How could a girl complain about that?

We'd been learning each other's bodies and what we liked. This was a first for us, though I was determined it wouldn't be the last. With every thrust of his dick there was a delicious little sliver of pain that was wracking my pleasure higher and I was so close to coming. A little lick of worry entered my brain. The intensity of the sensations was overwhelming and I wasn't sure I would survive it.

There was no stopping it. No stopping him. Not that I actually wanted that. My orgasm barreled down on me like a car and ran me over with its intensity. I screamed, pleasure drowning me from the inside out. My body was shaking and my mind soaked it all up. I'd been reduced to gasping moans.

I almost didn't hear him huff a long groan. Almost didn't feel him slam his cock as far into me as he could as he came. I nearly passed out. All I could do was hold on to him, my anchor in a storm.

Unsure of how long we stood there—well, he stood—I slowly came back to awareness. His large hands were cupping my ass and his top half leaned into me, pinning me to the wall and keeping him on his feet too. He was still chugging air, so I couldn't have been out of it for too long.

Kissing his cheek, I closed my eyes and waited for my heart to return to a normal rhythm.

"Jesus."

It was the first thing he'd said since he'd accused me of withholding information from him. "Yeah."

Rat sighed and let me unhook my legs from his waist. He slid out of me and I winced, knowing I was going to be sore later. Then again, he would be too. I cringed as he bent and pulled up his boxers and jeans and I saw the bloody welts on his back. *Oops.*

I searched around for my clothes and pulled them on. *Shit.* I felt his cum leak out of me and I had to take a steadying breath. We'd been using condoms because I hadn't had a chance to get to the doctor to get on birth control yet.

We'd have to deal with that later. What was done was done and the last thing on our minds had been a condom. I could see the turmoil roiling in his eyes, but I knew it wasn't from lack of birth control.

He raked his hand through his hair, making it stand in blond tufts. "Fuck, Ari. I'm so sorry."

I was getting used to my husband's moods. Most of the time he was a mellow guy, but that temper of his could crack like a whip, fast and sharp. I knew—without a doubt—he'd never hurt me, so it didn't frighten me anymore. The only thing I wasn't sure of was what he was apologizing for. He didn't keep me wondering for long.

"I shouldn't have just accused you like that." He scrubbed his hands over his face. "It wasn't fair. And this," his eyes clouded over when he looked down at me then himself.

Stepping forward, I covered his mouth with my hand, silencing whatever he'd been about to say. "This was hot. I loved it and will probably start picking fights with you so we can do it again."

Heat flared in his eyes and he nipped my palm. I smiled because it was his way of agreeing with me. He wrapped his fingers around my wrist and put his lips near my ear. His whispering breath made me shudder and my pussy clench. Just like that, I was ready to go again.

"I'm going to goad you into it if this is how it ends," he promised.

A smile played over my lips, but I schooled my face into a serious look and pulled back. "As for the other thing. I can't blame you for coming to that conclusion. I was helping Papa with stuff like that." I hurried on when his face clouded over. "It wasn't me, though. I promise. I would have told you the same day I told you about adjusting the video feed at the Guzman compound. That's the only thing I know about that I worked on for him that connected to you."

"I believe you," he said huskily, pulling me back into his arms, cuddling me close. "I should have trusted you from the get-go."

"So, how did your brother take that news? Do you know who it was that betrayed your family?" My curiosity was killing me.

"Shit!" Rat pulled out of my arms and headed for the door.

"Where are you going?"

"Ivan came with Enzo tonight. If I don't get down there Enzo and Alexis will gut him," he told me, pausing by the door.

I frowned. "You don't want him killed?"

Rat's smile was dark. "I don't want them to kill him before I have a chance to help."

I started to follow after him, but stopped in my tracks when my phone rang. Staring down at the name on the screen I debated on whether I should answer it or not. But, as we had just demonstrated, trust is important. I answered.

CHAPTER 32

Ari

"Uncle Nico!" I forced my voice to be bright and cheery even though I was feeling anything but that.

Desperately I ran through my options. Should I tell Uncle Nico what was happening with Abel and Papa? I quickly discarded that idea. Uncle Nico and Papa had known each other a long time. I wasn't sure what side of the fight he was going to come down on. He may have known Papa for most of his life, but he'd known us *all* of ours.

Uncle Nico was a very practical man. I had hope that if Abel could talk to him, Abel could make him understand why he had done this—that it was necessary.

"Hey, Ragazzina. I'm so sorry I missed your wedding."

The smile broke out over my face. He'd been using the Italian word for little girl as my nickname for as long as I could remember. Out of all the people my family was 'close' to, I'd always loved Uncle Nico and Uncle Dante most.

"Oh," I made a psfting sound, telling him without words that it didn't matter that he hadn't been able to make the trip. Maybe if the ceremony had been the one I'd wanted it would've mattered more, but as it was I didn't care. It had been Mama's vision, not mine. I'd gotten what I'd wanted from it, though—Rat.

"I'm also sorry that I don't have long to talk. I promise once I wrap everything up I'll come out for a visit. I need to meet your husband and make sure he's up to my standards."

I couldn't help but laugh. This was typical for him. He'd always been overprotective. Whereas Ada was Mama's favorite and Alex was Papa's I was pretty sure I was Uncle Nico's. My heart warmed in my chest. I just hoped he'd forgive us once he found out about Papa. I didn't want to lose this man from my life.

"It's a little late if he isn't, Uncle Nico. We're already married," I told him playfully.

"I know how to make things happen," he said.

He'd made the comment so deadpanned I couldn't tell if he was joking or not. I lapsed into horrified silence.

His laugh was short, but sharp and I joined him. I still wasn't sure that he wasn't dead serious. I knew exactly what Uncle Nico was capable of. If we hadn't grown up together—he wasn't that much older than me—and he'd proven that he would never hurt us, I'd probably be more scared of him than of Papa.

"Listen, I need your help."

"Oh, sure, Uncle Nico. What can I do for you?" I'd do anything for him under normal circumstances. These weren't usual situations that we were facing, so if helping him made him more likely to forgive Abel, I'd do whatever he asked of me.

"Dante's missing-"

I gasped "Oh my God! What happened?"

"Someone took him. I need your help finding him."

"Of course I'll help," I told him, then listened as he filled me in on what'd happened. When Raul Guzman's name popped up I swallowed hard. These Guzmans seemed to be everywhere.

"I'm so sorry," I whispered, my heart breaking. I hoped Dante was okay. "That's crazy. I'll do what I can, Uncle Nico. But-"

"What?" he asked when I hesitated.

"If I can't... if I can't find him, can I ask Viktor for help?" Rat had told me that he'd helped Papa once before to find someone that Uncle Nico had needed to track down. Probably asked the favor to make the Club more trusting of him. It felt like that was lifetimes ago and really it was only a little over two months prior. I waited silently as Uncle Nico considered that. It was hard for the mafia to trust those who weren't mafia. I was still considered to be a part of the family and through me, so was Rat.

"Do you trust him?" he finally asked.

"I do. He wouldn't tell your secrets," I insisted. "Well, to anyone other than his motorcycle club. He'd have to tell his president, probably. Since it could end up involving them. They wouldn't tell anyone else, though, and they're no friends to the Guzmans." *Trust me.* I didn't tell Uncle Nico about the trouble they were having with the Guzman brothers. I'd wait and speak with Rat about it first. Uncle Nico could be another powerful ally against them.

"Alright, whatever it takes to find him. Everything of mine is at your disposal, for both of you."

"I understand. I'll see what I can do and if I'm not having any luck in a few days I'll talk to Viktor." Relief coursed through me. I was a talented hacker, but with Uncle Dante's life on the line I didn't want to mess up and have him pay the price. Not for the first time, I was overwhelmingly grateful to have a husband even more skilled than I was.

My lips pursed together to remain silent as Uncle Nico told me everything that'd happened in New York in the last few days. I didn't want to interrupt.

"Thanks, Ragazzina," he finally said once the story was over.

Growing up in a mafia household, I'd seen things. That was inevitable, but it was like my world had vomited violence and death since meeting the MC. I didn't blame them, most of it was coming from my own family. I was surprised to realize it didn't bother me as much as it probably should.

Once—what felt like a lifetime ago even though it'd been mere weeks—I wanted out of this lifestyle. Going to school, getting a job, having a *normal* life, was my main goal. It was just hitting me now that being married to Rat meant I'd never reach that level of normal. I was fine with it. That had been a pipe dream anyway. I wasn't even sure I *could* be normal. The last month, despite the chaos, had its own smooth flow. The ups and downs felt so natural.

Worry had coated Uncle Nico's voice, even though he'd tried to conceal it. "We'll find him," I whispered. "I love you, Uncle Nico."

"Love you too."

As I hung up, I heard cheers and bellowing from downstairs. Remembering what'd happened before this phone call had me debating. Should I go fill in Rat on what I'd learned? Or start searching for Uncle Dante? Biting my lip, I thought about the look on his face when he'd thought I'd purposefully not told him about the documents that were still laying on the floor where I dropped them. This wouldn't be a secret, and it's not exactly withholding information, but...it was close enough to make me uncomfortable.

Mind made up, I went downstairs. It didn't matter if I told him now or in a few days, Uncle Nico would just have to realize that my loyalty for my husband came first. He would understand that. Anything he told me would be entrusted to Rat as well.

My steps faltered at the bottom of the stairs and my eyes widened at the scene in front of me. Someone had nailed boards into the wall and they had a man tied to them. He was already bleeding from a multitude of cuts. His eyes were nearly swollen shut and his head hung down—chin to chest. I could see his chest moving so he was alive, but passed out.

"Wake him up," Enzo roared at one of his men. The big burly fellow took a bucket of water and splashed it on the unconscious man.

My eyes moved from Enzo's ripped and very naked chest to where the water ran down onto the wooden floors of the clubhouse. It mixed with copious amounts of blood, staining the floorboards.

"Go back upstairs, Ari," Rat's voice called from across the room and every eye in the place shot over to me.

My eyes locked onto my husband. He was standing there—he'd also stripped out of his shirt—holding a wicked looking blade. Blood dripped down his forearm. It hadn't taken long at all for his Russian roots to surface. The look on his face was uncertainty mixed with anger. He didn't know how I'd feel about what he was doing. I could read it on his handsome face.

At least he'd gotten his pound of flesh.

I sauntered over to him, adding a little sway to my hips to add to the show a bit. "You think I haven't seen something like this before?" I asked him and fluttered my lashes when the spectators chuckled. "I watched my first man be tortured to death at twelve years old," I purred and ran my hand down his chest. He needed my permission to finish this and I was more than happy to give it to him. The man hanging there may not have physically raped and ended his mother's life, but he'd given the information to the men who had. He'd sentenced Rat to a childhood that no one deserved. For that, he deserved everything Rat and Enzo were about to give him.

Laying my lips lightly on his, I stepped back and stood near Cade and Riggs. Everyone was watching eagerly. Maybe I wasn't so different from these men after all. I had a bloodthirsty side to myself that I hadn't realized was there. The need to see these men avenged rode me hard, made me just as eager to see the end.

Ivan's begging—at least that's what the tone sounded like, but it was all a babble of Russian—died down into soft cries as the brothers took turns slashing and bleeding him.

Finally, Rat handed the knife to Enzo and told him to finish it. Enzo's men shuffled closer and we gave them space. This was the man who'd started the chain reaction that ended their beloved Pakhan's wife's life and lost him his youngest son. Rat told me that his father had died a few years later still searching for his missing son. Enzo had lost his entire family and Rat had never known them.

Enzo plunged the knife into Ivan's heart, and I watched as the light died from his eyes. Maybe later, when the bloodlust died down I'd feel guilty about my part in this. I watched as Rat walked over and reached up to touch my face. He paused when he saw the blood on his hands. The anguish on his face hardened my heart, and I knew I wouldn't feel sorry for the corpse they were dragging out of the clubhouse.

CHAPTER 33

Rat

I woke up the next morning feeling lighter than I knew was possible. Ivan and the Sidorovs were dead. Sully was behind bars and when he was eventually released he wouldn't live long. The man who'd raped my friend all those years ago had died a horrible—yet justified—death and was long gone. I had gotten answers, and more importantly, closure. I was working through my issues and there was finally a light at the end of that long dark tunnel.

Glancing down at my wife sleeping in my arms, I stroked her dark hair off her face. She had accepted me fully and willingly despite my faults. All we needed was to deal with Sal and the Guzmans and things would finally calm down. *As if that were some minor affair.*

Ari's green eyes fluttered open and she yawned, her cute nose wrinkling. I reached out and jabbed my finger into her open mouth, making her gag. She glared at me while I roared in laughter.

"Jerk," she muttered, smacking my chest, but she fought back a smile.

We laid there silently for a short time and I brushed my fingers up and down her back. Her skin was like silk. My internal debate on whether to stay like this or roll her over and fuck her was interrupted when she spoke.

"I have something to tell you."

My muscles stiffened. One day I might not have this reaction when she said things like that, but for now, there was too much happening for me to stay relaxed.

"I got a call from my Uncle Nico last night." She shifted up onto her forearms so she could see my face.

Frowning, I searched my memory. The name Nico sounded familiar.

"He's the man you sent information to for Papa... In New York," she told me and the lightbulb finally turned on. I nodded and waited for her to continue.

"I've known him and his brother—my Uncle Dante—my whole life."

Okay. I waited for her to get to the point. Why was the Don from New York City calling her? I'd done an extensive search into him before Cade and I had agreed to help Sal. Nico Romano was a fucking force of nature and we'd figured it wouldn't hurt to have him owe us a favor.

"He needs my help. Uncle Dante was taken and they can't find him. I asked him if I could ask you for help, and he consented." She blew out a breath before she told me the rest. "Raul Guzman is the one who took Uncle Dante."

My eyes narrowed on her face. "How do you know that?"

She shrugged her shoulders and smiled. "Uncle Nico has a way of always finding out what he needs to. If you think Papa's powerful, he's nothing compared to Nico."

We didn't think Sal was powerful, and he'd proved it by losing his position and wealth to his son. You can't stay in power when all you care about *is* power. He was paranoid and yet disloyal to every ally he tried to make. Which would actually explain the paranoia.

"Anyway, I thought you should know. Uncle Nico killed Raul Guzman. They didn't find Uncle Dante at his home, though, so he wanted me to help." Determination lit her green eyes. "I'm helping him," she told me.

Did she think I was going to talk her out of it? I wouldn't. I could see how much she cared for her uncles. It was written all over her face. Besides, this was yet another favor that Nico Romano would owe our MC. When we were racking up enemies left and right, it helped to have powerful men in our corner, or at the very least, not have another enemy.

"I'll help you," I told her and laughed when shock flooded her face. "They're your family, right?"

"Sort of an adopted family," she murmured, "but, yes."

Rubbing my thumb over her cheek, I nodded. I'd get more information about them later. For now, I needed to let Cade know about Raul Guzman. Another enemy had just been erased from our list and we hadn't even had to raise a hand to do it. I rolled out of bed.

"I'll be back. I need to talk to Cade."

Pulling on my jeans and a clean t-shirt, I glanced over to where Ari was kneeling on the bed—naked—watching me. My dick hardened at the sight of her. Groaning inwardly, I leaned over and gave her a quick peck on the lips. I couldn't linger or I'd never get out of there.

* * *

IT WAS an hour before I got back upstairs. When I entered our apartment, I found Ari furiously tapping on her keyboard. Her legs were tucked up underneath her in the chair, her shorts hiked up so that I could see a flash of her ass.

I wondered how hard it'd be to talk my wife into bed. Going to stand behind her, I stared at the screen and knew it wasn't happening. She was already looking for Dante.

Scanning the screen, I saw that she was looking through Raul Guzman's bank records. I shouldn't have been surprised, I knew she was a skilled hacker. There just hadn't been time to really see what she could do. I dragged my chair over and watched as she flew through screens, searching for anything that could help us locate Dante.

I saw her peek at me through the corner of her eye and rubbed my hand over her back. She paused and tugged the headphones off.

"There's so much to go through. The Guzmans have multiple properties scattered throughout the U.S. and Mexico and that's just the stuff that's legally theirs. There's no telling how many other places we'll find." She sounded defeated.

"Hey." My fingers grasped her chin, forcing her to meet my eyes. Desperation and worry mixed there in the green depths. "We'll find him. Okay?"

She blew out a sharp breath, then nodded. Smiling at her I brushed my lips over hers before I started up my own computer. We sat there for hours, pouring over every inch of Raul and his brothers' lives. Some of the information we found was going to help us with this war. My pride and respect for Ari grew by the minute as she dug up little nuggets of information that most of the hackers I knew would've never found.

She worked tirelessly. She was determined and motivated. This was where she could help us the most. Her skills had been downplayed, I realized, and I wondered if her father knew half of what she was capable of. I doubted it, or he would have had her doing far more for his organization than she had.

I came back up the stairs hours later and placed a plate with some sandwiches on it next to her. The clock shone bright, flashing the late hour. We'd been at this all day and well into the night.

"You need to eat."

Her bloodshot eyes met mine and she nodded absently. "In a minute."

"No," I told her firmly and grasped the handle of her chair, rolling her away from her desk.

Her angry gaze flashed to mine. Before she could argue, I cut her off.

"You're going to eat, shower, then we're getting some sleep. It's past midnight, Ari. I'm sorry, but your uncle is a big boy. He's going to have to hold out and wait until we can locate him. I won't let you run yourself into the ground searching, though."

"He could be hurt!" She raged at me, but then her full bottom lip trembled. "Or dead." It came out as a whisper.

I tugged her out of the chair and into my arms. "You can't help him if you're so exhausted that you miss something. He needs you fully rested and alert, that's how you'll find him."

Her stiff body relaxed against me so suddenly it was like she was melting in my arms. "Okay," she agreed with a sniffle.

After we'd eaten and washed, I lay with her in my arms. The minute her head hit the pillow she was out like a light. I remained awake, listening to her breathe, racking my brain for any little detail we might have missed. Not that we'd gotten through all of the information out there on the Guzmans, not by a long shot.

Sleep came, despite my best efforts to fight it off and with it came dreams. Not the nightmares of my past, it was the worries of what the future held that dipped into my subconscious while I slept.

CHAPTER 34

Ari

It'd been three weeks. Three long weeks of searching for Uncle Dante and still coming up blank. How were the Guzmans hiding him from us? All of Uncle Nico's resources had come up empty. The New York City Police Department hadn't had any more luck than we'd had. It was like he'd disappeared off the face of the Earth.

I sighed and hugged my knees to my chest as I stared out at the forest behind the clubhouse. This was my spot now. I'd claimed it. The picnic tables weren't as comfy looking as that wooden chair on the hill—which I now knew was Axel's—but they worked for me. Birds fluttered through the air and sang their hearts out in the early morning light.

Something made a chuffing noise down near the ground and I glanced down into a pair of mischievous brown eyes.

"Roo!" I scolded the little Boxer pup. "What are you doing out here alone?"

She put her front feet up on the bench, her nub wagging like mad. It created this whole body shake that had her wiggling around. I laughed and hauled her up onto the table with me. She instantly laid in my lap, letting out a contented sigh.

Ming's puppy had been a constant companion the last few days. I'd finished up the winter semester and was on a break. I'd offered to watch the pup while Ming worked. It gave me some company when Rat had to take time away for his job.

He still had clients to help and it was important that he keep those relationships strong. His business couldn't be put on hold for this. He worked like a man possessed when he wasn't busy with his regular job or handling club business and it humbled me. He didn't know Uncle Nico or Uncle Dante. He was doing this for me.

I cuddled the Boxer close and went back through everything in my mind. What was I missing? I'd found every property that each of the Guzmans owned. I'd poured over every asset they had to their names.

Warm, muscular arms wrapped around me from behind as Rat hopped on the table behind me. His legs bracketed my hips and he surrounded me. His lips brushed over the crown of my head.

"I'm at a dead end," I told him. Leaning back against his chest, I took comfort in his arms. His heartbeat was steady and strong against my back.

"We'll find him. It's only a matter of time." His deep voice rumbled through me.

I sighed. "I know. I just wish we could skip forward to that part."

"I know, baby. Me too."

I felt his hesitation. "What is it?"

"Marco landed in Austin an hour ago."

Rat had been keeping an eye out on all the local airports. Not even powerful mafia or cartel leaders could circumvent having to file a flight plan with the FAA. Ironically, a man in his position couldn't just sneak in. Too many eyes were on him, if he tried to enter illegally he would be caught. So instead, he just flew his private jet straight in.

Frustration ripped through me. If Marco was here, they were confident no one was going to find Uncle Dante. "Damn these Guzmans," I muttered. "I wish I could curse their names and them to the depths of-" I froze as something occurred to me. It couldn't be that easy, could it? I'd searched everything in their names. In their family's name. But what if?

"What?"

"Where's Axel and Diego?" I turned in Rat's arms and the look on his face told me I had a deranged gleam in my eye.

"Uhhh, kitchen, I th-"

I was off the table in one bound. Luckily, I'd taken the dog with me and hadn't flung her off my lap. She swayed groggily and glared at me as I plopped her on the ground then rushed off while she tried to find her footing.

Rat caught up with me easily. "What's going on?"

Giving him a wicked grin, I ripped open the door to the clubhouse. Everyone stared at me in surprise. My eyes zeroed in on the Juárez brothers and they glanced at each other with worried expressions.

"Are any of them married?"

"¿Mande?" Diego asked.

"What?" Axel said at the same time as his brother.

"The Guzman brothers," I said impatiently. My mind was going a million miles a minute and it was hard for me to slow it down to explain to them. "Do any of them have wives?"

"No," Diego said with a shake of his head.

My heart plummeted. I'd been so sure this was the missing piece of the puzzle.

"Wait," Axel said with a frown. "Doesn't Raul have a wife and a kid?"

"No, he never had children," Diego insisted.

Axel's frown deepened. "I thought he married some chick who had a kid. He eloped or some shit. His family didn't approve. She wasn't willing, but her family basically sold her to him since she was pregnant out of wedlock."

Diego's eyes narrowed on his brother's face. "That sounds familiar. Was that Raul?"

Both brothers sat searching their memories and I bounced from foot to foot while I waited. "Do you know her name?" I finally let the question burst out of me.

Their eyes focused on me.

"Uhhh, Carmen?" Axel muttered, "No, that's not right. Carmela...yeah, I think that's it."

"Where would they have eloped?" I asked, excitement nearly choking me.

"Reynosa," Diego replied.

"I don't know her last name," Axel said, the apology clear in his tone.

"I don't need it." I met Rat's gaze. His blue eyes were as triumphant as my own. "I can find her with what you gave me." Before either brother could dodge, I walked over and kissed each of their cheeks.

Bolting up the stairs, I heard Axel ask, "Seriously? She can find someone with a first name and a city?"

"Oh yeah," came Rat's proud reply. "She can."

* * *

"I FOUND HIM," I breathed out the sentence to the empty room. It'd taken me three hours from the time Axel had given me Carmela's name. Raul Guzman had put a property in upper New York in his wife's maiden name.

Quickly, I shot off an encrypted email to Uncle Nico then ran out of the room.

"I FOUND HIM!" I jumped off the last stair and launched myself into Rat's arms. Our bodies thudded together as he caught me with a grunt. My lips locked onto his and I kissed him long and deep as the men sitting in the common area looked on in amusement.

Rushing through the explanation, I laughed when Rat twirled me around.

"I knew you could do it," he murmured in my ear. "We need to talk about you and I working together once you graduate."

I pulled my head back and stared down into his face. "Really?"

"Fuck yeah, you're better than anyone I've interviewed recently."

He'd been trying to find someone he could hire to take off some of the workload. Business was booming and he was turning away more customers than he wanted to because he was only one man.

Rat walked out the door—while I clung to him like a baby monkey—giving us some privacy from the others.

"You want me to work for you?" I asked him, still amazed that the most talented man I knew thought I was good enough for that.

"With me," he corrected. "This is our business. What's mine is yours." His brows drew low over his eyes. "Speaking of, I haven't mentioned that we're multi-millionaires now, have I?"

A strangled sound escaped my lips. I licked them and tried again. "What?"

"Yeah, courtesy of Enzo. There was no denying him."

I shook my head in disbelief. The information wouldn't process, not after so many sleepless nights and the exuberance once I'd found Uncle Dante. My brain couldn't retain what he was telling me.

Burying my head in the spot where his neck and shoulder met, I groaned. "Tell me that again later. Can I have a nap now?"

He chuckled and stroked a large hand over my hair, sending goosebumps down my arms. I loved when he did that. "Sure, baby. I'd say you deserve it."

He walked me upstairs and tucked me into bed. I watched as sleep crowded my brain while he hung a sheet over the window to blacken the room for me. One last thought pushed through my sluggish mind. "I should call Uncle Nico. Make sure he sees the email."

"I'll call him," Rat told me and sat on the bed next to me. "You sleep." His large hand stroked my hair and I let my heavy eyelids finally close.

*　*　*

"Ugggghhh!"

I glanced up at Remi. "What?"

"I can't take all this *waiting*!" She wiggled her toes and I leaned back. Painting her toenails was impossible while she was squirming around.

"Hold still," I finally told her with a laugh.

She sighed, but dutifully went still so I could swipe more of the murder red polish on her toes.

"Well, I—for one—am enjoying the peace and quiet. You napped through the last shoot out we were in," Bridget said, then proceeded to bite her lip as she concentrated on smoothing the pink glossy color over my toes.

I knew from their recounts of it that Remi had actually been knocked unconscious, but they never let her live it down.

"Actually, you all were safe here during the last shoot out," Ming corrected.

"Fine," Remi conceded. "The waiting is still killing me."

It'd been a couple of weeks since I'd found Uncle Dante's location and Marco Guzman had shown up in Austin. We were all a little antsy, waiting on the other shoe to drop. The MC and their allies had been going out each night, searching for their enemies. So far, they'd been unsuccessful at finding Marco or my father.

It was a rare day that all us women had no obligations so we'd been having a movie marathon and were painting each other's toes. It was amazing to me how quickly and seamlessly these women had welcomed me into their group. My heart was so full it felt like it could burst at any moment. It didn't matter that I hadn't heard from Mama or Alex, or that Papa was still out there somewhere—watching. Being here with Rat, and these others who'd quickly become my family, was everything I'd ever hoped for.

I couldn't wait for Toni and Ada to get home so they could be a part of it, too.

"No! No, no, no," Ming laughed as she snatched up Roo, who had been face first in the popcorn bowl. We all chuckled as she put the bowl up and scolded the unrepentant puppy. Roo gave her trademark growl "ROOROOROO!" She gave us a long look to make sure we were focused on her, then wiggled off and farted. That got another laugh.

Sounds of motorcycles had all of us perking up. Frowning, I glanced down at my watch. We all came out onto the porch and watched as all the officers pulled in. I recognized Abel's car behind them, but there was another car in line.

"What are they doing home so early?" Julie asked.

"And who's with them?" Bridget frowned and shaded her eyes, as though that would help her peer into the darkened windows.

As soon as they parked and the man stepped out of the car I gasped and bolted off the porch.

"Ari!" the women called in shock and uncertainty.

I flung myself into Uncle Nico's arms and he chuckled, whipping me around in a circle. This had been a tradition of ours for far too many years to stop just because we were older.

"Hi, Ragazzina," he murmured.

I hugged him tightly and inhaled his scent. Cigars and sandalwood, it always reminded me of him. I pulled back and searched his face. "Uncle Dante?"

"Safe. He asked me to thank you and to tell you he's sorry he couldn't make this trip."

"What are you doing here, Uncle Nico?"

His smile was dark, dangerous. "I told you I'd be stopping by to make sure your new husband was worthy." His hazel eyes flicked over to where Rat was leaning against his bike, watching us.

I smacked his chest lightly. "Oh stop. He's good. I'm happy," I told him.

"Good. Then I can focus on the other reasons I'm here."

"Which are?" I asked, crossing my arms over my chest and raising my brows at him.

"To help Abel and to kill Marco Guzman." He watched me closely for my reaction.

I'd been so excited to see him I hadn't even thought about his reaction to Abel overthrowing Papa. Swallowing hard, I glanced over and found my brother at my side.

"I've been working with Nico for quite some time," he told me.

My mouth dropped open. "I thought you and Papa were..." Close. Was what I'd been about to say, but I didn't want to offend him.

Uncle Nico chuckled. The low rumbly sound didn't inspire any confidence. It was as much a warning as a growl from a wolf.

"I had to stay close to him. I knew one day he would try to betray me. Better to stay close so I could see it coming. When your brother approached me...well it only made sense for us to work together."

Shaking my head, I huffed out a breath. They'd all kept so much from me. I understood it. I wasn't a part of the 'business'. Personally, I appreciated how the Vikings did things. They had their women at their meetings and kept them apprised of what was going on. Apparently, it hadn't started out that way, though. I imagine that the girls bullied them into it. It seemed like something they would do. My need to be included was still there and I was much happier now that I was.

"Isn't there something else you came here to do?" A feminine voice asked.

A beautiful brunette stepped forward through the throng of people. All the bikers and women had gathered around to find out what was going on. She and I studied each other. Her gorgeous blue eyes were the color of the deep depths of the ocean. Finally, she smiled at me.

"I'm Havoc," she told me and held a hand out. I winced at how tightly she gripped mine and shook. She was strong. I felt like a midget staring up at her Amazonian glory.

"Hi, I'm Ari. It's nice to meet you."

"Ari, this is my fiancée," Uncle Nico told me.

My mouth dropped and before she could stop me I pulled her into a hug. "Oh my gosh! Now I'm really happy to meet you," I told her tearfully. When Uncle Nico's wife had been murdered I wasn't sure he would ever be the same. He'd grown colder, more harsh, even with his family. It'd broken my heart. Seeing him now, the change—however slight since Uncle Nico wasn't a mushy kind of guy—made me so happy.

Havoc laughed and squeezed me back. "Thanks."

"I know you!" Bridget gasped, as though she'd been trying to puzzle something out.

Havoc pulled out of my arms and smiled at her.

"You're Lyn!"

"I go by Havoc now," she said as she nodded, confirming Bridget's suspicions.

"I have to see your tattoo." When we frowned at her she continued, "Gunnar gave her this gorgeous tattoo, but I never got to see the end product."

Lyn started to lift her shirt only to glare at Uncle Nico when he gripped her wrist hard.

"No," he growled.

All of us women rolled our eyes because of his demand. He didn't want his woman to lift her shirt in front of the other men. I knew Rat wouldn't have reacted any differently.

"Come inside," Ming offered and everyone migrated into the building.

CHAPTER 35

Rat

"We appreciate the assistance," Cade told Nico.

The Mafia Don's gaze locked on mine. "As did I when Viktor helped me out."

I shrugged. "Ari was the one who found your brother."

"She told me that you helped and there was that other...thing you assisted with." His gaze shot over to where Havoc was standing with the other women.

The woman I'd tracked down for him had been Havoc. I'd just been doing a favor for my future father-in-law at the time, but it seemed to have worked out well for Nico and Havoc in the end.

"Either way, I appreciate it," Nico continued. "Besides, I have a score to settle with the Guzmans."

Cade raised a brow. "Get in line, brother."

Nico's grin was feral. "I figured I'd help you with Marco, then I'd do you a favor by taking out the other brothers." He used the favor like it was a demand. He wasn't offering to kill the twins for us, he was stating a fact.

Cade leaned back in his chair, his gaze flicking lazily between Nico and Abel. "If you have a score to settle, that's not much of a favor to us."

Nico grinned. There was respect in his eyes. Cade had that effect on people. "I suppose you're right. Fine. What would you like? For services rendered?"

"I'm sure there will be something in the future we'll need help with. We'll let you know then what we need."

Nico considered this, then nodded his agreement. Favors were the most valuable form of currency and Cade never missed the opportunity to have someone owe us one.

The rest of the meeting went quickly. Our women were in the common area, chatting and hanging out, but Havoc joined us. Her arms were folded over her chest and she let the Don do the talking, but there was a dangerous air surrounding her. I had no doubts that she could hold her own.

When Nico told us she'd be coming with us when we went out looking for Marco no one objected. What he did with his woman was his own business. I was just glad mine would be staying here, safe.

"One hour, then we're on the move," Cade told us as we filed out of the room.

We piled into the common area and I watched quietly as Ari talked and laughed with her brother, Nico, and Havoc. She had this ability to charm damn near anyone and I was not immune to her. I was so far in over my head that the idea would scare the fuck out of me if the thought of losing her didn't freak me out more.

I stood and walked outside, needing a minute alone to sort out all the emotion roiling around within me. Shoving my hands into my pockets, I went to stand and look out over the forest Ari loved to watch so much.

"Didn't feel like partying?"

The corner of my mouth tipped up as Bass walked out of the late evening shadows and stood shoulder to shoulder with me.

"How do you always know when something's eating at me?" I asked him.

He laughed and hopped up onto the picnic table. "That's what brothers do, right?"

That was probably true, though I wasn't one who would really know. The world I'd grown up in was one where you had to fight for everything you needed. If you didn't steal food, you didn't eat. Oftentimes, I went hungry to ensure that the younger kids had dinner. I'd known—even then—that kids shouldn't have to adopt that kind of mentality so early on in life. The only time our group banded together was at night. It was safer that way—for everyone. In the daylight hours, it was every man for himself.

"So, what is it?"

I looked over at him in confusion.

"What's bothering you?" He gave me his signature grin. The one that drew all the ladies to his side. It was a gift, that was for fucking sure. The single members of the club had celebrated when he'd started pursuing Julie. It was hard for them to get any action when the resident pretty boy flashed that smile in a woman's direction.

It occurred to me that I'd never seen Ari respond to him in any way other than with sibling type affection. Not that I suspected Bass would ever cross that line. It was almost as though my woman didn't see anyone else that way. How the fuck had I gotten so lucky?

Bass nudged me as I took the place next to him on the table. I leaned forward with my elbows resting on my knees. Just because I was in therapy didn't mean I wanted to talk, or knew how to put my feelings into words. Shit, who knew it was possible to have this many emotions? I took a page from Hush's playbook and shrugged.

Bass shook his head at me and then turned to study the property. "It's not a bad thing to talk shit through, you know. Sometimes it helps."

I shot him an irritated glance. Bass was much more outgoing and outspoken than I was. Maybe that was why we gravitated toward each other. We were polar opposites.

The sound of laughter floated on the night breeze.

"She's a good woman."

I nodded. "She is," I said.

"When we found out it was you getting married..." He paused

looking for a way to phrase it that wasn't offensive as hell.

I laughed. "You thought I was fucked."

Bass had the decency to look sheepish. "Yeah, Bro. Then I saw Alexandria and I swear I was planning your eulogy in my head."

We both chuckled at that.

"But even in that situation you managed to find the right girl for yourself." He shook his head in amazement. "You're like a cat."

I shot him a disgusted look. "What the fuck does that mean?"

"You have nine lives and you always land on your feet," he told me with a half-smile. "Plus, you're pretty cute." He batted his lashes and puckered his lips my way.

"Fuck you," I said, laughing. He was such an asshole.

"Nah, but seriously. I'm glad you found someone to love. If anyone deserves that shit, it's you." With that he stood and walked back in to join the others.

There wasn't much I could say since his words had hit me like a boot in the gut. As soon as he said it, it clicked. Love. That was what this was. No wonder I hadn't recognized the feelings rolling around inside of me. I hadn't been shown a lot of that particular emotion in my life. Not that I could remember anyway.

I followed the sounds of laughter back into the clubhouse. It didn't take me long to find Ari. Linking our fingers together, I led her upstairs to our room. I wasn't ready to put myself out there and tell her what I'd just discovered, and I knew Bass would keep my secret. That didn't mean I couldn't show her, in the only way I knew how.

Threading my fingers through her hair, I lowered my head and kissed her. When her lips softened, I took it deeper, stroking her tongue with mine.

"Rat," she moaned and pulled back. "What are you doing? You guys are leaving in a bit."

"There's time," I told her and pulled her into the bedroom. I laid her down on the bed, taking my time stripping her of her clothes. I kissed each inch of skin that I bared—taking extra time to swirl my tongue around her nipples. She was practically vibrating by the time I buried my head between her legs.

Her soft sighs and needy groans were like music to my ears. Flicking her clit with my tongue, I slid a finger inside her wet heat and had to bite back my own hoarse growl. She was so fucking tight. My dick hardened further and I had to fight to keep things slow.

Ari was grinding her hips, rubbing her pussy against my face, and I fucking loved it, but we were going at my pace. To punish her for trying to take her pleasure into her own hands, I lifted my head and licked my lips.

"Please," she moaned then threw her head back onto the bed in frustration when I kissed the inside of her thigh. Her hands went to my hair and she tried to direct me back to where she desperately needed my attention and focus.

Prying her hands off my hair, I pushed them down to the bed and held them there. Her head lifted and those green eyes flashed at me angrily. She wanted to come. I chuckled and ran my tongue from the bottom of her pussy all the way up to her clit. I soaked in her gasp, her scent, her taste. She was mine, all fucking mine.

Releasing her wrists, I used my hands to spread her thighs wide and dipped my head again.

"Rat!" she squealed and bucked in my arms when I licked her asshole.

I locked an arm over her hips to hold her in place and arched a brow at her. "Didn't like it?"

Her mouth was hanging open, shock written all over her face. "I… I don't know. You shouldn't do that."

"Why not? Did you not like it?" I asked her again.

Her face turned beet red. Slowly she shrugged. "I don't know, it's… dirty."

I smirked at her. "That's what makes it hot. It's alright, Baby. We'll try that again some other time." *When she is more comfortable with me,* I thought. Her ass was entirely too sexy for me not to pay it any attention. I lightly bit the inside of her thigh and grinned to myself when she jumped.

Going back to my original task, I ate her out like a fat kid eating cake. Ari was thrashing her head on the bed, moaning and urging me on, not that I needed the encouragement. She was drenched for me, and I fucking loved it.

I knew she was close and I kept up the steady rhythm of flicks with my tongue until her body arched off the bed. I wasn't entirely sure that if my arm wasn't anchoring her down she wouldn't have flown off it in her ecstasy. I slid my finger inside her again so I could feel her walls squeeze and convulse around it.

Reaching over, I grabbed a condom, shucked my clothes and rolled it on. Her eyes were opening lazily when I thrust inside her and her mouth formed a perfect little *o* at the sensation of my dick filling her up. It felt amazing for me as well.

Her silky-smooth legs wrapped around my hips, pulling me closer. With a groan I started moving. She used her legs and hips to match my thrusts and I felt a savage grin split my face when the headboard started bashing into the wall.

It didn't matter that she'd just finished, I could tell Ari was building back up to another orgasm. Her pussy walls were fluttering around my cock. Reaching between us I rubbed her clit and watched in fascination as she broke apart around me again. The squeezing of her inner muscles was too much, and I came right along with her.

She pulled me down so that I was laying on top of her, head pillowed between her breasts as we both caught our breath. Her nails scratched against my scalp and every time she did it I felt my dick kick in response. She experimentally squeezed her pussy and then laughed softly when she caused aftershocks to roll through my body again. It drew out the pleasure of my own orgasm and I laid there, completely wrung out—undone by the woman beneath me.

I groaned and glanced over at the clock. "I have to go." My voice sounded guttural, even to me.

She sighed. "Okay. Be safe, alright?"

I leveraged up on my forearms and gave her a long slow kiss. "Always."

Ari was already asleep by the time I finished dressing. I paused in the doorway and watched her sleep for a minute. Shutting the door behind me, I walked out to go join my brothers for the hunt.

CHAPTER 36

Ari

I jerked awake and laid there in the dark listening for what woke me. There was no rumble of motorcycles to indicate the guys were back yet. They'd been going out each night trying to find Marco and hadn't had much luck so far. I grabbed my phone, it read one a.m. I set it back down and groaned. They wouldn't be home for another few hours.

Getting out of bed, I pulled on my jeans, a black sweatshirt Rat had left on the end of the bed, and my sneakers. The hairs on the back of my neck were standing on end. I wasn't sure why. I clipped my switchblade to my waistband.

Going downstairs, I made a mental note to ask Rat for a gun for myself. It would've come in handy right now as my anxiety and the feeling that something was very wrong weighed on me. It was dark and quiet inside the clubhouse, so I wasn't sure why I was feeling this way.

Trying to shake off the uneasy feeling, I stepped out onto the back porch. Crickets sang and the light breeze brought that wonderful, clean smell that I'd come to love. You didn't get that fresh scent in the city, it was only out here where there was grass and trees.

Sighing, I started across the yard toward Cade's house. The others had fallen asleep in his living room in the middle of tonight's extended movie marathon. We'd moved it over there after the guys had left. We were watching all of the Marvel movies in order and Cade's house was more comfortable. I'd wanted to sleep in my own bed and had gone back to the clubhouse. I'd also wanted to be there for when Rat got home.

Pop, pop, pop.

I froze and dropped to a kneeling position. Holy shit. That was gun fire and it was coming from the front of the property. I needed to get out of the open. Surging to my feet, I sprinted hard toward Cade's.

Before I knew it, I was up on his porch and the door jerked open. Remi slammed into me and Bridget screamed when she rammed into her friend's back.

"Shhhhhh," Remi and I hissed at her. Bridget slapped her hands over her mouth, her wide blue eyes staring at us over them.

"Sorry," I whispered. "Did you hear that?"

"Yeah," Ming said in a grim voice. Anna and Julie were behind her and we were all standing by the door.

"You don't think that's Marco? Do you?" Anna asked.

"Or Papa," I said darkly. "I bet it's one of them. Why would our own guys be shooting off their weapons?" Cade had left six men behind—a mix of MC members and Zetas—to guard the clubhouse while they went out searching for our enemies. The men had gotten sick of playing defense and decided to go on the attack. In order to do that they needed to figure out where Marco was hiding.

"Maybe they got bored?" Julie asked, hope threaded through each syllable.

Gunshots rang out again, and we turned and saw dark figures running toward the clubhouse. I counted at least eight, too many to be the guards Cade left behind. The guys had been certain neither Papa nor Marco would come for anyone here. Clearly, Marco didn't believe in not attacking families. As for Papa...well he never used to do things like that. Who knew now what he was capable of?

"Does anyone have their phone? Someone call the guys," I hissed, cursing that I didn't bring mine.

Before anyone had a chance to do so, one of the shadows paused and we all sucked in audible breaths and held them.

Bridget squealed softly—her hands muffling some of the sound—when the man made a quick motion and the whole group started sprinting our way. They'd spotted us.

"Run!" Ming called out.

"Split up," I suggested and then ran to the side railing and vaulted over it. I wasn't wasting time with the steps.

"Zig zag if you can," Remi panted as we moved away from the clubhouse, then we all spread out as we sprinted toward the forest.

The moon was bright, but as soon as I entered the tree line the shadows deepened. I heard the shouts of the men following us and winced as the cracks of gunfire split the air. They were far too close for comfort and I heard a few bullets go zipping past.

Keeping an eye out around me, I ran, lungs burning. Stopping meant death. These weren't our men, there was no way they'd shoot at anyone on this property until they knew who it was for fear of hitting one of their own.

A sob of gratitude caught in my throat as I spotted a tree with a low hanging branch. Daring a glance over my shoulder, relief poured over me when I didn't see anyone directly behind me. They were back there though. I could hear them crashing through the forest over the sound of my heartbeat in my ears.

Reaching the tree, I jumped and grabbed the limb, using my other arm to wrap around the trunk. I scurried up and went one limb higher to be on the safe side. Pressing my back to the trunk I hid in the foliage as two men ran into view. They paused beneath the tree and I placed a hand over my mouth. They were listening, trying to determine the direction I went and it felt like my heaving breaths would give away my position.

"Where the fuck did she go?"

"To ground, most likely. She's hiding somewhere around here," the second man answered his friend.

"Split up. If you find her and it's Sal's kid, don't kill her. We're supposed to bring her to the meeting place."

"What if I find one of the other women?"

"Kill them. Marco's orders."

"Why does Marco give a shit about *this* girl?"

The second man didn't answer. Instead, they split up and ran off. I listened to the sound of them gaining more distance from my hiding spot. I thanked everything holy that I'd enjoyed climbing trees as a kid, but I needed to get back down and go find the other women. My family was in danger and I couldn't hide up in a tree all night when they were. *MY family. My new family. How quickly my life changed.*

Hearing that my father and Marco had teamed up made me so angry I wanted to scream. That wouldn't help anyone right now, though, so I stayed quiet and seethed on the inside. The absolute lows that my father had sunk to disgusted me.

I was about to hop down to the lower branch when the sound of footsteps crashing through more brush made me pause.

"Gotcha." A man laughed, low and evil.

I froze and scooted further out onto the limb I was on, so I could see what was going on. Below me Julie had a gun trained on one man while another circled behind her.

"I'll shoot you. Don't come any closer," she told them. Her voice was steady, strong, but the gun shook lightly in her hand. "I'll get at least one of you bastards," She promised.

The men chuckled and continued circling her. They were enjoying toying with her. The anger that'd been building inside of me exploded from every pore. Ada wasn't the only one like Papa. I had that psycho's blood running through my veins, too. I glanced down at the ground then at the man standing nearby.

Taking my switchblade out of the sheath—I'd started carrying it with me everywhere once Marco had come to town—I flicked it open and prayed I didn't misjudge the distance.

Everything happened in slow motion for me. I leaped off the tree branch and my heart crawled its way into my throat. I had to grit my teeth together to hold in the scream that gravity was trying to force out. It felt like my fall took forever. Thankfully, I collided into the man's body and wrapped my legs around him, my arms dropping over his shoulders, knife hand sinking the blade into his chest. It was a testament to his size that me crashing into him didn't send him immediately to the ground.

The impact knocked some of the wind out of me, but I didn't have the luxury of recovering. I screamed loudly, angrily, pulling the knife from his chest. I grabbed a fistful of his hair and yanked his head to the side and felt my knife bite into his flesh once again. Dragging the edge across his throat was the easiest thing in the world to do as I watched his friend—whose mouth was open in shock—finally snap out of his trance and lift his gun toward Julie.

There wasn't time to call out to her. Three shots rang out—deafening in the still night. My ears were ringing as the man slumped below my weight and we crashed to the ground. I felt his wet, hot blood on my hand and arm, but I ignored that.

"Julie!"

Scrambling to my feet, I raced forward, then stopped next to her. She stood over the man she'd killed, staring down at him with a blank look on her face.

Touching her arm, I caught her attention. Her brown eyes met mine and she blinked. "Gunnar's been teaching us all to shoot," she said in a monotone voice. She looked back down at the man.

"You did so good," I told her in a soothing tone. She was in shock.

That seemed to snap her out of her stupor and I was glad she recovered quickly. Determination filtered over her features, and I breathed a sigh of relief. These women were strong and I was damn proud to call myself one of them.

I bent and tugged the gun out of the man's lifeless hand after putting away my knife. Pulling the magazine out, I checked how many rounds were left.

A scream sounded off to our left followed by more gunshots. Julie and I exchanged glances and ran off in that direction. I wasn't about

'TIL ENCRYPTION DO US PART

to let these assholes kill my family. I shoved the magazine back inside the gun and pulled the slide back just enough to see brass before releasing it forward. I was locked and loaded.

We burst into a clearing and three gun barrels swung our way. I instantly shoved Julie's arm down. She'd reflexively pointed her weapon at the people in front of us.

"Whoa! It's us. Don't shoot," I called out in a low voice. I didn't want to alert any of Marco's men who might be nearby.

Remi swore and lowered her gun. Anna and Bridget followed suit. "Fuck. Are you two okay?"

"Yeah, we're fine. Where's Ming?" Julie looked around for her sister.

"We haven't found her yet," Anna said softly. She moved toward me and her eyes widened. "Are you sure you're not hurt?"

Glancing down, I realized I still had the man's blood all over me. "It's not mine."

Anna nodded silently.

"She would've circled back to the house," Julie said. There was confidence and pride on her face.

"Why would she do that?" I asked. It was suicide to go out into the open with these guys hunting us. "Marco's men are out there."

"How do you know it's Marco's men?" Remi asked, checking the guy's pockets that they'd killed.

"I heard them talking while I hid up in a tree."

She looked up and she and Anna exchanged a surprised glance.

"I know how to climb," I said dryly. I may have grown up a rich girl, but I'd still been a kid...and a mobster's kid at that.

"You should have seen her. She jumped off a branch and landed on a guy's back. Slit his-" Julie broke off and swallowed. "I'm going to throw up later," she told me.

"You and me both. Let's go find your sister," I replied. I couldn't dwell on what I'd done or I might puke right along with her. I knew I wasn't going to forget the feel of a knife slicing a throat anytime soon.

"Let's go. She would have gone back to find anyone who might have been hurt," Julie said as we all started jogging back toward the clubhouse.

"Of course she would," Remi grumbled.

"She's a doctor," Bridget said, as if we didn't all know that. "She's sworn to help people. She wouldn't be able to hide while they were injured."

"That puts her at even more risk," I told them. It made her a vulnerable target, and I assumed most doctors wouldn't hurt anyone.

"No. If someone tries to kill her, she'll fight back," Anna huffed as she trotted next to me. "She took out a bunch of guys with a homemade firebomb thingy down in Mexico."

My brows shot up. *Damn.* Ming was a badass. That made me feel better about her odds if she had circled around.

"Plus, Gunnar has taught us all how to shoot guns now," Bridget said.

"Shhhh," Remi whispered as we approached the tree line.

We squatted down and surveyed the open area silently for a moment.

"This is going to be the dangerous part," I whispered, keeping my voice low. "There's zero cover until we get back to the buildings."

"Maybe we should keep someone here to like… I don't know snipe people or something?" Bridget suggested.

Remi and I exchanged an amused glance. She was trying to help, but it was clear Bridget still thought the action scenes in movies were real.

"We'd need a rifle for that, Bridge," Remi told her. "These pistols won't be accurate enough."

"Plus, it's too dark out here to see our targets," I added.

"Was worth a shot," she grumbled, and I squeezed her hand in support. It hadn't been a terrible idea. We just weren't equipped to execute it.

"What do we do?" Anna asked.

"I think you and I should go search for Ming. These three should go find a spot to hide in the woods until we come back for them," I said, addressing Remi.

"Agreed," she said solemnly.

"Not agreed," Julie hissed. "That's my sister out there and we're not letting you go alone."

"The less of us, the better," I insisted. "We're a smaller target that way."

"Jules. Please," Remi said. Anna and Bridget were wearing matching stubborn expressions, but all three women softened at that.

"We can't send you off alone," Bridget said, her voice breaking in the middle of the sentence. This wasn't easy for them.

"We're the better shooters, and out of you three you're good enough to protect these two," Remi told her. "We need you to stay with them and keep them safe."

"I'll watch out for Remi. I swear," I added.

Julie glared at me. "We don't want you getting hurt either, you idiot."

She really wasn't happy with this plan, but something warm and fluttery filled my stomach. It felt really nice to have friends who cared about your wellbeing.

"Go hide. We'll find you later," Remi said.

We hugged them and then faced the open space between the woods and house again.

"Ready?" Remi asked. It sounded like her teeth were clenched together.

I didn't blame her. This was possibly going to suck big time. It just depended on how many of Marco's men were hiding out there in the dark.

"GO!" I hissed and bolted from the tree line with Remi right on my heels.

CHAPTER 37

Rat

"Whoa, whoa, slow down, Scout," Cade barked into his phone. His shoulders stiffened and his eyes shot around the circle of men standing around him.

He hung up the phone and without another word sprinted for his bike.

"What the fuck is going on?" Nico yelled as we all raced behind him. Cade was fucking fast and out distanced us easily.

"Guzman's men attacked the clubhouse!"

My steps faltered and I nearly fell as Abel slammed into me from behind. We'd been checking out a warehouse. One of Enzo's informants had said that they suspected something was happening there. We'd found signs that Sal had likely been holed up there, but he was long gone now. I found my footing and raced for my bike.

"Fuck!" I couldn't help the shout. All the women were at home—sleeping. If anything happened to them... The thought was too fucking horrific to even think about. Cade and I were the first on our bikes—despite my stumble I was faster than all of these men, including Cade—and out of the lot as the rest of us reached theirs in a large pack.

Glancing over my shoulder, I saw Abel's car as it skidded out of the lot, Nico and Havoc riding with him. Enzo, Diego, and his men were checking another area of the city. There was no time to call them and we were riding too fast to try a call on our bikes. Hopefully, Abel or Nico would contact them. We could use all the help we could get.

It was a race now, and we were way behind. The throttle was pegged, but it felt like we were crawling. Gritting my teeth, I took a corner faster than I should have and nearly tipped over. Sparks flew off the pipe as it scraped across the pavement. Muscling it back into line, I poured on more speed on the straight away.

We didn't bother with stealth. We'd left guards at the clubhouse, but the idea that these men would go after families—innocents—was beyond evil. As far as they knew they were attacking a place where women were home, sleeping soundly. All they saw were easy targets.

When we roared into the parking lot to our property we saw Scout come running up. "Ming and I have three of our guys over here. She's patching them up. Mostly flesh wounds."

We hurried over and found Ming working against the side of Cade's house, her back to it as she stitched up one of the men. He and the others—despite being hurt—had their guns drawn, eyes watchful.

"We sent Ramón and Trip to try to find the others," Scout told us.

"They weren't in the buildings?" Cade asked sharply.

"No, they ran into the forest. We did our best to try to take out as many of the Guzman men as possible, but we lost track of everyone."

"How many were there?" Steel asked.

"And how many are left?" Came Gunnar's question.

"Twelve total. Four had us pinned down out front when the other eight took off toward the forest. We managed to kill these four." He motioned to the bodies scattered around the grounds. "We heard one of the women scream and the way the men took off we figured it was to go after them."

"Move and we'll splatter your fucking brains all over this driveway."

We all froze as someone called out to us from the dark. As one unit we turned to face them, but I already had a smile on my face. I recognized her voice. "Julie! It's us. It's safe to come out," I called out to her.

The relief was strong when Julie, Anna, and Bridget ran out of the dark and into the arms of their men. It was comical to watch Anna pause in front of Riggs before my brother in arms jerked her forward and crushed her against his massive chest.

I glanced around. "Where are Ari and Remi?"

The women shot each other worried looks. "They came up here to find Ming," Bridget said.

Julie was already crouching by her sister's side, checking on her.

"We split up because they said it would be safer," Anna said, her words muffled in Riggs's hold.

"That was," Julie paused and looked down at her watch, "over twenty minutes ago." The last part of the sentence was whispered in horror. "We waited too long. Did they come out here?" Her eyes darted between Ming and Scout.

"No," Scout said grimly. "We tried to go look for all of you. Two of our guys are still out in the woods-"

"Jefe!"

We all turned and watched as Ramón and Trip appeared out of the dark. They were dragging one of Marco's men by the feet.

"This fucker weighs a ton," Trip huffed and dropped his foot as they stopped in front of us. "He's the only one we found out there—alive anyway. Was that you girls?" he asked with a grin.

"Yeah," Bridget responded. "Remi, Julie, and I each shot one. Ari slit the throat of another."

All the men in the circle focused on her—shocked. We shouldn't be. Time and time again these women had proven what they were capable of when backed into a corner.

"Where the fuck is my sister then?" Abel growled, shoving his hands through his hair in agitation.

I walked over and bent down toward the unconscious man. I slapped his face a few times until his eyes fluttered and he moaned. "Where are our women?" I asked him once his eyes opened and focused on me.

His grin showed bloodied teeth. "With her dear ole' Papa." His eyes rolled back.

"Nope, fuck that," I muttered and grabbed him by his shirt, hauling him into a seated position. I drew back and punched him in the face. That knocked him out of his stupor. Blood sprayed, but I ignored it. He groaned and his eyes rolled wildly as he looked for an escape route.

"Where the fuck are they?" I asked again.

"These aren't Sal's men," Abel said from directly behind me. "Either this guy has no fucking clue what he's saying or our father is working with Marco."

"In the desert," the man moaned, realizing keeping shit from us was only going to earn him an ass kicking.

"They're out in the desert?" Nico asked, crouching next to us.

"Where?" Steel barked. We'd all surrounded the man now and his eyes widened seeing so many pissed off faces around him.

"I can take you." It was his last pathetic attempt to get out of this alive.

*　*　*

WHY DID time move so slowly when you were desperate to get somewhere? The drive out to the desert meeting spot that Marco and Sal had set up only took us thirty minutes, but it felt like we rode for an hour.

We parked far enough away that we wouldn't alert whoever was there that we'd arrived. After getting off his bike and getting directions from Marco's man, Steel stepped up to the man, putting a hand on either side of his head. The man's mouth opened wide as he started to plead for his life. He didn't get the chance as Steel jerked and snapped his neck. He let his body crumple to the ground.

"Let's go," Cade said to the others and followed behind me. I'd already started off into the desert.

We ran most of the way, the moonlight guiding us. Once we got closer we slowed down and crept up to the circle of cars.

Steel made a low sound in his throat when he saw Remi laying on the ground—out cold. Cade grabbed his arm with what I assumed was a vice like grip. Steel looked over at him like he was about to chew Cade's arm off, then composed himself.

No sound could escape my throat since it felt like it'd closed up when I saw Ari kneeling in front of Remi. She was awake and had placed her body in front of her friend. Her father stood in front of her, gun pointed at her forehead.

There were about twenty men standing around in a circle. Cars and SUVs were providing light for them and cover for us as they sat idling around the cartel. It was going to be impossible to get in there without a shoot-out and with Sal pointing that gun at Ari, I didn't want to take the chance.

"What the fuck should we do?" Havoc asked.

"We need some kind of distraction," Cade muttered.

"I have an idea," I told him.

"What's-"

I shoved my gun into the back of my jeans and ran—stooped over—away from my group. I ignored Cade's hissing commands to come back. Once I was across the outer edges of the circle from our men, I stood tall.

"Sal! Give the women back and I won't kill you," I called out to him as I walked into the lights of the cars. Bass stepped up next to me and I cursed inwardly that the fucking idiot had followed me. I was willing to die for my woman. He still had his waiting back at the clubhouse for him.

Just as I had hoped, Sal's gun swung in our direction. A quick glance at Ari showed shock and fear on her face, but she didn't move.

CHAPTER 38

Ari

My heart sank as I watched Rat and Bass step—alone and vulnerable—into the circle. It was two of them—and me—against all these men.

They all chuckled at his demand since they vastly outnumbered us. I scooted backwards and checked on Remi. She was breathing. One of the men had pistol whipped her as soon as we'd gotten here. I was just thankful they hadn't shot her. Papa had been about to when I'd moved in front of her. Honestly, I was surprised he'd hesitated to shoot me.

"You and your fucking club lost me my men," Papa shouted, his face an angry red in the headlights.

"You lost your crew for yourself," Rat said, scoffing in the face of danger.

My heart leapt into my throat. My hand closed around Remi's gun and I breathed a sigh of relief. Everyone was focused on Rat and not paying attention to me. They'd taken my gun from me, but hadn't found Remi's. They probably figured they didn't need to search her since she'd be killed immediately. The thought made bile rise in my throat.

Rat was focused on Papa, and the man who stepped up next to him. I couldn't catch his attention. I tried to peer around in the darkness, but the cars' headlights were too bright and it was too dark past them to see much. The others must be around? Rat and Bass wouldn't have come here alone. Would they?

My eyes shot back to my husband and with a sinking feeling I knew they would if they'd had no other chance. The three of us were going to have to take on all these cartel and mafia men. Gritting my teeth, I stored up my courage and waited for some kind of signal from Rat.

"And my brother?" Marco asked smoothly. He had this cool, calm exterior, but the look in his eyes was pure rage. "Did he bring his death upon his own head as well?"

"OOHHHH YEAH, he practically begged for it." Every eye swung in my direction and it took me a moment to realize I'd said that out loud. Thankfully, I had the gun behind my back and no one was standing behind me. Since the focus was on me, I played it up. Ignoring Rat's indication to shut up, I kept going. Maybe if I could keep their attention on me it'd give the other men a chance to make a move.

"He kidnapped the girlfriend of one of the MC members, attacked the Zetas, lured them and the MC to Reynosa, came back to the Zetas Compound with the intention of killing Diego—and anyone else there, one of who was another girlfriend of an MC member," I ticked off each thing like it was a checklist. "So, to answer your question," I met Marco's eyes. They looked pitch-black in this lighting. "Yes, Miguel brought about his own death with his actions. Just like you're doing."

I was taunting him and it was working. He took a step toward me, fury on his face, only to be stopped short by my father's hand on his shoulder. Shock swept my system. My father was going to help me?

"If anyone is going to kill this little bitch, it's going to be me," said the man who'd sired me.

And there it is, the sociopath is back. All hope of him turning over a new leaf and becoming the man my family deserved died with that sentence. I remembered a time when Papa had killed one of his men for exacting revenge on the family members of an enemy. He'd gutted his own man, telling the others that they were above hurting women and children.

Oh, how the mighty had fallen. Abel's words of Papa spiraling out of control, of being fueled by fear and desperation echoed in my head. This was what he'd become. A man who was gleeful in the face of murdering his own daughter. Disgust for him washed over me.

Marco snapped a finger and three men stepped over to Rat and Bass. A brutal, yet short fight ensued. There was no way for them to win against the kind of odds that surrounded us. Marco's eyes slid from me to my husband. "You can watch your wife die. Then the other," he said, nodding to Remi. "Then we will kill you both."

Rat struggled against his captors, who held him back as Papa raised his gun again. He cocked his head at me as he walked forward until he was standing directly in front of me. "I should have drowned you as a baby," he told me.

At some point in my past, hearing those words from him would have ripped my soul from my body. That's how badly I'd wanted his approval and love. Now? I knew what it was to really love someone with no conditions placed upon the emotion. I knew what it meant to have a real family.

Tipping my chin up defiantly, I spat at his feet. I wouldn't give him the satisfaction of seeing me beg. I refused to show the fear that was threatening to drown me. If it was my time to die, so be it, but this man wouldn't break me in the process. I was still kneeling on the ground and he had the upper hand. That didn't mean I would die without dignity. Without a gesture that told him what I thought of him.

Papa's lip lifted in a snarl as his finger went to the trigger. After that it seemed like everything slowed down again—just like when I'd jumped out of the tree.

I saw bodies flying into the circle from the darkness and caught sight of Abel. He was lunging for Papa. Cade and Riggs were steps away from Marco while various MC members, Zetas, and Abel's men fought with Marco and Papa's crews. It was chaos.

Papa must have seen Abel out of the corner of his eye because as his body turned he swung his gun in the direction of my brother. Without thinking about it I pulled Remi's weapon out from the waistband of my jeans and leveled it on my father. I couldn't lose my brother. There wasn't time to hesitate.

The gun kicked twice in my hand as I pulled the trigger. For the second time that night, my ears were ringing from the noise. Movement caught my attention and I threw myself over Remi's body as Bene rushed over and pointed his weapon down at us.

I tucked my body around her as much as possible and closed my eyes, waiting for the shot. I probably wouldn't hear it coming the way my ears were—the ringing was stopping and now everything was muffled—but I'd feel the bite of the bullet, the hot flashing pain. I'd never been shot, but these were the images my imagination was coming up with while I waited.

When nothing happened, I dared to look up. Rat had a hand around Bene's wrist, forcing the gun away from us. I couldn't do anything but watch as my husband pulled his own gun out and fired five shots into the man's abdomen.

Gunshots reverberated all around me as I remained draped over Remi, trying to protect her as much as possible. We'd be lucky if no one caught a bullet from one of our own as they fought the cartel. It was much better than the alternative, though, and I was so grateful they'd shown up for us that tears slid silently down my cheeks.

Strong hands gripped my shoulders and tried to rip me away from Remi. It didn't occur to my shock filled brain that this was anyone other than an enemy. I tried to fight them, but they were too strong. I brought my gun around and clubbed the man in the face with it.

I stared in horror as Rat stumbled back a few steps, rubbing his jaw where I'd just clocked him with the pistol. "Oh my God! Rat! I'm so sorry." I looked around and realized that the fight was over. How long had it lasted? My sense of time was shot to hell. It could've been seconds or hours and I wouldn't have known.

'TIL ENCRYPTION DO US PART

Bene was dead. The other men that made up Marco and Papa's crews were dead. Marco himself was on his knees in the middle of the circle, hands on his head, glaring up at Cade, Nico, and Havoc as they all stood with weapons drawn on him.

Abel rushed over and pulled me up into a bone-crushing hug. "You idiot. Are you alright?"

I didn't have a chance to answer before my husband was ripping me from my brother's arms and smothering me in a hug as well.

"What?" I asked Abel. Although the muffled sounds were fading and I was getting my hearing back, I needed a moment to process his question.

"You could've been killed," Rat shouted.

I winced because it was directly into my ear. I wasn't sure if he was shouting because he thought I couldn't hear him or because he was angry. I looked up into those gorgeous blue eyes. Angry. It was definitely because he was angry.

"I had a plan," he told me as he shook me slightly. "That plan wasn't for you to help and almost get yourself killed." He jerked me against his chest again.

Jeez, a girl could get whiplash this way. But my heart swelled with love. He and my brother looked like they wanted to throttle me and I knew it was because I'd scared them.

"Like I was going to let either of you get shot without helping-" I broke off with a gasp and searched the spot where my father had last stood.

Numbness blanketed my body as I stared into his eyes. They were blank—dead—and I sucked in a breath. I'd killed my own father. Abel stepped over, blocking my view.

"You saved my life, Ari," he told me, searching my gaze as he accurately read my emotions. "That man didn't deserve any of our loyalty and he tried to kill us both."

I was still the woman who'd killed her own father. I wasn't so much like him that I could deal with that easily, despite the fact that he'd taken such joy in the thought of killing me.

Rat scooped me into his arms and started walking away from the lights. I glanced back over his shoulder in time to watch Marco jolt to his feet and listened to the triple shots ring out in the otherwise still night. His body froze, then crumpled to the ground.

I hadn't known Marco. He was the club's enemy, Uncle Nico's enemy, and therefore mine, but I didn't feel one way or another about his death. I hadn't lied when I told him he and his brother had earned their deaths. Maybe his remaining brothers would realize how stupid it was to come after us.

A thought occurred to me and I searched for Remi. Only once I saw Steel carrying her and following us did I relax. Burying my face in Rat's neck, I let exhaustion and the blackness creep over me.

CHAPTER 39

Rat

I laid Ari's limp form gently in the back seat of Abel's car. Sitting her up against the seat, I brushed my hands over her body, searching for wounds. She had blood and dirt covering her. Steel did the same with Remi. His girl was awake now and spitting mad.

"Those assholes hit me," she said indignantly.

I would've smiled if I wasn't so worried about Ari. She'd passed out on the way back to the cars and I still hadn't figured out why.

Ming rushed over and shoved Steel out of the way so she could hug Remi. The Doc had insisted on coming with us. We'd agreed and left her and a few guards in a hiding spot a little ways away from where we'd parked. I was grateful she was here now.

She poked and prodded at the gash on Remi's head before she declared she'd deal with it when we got back to the club. Then, with a soft smile she came around to the other side and stood next to me.

"Can I look her over?" she asked, putting a hand on my shoulder.

It wasn't until she asked that I realized I was hovering over her—guarding her like a territorial dog. I moved from where I'd been kneeling next to my wife and gave Ming space. After a few minutes of checking her over she smiled again. "It's just shock and exhaustion. She's fine."

Already Ari's eyelids were starting to flutter open and intense relief nearly buckled my knees.

"Hey." Her soft green eyes found mine as she spoke.

I kneeled down again and brushed a lock of hair off her forehead. "Hey, Baby."

Her head lolled back on the seat. "I'm so tired all of a sudden."

"Sleep," I told her. "I've got you. You're safe."

It took another hour or so to get everyone organized and to toss all the bodies in the back of a truck. Enzo had arranged for them to be taken to someone who owed him a favor. Apparently, the man ran a crematorium. It would be an effective way to quietly dispose of twenty-eight bodies.

Abel told us he'd be taking care of his dad's body. He wanted to give him a funeral. It was more than the man deserved, but he was doing it for his mother and sisters. We could all understand that. He assured us he would take care of everything so that there was no question about Sal's death.

The rest of the men working for Marco and Sal had split. Enzo and Diego had found where Marco had been hiding prior to tonight's attack. We didn't need to worry about the cartel or Sal's men coming back in the next few weeks. We'd made a lasting impression on why they shouldn't fuck with us.

Ari slept through it all and the ride home. She stirred momentarily when I placed her in our bed, but fell back asleep as I brushed my hand over her head. I hadn't bothered to bathe her or pull her clothes off. I'd toss the sheets and blankets tomorrow and buy more. She needed rest more than anything. As dirty as she was, I didn't have the heart to wake her. She was already going to have to learn to handle the fact that she'd been the one to put her father down like the rabid dog he was. But he was still her father. My girl had a soft heart, she would struggle with what she'd been forced to do, but I'd help her move past it. All of us would, we were family.

I left her in our darkened room and went downstairs to help finish cleaning up the mess outside. There was a lot to do in order to stay off the cops' radar. We still weren't sure what was going on there, but the police chief was sure to notice that Sal had gone missing and the change in leadership. We'd deal with that when it came.

* * *

Two days later we all crowded into Abel's massive dining room and took a seat at the table that used to be Sal's. It'd only been a short time ago when I'd sat at this table and been told that I'd have to choose a wife. Then I'd sat here again and actually said Arianna's name. Fuck... it felt like that was a lifetime ago.

"Thank you all for coming," Abel told the room.

Later today everyone would be dispersing back to their homes. Nico and Havoc were going back to New York to continue hunting the other Guzman brothers. Diego and the Zetas would head back to Mexico. Enzo and his men would go back to their normal routine, and we'd finally be free to start up some kind of new normal for our club.

It felt fucking weird not to have the Guzmans hanging over our heads anymore like a never-ending dark shroud. It was over. Marco, Miguel, Raul, and Lorenzo were dead—Nico had told us Lorenzo had been killed by Dante. It was only a matter of time before the twins joined them six feet under. The look on Havoc's face told me that was a truth I could bet on.

"The last few weeks have been a bit...fucked up."

Everyone in the room chuckled.

"A few of you went above and beyond in order to protect the women," as Abel said it his eyes found Drew, and two Zetas who'd taken bullets during the fight against Marco's men.

"The women did a damn fine job helping to protect themselves and us," Diego said. A round of murmurs agreed with him.

"That they did," Abel said with a grin. "I hope to one day find one as brave as yours." His eyes met mine and the pride in them was unmistakable. I understood it completely. Ari had surprised the hell out of me, but in the best way possible. Not for the first time, I felt grateful to whatever sense of self-preservation had me choosing her.

The next few hours were spent going over details, making sure nothing could be traced back to us. I'd have a big part to play in that—though I planned to have Ari help me. I needed to hack into the FAA's systems and erase Marco's flight plan back to Mexico. I had every intention of making him disappear digitally as thoroughly as we had disposed of his body. Once all the Guzman brothers were dead, the world would never know they'd existed. To anyone searching, Rosario would be the only one they found.

We split up and accompanied the various groups to the airport and border, making sure our allies got home safely. The sun was already sinking below the horizon by the time I got home.

The clubhouse was lit up, but no one was partying tonight. I nodded to the various men—all armed to the teeth—who were watching over our women. Just because this was over didn't mean we were going to relax any time soon.

I opened my apartment door and Ming looked up from where she and Hush were sitting on the couch.

"Hey," she called softly.

I went over and gave her a hug. "You alright?"

She smiled at me. "Just fine, although I'm going to go find my biker and our bed now that you guys are back."

"Thanks for looking after her," I told Ming, following her to the door. She gave me a peck on the cheek and let herself out.

"I'm headin' out, too," Hush told me. He grunted when I thanked him.

I was too tired to laugh. Trudging into my bedroom I stripped out of my clothes and climbed into bed. Ari sighed as I pulled her into my arms and let exhaustion drag me under.

CHAPTER 40

Ari

Mama and Alex glared at us from the driveway. They had on black dresses and were heading to Papa's funeral.

"It's disgraceful," Mama hissed at us. "You should be attending your father's funeral."

I felt shame roll over me in waves. How would she feel if she knew it'd been me that ended her husband's life? We'd decided not to tell her or my sisters that I'd killed him, or that he'd tried to kill both of us. It wouldn't help and there was no reason to lay that burden on them. It was for us to bear.

Abel shot me an amazed look. *This* was what she thought was disgraceful, his look said. I understood completely. It was beyond amazing that Mama was embarrassed by *our* behavior, but not the fact that her husband had treated his son the way he had for all those years? Nor the fact that our father had tried to murder us a few days ago—his own children? To be fair, she didn't know that part. Then again, she didn't deserve the consideration, I decided when she spoke next.

"What will people think?"

"You're such a hypocrite, Mama," I told her. I'd spent too many years calling them Mama and Papa to change now, but I felt nothing for the woman who'd given birth to me. Not even anger. That'd bled out of me as surely as my father's blood had seeped from him to wet the earth in front of me.

Her chin tilted up. "If you think you can speak to me that way in my own house-"

"It's no longer your house," Abel said, calm and cool as ever. I'd already altered the deed for him. "You're not welcome here."

Mama's jaw dropped as she looked back and forth between us. Abel's arm went around my shoulders. We were a united front against her.

"You'd throw us out on the streets?" Alex screeched.

I'd wondered how long it would take for her to interfere. I should've known it would happen once money was involved.

"I'll send you an allowance," Abel said in a tight, angry voice. "You'll only get what I give you each month, not a cent more." His eyes pierced Alex. "So don't bother asking for more and don't waste it."

"You will not contact any of us. If the girls want to speak to you, they'll be welcome to, but they'll call you," I told her, cutting off her protest before she had a chance to speak.

My sisters were on their way home, and I couldn't wait to see them. Now that this was over, Antonia and Ada would be free to choose their own husbands someday.

I was thrilled for them. I couldn't lie and say that the arranged marriage deal hadn't worked for me. It had. I was partnered with the most wonderful man and I loved him dearly—not that we'd told each other that yet. We'd get there, though.

It didn't matter that it'd worked for me. What were the odds that lightning would strike two, then three times and my sisters would find happy unions in that way? This way they got to choose. It made me so hopeful for their futures.

Gravel flew as Mama peeled out of the driveway. I'd been lost in my thoughts and hadn't realized she and Alex had stomped over to the car. *Hell, when was the last time that Mama had driven anywhere?*

"She might end up being trouble," I told Abel.

"I'll handle whatever comes."

"We will," I said looking up at him. "Together. Promise?" I held out my pinky.

He chuckled. We hadn't made a pinky promise since we were kids, but he looped it with his own. "Promise."

With a contented sigh I watched my mom and sister drive off.

* * *

I LEANED back into Rat's arms, my hands still gripping the bike's handles. Letting out a huff of breath I decided—probably stupidly—that now was the time. I'd promised not to lie to my husband anymore. Not since that first time when I'd withheld that I'd helped my father, but I'd been keeping something from Rat.

It'd been two weeks since we defeated Marco and my father. Uncle Nico and Havoc had gone home to New York, promising to exterminate the rest of the Guzman brothers. Abel had fully taken over the mafia here. The men who'd followed my father had either been killed or left the city. They knew better than to stick around. Things were settling down and everyone had been ready to take a breather and relax a little.

That time had proven to be so important for Rat and me, and he'd actually taken a week off work to spend with me. He'd been teaching me to ride his motorcycle and promised to get me one of my own. The freedom of riding one soothed my soul. I could only imagine how being in control of the powerful machine would make me feel. I was still having some trouble with the hand clutch and shifting. It shouldn't have been that different than shifting a car. In fact, you'd think it would be easier since I have more coordination in my hand, but I just kept letting it out too fast and stalling.

Rat was seated behind me, demonstrating—again—how to do it. I loved having his strong arms wrapped around me. It made me feel safe and like I could face anything. That was probably why I'd chosen now.

"I need to tell you something."

I felt him tense up against me. That may not have been the best way to start this conversation, but I was nervous. Sue me.

"What's wrong?" His deep voice was full of suspicion.

"Hopefully nothing," I hedged.

"Just tell me, Ari."

"I'm pregnant." My voice was low, hushed, and I cringed as I said it, waiting for his reaction.

When he didn't say anything—or move—I snuck a peek over my shoulder.

Rat's lips were parted, eyes wide, and all the color had leached out of his face. I'd have laughed if I wasn't so worried about what he was going to say.

"You're-" his voice cracked and he cleared his throat. "You're sure?"

I nodded. "Five positive at home tests. Of course, I'll have to go to the doctor to get the official diagnosis, but I don't think five tests in a row would lie."

"How..." He flinched. "I mean I know how, but we've been using protection."

I still hadn't found the time between school, uncles going missing, and being shot at to get on the pill. "Remember that night? Against the wall." I flushed as I said it.

The grin that slowly formed on his face told me he remembered. His eyes flashed to mine. It was hard to read the emotion there. His large hand slid down to my stomach and I covered it with mine.

"We're going to have a kid?" He sounded shocked, amazed, and slightly...hopeful.

"Yes."

His growl was so loud behind me it hurt my ear. Kicking down the stand, Rat tugged me off the bike and into his arms. "How long have you known?"

"Uhhh..." I wasn't sure why he suddenly looked angry. "I've suspected for a few weeks."

His eyes narrowed and my stomach clenched under his scrutiny. "Did you *suspect* when you flung yourself out of a tree and onto a homicidal maniac?"

I bit the insides of my cheeks to keep my facial expression neutral. "Maybe," I told him.

His glare heated up with his anger.

"What was I supposed to do?" I asked in amazement. "Let the guy kill Julie? Then myself?"

The anger faded off his face. "No."

I gave him a sweet smile, trying to get him to smile. It didn't work. "We're fine. I promise." I patted my belly.

"How do you know?" He scowled at me. "You're going to one of those baby doctors."

My mouth dropped open. "What, now?"

"Right now," he growled. He wasn't pissed anymore. There was a mix of dominance and playfulness in his eyes.

I ran my finger over his chest. "Maybe after we..." Wiggling my eyebrows suggestively, I scooted in closer to him.

"Nope. Now."

"Spoil sport," I muttered.

He reached out and hooked his arms around me as he hugged me fiercely. "I love you, Ari." His breath tickled my neck, stirring my hair, as his words imploded my heart.

"I love you, too," I said, tears leaking out from the corners of my eyes. Sniffling, I shoved my face into his neck.

"Then why are you crying?" He laughed, bad mood forgotten.

"Happy tears? Hormones? Weeks of people trying to kill me? I don't know," I said as a flood of tears washed down my face.

He kissed my cheeks, then picked me up in his arms.

"Rat!" I clutched onto his shoulders. "What are you doing?"

"Like I said, you're going to the doctor," he told me. "I need my keys." He strode with me in his arms toward the clubhouse.

We didn't make it past the kitchen. There were too many people in there and we were too excited to keep it quiet. I had zero doubts that he'd be dragging me to the doctor the first chance he got, but that was fine by me. We ended up celebrating in the clubhouse kitchen with our family gathered around. I'd finally found where I belonged.

CHAPTER 41

Rat

I accepted the beer Cade handed to me with a gratefulness that bordered on insanity. Everything felt like it was spiraling and I wasn't sure how to handle it.

Ari'd gone outside to watch the sunset. She and Hush usually watched together and talked. I let them have their time. She was drawing our usually silent brother out of his shell and I knew she thought of him like a father figure. After everything that'd happened over the last few weeks she could use the extra guidance and comfort.

I avoided Cade's direct gaze as he sat down across from me. Looked like I was about to get some guidance and comfort of my own—whether I wanted it or not. "What?" I growled at him, taking a swig of my beer. I knew what. I was just hoping to avoid this conversation.

"Just checking in," he said in amusement.

"I'm fine," I said quickly. Too quickly.

Cade's eyes narrowed and I sighed inwardly.

"That's some big news you two had," he said calmly, as though we weren't discussing something huge. Something that was so over the top for me. I felt out of control and out of my depth. Like I was drowning in a sea of uncertainty.

How was I supposed to raise a kid? I knew nothing about babies. I couldn't even remember my own parents. In all reality my life started when I was twelve and met Cade. Before that was nothing but nightmares.

"What's bugging you, Rat?"

I scoffed. "I'm thrilled." My eyes slid over to him then darted away. "Really, I am. I'm also…"

"Terrified?"

I grimaced. All these men surrounding me were always so fucking sure of themselves and confident. It sucked to be the one with so many issues that you couldn't function in the same way as them.

"You realize there's nothing wrong with being afraid?" Cade said in a short, clipped tone.

I snorted and took another swallow of beer. "You never are."

His laugh was loud and harsh. "Bullshit."

Now I focused on him. His green eyes held some deep emotion I couldn't identify. "You think I don't fear anything?" When I nodded a smile tipped his lips. "I'll let you in on a secret, Kid. Stepping up and leading? That puts the responsibility of your men's lives on your shoulders. You think I'm not afraid for every one of you each time we go into a fight?"

He shook his head and stared down at the floor. "I'd give my life to make sure you're all safe. Add on top of that the knowledge that you're only there because I've asked you to be. If you don't come home, I'm the one who has to tell your old lady. I know about fear."

That'd never occurred to me. I thought about what it would mean for men to follow me into a battle and maybe not make it out. The devastation that would cause for their wives and children, and for our club. I didn't envy Cade his position. I never had, but even more now. I knew I wouldn't want to be the one making these heavy decisions for our club.

He took a long pull from his own bottle then met my eyes. "That's not the way life works out, though. I guarantee you not one of these men do what needs to be done without fear. Going into the situations we do without it either makes you delusional, psychotic, or an idiot. The key is not to let fear control your actions. Take Sal for example. He was so scared of losing his empire that he brought on the loss himself."

That made sense. He treated Abel the way he had because he knew one day his son would take over. If he hadn't taught Abel to hate him —which he did out of fear—his son wouldn't have overthrown him. Being afraid had also caused Sal to double cross every one of his allies and look where that had gotten him.

"So...suck it up and deal," I summarized with a grin, trying to lighten the mood a little.

Cade laughed. "Rat...I don't think you realize how strong you are. It's true most of us have fucked up pasts, but I think yours takes the cake on the worst out there. Yet, here you are. You've persevered and risen above all of that bullshit."

I cocked my head as I thought about that. "What was the alternative? Give up?" I scoffed at the idea.

"Some might have. Others would've looked for someone to blame. You just moved forward and made something of yourself. Now you have a wife—that you love and who loves you—and you two are going to have a kid."

The declaration settled around me, but it didn't carry the weight it had even a few minutes ago. "What if I fuck up?" I asked, meeting his eyes.

Cade chuckled. "We can't get through life without fucking up here or there, but you'll fix it when you do."

"I want to be a good father."

His smile was genuine and spread across his face. "You will be. You know why?"

I shook my head.

"Because you want to be, so you'll learn, and you'll try. That's the important part. Besides, we'll be there to help... Not that any of us have any clue how to raise a kid," he said with a sardonic smile. "And you have Enzo. At least there's one man around who knows what he's doing on the baby front."

That was true. Knowing I had Enzo as back up eased my mind a little. Even more importantly, knowing that my MC was going to be there, no matter what I needed, completely disintegrated any worry that had been plaguing me.

I came to them as a homeless orphan, now I had a brother—multiple brothers, and sisters really. A wife, and soon a kid. A real family.

CHAPTER 42

Ari

I wandered out to my spot and smiled when I saw Hush sitting there, waiting for me.

"Hey," I called out softly.

"Hey, yourself," he replied with a devastating grin. I knew that one day—when he was ready—some woman was going to snatch him up in a heartbeat. I couldn't wait to see my friend be happy.

We'd taken to sitting out here, watching the sun sink below the horizon. I sat on the picnic table next to him and sucked in a deep breath of the fresh, cool air.

"I hear congratulations are in order?" He pointed at my belly.

Smiling over at him, I nodded. He'd been on the road, picking up my sisters when we told everyone the news. Hush leaned over and hugged me. I inhaled his cologne and wondered what might have happened if we'd had a man like this as our father? Someone strong and brave. Someone who was loyal and kind, although maybe not to his enemies.

"Hush… I don't know if you're Catholic, or even religious." I frowned. "I'm not really sure I even am, but... Would you be our baby's Godfather?"

I'd already spoken with Rat about this choice and we'd both agreed that there wasn't anyone else—other than maybe Cade—who we'd want to raise our baby if something happened to us. This man would protect our kid with his entire being.

His eyes widened comically and he was at a loss for words. I think. He spoke so seldom it was hard to tell.

Finally, he nodded and looked away quickly. There might have been a sheen of tears in his eyes. He tucked me up under his arm and I laid my head on his shoulder as we watched the sun start to sink. It was hard to imagine that my life could be so perfect.

Once we went our separate ways, I headed back to the clubhouse. An SUV pulling into the lot had me walking around front. It wasn't so dark yet that I couldn't see the people who got out of the vehicle. I eyed the blonde woman and dark-haired man as they approached. They were both in suits and were equally gorgeous. Seriously, they looked like Barbie and Ken.

I didn't need to let my gaze drop to the shiny gold badges on their belts to know what they were—cops.

"Good evening," the woman said, her blue eyes surveying me shrewdly.

I folded my arms over my chest and raised my brows, saying nothing. That'd been rule number one I'd been taught as a kid. You never spoke to cops. As an adult I could obviously employ that rule as I saw fit.

The woman's lush lips lifted into an amused smile. "Is Cade here?"

"Maybe. Maybe not," I told her. "Who are you?"

"I'm Special Agent Flynn."

FBI, I thought with an inward sneer. Worse than cops.

"This is my...partner, Austin PD Detective Zane Gallagher."

Interesting. Why were an FBI Agent and a Detective together—and here?

I waited. "What do you want?"

Her blue eyes narrowed on me. "To speak with Cade."

"Well, he's not available. I'll tell him you stopped by."

"Little girl-"

Before she could finish the sentence, or I could correct her I heard the door of the clubhouse slam shut. Familiar arms wrapped around me and I leaned back into Rat. He had a thing for protecting my back and I couldn't say that I minded. If anything went down, I knew he'd be shoving me behind him in order to shield me, and I'd do the same for him.

"Flynn," Cade said as he stepped up next to us. His eyes focused on her after he took the detective's measure. I glanced around and saw all the club officers and their women standing together—an army against the two interlopers.

"Hey, Sis," Flynn said with a devious smile. I followed her gaze and was shocked to find them locked on Bridget.

Bridget's eyes met mine and she shrugged. She mouthed 'I'll tell you later.'

I turned back to the cops.

"I need to speak with you," Flynn told Cade. "Alone."

"It's not alone with him there," Rat rumbled from behind me. His hard gaze was focused on Zane.

Zane smirked. "I knew there was no way you were a computer programmer. As soon as I saw you in the precinct that day, I knew there was something more to you."

Riggs stepped forward menacingly and started taunting the cop. Rat didn't bother to answer, though I felt how tense he was.

Flynn sighed and pinched the bridge of her nose. "Alright, everyone shut up." Her blonde brows rose as she shot a challenging look at Cade. "You want to do this here?"

"Yes." He folded his muscular arms.

Flynn shrugged then those bright blue eyes shifted off Cade and locked onto Bass. "Tommy Higgins. I'm sorry to tell you that your sister, Tiffany Higgins, is dead."

Her voice was cold, but a spark of empathy shone in her eyes. She wasn't playing this time, not like how the girls described her usual encounters.

Bass's mouth dropped open and everyone froze in shock. That wasn't what anyone was expecting. Why was an FBI Agent handling a death notification? I watched enough murder documentaries to know that it would normally be a pair of officers, not the FBI, and not a detective.

I didn't know Bass had a sister, but tears welled in my eyes for his loss.

"That's...not all," Flynn continued. She arched a brow at Cade. "Maybe now you'd like to follow me? There's something I need to show you." She stalked over to her SUV with Cade, Bass, and Julie following.

Rat kissed my head then caught up with them. He put a hand on Bass's shoulder and said something, too low for any of us to hear.

The hair on my nape prickled with awareness. We'd thought things were finished. Something told me we were just getting started.

Thanks for reading!

Bass & Trouble is available for pre-order today! Keep reading for a sneak peek.

SNEAK PEEK

BASS & TROUBLE

TIFFANY

The red light shone bright in front of me, mocking me. It felt like the world was working against me right now, conspiring to make me fail. My heart galloped in my chest. They were going to catch me too soon. Making a quick, and likely dangerous, decision, I stomped on the gas pedal. The engine revved loudly as I blew through the light, barely missing the oncoming traffic that swerved around me. Horns blared, angry and frightened as people tried to avoid crashing into each other.

I turned hard onto the freeway entrance, tires squealing with the effort. I knew the red light wouldn't slow them down, but maybe the traffic jam I caused would give me a few second's lead. Those seconds gave Dario more precious time to carry out our plan. Nothing else mattered except that he succeeded—nothing.

I dared to glance at my phone. It was a burner that Dario had given me. There was only one number on it. No messages.

Damn.

Looking in my rearview mirror, I saw headlights in the distance as they swerved onto the freeway. They were getting closer, and we were running out of time.

Dario had tried to make arrangements for me. To get me out. To get *us* out. Me, him, and our babies. Our precious babies. He couldn't have known it would all go so wrong. Maybe it'd been stupid to think we could outrun his old life, but we hadn't had any other options. We'd finally realized that The Texas Syndicate would never let us go. Dario's former gang was ruthless and we were desperate.

I took the next exit, hoping that I could lose them on the back roads. Maybe there was a spot I could pull off and blend in. It was so desolate out here, away from the city, it gave me a moment of hope. Only a moment, as it was lost almost immediately.

They followed me off the exit. My back window shattered suddenly and the scream spilled from my lips involuntarily. They were shooting at me. I turned down another road. Where could I go? My eyes scanned the landscape, but there was nothing here. No hope. No escape.

I could hear the bullets pinging off the car. I made another rapid right turn. This time I heard a loud pop and the car started to swerve uncontrollably. They must have hit a tire. The steering wheel jerked in my hands so hard I couldn't control it and I ran right off the road into a ditch. I was lucky that we didn't roll over.

No time to consider my luck. I leaped out of my seat and opened the back door, quickly scooping up the little bundles in the back out of their car seats, before heading off into the desert. I was running hard for a grove of trees that could offer some protection. Glancing over my shoulder, I saw their car stop behind mine, they were getting out. It wouldn't be long now.

I felt a vibration in my pocket and my heart surged into my throat. Hope was threatening to suffocate me. The men were closing in. I couldn't spare a second—but this message—this message was worth it. I shifted the bundles to one arm and with my free hand checked the phone as I slowed a little so I wouldn't trip as I ran. No words. That would have been too risky. Just an emoji. A thumbs up. He did it. A relieved smile split my face.

BANG. The smile disappeared as my steps faltered to a stop. I looked down and saw the blood oozing out from a small hole in my stomach. Funny. I'd always assumed being shot would hurt. Why couldn't I feel anything? I dropped the phone while my other arm tightened around the two bundles. Falling to my knees, I wrapped both arms around them and held them tight to my breast.

The men were closer now. I could hear their footsteps, not that it mattered. There was no escaping a stomach wound. It was only a matter of minutes, maybe seconds, before I would bleed out. Not that it mattered, they'd be right on top of me any moment.

The tears started flowing. My babies. My precious, innocent babies. I would never see them again. They would never see me. They're so young...would they remember me? Would they know how much I loved them? Would they understand? Would they forgive me? Forgive us for what we had to do?

Everything was blurry, I couldn't make my eyes seem to focus and I was so cold. Each breath was like an icicle stabbing into my lungs. Texas was in the middle of winter and contrary to popular belief it did get cold here. Add to that my imminent death and fear had full body shudders wracking me.

They were upon me now, laughing at me. I remembered the text message. A thumbs up. My tears eased for a moment. One of the men grabbed the bundles out of my arms.

"What the fuck is this!" he screamed. "They're fucking dolls!" He cast them aside and kicked me square in the stomach.

I bent over, breath whooshing out of me, but there was no pain. Everything was fading out. "Ha ha ha, fuck you," I choked out. I couldn't resist taunting them now that they knew what I had when this chase began; my babies were safe. I'd given my life to ensure that they'd be safe from these men. That was enough. I clung to that as the man snarled at me.

I wanted to sob, to cry out and scream. My babies would grow up without their mother. They *would* grow up, though. They were safe. Tommy would make sure of it. He'd always been such a good kid. His handsome smile flashed before my eyes. He was going to be so pissed at me for this. For dying and leaving him. For gifting him the only two things that had any meaning in this world to me—besides him. He probably wouldn't see it as a gift. A smirk lifted my lips even as the tears streamed down my face.

The gang member grabbed my foot and started dragging me toward the trees. Desperately, I reached out, clawing the ground. I wasn't trying to stop him from taking me, I was already too far gone to care. My frantic motions stopped when my hand wrapped around the blankets. The dolls rolled from them as he dragged me along.

Pressing the cotton to my face, I inhaled the warm scent of my babies. It comforted me, just as the knowledge that they'd grow, find love, get married, comforted me.

The man dragging me shoved my foot away as soon as he stopped. My gaze shifted to him, but black dots were dancing in front of my eyes. I was still able to make out the shining barrel of the gun as he pointed it at me. Apparently, waiting for me to bleed to death was too slow for him. Closing my eyes, I clutched their blankets to my heart, their scent surrounded me. The sound of the gunshot and the blackness collided together on my last thought.

ACKNOWLEDGMENTS

A huge thank you to my partner in crime and Co-Author, Frank Jensen. I couldn't do this without you.

To my amazing beta readers Heather Ashley and Aurora Welkin, thank you so much for all of your time and effort you spent helping me make these books the best they can be!

A huge shout out to my editor, Ce-Ce Cox of Outside-Eyes Editing and Proofreading! Thank you for catching everything I always seem to miss, especially those pesky commas.

Thank you to the awesome Kari March of Kari March Designs for giving me gorgeous covers each and every time.

To my wonderful and perfect fans! Thank you all for giving an unknown author a shot and for reading my books! I hope you love them and I can't show my gratitude for you enough.

Lastly, to my family, you're the best. Thank you for the love and support.

ABOUT THE AUTHOR

Cathleen Cole currently lives in Utah with her husband Frank, their six dogs, four goats, and flock of chickens. Cathleen and Frank have nomadic souls, so they don't expect to be tied down to one place indefinitely.

Animals, dog sports, traveling, scuba diving, and everything books are just a few of Cathleen's passions in life. She measures her quality of life based off the different experiences and adventures she gets to have. The one phrase that has always struck a resounding chord within her has been, "The woods are lovely, dark, and deep. But I have promises to keep. And miles to go before I sleep. And miles to go before I sleep." ~ Robert Frost. She has always used that as an internal compass to guide her on her way.

You'll see every book written by either Cathleen Cole or Frank Jensen will always credit the other as co-author and that is because they use each other as sounding boards during their writing processes as well as they are each other's main beta readers. As husband and wife, they insist on sharing all successes and failures equally.

ALSO BY CATHLEEN COLE

The Vikings MC Series
Heart of Steel
The Viking's Princess
All's Fair In Love & Juárez
'Til Encryption Do Us Part
Bass & Trouble
War & Pieces

The Discord Series
Havoc
Inferno
Deviant